*For Bill Massey, Laura Gerrard, Shelley Power,
and all the copy editors and proofreaders
who make these books work.*

Glossary

I am an *amateur* Greek scholar. My definitions are my own, but taken from the LSJ or Routledge's *Handbook of Greek Mythology* or Smith's *Classical Dictionary*. On some military issues I have the temerity to disagree with the received wisdom on the subject. Also check my website at www.hippeis.com for more information and some helpful pictures.

Akinakes A Scythian short sword or long knife, also sometimes carried by Medes and Persians.

Andron The 'men's room' of a proper Greek house – where men have symposia. Recent research has cast real doubt as to the sexual exclusivity of the room, but the name sticks.

Apobatai The Chariot Warriors. In many towns, towns that hadn't used chariots in warfare for centuries, the *Apobatai* were the elite three hundred or so. In Athens, they competed in special events; in Thebes, they may have been the forerunners of the Sacred Band.

Archon A city's senior official or, in some cases, one of three or four. A magnate.

Aspis The Greek hoplite's shield (which is not called a hoplon!).

The *aspis* is about a yard in diameter, is deeply dished (up to six inches deep) and should weigh between eight and sixteen pounds.

Basileus An aristocratic title from a bygone era (at least in 500 BC) that means 'king' or 'lord'.

Bireme A warship rowed by two tiers of oars, as opposed to a *trireme*, which has three tiers.

Chiton The standard tunic for most men, made by taking a single continuous piece of cloth and folding it in half, pinning the shoulders and open side. Can be made quite fitted by means of pleating. Often made of very fine quality material – usually wool, sometimes linen, especially in the upper classes. A full *chiton* was ankle length for men and women.

Leonidas, best of the Spartans, held the pass at Thermopylae. And we, as ragtag a fleet as ever put oar to water, held the waters off Artemisium – day after day. Storms pounded the Persians. We pounded the Persians. Once we fought them to a standstill, and on the last day we beat them.

But at our backs, a traitor led the Medes around the Spartan wall, and King Leonidas died.

The so-called Great King desecrated his body and took his head. The Great King's soldiers did the same to all three hundred Spartans and to others besides. Dogs ripped the body of my noble brother-in-law, Antigonus. My sister would weep for his shade, and I would weep too.

No gods laughed. The week after Thermopylae was the worst of the Long War – the worst week many of us had ever known.

Calliades was archon in Athens, and the Eleians celebrated the Seventy-fifth Olympiad, that in which Astylus of Syracuse won the stadion. It was in this year that King Xerxes made his campaign against Greece. It was the year of the climax of the Long War.

I was there.

Christian Cameron is a writer and historian. He is a veteran of the United States Navy, where he served as both an aviator and an intelligence officer in the first Gulf War, Somalia and elsewhere, with degrees in History and Classics. He lives in Toronto with his wife and daughter, writing his next novel, while preparing to re-enact the Battles of Marathon and Castagnaro. He's currently learning Italian.

Find out more at: www.hippeis.com

Also by Christian Cameron

Salamis

CHRISTIAN CAMERON

An Orion paperback

First published in Great Britain in 2015
by Orion Books
This paperback edition published in 2016
by Orion Books,
an imprint of The Orion Publishing Group Ltd,
Carmelite House, 50 Victoria Embankment,
London EC4Y 0DZ

An Hachette UK Company

1 3 5 7 9 10 8 6 4 2

A CIP catalogue record for this book
is available from the British Library.

ISBN 978 1 4091 1813 8

Typeset by Deltatype Ltd, Birkenhead, Merseyside

Printed in Great Britain by CPI Group (UK) Ltd,
Croydon CR0 4YY

The Orion Publishing Group's policy is to use papers
that are natural, renewable and recyclable products and
made from wood grown in sustainable forests. The logging
and manufacturing processes are expected to conform to
the environmental regulations of the country of origin.

www.orionbooks.co.uk

Chitoniskos A small *chiton*, usually just longer than modesty demanded – or not as long as modern modesty would demand! Worn by warriors and farmers, often heavily bloused and very full by warriors to pad their armour. Usually wool.

Chlamys A short cloak made from a rectangle of cloth roughly 60 by 90 inches – could also be worn as a *chiton* if folded and pinned a different way. Or slept under as a blanket.

Corslet/Thorax In 500 BC, the best *corslets* were made of bronze, mostly of the so-called 'bell' *thorax* variety. A few muscle *corslets* appear at the end of this period, gaining popularity into the 450s. Another style is the 'white' *corslet*, seen to appear just as the Persian Wars begin – re-enactors call this the 'Tube and Yoke' *corslet*, and some people call it (erroneously) the *linothorax*. Some of them may have been made of linen – we'll never know – but the likelier material is Athenian leather, which was often tanned and finished with alum, thus being bright white. Yet another style was a tube and yoke of scale, which you can see the author wearing on his website. A scale *corslet* would have been the most expensive of all, and probably provided the best protection.

Daidala Cithaeron, the mountain that towered over Plataea, was the site of a remarkable fire-festival, the *Daidala*, which was celebrated by the Plataeans on the summit of the mountain. In the usual ceremony, as mounted by the Plataeans in every seventh year, a wooden idol (*daidalon*) would be dressed in bridal robes and dragged on an ox-cart from Plataea to the top of the mountain, where it would be burned after appropriate rituals. Or, in the *Great Daidala*, which were celebrated every forty-nine years, fourteen *daidala* from different Boeotian towns would be burned on a large wooden pyre heaped with brushwood, together with a cow and a bull that were sacrificed to Zeus and Hera. This huge pyre on the mountain top must have provided a most impressive spectacle; Pausanias remarks that he knew of no other flame that rose as high or could be seen from so far.

The cultic legend that was offered to account for the festival ran as follows. When Hera had once quarrelled with Zeus, as she often did, she had withdrawn to her childhood home of Euboea and had refused every attempt at reconciliation. So Zeus sought the advice of the wisest man on earth, Cithaeron (the eponym of the mountain), who ruled at Plataea in the earliest times. Cithaeron advised him to make a wooden image of a woman, to veil it in the manner of a bride, and then to have it drawn along in an ox-cart after spreading the rumour that he was planning to marry the nymph Plataea, a daughter of the river god Asopus. When Hera rushed to the scene and tore away the veils, she was so relieved to find a wooden effigy rather than the expected bride that she at last consented to be reconciled with Zeus. (Routledge *Handbook of Greek Mythology*, pp. 137–8)

Daimon Literally a spirit, the *daimon* of combat might be adrenaline, and the *daimon* of philosophy might simply be native intelligence. Suffice it to say that very intelligent men – like Socrates – believed that god-sent spirits could infuse a man and influence his actions.

Daktyloi Literally digits or fingers, in common talk 'inches' in the system of measurement. Systems differed from city to city. I have taken the liberty of using just the Athenian units.

Despoina Lady. A term of formal address.

Diekplous A complex naval tactic about which some debate remains. In this book, the *Diekplous*, or through stroke, is commenced with an attack by the ramming ship's bow (picture the two ships approaching bow to bow or head-on) and cathead on the enemy oars. Oars were the most vulnerable part of a fighting ship, something very difficult to imagine unless you've rowed in a big boat and understand how lethal your own oars can be – to you! After the attacker crushes the enemy's oars, he passes, flank to flank, and then turns when astern, coming up easily (the defender is almost dead in the water) and ramming the enemy under the stern or counter as desired.

Doru A spear, about ten feet long, with a bronze butt-spike.

Eleutheria Freedom.

Ephebe A young, free man of property. A young man in training to be a *hoplite*. Usually performing service to his city and, in ancient terms, at one of the two peaks of male beauty.

Eromenos The 'beloved' in a same-sex pair in ancient Greece. Usually younger, about seventeen. This is a complex, almost dangerous subject in the modern world – were these pair-bonds about sex, or chivalric love, or just a 'brotherhood' of warriors? I suspect there were elements of all three. And to write about this period without discussing the *eromenos/erastes* bond would, I fear, be like putting all the warriors in steel armour instead of bronze . . .

Erastes The 'lover' in a same-sex pair bond – the older man, a tried warrior, twenty-five to thirty years old.

Eudaimonia Literally 'well-spirited'. A feeling of extreme joy.

Exhedra The porch of the women's quarters – in some cases, any porch over a farm's central courtyard.

Helots The 'race of slaves' of Ancient Sparta – the conquered peoples who lived with the Spartiates and did all of their work so that they could concentrate entirely on making war and more Spartans.

Hetaira Literally a 'female companion'. In ancient Athens, a *hetaira* was a courtesan, a highly skilled woman who provided sexual companionship as well as fashion, political advice and music.

Himation A very large piece of rich, often embroidered wool, worn as an outer garment by wealthy citizen women or as a sole garment by older men, especially those in authority.

Hoplite A Greek upper-class warrior. Possession of a heavy spear, a helmet and an *aspis* (see above) and income above the marginal lowest free class were all required to serve as a *hoplite*. Although much is made of the 'citizen soldier' of ancient Greece, it would be fairer to compare *hoplites* to medieval knights than to Roman legionnaires or modern National Guardsmen. Poorer citizens did serve, and sometimes as *hoplites* or marines, but in general, the front ranks were the preserve of upper-class men who could afford the best training and the essential armour.

Hoplitodromos The *hoplite* race, or race in armour. Two *stades* with an *aspis* on your shoulder, a helmet and greaves in the early runs. I've run this race in armour. It is no picnic.

Hoplomachia A *hoplite* contest, or sparring match. Again, there is enormous debate as to when *hoplomachia* came into existence and how much training Greek *hoplites* received. One thing that they didn't do is drill like modern soldiers – there's no mention of it in all of Greek literature. However, they had highly evolved martial arts (see *pankration*) and it is almost certain that *hoplomachia* was a term that referred to 'the martial art of fighting when fully equipped as a *hoplite*'.

Hoplomachos A participant in *hoplomachia*.

Hypaspist Literally 'under the shield'. A squire or military servant – by the time of Arimnestos, the *hypaspist* was usually a younger man of the same class as the *hoplite*.

Kithara A stringed instrument of some complexity, with a hollow body as a soundboard.

Kline A couch.

Kopis The heavy, back-curved sabre of the Greeks. Like a longer, heavier modern kukri or Gurkha knife.

Kore A maiden or daughter.

Kylix A wide, shallow, handled bowl for drinking wine.

Logos Literally 'word'. In pre-Socratic Greek philosophy the word is everything – the power beyond the gods.

Longche A six to seven foot throwing spear, also used for hunting. A *hoplite* might carry a pair of *longchai*, or a single, longer and heavier *doru*.

Machaira A heavy sword or long knife.

Maenads The 'raving ones' – ecstatic female followers of Dionysus.

Mastos A woman's breast. A *mastos* cup is shaped like a woman's breast with a rattle in the nipple – so when you drink, you lick the nipple and the rattle shows that you emptied the cup. I'll leave the rest to imagination . . .

Medimnos A grain measure. Very roughly – 35 to 100 pounds of grain.

Megaron A style of building with a roofed porch.

Navarch An admiral.

Oikia The household – all the family and all the slaves, and sometimes the animals and the farmland itself.

Opson Whatever spread, dip or accompaniment an ancient Greek had with bread.

Pais A child.

Palaestra The exercise sands of the gymnasium.

Pankration The military martial art of the ancient Greeks – an unarmed combat system that bears more than a passing resemblance to modern MMA techniques, with a series of carefully structured blows and domination holds that is, by modern standards, very advanced. Also the basis of the Greek sword and spear-based martial arts. Kicking, punching, wrestling, grappling, on the ground and standing, were all permitted.

Peplos A short overfold of cloth that women could wear as a hood or to cover the breasts.

Phalanx The full military potential of a town; the actual, formed body of men before a battle (all of the smaller groups formed together made a *phalanx*). In this period, it would be a mistake to imagine a carefully drilled military machine.

Phylarch A file-leader – an officer commanding the four to sixteen men standing behind him in the *phalanx*.

Polemarch The war leader.

Polis The city. The basis of all Greek political thought and expression, the government that was held to be more important – a higher god – than any individual or even family. To this day, when we talk about politics, we're talking about the 'things of our city'.

Porne A prostitute.

Porpax The bronze or leather band that encloses the forearm on a Greek *aspis*.

Psiloi Light infantrymen – usually slaves or adolescent freemen who, in this period, were not organised and seldom had any weapon beyond some rocks to throw.

Pyrrhiche The 'War Dance'. A line dance in armour done by all of the warriors, often very complex. There's reason to believe that the *Pyrrhiche* was the method by which the young were trained in basic martial arts and by which 'drill' was inculcated.

Pyxis A box, often circular, turned from wood or made of metal.

Rhapsode A master-poet, often a performer who told epic works like the *Iliad* from memory.

Satrap A Persian ruler of a province of the Persian Empire.

Skeuophoros Literally a 'shield carrier', unlike the *hypaspist*, this is a slave or freed man who does camp work and carries the armour and baggage.

Sparabara The large wicker shield of the Persian and Mede elite infantry. Also the name of those soldiers.

Spolas Another name for a leather *corslet*, often used for the lion skin of Heracles.

Stade A measure of distance. An Athenian *stade* is about 185 metres.

Strategos In Athens, the commander of one of the ten military tribes. Elsewhere, any senior Greek officer – sometimes the commanding general.

Synaspismos The closest order that *hoplites* could form – so close that the shields overlap, hence 'shield on shield'.

Taxis Any group but, in military terms, a company; I use it for 60 to 300 men.

Thetes The lowest free class – citizens with limited rights.

Thorax See *corslet*.

Thugater Daughter. Look at the word carefully and you'll see the 'daughter' in it . . .

Triakonter A small rowed galley of thirty oars.

Trierarch The captain of a ship – sometimes just the owner or builder, sometimes the fighting captain.

Zone A belt, often just rope or finely wrought cord, but could be a heavy bronze kidney belt for war.

General Note on Names and Personages

This series is set in the very dawn of the so-called Classical Era, often measured from the Battle of Marathon (490 BC). Some, if not most, of the famous names of this era are characters in this series – and that's not happenstance. Athens of this period is as magical, in many ways, as Tolkien's Gondor, and even the quickest list of artists, poets, and soldiers of this era reads like a 'who's who' of western civilization. Nor is the author tossing them together by happenstance – these people were almost all aristocrats, men (and women) who knew each other well – and might be adversaries or friends in need. Names in bold are historical characters – yes, even Arimnestos – and you can get a glimpse into their lives by looking at Wikipedia or Britannica online. For more in-depth information, I recommend Plutarch and Herodotus, to whom I owe a great deal.

Arimnestos of Plataea may – just may – have been Herodotus's source for the events of the Persian Wars. The careful reader will note that Herodotus himself – a scribe from Halicarnassus – appears several times ...

Archilogos – Ephesian, son of Hipponax the poet; a typical Ionian aristocrat, who loves Persian culture and Greek culture too, who serves his city, not some cause of 'Greece' or 'Hellas', and who finds the rule of the Great King fairer and more 'democratic' than the rule of a Greek tyrant.

Arimnestos – Child of Chalkeotechnes and Euthalia.

Aristagoras – Son of Molpagoras, nephew of Histiaeus. Aristagoras led Miletus while Histiaeus was a virtual prisoner of the Great King Darius at Susa. Aristagoras seems to have initiated the Ionian Revolt – and later to have regretted it.

Aristides – Son of Lysimachus, lived roughly 525–468 BC, known later in life as 'The Just'. Perhaps best known as one of the commanders at Marathon. Usually sided with the Aristocratic party.

Artaphernes – Brother of Darius, Great King of Persia, and Satrap of Sardis. A senior Persian with powerful connections.

Behon – A Kelt from Alba; a fisherman and former slave.

Bion – A slave name, meaning 'life'. The most loyal family retainer of the Corvaxae.

Briseis – Daughter of Hipponax, sister of Archilogos.

Calchus – A former warrior, now the keeper of the shrine of the Plataean Hero of Troy, Leitus.

Chalkeotechnes – The Smith of Plataea; head of the family Corvaxae, who claim descent from Herakles.

Chalkidis – Brother of Arimnestos, son of Chalkeotechnes.

Cimon – Son of Miltiades, a professional soldier, sometime pirate, and Athenian aristocrat.

Cleisthenes – A noble Athenian of the Alcmaeonid family. He is credited with reforming the constitution of ancient Athens and setting it on a democratic footing in 508/7 BC.

Collam – A Gallic lord in the Central Massif at the headwaters of the Seine.

Dano of Croton – Daughter of the philosopher and mathematician Pythagoras.

Darius – King of Kings, the lord of the Persian Empire, brother to Artaphernes.

Doola – Numidian ex-slave.

Draco – Wheelwright and wagon builder of Plataea, a leading man of the town.

Empedocles – A priest of Hephaestus, the Smith God.

Epaphroditos – A warrior, an aristocrat of Lesbos.

Eualcides – A Hero. Eualcides is typical of a class of aristocratic men – professional warriors, adventurers, occasionally pirates or merchants by turns. From Euboea.

Heraclitus – c.535–475 BC. One of the ancient world's most famous philosophers. Born to an aristocratic family, he chose philosophy over political power. Perhaps most famous for his statement about time: 'You cannot step twice into the same river'. His belief that 'strife is justice' and other similar sayings which you'll find scattered through these pages made him a favourite with Nietzsche. His works, mostly now lost, probably established the later philosophy of Stoicism.

Herakleides – An Aeolian, a Greek of Asia Minor. With his brothers Nestor and Orestes, he becomes a retainer – a warrior – in service to Arimnestos. It is easy, when looking at the birth of Greek democracy, to see the whole form of modern government firmly established – but at the time of this book, democracy was less than skin-deep and most armies were formed of semi-feudal war bands following an aristocrat.

Heraklides – Aristides' helmsman, a lower-class Athenian who has made a name for himself in war.

Hermogenes – Son of Bion, Arimnestos's slave.

Hesiod – A great poet (or a great tradition of poetry) from Boeotia in Greece. Hesiod's *Works and Days* and *Theogony* were widely read in the sixth century and remain fresh today – they are the chief source we have on Greek farming, and this book owes an enormous debt to them.

Hippias – Last tyrant of Athens, overthrown around 510 BC (that is, just around the beginning of this series). Hippias escaped into exile and became a pensioner of Darius of Persia.

Hipponax – 540–c.498 BC. A Greek poet and satirist, considered the inventor of parody. He is supposed to have said, 'There are two days when a woman is a pleasure: the day one marries her and the day one buries her.'

Histiaeus – Tyrant of Miletus and ally of Darius of Persia, possible originator of the plan for the Ionian Revolt.

Homer – Another great poet, roughly Hesiod's contemporary (give or take fifty years!) and again, possibly more a poetic tradition than an individual man. Homer is reputed as the author of the *Iliad* and the *Odyssey*, two great epic poems which, between them, largely defined what heroism and aristocratic good behaviour should be in Greek society – and, you might say, to this very day.

Idomeneus – Cretan warrior, priest of Leitus.

Kylix – A boy, slave of Hipponax.

Leukas – Alban sailor, later deck master on *Lydia*. Kelt of the Dumnones of Briton.

Miltiades – Tyrant of the Thracian Chersonese. His son, Cimon rose to be a great man in Athenian politics. Probably the author of the Athenian victory of Marathon, Miltiades was a complex man, a pirate, a warlord, and a supporter of Athenian democracy.

Penelope – Daughter of Chalkeotechnes, sister of Arimnestos.

Polymarchos – ex-slave swordmaster of Syracusa.

Phrynicus – Ancient Athenian playwright and warrior.

Sappho – A Greek poetess from the island of Lesbos, born sometime around 630 BC and died between 570 and 550 BC. Her father was probably Lord of Eressos. Widely considered the greatest lyric poet of Ancient Greece.

Seckla – Numidian ex-slave.

Simonalkes – Head of the collateral branch of the Plataean Corvaxae, cousin to Arimnestos.

Simonides – Another great lyric poet, he lived c.556–468 BC, and his nephew, Bacchylides, was as famous as he. Perhaps best known for his epigrams, one of which is:

Ω ξεῖν᾽, ἀγγέλλειν Λακεδαιμονίοις ὅτι τῇδε
κείμεθα, τοῖς κείνων ῥήμασι πειθόμενοι.
Go tell the Spartans, thou who passest by,
That here, obedient to their laws, we lie.

Thales – c.624–c.546 BC. The first philosopher of the Greek tradition, whose writings were still current in Arimnestos's time. Thales used geometry to solve problems such as calculating the height of the pyramids in Egypt and the distance of ships from the shore. He made at least one trip to Egypt. He is widely accepted as the founder of western mathematics.

Themistocles – Leader of the demos party in Athens, father of the Athenian Fleet. Political enemy of Aristides.

Theognis – Theognis of Megara was almost certainly not one man but a whole canon of aristocratic poetry under that name, much of it practical. There are maxims, many very wise, laments on the decline of man and the age, and the woes of old age and poverty, songs for symposia, etc. In later sections there are songs and poems about homosexual love and laments for failed romances. Despite widespread attributions, there was, at some point, a real Theognis who may have lived in the mid-6th century BC, or just before the events of this series. His poetry would have been central to the world of Arimnestos's mother.

Vasileos – Master shipwright and helmsman.

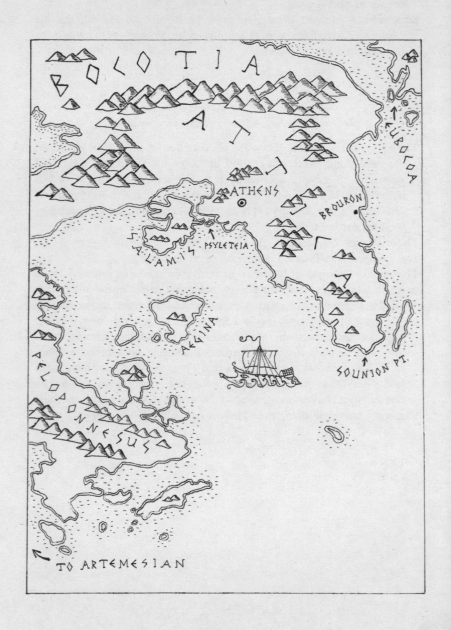

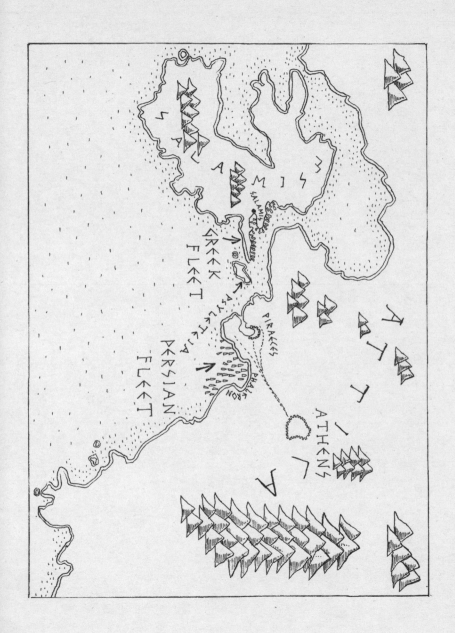

Prologue

Here we are again – the penultimate night of my feast. Quite a crowd for an old man's ravings.

But this is the best of tales since Troy – with sorrow and joy, men and women, heroes and traitors and men, like Themistocles, who were both. May you never see such times, thugater.

The first night, I told you of my youth and how I went to Calchus the priest to be educated as a gentleman, and instead learned to be a spear fighter. Because Calchus was no empty windbag, but a Killer of Men, who had stood his place many times in the storm of bronze. And veterans came from all over Greece to hang their shields for a time at our shrine and talk to Calchus, and he sent them away whole, or better men, at least. Except that the worst of them, the Hero called for, and the priest would kill them on the precinct walls and send their shades shrieking to feed the old Hero, or serve him in Hades.

Mind you, friends, Leithos wasn't some angry old god demanding blood sacrifice, but Plataea's hero from the Trojan War. And he was a particularly Boeotian hero, because he was no great man-slayer, no tent-sulker. His claim to fame is that he went to Troy and fought all ten years. That on the day that mighty Hector raged by the ships of the Greeks and Achilles sulked in his tent, Leithos rallied the lesser men and formed a tight shield wall and held Hector long enough for Ajax and the other Greek heroes to rally.

You might hear a different story in Thebes, or Athens, or Sparta. But that's the story of the Hero I grew to serve, and I spent years at his shrine, learning the war dances that we call the Pyrrhiche. Oh, I learned to read old Theognis and Hesiod and Homer, too. But it was the spear, the sword and the aspis that sang to me.

When my father found that I was learning to be a warrior and not a man of letters, he came and fetched me home, and old Calchus – died. Killed himself, more like. But I've told all this – and how little Plataea, our farm town at the edge of Boeotia, sought to be free of cursed Thebes and made an alliance with distant Athens. I told you all how godlike Miltiades came to our town and treated my father, the bronze-smith and Draco the wheelwright and old Epictetus the farmer like Athenian gentlemen – how he wooed them with fine words and paid hard silver for their products, so that he bound them to his own political ends and to the needs of Athens.

When I was still a gangly boy – tall, and well-muscled, as I remember, but too young to fight in the phalanx – Athens called for little Plataea's aid, and we marched over Cithaeron, the ancient mountain that is also our glowering god, and we rallied to the Athenians at Oinoe. We stood beside them against Sparta and Corinth and all the Peloponnesian cities – and we beat them.

Well, Athens beat them. Plataea barely survived, and my older brother, who should have been my father's heir, died there with a Spartiate's spear in his belly.

Four days later, when we fought again – this time against Thebes – I was in the phalanx. Again, we triumphed. And I was a hoplite.

And two days later, when we faced the Euboeans, I saw my cousin Simon kill my father, stabbing him in the back under his bright bronze cuirass. When I fell over my father's corpse, I took a mighty blow and when I awoke, I had no memory of Simon's treachery.

When I awoke, of course, I was a slave. Simon had sold me to Phoenician traders, and I went east with a cargo of Greek slaves.

I was a slave for some years, and in truth, it was not a bad life. I went to a fine house, ruled by rich, elegant, excellent people: Hipponax the poet and his wife and two children. Archilogos, the eldest and a boy, was my real master, and yet my friend and ally, and we had many escapades together. And his sister, Briseis—

Ah, Briseis. Helen, returned to life.

We lived in far-off Ephesus, one of the most beautiful and powerful cities in the Greek world, yet located on the coast of Asia. Greeks have lived there since the Trojan war, and the temple of Artemis there is one of the wonders of the world. My master went to school each day at the temple of Artemis, and there the great philosopher, Heraclitus, had his school, and he would shower us with questions every bit as painful as the blows of the old fighter who taught us pankration at the gymnasium.

Heraclitus. I have met men, and women, who saw him as a charlatan, a dreamer, a mouther of impieties. In fact, he was deeply religious – his family held the heredity priesthood of Artemis – but he believed that fire was the only true element, and change the only constant. I can witness to both.

It was a fine life. I got a rich lord's education for nothing. I learned to drive a chariot, and to ride a horse and to fight and to use my mind like a sword. I loved it all, but best of all . . .

Best of all, I loved Briseis.

And while I loved her – and half a dozen other young women – I grew to manhood listening to Greeks and Persians plotting various plots in my master's house, and one night all the plots burst forth into ugly blossoms and bore the fruit of red-handed war, and the Greek cities of Ionia revolted against the Persian overlords.

Now, as tonight's story will be about war with the Persians, let me take a moment to remind you of the roots of the conflict, because they are ignoble, and the Greeks were no better than the Persians, and perhaps a great deal worse. The Ionians had money, power, and freedom: freedom to worship, freedom to rule themselves under the Great King, and all it cost them was taxes and the 'slavery' of having to obey the Great King in matters of foreign policy. The 'yoke' of the Persians was light and easy to wear, and no man alive knows that better than me, because I served, slave though I was, as a herald between my master and the mighty Artaphernes, the satrap of all Phrygia. I knew him well; I ran his errands, dressed him at times, and one dark night, when my master Hipponax caught the Persian in his wife's bed, I saved his life when my master would have killed him. I saved my master's life, as well, holding the corridor against four Persian soldiers of high repute – Aryanam, Pharnakes, Cyrus and Darius. I know their names because they were my friends, in other times.

And you'll hear of them again. Except Pharnakes, who died in the Bosporus, fighting Carians.

At any rate, after that night of swords and fire and hate, my master went from being a loyal servant of Persia to a hate-filled Greek 'patriot'. And our city, Ephesus, roused itself to war. And amidst it all, my beloved Briseis lost her fiancé to rumour and innuendo, and Archilogos and I beat him for his impudence. I had learned to kill, and to use violence to get what I wanted. And as a reward, I got Briseis – or to be more accurate, she had me. My master freed me, not knowing that I had just deflowered his daughter, and I sailed away with Archilogos to avoid the wrath of the suitor's relatives.

We joined the Greek revolt at Lesvos, and there, on the beach, I met Aristides – sometimes called the Just, one of the greatest heroes of Athens, and Miltiades' political foe.

That was the beginning of my true life. My life as a man of war. I won my first games on a beach in Chios and I earned my first suit of armour, and I went to war against the Persians.

But the God of War, Ares, was not so much in charge of my life as Aphrodite, and when we returned to Ephesus to plan the great war, I spent every hour that I could with Briseis, and the result, I think now, was never in doubt. But Heraclitus, the great sage, asked me to swear an oath to all the gods that I would protect Archilogos and his family, and I swore. Like the heroes in the old stories, I never thought about the consequence of swearing such a great oath and sleeping all the while with Briseis.

Ah, Briseis! She taunted me with cowardice when I stayed away from her and devoured me when I visited her, sneaking, night after night, past the slaves into the women's quarters, until, in the end, we were caught. Of course we were caught.

And I was thrown from the house and ordered never to return, by the family I'd sworn to protect.

Three days later I was marching upcountry with Aristides and the Athenians. We burned Sardis, but the Persians caught us in the midst of looting the market and we lost the fight in the town and then again at the bridge, and the Persians beat us like a drum, but I stood my ground, fight after fight, and my reputation as a spear fighter grew. In a mountain pass, Eualcides the Euboean and I charged Artaphernes' bodyguard, and lived to tell the tale. Three days later, on the plains north of Ephesus, we tried to face a provincial Persian army with the whole might of the Ionian Revolt, and the Greeks folded and ran rather than face the Persian archery and the outraged Phrygians. Alone, on the far left, the Athenians and the Euboeans held our ground and stopped the Carians. Our army was destroyed. Eualcides the hero died there, and I went back to save his corpse, and in the process found that Hipponax, my former master, lay mortally wounded. I gave him the mercy blow, again failing to think of the oath I'd sworn, and my once near-brother Archilogos thought I'd done it from hate, not love. And that blow stood between us and any hope of reconciliation. To Archilogos, I'd raped his sister and killed his father after swearing an oath to the gods to protect them. And that will have bearing on tonight's tale.

From the rout of Ephesus, I escaped with the Athenians, but the curse of my shattered oath lay on me and Poseidon harried our ship, and in every port I killed men who annoyed me until Hagios, my Athenian friend, put me ashore on Crete, with the King of Gortyn, Achilles, and his son Neoptolymos, to whom I was war tutor. I tutored him so well that, in the next great battle of the Ionian War, Neoptolymos and I were the heroes of the Greek fleet, and we helped my once-friend Archilogos break the Persian centre. It was the first victory for the Greeks, but it was fleeting, and a few days later, I was a pirate on the great sea with my own ship for the first time. Fortune favoured me – perhaps, I think, because I had in part redeemed my oath to the gods by saving Archilogos at the sea battle. And when we weathered the worst storm I had ever seen, Poseidon had gifted me the African-Greek navigator Paramanos and a good crew in a heavy ship. I returned to Lesvos and joined Miltiades, the same who had wooed the Plataeans at the dawn of this tale. And from him I learned the facts of my father's murder and I determined to go home and avenge him.

I found Briseis had married one of the architects of the Ionian Revolt, and he was eager to kill me – the rumour was that she called my name when he was with her at night. And I determined to kill him.

After two seasons of piracy with Miltiades and further failures of the rebels to resist the Persians, I found him skulking around the edge of a great melee in Thrace and I killed him. I presented myself to Briseis to take her as my own – and she spurned me.

That's how it is, sometimes. I went back to Plataea an empty vessel, and the Furies filled me with revenge. I found Simon and his sons sitting on my farm – Simon married to my mother, planning to marry his youngest son Simonalkes to my sister Penelope.

I'll interrupt my own tale to say that I did not fall on Simon with fire and sword, because four years of living by the spear had taught me that things I had learned as a boy from Calchus and heard again from Heraclitus were coming to seem important and true – that justice was more important than might. I let the law of Plataea have its way. Simon hanged himself from the rafters of my father's workshop, and the Furies left me alone with my mother and my sister.

*

5

That would make a fine tale, I think, by itself, but the gods were far from done with Plataea, and by the next spring there were storm clouds brewing in all directions. An Athenian aristocrat died under my hypaspist's sword – Idomeneus, who comes all too often into these stories, a mad Cretan – he had taken up the priesthood of the old shrine. I went off to see to the crisis and that road took me over the mountains to Athens and into the middle of Athenian politics – aye, you'll hear more of that tonight, too. There I fell afoul of the Alcmaeonidae and their scion Cleitus, because it was his brother who had died in our sanctuary and because my cowardly cousin Simon's sons were laying a trap for me. He stole my horse and my slave girl, but that's another story. Because of him, I was tried for murder and Aristides the Just got me off with a trick. But in the process, I committed hubris – the crime of treating a man like a slave – and Aristides ordered me to go to Delos, to the great temple of Apollo, to be cleansed.

Apollo, that scheming god, never meant me to be cleansed, but instead thrust me back into the service of Miltiades, whose fortunes were at an all-time ebb. With two ships I re-provisioned Miletus, not once but twice, and made a small fortune on it, and on piracy. I took men's goods, and their women, and I killed for money, took ships, and thought too little of the gods. Apollo had warned me – in his own voice – to learn to use mercy, but I failed more often than I succeeded, and I left a red track behind me across the Ionian Sea. And in time, I was a captain at the greatest sea battle of the Ionian Revolt – at Lade. At Lade, the Great King put together an incredible fleet, of nearly six *hundred* ships, to face the Greeks and their allies with almost three hundred and fifty ships. It sounds one-sided, but we were well trained; we should have been ready. I sailed with the Athenians and the Cretans and we beat the Phoenicians at one end of the line and emerged from the morning fog expecting the praise of our navarch, the Phocaean Dionysus – alongside Miltiades, the greatest pirate and ship-handler in the Greek world. But when we punched through the Phoenicians, we found that the Samians, our fellow Greeks, had sold out to the Persians. The Great King triumphed, and the Ionian revolt collapsed. Most of my friends – most of the men of my youth – died at Lade.

Briseis married Artaphernes, who had slept with her mother – and became the most powerful woman in Ionia, as she had always planned.

6

Datis, the architect of the Persian victory, raped and plundered his way across Lesvos and Chios, slaughtering men, taking women for the slave markets, and making true every slander that Greeks had falsely whispered about Persian atrocities.

Miletus, that I had helped to hold, fell. I saved what I could. And went home, with fifty families of Miletians to add to the citizen levy of Plataea. I spent my fortune on them, buying them land and oxen, and then ... then I went back to smithing bronze. I gave up the spear.

How the gods must have laughed.

A season later, while my sister went to a finishing school to get her away from my mother's drunkenness, I went back to Athens because my friend Phrynicus, who had stood in the arrow storm at Lade with me, was producing his play, *The Fall of Miletus*. And Miltiades had been arrested for threatening the state – of which, let me say, friends, he was absolutely guilty, because Miltiades would have sold his own mother into slavery to achieve power in Athens.

At any rate, I used money and some of the talents I'd learned as a slave – and a lot of my friends – to see that Phrynicus's play was produced. And, incidentally, to win my stolen slave-girl free of her brothel and wreak some revenge on the Alcmaeonidae. In the process, I undermined their power with the demos – the people – and helped the new voice in Athenian politics – Themistocles the Orator. He had little love for me, but he managed to tolerate my success long enough to help me – and Aristides – to undermine the pro-Persian party and liberate Miltiades.

I went home to Plataea feeling that I'd done a lifetime's good service to Athens. My bronze-smithing was getting better and better and I spent the winter training the Plataean phalanx in my spare time. War was going to be my hobby, the way some men learn the diaulos or the kithara to while away old age. I trained the young men and forged bronze. Life grew sweeter.

And when my sister Penelope – now married to a local Thespian aristocrat – decided that I was going to marry her friend Euphonia, I eventually agreed. I rode to Attica with a hunting party of aristocrats – Boeotian and Athenian – and won my bride in games that would not have disgraced the heroes of the past. And in the spring I wed her, at a wedding that included Themistocles and Aristides and Miltiades – and Harpagos and Agios and Moire and a dozen of my other friends from every class in Athens. I went back over the mountains with my bride and settled down to make babies.

But the storm clouds on the horizon were coming on a great wind of change. And the first gusts of that wind brought us a raid out of Thebes, paid for by Cleitus of the Alcmaeonids and led by my cousin Simon's son Simonalkes. The vain bastard named most of his sons after himself – how weak can a man be?

I digress. We caught them – my new Plataean phalanx – and we crushed them. My friend Teucer, the archer, killed Simonides. And because of them we were all together when the Athenians called for our help, because the Persians, having destroyed Euboea, were marching for Athens.

Well, I won't retell Marathon. Myron, our archon and always my friend, sent us without reservation, and all the Plataeans marched under my command – and we stood by the Athenians on the greatest day Greek men have ever known, and we were heroes. Hah! I'll tell it again if you don't watch yourselves. We defeated Datis and his Persians by the black ships. Agios died there on the astern of a Persian trireme, but we won the day. Here's to his shade. And to all the shades of all the men who died at Lade.

But when I led the victorious Plataeans back across the mountains, it was to find that my beautiful young wife had died in childbirth. The gods stole my wits clean away – I took her body to my house and burned it and all my trappings, and I went south over Cithaeron, intending to destroy myself.

May you never know how black the world can be. Women know that darkness sometimes after the birth of a child, and men after battle. Any peak of spirit has its price, and when a man or woman stands with the gods, however briefly, they pay the price ten times. The exertion of Marathon and the loss of my wife unmanned me. I leapt from a cliff.

I fell, and struck, not rocks, but water. And when I surfaced, my body fought for life, and I swam until my feet dragged on the beach. Then I swooned, and when I awoke, I was once again a slave. Again, taken by Phoenicians, but this time as an adult. My life was cruel and like to be short, and the irony of the whole thing was that now I soon craved life.

I lived a brutal life under a monster called Dagon, and you'll hear plenty of him, tonight. But he tried to break me, body and soul, and nigh on succeeded. In the end, he crucified me on a mast and left me to die. But Poseidon saved me – washed me over the side with the mast and let me live. Set me on the deck of a little Sikel trading ship, where I pulled an oar as a near-slave for a few months. And then I was taken again, by the Phoenicians.

The degradations and the humiliations went on, until one day, in a sea fight, I took a sword and cut my way to freedom. The sword fell at my feet – literally. The gods have a hand in every man's life. Only impious fools believe otherwise.

As a slave, I had developed new friendships; or rather, new alliances, which, when free, ripened into friendship. My new friends were a polyglot rabble – an Etruscan of Rome named Gaius, a couple of Kelts, Daud and Sittonax, a pair of Africans from south of Libya, Doola and Seckla, a Sikel named Demetrios and an Illyrian kinglet-turned-slave called Neoptolymos. We swore an oath to Poseidon to take a ship to Alba and buy tin and we carried out our oath. As I told you last night, we went to Sicily and while my friends became small traders on the coast, I worked as a bronze-smith, learning and teaching. I fell in love with Lydia, the bronze-smith's daughter – and betrayed her, and for that betrayal – let's call things by their proper names – I lost confidence in myself, and I lost the favour of the gods, and for years I wandered up and down the seas, until at last we redeemed our oaths, went to Alba for the tin, and came back rich men. I did my best to see Lydia well suited, and I met Pythagoras's daughter and was able to learn something of that great man's mathematics and his philosophy. I met Gelon the tyrant of Syracuse and declined to serve him, and sailed away, and there, on a beach near Taranto in the south of Italy, I found my friend Harpagos and Cimon, son of Miltiades, and other of the friends and allies of my youth. I confess, I had sent a message, hoping that they would come. We cruised north into the Adriatic, because I had promised Neoptolymos that we'd restore him to his throne, and we did, though we got a little blood on it. And then the Athenians and I parted company from my friends of Sicily days – they went back to Massalia to till their fields, and I left them to go back to being Arimnestos of Plataea. Because Cimon said that the Persians were coming. And whatever my failings as a man – and I had and still have many – I am the god's own tool in the war of the Greeks against the Persians.

For all that, I have always counted many Persians among my friends, and the best of men – the most excellent, the most brave, the most loyal. Persians are a race of truth-telling heroes. But they are not Greeks, and when it came to war . . .

We parted company off Illyria, and coasted the Western Peloponnese. But Poseidon was not yet done with me, and a mighty storm blew up off of Africa and it fell on us, scattering our little squadron and sending my ship far, far to the south and west, and when the storm blew itself out, we were a dismasted hulk riding the rollers, and there was another damaged ship under our lee. We could see she was a Carthaginian. We fell on that ship and took it, although in a strange, three-sided fight – the rowers were rising against the deck crew of Persians.

It was Artaphernes' own ship, and he was travelling from Tyre to Carthage to arrange for Carthaginian ships to help the Great King to make war on Athens. And I rescued him – I thought him a corpse.

So did his wife, my Briseis, who threw herself into my arms.

Blood dripped from my sword, and I stood with Helen in my arms on a ship I'd just taken by force of arms, and I thought myself the king of the world.

How the gods must have laughed.

Last night I told you of our lowest ebb. Because Artaphernes was not dead, and all that followed came from that fact. He was the Great King's ambassador to the Carthaginians, and our years of guest-friendship – an exchange of lives going back to my youth, if you've been listening – required me to take him and my Persian friends, his bodyguards, and Briseis, my Helen reborn, to Carthage, though my enemy Dagon had sworn to my destruction in his mad way, and though by then Carthage had put quite a price on my head.

Hah! My role in taking part of their tin fleet. I don't regret it – the foundation of all our fortunes, thugater.

At any rate, we ran Artaphernes – badly wounded – into Carthage, and escaped with our lives after a brilliant piece of boat handling and the god's own luck. Possibly *Lydia's* finest hour. And I saw Dagon.

We ran along the coast of Africa and stopped at Sicily, and there I found my old sparring partner and hoplomachos Polymarchos. He was training an athlete for the Olympics and in a moment I made peace with the gods and took Polymarchos and his young man to Olympia, where we – my whole ship's crew – watched the Olympics, spending the profits of our piracy in a fine style, and making a wicked profit off the wine we brought to sell. There, we played a role in bridging the distance between Athens and Sparta, and there I saw the depth of selfish greed that would cause some men – like Adeimantus of Corinth

– to betray Greece and work only for his own ends. I hate his memory – I hope he rots in Hades – but he was scarcely alone, and when Queen Gorgo – here's to the splendour of her, mind and body – when Queen Gorgo of Sparta called us 'a conspiracy to save Greece' she was not speaking poetically. Even the Spartans had their factions and it was at the Olympics that I discovered that Brasidas, my Spartan officer, was some sort of exiled criminal – or just possibly, a man who'd been betrayed by his country, and not the other way around.

With only a little jiggling of the wheel of fate, we made sure Sparta won the chariot race and we left the Olympics richer by some drachmas and wiser by as much, as we'd had nights and nights to thrash out plans for the defence of Greece.

So it was all the more daunting when King Leonidas and Queen Gorgo of Sparta asked me to take their ambassadors to the Great King, the king of Persia. That's another complex tale; the old Spartan king had killed the Persian heralds, an act of gross impiety, and Leonidas sought to rid Sparta of that impiety. So he sent two messengers to far-off Persepolis, two hereditary heralds.

And me.

Well, and Aristides the Just of Athens, who was ostracised – exiled – for being too fair, too rigid, too much of a prig ...

I laugh. He was probably my closest friend – my mentor. A brilliant soldier – his finest hour will come soon – and a brilliant speaker, a man who was so incorruptible that ordinary men sometimes found him easy to hate. An aristocrat of the kind that makes men like me think there might be something to the notion of birth; a true hero.

We went to the Great King by way of Tarsus, where I was mauled by a lion, and Babylon, where I was mauled by a woman. Of the two, Babylon was vastly to be preferred. In Babylon we found the seed of the revolt that later saved Greece. When we arrived at Persepolis, I knew immediately that our embassy was doomed – the arrogance of the Persians and Medes was boundless, and nothing we could do would placate or even annoy them. I told you last night how the Spartan envoys – and Brasidas, my friend – and I danced in armour for the Immortals, and were mocked.

Our audience with the Great King was more like staged theatre, intended by his cousin Mardonius to humiliate us before the King had us executed.

But, luckily, my friend Artaphernes had a long arm and his own allies. In other places I have discussed him – another great man, another hero, another mentor. The greatest of my foes, and one I never defeated. But in this we were allies; he did not want Mardonius to triumph, nor did he seek to destroy Athens or Sparta. Because of Artaphernes, we had a few friends in Persepolis, and we were rescued from death by the Queen Mother, who smuggled us out of the city and let us free on the plains; not because she loved Greece, but only because she feared Mardonius and his extreme, militaristic policies.

We ran. But in running, with our Persian escort of Artaphernes' picked men (and my boyhood friend Cyrus!), we left Brasidas to fan the flames of revolt in Babylon, and we slipped home.

In Sardis, after weeks of playing cat and mouse with all the soldiers in Asia, I saw Artaphernes. He was sick and old, but strong enough to ask me for a last favour – that when I heard he was dead, I should come and take Briseis. Yes, the love of my life was his wife, the Queen of Ionia as she had always meant to be. Artaphernes' son, also called Artaphernes, hated her, and hated me.

At any rate, we made it to my ships, and sailed across the wintry sea to Athens. In the spring, the Revolt of Babylon saved Greece from invasion, and the leaders of the Greek world gathered at Corinth and bickered. Endlessly. My ships made me rich, bringing cargoes from Illyria and Egypt and Colchis and all points in between, and I sailed that summer, going to the Nile delta and back, and ignoring the cause of Greek independence as much as ever I could.

But in the end, the Persians came. Last night I told you all of the truth: the internal divisions of the Greeks, and their foolish early efforts – the march to the Vale of Tempe and its utter failure, and the eventual arrangement for a small land army to hold the Hot Springs of Thermopylae while the great allied fleet held Cape Artemisium.

Leonidas, best of the Spartans, held the pass at Thermopylae. And we, as ragtag a fleet as ever put oar to water, held the waters off Artemisium – day after day. Storms pounded the Persians. We pounded the Persians. Once we fought them to a standstill, and on the last day we beat them.

But at our backs, a traitor led the Medes around the Spartan wall, and King Leonidas died.

The so-called Great King desecrated his body and took his head. The Great King's soldiers did the same to all three hundred Spartans and to others besides. Dogs ripped the body of my noble brother-in-law, Antigonus. My sister would weep for his shade, and I would weep too.

No gods laughed. The week after Thermopylae was the worst of the Long War – the worst week many of us had ever known.

Calliades was archon in Athens, and the Eleians celebrated the Seventy-fifth Olympiad, that in which Astylus of Syracuse won the stadion. It was in this year that King Xerxes made his campaign against Greece. It was the year of the climax of the Long War.

I was there.

Part I

The Wooden Wall

When the foe shall have taken whatever the limit of Cecrops
Holds within it, and all which divine Cithaeron, shelters,
Then far-seeing Jove grants this to the prayers of Athene;
Safe shall the wooden wall continue for thee and thy children.
Wait not the tramp of the horse, nor the footmen mightily moving
Over the land, but turn your hack to the foe, and retire ye.
Yet shall a day arrive when ye shall meet him in battle.
Holy Salamis, thou shalt destroy the offspring of women,
When men scatter the seed, or when they gather the harvest.

Prophecy of the Oracle of Delphi, 480 BC

When morning broke, we prepared our ships to put to sea. Unbeaten, we prepared to disperse and run.

It didn't matter particularly just how the Spartans had come to lose such an impregnable position. It's a well-known story now and I won't shame us all by telling it. And at the time I did not yet know that my brilliant brother-in-law, Antigonus, had died at the head of his Thespians, taking forty Marathon veterans to die beside the Spartans. They stripped and desecrated his body too, the cowards.

I didn't know, yet. But I knew that Themistocles was grey with fatigue and shattered hopes, and I knew that Adeimantus scarcely troubled to hide his delight. The great fleet was breaking up. Nothing had been decided except that all the Boeotians – Plataeans like me – were to run for their homes and clear the plains of Boeotia before the Great King came with fire and sword. We knew, even then, what was coming. With the Hot Gates lost there wasn't another place to stop the Medes. Eurybiades said that there would be another army to fight for Boeotia, but none of us believed him.

Aristides told me in that awful dawn that the Thebans had already offered earth and water to the Great King. I spat, somewhat automatically.

'We were *winning*,' I said. It was said in the sort of voice that young men comment on the ultimate unfairness of the world.

Aristides looked at Brasidas, who happened to be there, cleaning the blood from his greaves in seawater. They exchanged a look.

'It is the will of the gods,' Aristides said.

'Fuck the gods,' I spat.

Brasidas stepped back and met my eye. 'You sound like a child,' he said – a long speech, for him.

But to a Spartan, the essence of nobility is in not showing weakness

– and almost *any* show of emotion, even anger, rage or love – all of these are signs of weakness. A true Spartan hides his thoughts from men.

It's not an ideal I've ever striven for, but I understand it.

Aristides was an aristocratic Athenian and he clearly shared Brasidas's views. 'Blasphemy,' he said.

Together, they made me feel like a small boy who had fled rather than face a beating.

I remember all this because of what Aristides said.

First, he put a hand on my shoulder – an unaccustomed familiarity.

Then he said, 'Most men praise the gods when they are happy and curse them when they are sad. But piety lies in obeying the will of the gods all the time. It is easy to be a just man when all of your decisions go well and all the world loves you. It is when all is lost that the gods see what you really are.'

I spat again. 'Let the gods note that I'm tired and wounded, then,' I said. I had lost fingers on my left hand, and they ached – the ends hurt all the time, making sleeping difficult, and I had trouble closing my hand.

Briseis was lost. For ever, as far as I could tell. Again.

Let me tell you a thing, thugater. I had determined that if the Greeks lost I would not return alive. I had seen too many defeats. My house was too empty, despite my daughter. Yes – despite her.

But we had *not* lost. Beyond all fears, it was the *Spartans* who lost. And now I was alive and all my hopes in ruins. In a way, it was worse then Lade.

At Lade, I felt Apollo betrayed us. At Artemisium, I felt as if the whole pantheon deserted us.

Aristides left his hand on my shoulder. 'Now we show the gods who we are,' he said.

Brave words, in a moment of despair.

Eurybiades summoned us as the sun rose. Some of the ships had already left – two Athenian dispatch boats, and a whole squadron of Athenians under Xanthippus, one of their navarchs.

We were a grim and silent lot – three hundred captains. Many of us had wounds from the day before, and there were gaps. We had lost almost fifty ships in four days.

Themistocles had his himation wrapped around him and the end pulled over his head, and seemed unwilling to speak. His bluff, man-of-the-people face looked bloated, and he himself seemed crippled.

In that dark hour it was Eurybiades who declined to crack.

'We will need a fleet rendezvous,' he said clearly. 'First, let us make sacrifice to the immortal gods and then let us have some clear counsel.' He led us up on the headlands to the little temple of Artemis and there he sacrificed a pair of rams. Themistocles played no part, and Aristides hung back.

Adeimantus of Corinth held the sacrifices and walked with the Spartan navarch back down the hill to the small rise where we gathered to talk.

After prayers and some exhortations, Eurybiades raised his arms. 'Let me hear you,' he said. 'What is our next move?'

He looked at Themistocles. The Athenian democrat shook his head.

'Corinth!' said Adeimantus. 'We can hold the isthmus for ever, and if we should lose it, we have the Acrocorinth, which can host a mighty army and hold until the gods come to aid us.'

Themistocles twitched, like a wounded man who is wounded again.

No one was going to listen to me, so I walked around the circle of men slowly, hobbling a little on my second-best spear, until I reached the Athenian orator.

I poked him.

He ignored me.

'Themistocles!' I hissed. 'If you don't enter into this thing, they're going to sail away and leave Athens to its fate.'

Themistocles met my eye. 'Athens is already doomed,' he said. 'Don't you understand? Attica is open. The Persians will come at us now, as they have always desired. It is over.'

I frowned. I wanted to say what Aristides had said to me, but Themistocles was not the man to accept arguments about excellence and the gods.

'How great would men think you if you stopped the Persians now?' I asked him. 'The fleet is *not* beaten.' I pointed. 'Yesterday they flinched, not we Greeks.'

I'm not sure what I believed, thugater. What I meant. I hated that Themistocles would not even make a fight of it, even while I recognised the totality of our defeat.

Aristides had followed me. He and Themistocles hated each other, of course, but in that hour they were both Athenians.

'We must at least have the fleet to cover the movement of all the demos – the people – to Salamis,' Aristides said.

That shook me. Of course, they would empty Attica.

My daughter was at Brauron, dancing with the maidens. She was in Attica.

Aristides crossed his arms.

Themistocles slowly straightened, like a man waking from sleep. His voice was carefully pitched. He sounded as if he did not care.

'None of you can sail to Corinth in a single leg,' he said. 'You'll want to take water on the beaches of mighty Ajax, where Salamis brushes the sea.'

Adeimantus grinned. 'We can take on water while we watch Athens destroyed!' he said, and laughed like a boy, so that men turned their heads away in shame, and shuffled away from him. 'But then, we sail for Corinth.'

Themistocles shrugged as if it was a matter of little moment.

Eurybiades nodded sharply. 'Salamis it is. Day after tomorrow.' To the Corinthian, he said, 'It is not fitting to speak of the destruction of Athens. It is close to blasphemy.'

From the Spartan, these were strong words.

Adeimantus laughed, more of a bark than a laugh, a sound made to gain attention as a child, I'd warrant. 'Mighty Lacedaemon sent one king and a handful of men to protect Greece. Why pretend? Sparta wants Athens destroyed as much as Corinth does.'

Eurybiades' face grew red and his reserve showed the first sign of cracking that I had seen.

Adeimantus realised his error and held up a hand, like a man signalling defeat in a pankration bout. 'No – I spoke only in jest.'

'An ill jest,' I said.

Adeimantus turned on me. 'I do not speak to you.'

I let it go. I wanted to get to my daughter, not to have a fight on the beach.

The gloom engendered by the death of Leonidas stayed on us even as we got our hulls into the water and indeed, my thugater, it was on us for many days thereafter. But I reminded young Pericles, when he was going to return to Cimon, that Heraclitus said, 'Souls slain in war are purer than those that perish in disease.'

'What does that mean?' Pericles asked me. He had a way, comic in a man so young, and yet also a little terrifying, of asking the most direct questions with his big eyes boring into you.

I shrugged. 'Who am I to tell you what Heraclitus meant by

anything?' I said. 'But if I had to hazard a guess, I'd say he meant that as the basis of soul is fire, so, in combat, a man's soul is hottest, and if he dies then, he dies with his soul closest to its natural state. Whereas my master thought that moisture was the antithesis of the soul and that in sickness we become weak and our souls moist.'

Pericles shook his head. 'I would like to believe that the king of Sparta went straight to Elysium, to walk there with Achilles and Hector. But ...' He met my eye, this adolescent boy. 'Yet I do not think it is so simple. I think this is the sort of thing men tell each other to console themselves for the loss of a comrade.'

Then he bowed. 'I am sorry, Lord Arimnestos. I speak as if I was your peer.'

I had to laugh. Even through the pain of losing the king, even in the knowledge that my world was about to be destroyed, there was something antic in the serious, steady-burning arrogance of the boy.

'Go prate at Cimon,' I told him. 'I'll see you in Attica.'

I said the last because I had determined to go first to Brauron, which is close by the sea, to pick up my daughter. But my oarsmen were Plataeans almost to a man, and they made it clear that they had other priorities.

I couldn't be angry. First, I knew from Cimon that the great sanctuaries, like Brauron and Sounion, would be evacuated anyway. My daughter had many friends and I had guest friends in Attica. She was not going to be abandoned in the rush to the ships. Athens and Themistocles had been planning their resistance to the Great King for three years and every aspect of defence – and every option – had been examined. One of the few real advantages to democracy in the face of crisis is that the involvement of every free man means that many different points of view are brought to bear on a problem; admittedly, half of them are foolish or even fantastical, but many men bring new ideas and ready wit. Most of the rural population of Attica was already evacuated to Salamis and to the east coast of the Peloponnese. Troezen especially welcomed Athenian refugees, and little Hermione took many Attic farm families (and, as it proved, many Plataeans), but most of the people went across the narrow straits to the island of Salamis.

At any rate, my daughter was safe enough. Or so I had to hope, because unless I wanted mutiny and blood, my oarsmen wanted to go home. At Artemisium we were an easy day's rowing from the narrows where Euboea nearly connects to the mainland, just another day's walk or two from Plataea over to the west near Mount Cithaeron. As we had nearly the whole phalanx of Green Plataea and nearly every man of substance either rowing or serving as marines – and as the Persians would be at our gates in three days or less – Plataea represented the more immediate crisis.

We rowed with a will. But as we rowed, I marshalled my arguments for the rowers. When we camped on the beaches of Boeotia that night, I convinced Myron and both Peneleos and Empedocles, sons of Empedocles, and old Draco himself and Myron's rich friend Timaeus – and Hermogenes and Styges and Idomeneus and the rest – to give me one more day of rowing. I suggested that some men be sent ahead, walking, or riding. I sent Ka and his archers and they found mules and a pair of horses to carry our messengers. I didn't ask Ka too many questions about where the horses had come from.

'Let's take the ships around to Athens,' I said to the men on the beach. 'They need them for their evacuation. And we can go as swiftly over the mountains from Eleusis as across Boeotia from here.'

Myron nodded. 'There might already be Persian troops loose in Boeotia,' he said. 'Their cavalry—'

Hermogenes nodded. 'And the Thebans have already Medised,' he said, as everyone spat. 'They're between us and home, here.'

Styges glared. 'Traitors,' he said.

We chose a dozen steady men – well, Idomeneus was one, and no one ever called him steady, but they needed a killer to get them through if the going got rough. Ka stole more horses – let's call it what it was – and the messengers rode off with careful instructions and Timaeus to see they were obeyed.

The rest of us woke before dawn and rowed. We were in advance of most of the rest of the fleet, because we were rowing to save our goods and families. We passed the headland at Brauron south of Marathon under sail and I could see the temple and the old bridge and I was delighted to see that there was no one moving – no girls dancing in the courtyard, no children playing at goats on the old hill above the cave of the goddess. We had a beautiful wind and we ran towards Sounion on an empty coast, but towards afternoon, as we prepared to weather Poseidon's promontory, we saw the flash of oars behind us. We knew Cimon's squadron had stayed to watch the Persians and we guessed the Athenian's public ships were moving in a body under Xanthippus, rowing as hard for home as they could.

I feel I should explain that, in the years before Artemisium, the

Athenians had invested the whole output of their silver mines in building a fleet of more than a hundred well-built triremes. Five of them were being crewed by Plataeans, and had Plataean officers and marines. It seemed to me awkward – at best – to leave these five ships on the beaches of Boeotia while we ran home to save our furniture and I said so.

We were not, as it proved, the first ships of the Allied Fleet to reach the beaches at Phaleron. But we rowed past, despite the late hour, and swept into the narrow channel between the Island of Salamis and the mainland as the sun dropped into the sea beyond Megara to the west.

The Bay of Salamis was covered in ships. Fishing boats, merchant ships of every size, rowing boats, military pentekonters and even older triakonters of thirty-oared ships were going back and forth, turning the sea to froth by the beating of their oars, or so the poets liked to say.

I landed my ships on one of the north-facing beaches on the island of Salamis, and after borrowing a horse and making some hasty arrangements, we gathered the men together – all the Plataeans in one great council. It was, to all intents and purposes, a meeting of the City of Plataea.

Why Salamis? Because that's where most of the Athenians were. Like I said, I didn't want to leave their precious ships to rot on the beach or be captured. I handed the five public ships over to a member of the Athenian boule and he was already finding rowers for them while Myron negotiated our passage across to Attica – easy enough, as the Athenians' shipping was mostly empty going that way. We arranged for all our men to go to Eleusis.

Then I spent time putting my professional crews back together. I had men who were Plataean citizens, but my oarsmen, in several ships; we'd sent them out through the fleet to train other rowers. My *Lydia* had kept her crack crew, and now I left her under Seckla with a skeleton crew and no marines, but with Ka and all his archers and Leukas as his helmsman. Paramanos was dead but we'd retaken *Black Raven* and I gave her to Giannis with Megakles as *his* helmsman. In fact, *Black Raven* was not my property and eventually a probate court in Athens or Salamis would see to it that someone bought her and Paramanos's daughters were paid, but that was all in some hazy future where the rule of law applied. In the immediate future, Athens needed every ship. Paramanos had a mostly Athenian crew, including

Thracians, Cilicians, and men of Cyrenaica, his port of origin so to speak, but they had taken terrible casualties fighting three Egyptians at Artemisium and we had to refill the benches. Aristides was going to Corinth with his wife, but his helmsman Demetrios had his own long *Athena Nike* well in hand, and he'd made captures at Artemisium and seemed content. *Amastis,* our rebuilt Corinthian trireme that has been the source of so much trouble, had come through both battles untouched and her crew was professional and under Moire, who needed no help from me. But Moire, like many of his men, had taken up their Plataean citizenship and had homes or families in Plataea. For some oarsmen it was an empty honour and their families were already on Salamis, but others, and especially my old crews in *Lydia* and *Storm Cutter*, crewed by Chian exiles and other men who'd settled at Plataea, had deeper roots – and they were needed. Many of them wanted to go back to Plataea, even for a few hours, to see to their families.

Moire had adjusted to 'being Greek' better than many of my other foreign (or barbarian) friends. His name was an allegory for his acceptance. In his own tongue, Moire (or something that sounded that way) meant 'a jet black horse' or so he told us, but in Greek, Moira is the Goddess of Fate and Fortune and many newly enfranchised ex-slaves chose to call themselves 'Moiregeneus' or 'Born of Good Fortune'. Moire never changed his name. And that, I think, represents the man. He sacrificed to our gods, especially to Poseidon, Lord of Horses. But he always had his own gods, small images he carried with him at sea. It was his particular skill, or tact, that he seemed to like being Greek, but never 'needed' us particularly. In Athens or in Syracusa you could find him squatted down on his heels with a dozen other men of his kind, jabbering in their barbarous tongue and then he'd stand up, pull his himation around himself, and walk off for wine with another kubernetes or helmsman.

As usual, I digress. Harpagos offered to stay with the ships and he was the best kubernetes or trierarch of the lot. I left him in command with good officers and loafing warriors like Sittonax the Gaul and orders to keep the men who stayed busy every day, either training to fight or training to row. He had about three full crews when the rest of us headed for Plataea and I had almost four hundred men.

Brasidas shook his head. 'I'll stay and train the marines,' he said. He meant the ten best oarsmen he'd chosen to replace all the men who'd died on *Black Raven*. I pitied them. But I also knew I'd sleep better knowing that he and Seckla would run a tight camp with sentries and watchtowers – and that Brasidas, although it hurts me to say it, could command a respect from the Athenian oligarchs that Seckla would not. I was to regret not taking him, but that's the way decisions go.

That night on the beach we burned Paramanos. We'd saved his body, or rather, Harpagos and Cimon had, in hard fighting, and we put him on a funeral pyre as his people's traditions' demanded, sang the paean of Apollo and other hymns, and drank too much. He had been first my captive, then my not-very-willing helmsman; then a rival pirate under Miltiades and, only later, my peer and friend. He was the best navigator I ever knew, except perhaps Vasileus. He was a good father to his daughters and a right bastard to his enemies. Here's to his shade.

Aristides the Just was in exile. He wasn't even supposed to be on Salamis, but we all stretched a point. He was eager to get over the mountains to Plataea where his wife awaited, but he wept – openly – to see the whole of the population of Attica gathered on the beaches of Salamis, like a nation of beggars. His words, not mine.

The camps of the Athenians stretched inland, on every path of flat ground the island had to offer. Ajax the Hero may have come from Salamis but it is not the most prosperous place, nor well inhabited, and it lacked the resources to feed the whole population of Attica for any significant time.

But I digress like an old man, which I certainly am! We held our meeting, and our leaders – Myron and Draco, as Timaeus was already gone with the messengers – chose to take the Plataean people over the isthmus to the Peloponnese. Well, Myron had already made that decision and had sent messages to that effect, but sometimes democracy is retroactive tyranny.

In fact, the Spartan navarch had invited all of our people to go to Sparta – probably meant as an honour, it led to a lot of loud talk and some rough jests in our meeting. In the end, they decided to go to Hermione, a small town on the west coast, one of Sparta's allies, a member of her league. Hermione was five days' hard walking from Plataea and a man could pack a cart with enough food for that journey. Because many men had gone to Epidauros to be healed at the sanctuary of the God-Hero Asclepius, many knew the roads to Hermione. Myron hoped to find shipping at the isthmus, and although it plays almost no role in this story, I'll say that my three merchant ships never joined the fleet because they ferried Boeotians – first, people from Thespiae and then Plataeans – to Hermione from the Gulf of Corinth.

At any rate, that was the plan that seemed best. And the phalanx would march home under Hermogenes. I was determined to go to Plataea and come swiftly back over the mountains to the ships. The sight of thousands of Attic refugees crowding the beaches of Salamis taught me a lesson; I knew from the moment I saw them that Athens would fight. The Athenian fleet was not going to sail to the isthmus to defend Corinth and Sparta. It was going to fight right here.

Of course, there was another alternative that didn't bear thinking about – the possibility that Themistocles would sell the alliance out to the Medes. Thebes had, as I have said, already gone over to the Great King. Athens might make the same choice.

But I doubted it.

Aristides found all the Brauron girls after Paramanos's feast, when he met a friend of his wife's on the beach. The next morning, as the phalanx of Plataea loaded themselves into a dozen Athenian grain ships on our beach, I rode over the headland with my sons to find Euphonia as a *skope* in a small lookout tower, watching the waters of the Gulf of Salamis for Persians. All her Brauron sisters were living in a camp of Laconian severity, at the foot of the cliff. The girls were very proud of the orderly, military camp. They had stacks of firewood, simple tents, and when I came, they were practising dancing on the wet sand.

Euphonia laughed and embraced me, which brought a lump to my throat, and still does. She was becoming a young woman and not a slip of a girl – becoming, but not yet there, although her body was lean and hard from a summer of dancing and archery, riding and fighting and hunting. Brauron was like a Spartan academy, but for the girls of the wealthy. The women who ran it, the priestesses of Artemis, had been required to abandon their temple with its magnificent Pi-shaped stoa and its great dining hall where women learned to recline on couches like their brothers – and not spill their wine, I hope.

She began talking without sparing her brothers so much as a look. 'I love to be sentry,' she said. 'I pretend I'm Atlanta, running with Heracles. Or perhaps Achilles. And I want to be the first to spot the Persians. I saw your ships, Pater! I was on duty yesterday, too, and I sent my pais running to say that the fleet of Plataea was on the beaches! And I won the younger girls' dancing, but we had to dance on the sand and not in the great hall, because the Persians are going to burn it, and Mother Bear Europhile says that the dance counts anyway, but Eustratia said it wasn't fair. And next year I'll be allowed to wear the red cord! Unless the Persians burn the temple,' she said in sudden deflation.

I kissed her. 'Euphonia, this is your brother, Hipponax, and no doubt you remember Hector.'

Euphonia gazed at them her usual adoration. 'I saw them,' she said. She smiled. 'Hector is no longer anyone's hyperetes,' she added. 'I can tell, because Mother Bear Thiale lectured us on armour, and that thorax is a very good one. Anyway, I didn't need the lecture – you own lots of armour, and you even used to make it, so I raised my hand and said—'

At this point the boys crushed her in two manly, armoured embraces that stopped even her flow of words for a few moments.

She waved a red shield – a small thing of hide – down at the camp, and instantly, as if they were all Spartan peers, a girl sprinted out of the camp and up the ridge to us. She and Euphonia exchanged salutes – exactly like my own epilektoi! – and my daughter grinned.

'We want to carry swords or at least knives, but Mother Bear Thiale will not let us,' she said. 'I want to kill a Persian,' she added. 'Anyway, we're going to do our special "little bear" dances this morning, and I want you to see them. It's an honour even to be asked to see them,' she said to the two young men.

They chose – wisely, I feel – to look respectful and impressed.

What followed was better than a mere delight. Despite our hurry – and believe me, I felt the beating of the wings of time's winged horses with the passing of every moment – we sat on stools provided by the priestesses. Wine was brought us, and we poured libations to Artemis and heard them sing her hymns – three of them, one disturbingly like a marching paean.

Mother Thiale turned to me. 'You believe that is too warlike for women,' she said.

I cocked an eyebrow. 'No,' I said. 'I'm delighted to see what a little Titan you've made of my daughter.'

Thiale seemed ready for a different answer. She looked at me carefully. 'Report has it that you are a man of blood,' she said.

I shrugged. 'I am, at that. So I imagine my daughter bears the same blood that all the Corvaxae bear, and perhaps even the same daimon.'

She frowned. 'The girls are ready to begin,' she said.

The girls dancing were between the ages of eight and fifteen. Fifteen was quite old for an aristocratic woman to still be at Brauron – most of them were married by then. But some stayed – some stayed for ever as priestesses, and some remained as guides and junior teachers for the younger girls, summer after summer. In truth, it must have been a fine life for a girl who liked sport, and I know that some weep bitter tears when they leave the sanctuary for the last time. Who encourages women to run the two-stade race after they have borne a child? Who gives new mothers the time to dance the sacred dances or shoot a bow? What of the girls who excel at athletics the way boys do? Well might they be bitter when their fathers announce to them that they must put away childish things and bear children.

Well, I am not one of those fathers. I hope.

At any rate, there they were – big and small, tall and short, long-legged and short-legged, black-haired and brown-haired and red-haired – the height of fashion at the time, let me tell you – and golden-haired like Euphonia. They were beautiful in their coltish innocence, afire with the excitement of their exile and the adventure of the war, and in the rising sun, they looked like so many muses or naiads. Most wore a simple boy's chitoniskos, worn off one shoulder and thus exposing one breast on a few of the older girls. In the dawn, preparing for their dance, they were all stretching like boys in a gymnasium. In fact, the women's gymnasium at Brauron was a wonder throughout Attica, and perhaps until that moment I had never seen women as athletes. But closest to me was an older girl whose legs carried the same sort of muscle my legs wore when I could run two stades faster than all the other youths, and her arms showed the same ridges of muscle at biceps and triceps that any well-trained boy had.

My two boys were acting like clods, their mouths open, their teeth showing.

I leaned back on my stool and kicked Hipponax sharply in the shin even as I held my cup out to a young girl of perhaps ten years to have it refilled.

Let me add that if Hector and Hipponax had ever had a thought in their handsome heads about anything but war, I had assumed it was about each other. This is natural enough, especially in war – they were young and tough and together every minute. Perhaps I should have given it more thought. I suppose I assumed they were Achilles and Patrocles, or something like.

As it proved, they were just two boys who'd never seen a girl. Much less twenty girls all on the edge of womanhood, wearing an arm's length of transparent cloth that revealed one breast, one shoulder, and most everything else, especially when a girl stretched a leg high in the air in a manner than *no* boy could manage, or did a handstand.

I'll blush myself if I go on. These girls were young enough to be my daughters. If they were shameless, they were also utterly innocent. Their very shamelessness came of summers of high training with no men about to stare or pry.

Of course, the staring was not entirely one-sided, and one girl, crowned with a magnificent double braid of her own red-brown hair, seemed to need to stretch each of her legs repeatedly just a horse-length from Hipponax, who watched her with the attention he usually saved for an adversary in a ship fight.

'It's not polite to drool,' I said quietly.

Hipponax didn't seem to hear me.

Hector dug a thumb under his arm. Hipponax squirmed, but he and the girl seemed to have their eyes locked together. I think I actually saw the arrow of Eros's little bow go into his eye. He was slain dead on the spot.

Hah! That was a lovely morning.

At any rate, the girls began to dance – none too soon, for the boys. And there was nothing lovesome or erotic to their dance – they leapt and crawled, they kicked and growled, little bears indeed. Some of the girls were quite good – to my delight, Euphonia was one of them, her movements pure and graceful, her back straight. Once in a while she'd spoil it by taking her lower lip between her teeth in concentration, but she was *good*.

I must have been grinning. The priestess leaned over. 'She's very good, although a little arrogant.' She paused. 'Have you found her a husband already?' she asked.

Really, if the whole of the Persian fleet had rounded the promontory that instant, I wouldn't have been more surprised. 'No,' I said.

Mother Thiale smiled. 'Ah,' she said. 'She has much spirit,' she said. 'Is she to be a priestess?'

'In Plataea, Mother, most priestesses are wives,' I said. 'We are a small city. My mother was hereditary priestess of Hera.'

Mother Thiale looked non-committal. 'Ah,' she said.

The girl with the double braid wrapped around her head – a man's hairstyle meant to pad a helmet – was clearly one of the dance leaders. She did a movement with her legs and hips, exactly as we do it in Pyrrhiche, her feet both performing a sliding turn in place, her hips turning as if to face a new partner – or a new opponent.

All the other girls followed suit. In this portion of the dance, the braided girl did each figure alone, and then the rest of them would copy her. She kicked, jumped, stretched. While she was dancing, she was beautiful. When the figure was done and all the girls took water, she was revealed as being very tall and heavily built – almost as well built as a man. Proportioned – still pretty. But her beauty had been in her dance.

And she drank her water with her eyes on Hipponax.

After they drank water, the dancers came together for one more dance. This was a hymn to the sun and another girl led it, this one smaller, blonde and very serious and grave. But if the first girl's dancing had been beautiful, this girl's dancing was divine, or at least direct from the goddess. Her sense of the timing in the music was superb – in fact, I've never seen a professional dancer who was her equal. It was as if she understood something in the music that the other girls didn't hear.

My Euphonia danced well – her movements were crisp and to the music, and this time she didn't chew on her lip. But she was merely a devotee of the Goddess of the Bears. For the duration of the dance, the blonde girl was the goddess herself, and her legs flashed and moved with a precision that only the very best warriors could match.

They trained well, at Brauron.

The two girls – the braided one and the smaller one – were, as it always proves, best friends. Summers of competition at everything had only made them closer. You could see in the way they stood together, and the way they drank the water from their black ceramic canteens, and giggled.

Hipponax and Hector watched them with something like the adoration that dogs have for their masters.

Euphonia bowed low to her teachers, got a pretty hug from the blonde dancer, and came over to us.

'You are a very good dancer,' I said. The first duty of every parent – provide accurate praise. Empty praise is worthless, but children are like soldiers – they need praise to enable their work.

In fact, if you ask me, training soldiers and oarsmen is the very best training for being a parent. Except, come to think of it, women do neither of these things and seem to be very good at mothering, so perhaps my wits are astray.

At any rate, she hugged both her brothers, and accepted their praise.

Hector was the bolder of the two. 'Who is the blonde girl? The one who danced—'

Euphonia laughed. 'Heliodora? She's the best dancer they've ever had here.' She paused. 'At Brauron I mean. Pater, why is the fleet not fighting at Brauron? The Persians will destroy the temple.'

I suppose I smiled. 'My little bear, Athens will be lucky if the allied fleet agrees to make its stand here and defend Salamis.' I looked around at the bay in the growing September sunlight. 'If we could lure the Persians into fighting inside the bay—'

'Brauron has a rocky promontory on which all the Persian ships could wreck themselves.' She all but bounced while she spoke.

'Perhaps, with Poseidon's help, they will.' I tried to make light of it.

Euphonia caught sight of my left hand. I'd been hiding it inside my himation, and she caught me, as children do. She pulled it out.

'Oh, Pater!' she said.

Even the priestess winced.

I smiled. You learn, in time, how to play the hero, and how not to say, 'Yes, it hurts as if all the Furies had stung me themselves, and it's also clumsy for eating.' Instead, you smile and say, 'It's nothing. I never even needed those fingers.'

Or words to that effect.

Brasidas would, I'm sure, pretend that his hand was uninjured.

'It only hurts a little,' I said. To distract her, I drew lines on the sand. 'Look, Little Bear, if I want to fight the Persians – you know they have a much larger fleet?'

She nodded wisely. 'Everyone knows that. Everyone knows we beat them at Artemisium, too.'

The priestess smiled, proud of her charge.

'So we did, girl.' I went back to my drawing.

'One of our ships is worth ten of theirs,' Euphonia said.

That statement distracted Hipponax. He laughed. 'Don't you believe it, Little Bear,' he said. 'Their ships are mostly just like ours – as well trained, if not better. The Phoenicians are first-rate sailors, and the Ionians are no worse.'

Hector nodded. 'And either of them is better than the Corinthians,' he said. He spoke just a little too loudly and his head remained turned towards the two girls who were tying their sandals.

The girl with the braids spent quite a bit of time on her sandals.

The other girl seemed impatient – and unaware of the male attention that her friend was enjoying.

Euphonia put her hands on her hips. 'They can't be so good,' she said. 'They're horrible alien barbarians.'

Hector laughed aloud – a little too loud, and he won his wager, because both girls allowed themselves to look at him. 'The Ionian Greeks are our own cousins. In some cases, literally,' he said.

'Too true,' I said. 'Look, my sweet. If the Great King's ships catch us in open water, they can envelop a flank – perhaps even both flanks. They have six or seven hundred ships. All they have to do is back water in the centre and the rest of the ships can take all the time they want. Eventually – ' I drew arrows around the ends of my hypothetical allied line ' – eventually we lose. Brauron is a peninsula; we could only anchor one flank.'

'And anyway, silly, it doesn't have any beaches. Where would we camp? Where would all the ships start the day? We'd have to row from here!' Hector mocked her.

'I am *not* silly,' Euphonia said.

Hipponax had the good sense to look as if he wasn't there. Hector looked annoyed. 'War isn't for girls,' he said dismissively. 'It's complicated.'

Euphonia didn't burst into tears or anything of the sort. Instead, she crossed her arms. 'Not as complicated as having a baby,' she said. 'Or running a household. But it's funny that you want to insult me,' she added wickedly, 'as I know both their names, and I'm friends with them. And I doubt you'll convince them to come talk to you by staring like statues.'

Hector, stung, pretended adolescent indifference. 'Them? I don't know who you are talking about,' he said.

'Oh,' Euphonia said. 'Fair enough then.' She smiled, knowing her power.

I thought I had better step in before blood was shed. 'You should gather your things, Little Bear. We have a ship for the mainland—' I was in mid-sentence when I realised that taking Euphonia to Plataea was probably foolish. She would be caught in a column of refugees, dragged to Hermione ...

On the other hand, Penelope, my sister, would take her. That made me worry about Antigonus – of course I didn't know he was dead yet – and that made me think of Leonidas, dead. And other dark things.

Unbidden, I reached out and hugged Euphonia.

'But my summer isn't over for *two weeks!*' she said. 'I'm going to stay here and help fight the Persians!'

Unbidden, I had a whole series of pictures – of my daughter as a slave, of the rape of the island of Salamis. Of Adeimantus, delighting in the destruction of Athens.

On the other hand, I didn't want to drag her across Attica and Boeotia, especially if there really were already Persian cavalry patrols out in Boeotia.

'Please, Pater?' she said.

She didn't squeeze my hand or bat her eyelashes or any of the things you see women do in plays. She just looked at me steadily. 'Pater? I want to stay here and fight for Greece and dance with my friends,' she said.

Naturally, I agreed.

She jumped up and down and clapped her hands. Her priestess appeared pleased, too.

I smiled, and then nodded to my young men. 'Make your bows, gentlemen,' I said. 'Euphonia is in good hands and we will return here in a few days.' I made my own bow to the priestess. 'I expect to be five days at most. My ships are beached in the next bay and if my daughter needs anything – money, or other things – my friend Seckla has my purse and my ships.'

The priestess nodded with dignity. 'It is inspiring to the girls,' she said, 'for one of the men who fought at Artemisium to watch the dances.'

'We all three fought at Artemisium,' Hipponax said.

The priestess looked at him as if he was made of dung. 'Really?' she said. 'I'd have thought you too young.'

Both of them flushed.

Euphonia laughed.

I smiled, I confess. 'They fought very well – like heroes in the Iliad,' I said. 'The two of them cleared a Phoenician ship.'

'Oh,' the priestess said with renewed respect. 'You fought as marines!' She smiled – she was so dignified that her smile was a contrast and it spread like sunshine. 'My brother is a marine sometimes.'

The boys didn't hold a grudge. They bowed, and then turned, almost as one, to watch the two girls, who were still lingering, held by the power of attraction of Eros and youth.

'Last chance,' Euphonia whispered. 'I could introduce you.'

Hipponax looked at her. 'Please, little sister?'

'He has to say he's sorry,' Euphonia said. 'I'm not silly.'

Hector smiled and you'd have thought that he was the gift of the sun, his face was so bright. 'I'm sorry, Little Bear,' he said. 'You are not any sillier than the rest of us.'

She grinned. 'As long as you understand that they're way too good for either of you,' she said, in her mature age-ten wisdom. She ran over to the two girls and took their hands, swinging back and forth on the braided girl's long, muscular arm.

Both girls smiled and, without hesitation, came across the sand to us.

The priestess paused at my back. 'I don't let girls talk to boys,' she said. Then she smiled. 'But I suppose that if they fought for Greece, they're men, are they not?'

'I suppose,' I said. I tried to let her hear all of my lack of belief in their maturity. She laughed, and I laughed – we were old people of thirty-five or so.

But Hipponax and Hector were lost, aswim in a sea of Eros and Aphrodite. But my daughter, like the good girl she was, walked the two young women right past the boys and to me.

'Pater, this is Heliodora, the best dancer we have ever had. And this is Iris, who wins every sport.' She laughed. 'This is my father, Arimnestos.'

Heliodora looked at her friend and arched a brow. 'I think I have won *some* contests outside dancing.'

Iris laughed. 'Far too often. But it is a great honour to meet a man so famous. Indeed, my father calls you "Ship Killer" and says you are a living hero.'

Any woman's admiration is worth having. There's something remarkable about the pure admiration of the young. I smiled at her smile.

Heliodora bowed her head. 'I won't repeat what *my* father says of you, sir,' she said quietly. 'My father is Cleitus of the Alcmaeonids.' Then she raised her eyes.

My daughter nodded with surprising dignity. 'Heliodora and I decided that it's nothing to us that her father's men killed my grandmother,' she said. 'Women's lives do not need to involve revenge, do they, Mother Thiale?'

The priestess met my eye, not my daughter's. 'The principal role of women in revenge,' she said, 'is as convenient victims.'

'I've known a woman or two to exact a bloody revenge,' I said. 'Heliodora, your father and I have renewed our oaths of non-aggression until the Medes are defeated. Please accept my oath that I mean you no harm.'

She smiled. 'Oh, I like everything I hear about you, except killing our horses,' she said. She tried to say this with dignity and becoming modesty, all the while trying not to give her attention to young Hector – or Hipponax. It was a pretty fair performance for so young a woman.

I decided to take pity on all of them. 'Despoinai,' I said to the two young women, 'it would be rude of me not to introduce my son Hipponax and his inseparable warrior companion, Hector, son of Anarchos, both of whom serve me as marines. They fought quite well against the Persians.'

My son shot me a look of pure love.

Parenting. Much like military leadership. Certainly.

The next morning, a day behind Hermogenes and the phalanx, we crossed into Attica. We landed on the open beach where pilgrims going to the great mysteries landed, and there were still great crowds there – hundreds of families with their sheep or goats or oxen. And there were ships, two great Athenian grain freighters as big as temples, waiting to load the people and perhaps even the goats.

I purchased horses at the beach. It was a sudden inspiration, directly from Poseidon, no doubt. Many of the refugees waiting to take ship were prosperous people and, as I said, they brought all their animals, but there was no way that all the herds of Attica could fit into those ships, much less be fed on the grass of Salamis. I picked up six horses – all fine animals – for a song, and was blessed into the bargain by the gentleman who owned them. I think he really didn't want to slit their throats. And I had armour and weapons and three men to move quickly. I promised him that he could have them all back at the end, if all went well.

He was right to fear the slaughtering knife for his animals, though. That's just what a small body of hoplites was doing to any animal that could not be loaded, butchering them on the spot for meat, and burning the carcasses. Athens meant business: she was not leaving grain or animals to feed the Great King's army. She was, in a terrible way, destroying herself to hurt her enemy.

But once we left the shore, Attica was a strange land indeed. It was empty. Not only were all the people gone, but so were most of the animals. As we took the road for Plataea over the mountains, I remember passing the tower at Oinoe where my brother died and seeing a cat sleeping in the sun on a wall. That cat was almost the only living thing I saw that day.

Plataea was already emptying by the time I arrived. We made the ride in one day and came in the dark. But Eugenios was there to take my exhausted mare and there were beds made up and sweet-smelling blankets and we collapsed into them, and in the morning there was warm milk heavy with honey and fresh bread.

But there wasn't a hanging on any of the walls, and the chests that held all my spare armour and all my fine cups and plates, my bronze platters and some nice pieces of loot from my days of piracy – they were all gone. So were the better pieces of Athenian ware, like the krater with the painting of Achilles receiving his armour from his mother, and the kylix with Penelope weaving at her loom, from which our fresco painter took his model.

All gone.

Eugenios smiled in quiet triumph. 'I sent a mule train to the isthmus under Idomeneus's orders,' he said. 'The slaves packed as soon as your message came.' He bowed his head. 'I would like to come with you, lord, if you are going to fight the Persians.'

In fact, there were several dozen men who came that morning, slaves released from service, or sent by their masters. Plataeans are surprisingly generous – many men freed slaves to build the walls in Marathon year, you will recall, and now several of the richer men were freeing farm workers to help Athens. Slaves and servants have a world of their own – look around you, thugater – you think they only talk to you? And Eugenios, my steward, had organised it all.

But I never expected packing my house to be my real task. I had people for that, people trained by Jocasta. And in my very clean kitchen, the great lady of Athens looked me in the eye and said, 'Antigonus died with the King of Sparta. We heard yesterday. Your sister needs you.'

36

So I took my new mare and road over the Asopus to Thespiae, and there I found Penelope. She had already cut away a great slice of her hair in mourning and her eyes were red with weeping. She didn't say anything, certainly nothing accusatory.

She just stood in her house-yard with her arms around me while her slaves packed. She cried a little.

The first words she said were, 'They mutilated his body.'

By then, we had all heard that the mighty King of Persia, King of Kings, reigning over kings, was a petty tyrant who had ordered the heads of the last five hundred hoplites to fight all hacked off, and their bodies cut up. I won't even describe it. It was – atimnos. Dishonourable. Stupid, too. No Greek who heard of the mutilation of the King and his companions would ever forget it.

It is perhaps one of the curses of warfare that men do such stupid, horrible things and think themselves strong, when in fact, all they prove is that they are weak.

But it told us another story, too. That the Great King intended to mutilate us.

'Come with me to Salamis,' I said. 'Come and help me take care of Euphonia.'

Penelope didn't smile or laugh or make a joke. 'I'll be ready in the morning,' she said. She shrugged. 'I think people will need me at the isthmus,' she said. 'Your daughter is in good hands.'

'There's a rumour that there are Saka cavalry at Thebes.'

We both spat.

'Come with me now,' I said. 'I don't want to leave you for the Medes.'

She thought a moment, and then she nodded. With surprisingly little fuss she gathered two women and her children and their Thracian nurse and they all mounted horses. Ajax, one of my steadier men from former times and a near neighbour, gave me his handclaps that he'd see her goods safely to Corinth. The phalanx was marching all together, with a long column of baggage carts sandwiched in between, as we'd practised.

And I wasn't going with them.

I took my sister and her people back to Plataea as the sun went down, the fifth day since we'd left the beaches at Artemisium. There was a watch on the walls of my town and the only people left in it were the freedmen coming with me to row, the rest of my sailors, all armed and having a bit of a feast, and the rearguard of the phalanx under Alcaeus and Bellerophon. They had a hundred men, more or less, to cover the rear of the town's goods, which had left already.

They'd planned it all without me. Which was as well, because the roads from Thebes were choked with refugees, and Plataea's gates were shut for the first time in many years.

I left Jocasta with Pen and went to my forge. Styges was there, loading the last of his tools for the baggage train. He was not going back to Salamis with me; many of the Epilektoi were going to the isthmus to be the core of the Plataean phalanx in the new League army. I did not need so many marines on my remaining ships.

He looked up when I came in. Darkness had already fallen and he had a dozen lamps lit to provide light, wasting oil that he would lose anyway, I suppose.

'Eerie, isn't it?' he asked me. 'So quiet.'

I nodded and pulled out my greaves. In the last fight at Artemisium, someone had put a spear point into my left greave. Or, just possibly, my own sauroter – the bronze point on the butt of a Greek spear – had penetrated the armour. It can happen, when you shift grips. Either way, I had a hole in the armour the size of the tip of my little finger and I needed it repaired.

It was really just an excuse. I needed to do something with my hands. Mourning for loss is an odd thing. It can come and go. I knew that when the King of Sparta fell I had probably lost Briseis, and now, talking to Penelope, seeing her tears, feeling the weight of the loss of her husband – a good man – it was all more real to me.

I knew in my heart that the Athenians would fight for Salamis. I suspected that Adeimantus would make sure that the rest of the allies left them to die alone. I was determined to die with them.

I needed a little time with my god.

'Fire hot?' I asked.

Styges smiled. 'There were still coals when I came back. Tiraeus must have done some work when he came back, and the slaves have been steady. I sent a shipment of finished goods away yesterday.'

It was, after all, our business. We all shared it, although I had paid down the capital to put up the building.

'Where is Tiraeus?' I asked. He had not come out to fight at Artemisium. No shame to him – the town picked five hundred men by lot to stay.

'He took the first mule train towards Corinth, the night Idomeneus arrived.' Styges frowned. 'Why do I know all this and you do not?'

'I've been with my sister,' I said, and explained.

At any rate, I went to the bellows and pumped while he packed fine engraving tools into a leather bag. I told him about Xerxes mutilating the bodies and we both cursed. Probably helped me make the fire hot. When the fire was fierce enough, I rooted around the floor looking for some scrap bronze.

'This place is too clean,' I joked.

Styges shrugged. 'You haven't been here,' he said. 'What are you doing?'

'Patching greaves,' I said.

He nodded, looked at mine, and admired the perfection of the workmanship. 'You made this?' he asked.

'No,' I admitted. 'A man named Anaxikles, as young as you are yourself. The best armourer I've ever seen.'

Styges sniffed. 'Not so good that you didn't take a spear point through his work, however.' He tossed me a rectangle of neatly hammered bronze plate, thinner than parchment. I bent it back and forth between my hands and decided it was suitable.

He grinned. 'I reckon anything right for mending pots will mend armour.'

I spent a happy hour shaping and planishing my patch. It was a simple process, but soothing. I marked a line right on the greave with a scribing tool for the lower edge of the patch, so that it would always go to the same place as I tried it. Then I began to shape it, first with a simple crease down the middle to match the central ridge on the greave – see here, thugater, where the front of a good greave is like the prow of a ship? The prow of the ship turns water, but the sharp angle at the front of the greave mimics the line of a man's shin and turns the points of weapons, too.

But of course, the blow had struck where the sharp line of the shin bends away into the soft curve of the top of the foot – a very complex shape, and one that requires forming both by pushing and pulling the metal.

But it was a small patch and soon enough I had it where it would drop over the original like a mask on an actor's face.

Then I had to planish it to make it as smooth and nice as the original. Anaxikles had been a master at planishing whereas I always found it a little dull, but that night, in an empty Plataea, I worked the bronze willingly, tapping away to make it smooth with my best flat hammer, and then cutting the patch with a file and then polishing it again with a linen cloth full of pumice, and again with ash until it glowed.

And then I punched fourteen holes around the edges and used them to mark fourteen more in the damaged greave itself. By then, Styges was done and his two slaves were waiting for me while I drove the tiny rivets home, nipped them short and widened their ends into conical sockets I'd made with a tool. It was not master work, but it was good, solid work, and when I polished the rivets so flat that they were nothing but faint circles against the bronze, I felt that I had done honour to my god and to Anaxikles who made them. I poured a libation to Hephaestus, and sang one of his hymns, and then I sent a prayer that Lydia and Anaxikles were happy and healthy.

I looked at that greave with real satisfaction. I remember the darkness, the silence, the smell of the burning charcoal, and the spilled wine and the bronze.

Styges was the last man left. We had a ceremony to put out the fire.

'The Persians will no doubt destroy the town,' Styges said.

I nodded. 'Styges,' I said. 'I don't plan to come back. If – *when* Athens loses – I won't stay alive to see what comes after.'

Styges nodded. 'Idomeneus said the same, last night,' he said. 'Just so you know.'

Styges nodded again, his young face silhouetted against the darkness by the orange glow of the last of our forge fire.

Then we said the prayers and cursed the Persians. Fire has power, and so does darkness, and any time a man willingly extinguishes fire, he has power.

Or so Heraclitus said.

We walked down the hill in a sombre mood, to my house. North of us, near the small acropolis, I could hear oarsmen singing. I hoped they were welcoming our new freedmen ... who were only going to be free a few days anyway, before they died. I hoped a few days of wine and freedom had some value.

The world was as black as my forge.

We rose with the dawn and joined the rearguard at the gates. Styges closed the gate from inside and then came over the wall on an orchard ladder, which we broke to smithereens. No need to make it easy for the Medes to take our town.

Aristides took his wife and went with the column to Corinth. He had many friends there. There was a rumour that all the exiles were to be recalled and indeed he'd been with the fleet at Artemisium. But he meant to follow the law – he always followed the law.

'We might fight before you come back to us,' I said.

Aristides shook his head. 'I doubt it. The Great King's fleet will not move so fast, and besides, Themistocles will have to convince the Corinthians to fight at Salamis.'

I said nothing. Neither did he.

Neither of us believed that Corinth would fight.

In the end, Pen chose to go with Jocasta – mostly, I suspect, because they were both women.

I held her for a long time and then I gave her an ivory scroll tube that held my will and all my plans for Euphonia.

She bit her lip. 'I can't lose you, too!' she said.

I said nothing. Aristides turned his head away. Even Styges tried to be somewhere else.

'You think you will lose?' Penelope asked. 'You think ...'

I was in armour. I motioned to Hector to bring my shield. Penelope understood, and she took wine and blessed it – she was a priestess of Hera – and poured it on the face of my aspis, cleaning it. A little flowed through a place where a Persian arrow had penetrated, at Artemisium. Then she wiped it with a clean cloth, and I took it.

She was dry-eyed, as a proper matron must be.

She touched my hand once more, and then – we were gone.

I had one more encounter that morning. We rode away toward Cithaeron and Athens, and we passed my cousins on the road. Simonalkes, younger brother to the Simonides who Teucer killed, and Achilles, and Ajax. Simonides was tall and cautious, and Achilles – what a terrible name to give a boy – was not very bright and very aggressive. They had a wagon and two oxen and all their wives on donkeys. They were walking, and I was riding the opposite way.

I thought to ride by them, but it was too awkward. I was in armour, of course, on a horse. At any rate, I dismounted.

'You are going the wrong way,' Simonides said – with a little ill will, I thought.

'I'm returning to the allied fleet,' I said. 'The Greek ships are at Salamis.'

'As long as there's a fight, we can count on it that you'll be there,' Simonides said. 'Will the army ever form, do you think?'

It was a fair question and asked without malice. The Spartans were still slow in getting their army together, and that autumn, with Attica and Boeotia threatened, it seemed suspicious, to say the least.

'The Spartans said to form the allied army on the isthmus,' I said. 'Hermogenes should know more by the time you get there.'

'Hmmph,' Ajax said, his arms crossed. 'So you'll desert us again?'

Age does have its benefits. I didn't cut him down on the spot. I sighed – audibly. 'I'm deserting you to help Athens fight the Persians,' I said. 'The best of luck to you, cousins, and may the gods go with you.'

Simonides shocked me. 'And with you, cousin. You've been more than fair with us. May I have your hand?'

We shook.

'My brother,' he said quietly, 'is not much of a farmer and fancies he might be a soldier. Would you take him?'

I looked at Achilles, and saw nothing but a bag of blood and rage. Like many strong young men.

He narrowed his eyes. 'I don't need—' he began.

His brother shook his head. 'Be silent, brother. Arimnestos, I ask this of you, as head of our family, formally. Please take my brother where his arm may hack at enemies and not friends, and where, if he dies, his blood will go to the gods and not stain our threshold.'

Ouch. Achilles had really angered his brother. I wondered what he had done.

But blood truly is thicker than water. Simonides had referred to me as the head of the family. I had little choice.

'You have a panoply?' I asked Achilles.

He nodded.

'You think I'm mad?' Idomeneus said quietly.

I turned. 'This young man is all yours,' I said.

Idomeneus laughed. 'I walked into that,' he said. 'Lad! You'll need a mule for your kit!'

From the flanks of Cithaeron, we looked back over the fields of Boeotia. There was smoke rising towards Thebes – but it might just have been a farmer burning his fields. At our feet we could see the rearguard of the Plataeans moving out from the shadow of the old mud-brick walls, the glitter of the late-summer sun reflecting off their spear points and their bronze.

Over towards Thespiae we could see more metal and a cloud of dust.

Horses.

And closer to hand, as well.

Just for a moment, it was hard to get the senses around just exactly what we perceiving. There were matching dust clouds on a number of roads – on the ridge opposite Plataea, across the Asopus, there was one, and then over to my right, looking down towards Eleutherae, there was another.

It took as long as a hurried man might take three breaths.

'By Poseidon,' whispered Idomeneus.

It was a veritable *cloud* of cavalrymen. They were expanding like the ripples in a pond from Thebes, which lay at the centre of all the roads in Boeotia, less than a parasang – that's thirty-six stades – away. From high enough on Cithaeron, you can *see* Thebes.

We were seeing hundreds – *thousands* – of Persian cavalrymen pouring over the fields of Boeotia like water from a rising tide rushing over a beach.

More particularly, the different groups of horsemen on different roads were, at least some of them, converging on Plataea. And they moved – discernibly. Marching men scarcely seem to move, but these dust clouds moved quickly. I looked back at our rearguard, headed for Corinth by the lower Asopus road. The cavalry over by Thespiae would cut them off. No great matter – I expected a hundred hoplites would make short work of the horsemen. But not if they were then taken in the rear by the cavalrymen coming down the main road behind them.

I had almost five hundred men at my back – well-armed, fit men, veterans of a dozen fights. With oars.

'We need to go back,' I said. 'We need to sting this nearest group and draw them up Cithaeron behind us, rather than let them go by and sail into the backs of the hoplites.'

Men were already pulling their weapons off the donkeys and the mules. A few of us had horses and armour and shields, although I've never met a man who can manage an aspis and a horse at the same time.

I didn't fancy facing Cyrus and his war-brothers on a horse, anyway.

'Follow me!' I yelled, when I felt I had enough men armed. That's all the plan I made.

We came back down the mountain on the road past the shrine. There were a dozen of us mounted – all the best-armed men – and we left the rest behind immediately. It was my sense that we needed to do this thing immediately or not at all.

We went down the hill from the shrine to the stream that runs there, where Hermogenes and I swore our friendship many years before. That's where the mountain road meets the road to Eleutherae.

Only then did the idea strike me: we needed an ambush.

At the tomb, naturally.

I turned to Hector. 'Back to the men on foot,' I said. 'Get to the dip in the road just beyond the tomb and make an ambush. Both sides. Tell Moire to take command.'

Hector nodded. 'Moire to take command. An ambush from both sides of the road, where you killed the bandits before I was born.' He smiled to show he knew what I was ordering.

And to show how much fun he was having.

Young men, and war. It is a remarkable thing. I was ready to fall off my horse, my knees were shaking so hard – I was committing myself to be bait for a trap, and on *horseback*. And Hector was smiling. He didn't want to go, but he was *happy*.

He rode away.

My mounted men were a hodgepodge of Plataean gentry, like Teucer, son of Teucer, and Antimenides, son of Alcaeus, on the one hand, and sailors who happened to have armour and a horse, like Giorgos of Epidauros and Eumenes, son of Theodorus, an oarsman. And ten more, including a couple of reliable killers in the persons of Idomeneus and Styges, his apprentice. In war, anyway.

'We wait here,' I said. 'When we see the Persians, we turn and run up the hill. No heroics. All we want to do is lead them off this road.'

Idomeneus drew his sword.

I heard the hoof beats too.

'No heroics!' I said again.

'This from you?' Idomeneus asked.

They were coming quickly. I assumed they knew what they were about; that their prey was our baggage column. It only took a runaway slave or a traitor.

'Form across the road as if you mean business,' I said, and took my spear in my right hand. I didn't even have a shield, which made me feel naked, despite my shiny bronze armour.

We were on a good spot of road, with a big rock on the right and a bit of a drop on the left, so there was just room to form up two-deep, on horseback.

The lead Persian wore a beautiful scale shirt plated in gold, and a magnificent tiara. The man behind him wasn't Persian. He was a Saka. I knew his kind immediately from the long flaps on his leather cap and the sheer amount of gold he had. He saw us – and whooped.

That whoop could freeze your blood.

Then everyone did everything wrong.

I had never fought on horseback. That's not really true; I have been in some fights on horseback, but never willingly, and never against Saka.

If I was committed to this suicidal action, the worst thing I could possibly have done was to remain stationary. I have since learned that the only way to meet a charging horse is on another.

On the other hand, my adversaries should have uncased and loosed their bows. They are the greatest archers in the world. However, they are also the most enthusiastic horse thieves, and I'm going to guess that they didn't want to hit our horses. They thought we were easy marks.

The result of our mutually bad military decisions was a disastrously deadly melee. We had armour and spears and the Saka could actually ride and were coming fast, but had no armour. Most of them had short swords, a few had much longer swords, and at least one woman had a rope.

We should have run. But it was all too fast. They should have shot at us. But they were too excited.

The Persian slowed, but the Saka leader didn't *crash* into us. He threaded between Idomeneus and Hipponax, slashed at Hipponax with his little sword – an akinakes as I later learned – and vanished into the second rank, his superb horsemanship guiding his mount through the narrowest of gaps. Had he used his bow, we'd all have died.

As it was, Idomeneus, no great horseman, nonetheless put his spear point into the man's back and killed him.

Then the wave front struck us. There were a dozen of them – more – and they panicked our horses when they struck. My nice mare was an Attic riding horse and she had no notion of staying to fight. I struck one blow, a spear blow that missed my target against a man in the most outlandishly barbarous trousers I'd ever seen – purple and yellow diagonal checks. Perhaps he wore them to confuse his enemies. I certainly missed him and he caught the shaft and pulled and I almost lost my seat. The girl came up on my other side – she threw the open loop of her rope and my lovely mare pivoted on her back feet. The rope slid off my arm and I was free. The man in the foolish clothes slammed his spear sideways into my head and I covered it with my own spear and thrust. My spear went into his horse's neck.

My horse didn't stay to let me finish him, which is a pity, because now I know I was spear to spear with Masistius, the commander of all Xerxes' cavalry.

But even as his horse fell, blocking the road, other Saka were all around us. A blow clipped my back plate and another slammed into my helmet, but my good helmet held the point and I got a hand on my sword. Beside me, Hipponax landed a shrewd blow to a Saka's head and the man fell, although the blade cannot have cut through his heavy leather hat. Then Hipponax's horse spooked as mine had, and we were both moving down the road, away from the fight. This is why I have no love for horses. I could not get my horse to turn, and so I was fighting while rotated, trying to thrust over my shoulder and under my arm. Try it.

Two of my better-armed sailors were down. Teucer and another man were still fighting.

I had a pair of Saka racing with me. He was one of the men with the long swords, and his was slightly curved. He cut and I had to cover with my sword – my favourite, my long, straight xiphos.

His friend reached for his bow, a small, vicious recurve that sat, strung and deadly, in its own scabbard. A gorytos.

I knew where this was going to end. I also knew that the opening of the uphill road to the shrine was about to appear on my left. I leaned my weight back to slow my mare, and cut – one, two – at my opponent. Our swords rang together and sparks flew, and then I cut again, at shoulder height, and again.

And then, as he stayed with me stride for stride but seemed unable to regain the fighting initiative, I flicked a thrust overhand, my palm down. It just scratched his face – perhaps I took one of his eyes, or he was blinded by the cut, but he threw his arms up and my full back cut put him down – and then I was sawing the reins to slow my mount and turning hard. My second assailant with the bow vanished – still riding flat out at a gallop, he continued on the main road.

His arrow struck. He'd shot almost backwards over his saddle, but his aim was true, and the arrow dug a ridge in my best helmet and lodged between the crest box and the helmet. He turned his horse, reaching for another arrow, and I lost sight of him.

Idomeneus was emerging from the back of the melee, having left his usual red ruin. Another man in bronze armour was down in the road – Antimenides, son of Alcaeus. I knew him by his crest. Our Olympian.

Teucer's son was fighting over the body and, as I watched, he too was cut down. They were too many for us and we were bleeding good men – men who would rule them on the deck of a ship.

For a terrible, slow beat of my heart, my head was at war with itself. The hero in me longed to save Teucer. The leader in me – or was it the coward – said run. Indeed, we should never have fought. But the sons of my friends were dying.

In an agony of indecision, my hands pointed my horse up the hill and I rode for it. Styges was with me for ten strides and then his horse pulled ahead.

The Saka followed us.

My little mare took an arrow in the hindquarters and didn't falter, but we had only heartbeats to live.

Idomeneus was beside me, and he was angry. He hated to run.

I thought of Eualcides. *If you live long enough, you'll run too. The day comes, and the moment, and life is sweet.*

It was horrible. When you flee, you have no idea what the man behind you can do – or is doing. Is this your death blow? Is that arrow the one? You see nothing but the trees in front of you and the hope of the sky.

There were five or six of us left in a little pack and the Saka had lost a few strides on us at the turn. But now they were on a good road, headed uphill, and their superior riding skills, their light weight – most of them were small – and let's be fair, their better horses, began to tell.

Idomeneus took an arrow between the shoulder blades. He leaned forward and the pain showed.

But we had made it to the tomb. I suppose that Idomeneus wanted to die there.

He turned his horse.

'No, you mad Cretan!' I roared, and slapped his horse with the flat of my sword.

His horse ambled a few steps and fell against the side of the priest's house. The horse had six or seven arrows in him. Idomeneus managed to get to the ground without falling and he was hit again, although the arrow shattered against his helmet and I was showered in cane splinters.

He sat suddenly.

I saw the aspis hanging on the wall of the priest's house. It was Calchus's old one, and it had seen better days – the bronze face was now brown and green like sun dapple in the wood, and the face was no longer smooth, because a generation of aspiring warriors had used it as the target of their youthful attempts to be spearmen.

It was on my arm as fast as I could get off my mare.

I took the old spear that leaned next to it and stood over Idomeneus. There was a lot of blood.

The first Saka to burst into the clearing rode right past me, up the trail.

The next three all saw me and they all changed direction together, so fast that I almost missed my cast, but I didn't, and the heavy spear hit a horse and the horse fell. I took the second spear.

One of the Saka leaped the falling horse and one didn't.

The clearing was suddenly full of mounted men and they were coming both ways around the old priest's cabin – the Saka can ride through the woods as easily as riding on a road.

An arrow hit my aspis and shattered. And then another, like the blow of a rock thrown by an angry man, and then two together. And then it was like rain and shafts began to penetrate the surface and search for my arm and hand.

I was going to die, and it was just a matter of when. So I slammed my aspis into the man who had leaped the dying horse – into his mount, really. He cut at me and I cut at him, and we both missed, and he was past. I turned and threw my spear into the next man to come at me, and then I put my back against the priest's house. That bought me a few heartbeats, and then I slipped around the corner – the clearing was full of men on horseback and summer dust.

Just for a moment, the woods beckoned.

But I had made my decision. Briseis was lost. Greece was lost.

I ran in among them. I was not blood-mad – in fact, I was as fastidious as I have ever been. My long xiphos is a wonderful thrusting weapon, a killing tool beyond compare. Cuts are all very well when you are desperate, but when you want to kill, the thrust is the thing. I thrust quickly, putting the tip three or four fingers into a victim and then pulling it out and moving on. I didn't discriminate – I struck horses and men, whatever offered. I was determined to keep moving, to do all the damage I could.

Truly, I have no idea how long this went on. I took some cuts, and an arrow went right through my shield and struck my left hand in the antelabe, but by some joke of the gods it emerged where my two missing fingers weren't.

I remember fighting for hours. I'll be fair and assume I was in among the horses for as long as a man takes to sprint a stade. Perhaps two.

A horn sounded, and then another, and then all my sailors burst upon them like a wave.

Again, that's how I remember it. And a delicious thing happened – one of those moments that make you savour your role in the world.

The moment a horn sounded I remembered that I had friends – that I had, in fact, laid an ambush.

And in that moment I went from a serene and very deadly suicide to a man desperately eager to live.

You must laugh. I do now. I don't know if it was the best I had ever fought, but it was inspired – god inspired. I truly think Athena guided my hand as I passed from Saka to Saka, stabbing this one in the buttock and that one in the kidney and another in the face or arm, a horse in the arse, another in the breast – all while moving like a dancer through them.

But the horn sounded and my godlike powers fell away and left me, terrified and eager to live, in the midst of my enemies.

What saved me was that the sounding of the trumpet seemed to have the same effect on my adversaries. Perhaps they smelled a corpse. Since we moved here, thugater, we've come to know many noble Saka, or Sakje as they call themselves, and they are experts at ambush. Perhaps one of the leaders didn't like what he saw.

Anyway, as soon as the horns sounded, they began to flow away.

Hipponax burst into the clearing and threw his spear, knocking a man into the dust. The man fell from his horse and his head hit one of the boundary stones of the sanctuary and split open with an awful sound – one of the few things of that fight I remember clearly.

And then the clearing was full of my oarsmen and they were cheering. Hipponax says I looked like a hedgehog and that may indeed be true. Certainly I was carrying more than twenty Saka arrows in my aspis and I had blood trickling from two punctures that had come all the way through the shield's face.

I went back to Idomeneus. He was breathing – slowly, and in odd bursts, like a man snoring. Men took my aspis and other men pursued the Saka down the mountain. I stood and breathed and the sum of all my wounds began to sap at me. I had been hit repeatedly at Artemisium, I'd had very little sleep, and now I'd fought twenty horsemen and my skin was pierced in half a dozen places.

Hipponax got Idomeneus out of his fine thorax. He'd fallen on his back and the fall had broken the shaft of the arrow there. Or perhaps it had already broken – the cane shafts that the Persians and the Saka used were strong, but brittle once they cracked and any sort of resistance seemed to break them, especially when the weather was cold. I had the splinters of a dozen failed arrows in my forearms.

But Idomeneus was alive, if deeply unconscious. The arrow that penetrated his back plate had not gone far through the heavy muscle of his upper back.

Hector tore into the leather bag he wore and produced our salve, made of honey and oregano and a few other things, blessed by a priestess of Hera. He slathered it over the wound, wrapped the sticky stuff in his spare chiton, and he and Hipponax threw the wounded Cretan over the back of a spare horse. There were a dozen Saka horses milling about the clearing, and the more horse-oriented young men were catching them.

My mare, to my astonishment, came to me. She had an arrow standing proud of her rump, but she seemed immune to it. Nonetheless, as the salve was out, I said a prayer to Poseidon, Lord of Horses, and while a pair of my marines held the horse's head, I made a small cut with my scabbard knife and withdrew the arrow, and then used the salve. She was none too happy with the operation, I can promise you, but I already loved her – such heart! I had never really fancied a horse before. See what a good prayer to Poseidon can get you? Eh?

I realised in the next few minutes how used I had grown to being a great man with many officers. I was unused to having to figure out each aspect of the next step – I had men I trusted for that. But Idomeneus was down and Teucer, son of Teucer, was dead and none of the rest of the Plataeans was ready to command, much less to make the sort of decisions that would allow me to think about the larger issue.

In brief, the larger issue was that Boeotia was alive with Persian cavalry. I had to assume that they were headed for Attica by the same road we were going to use, and they would be much faster than we.

I had not, to be honest, expected Xerxes to move so fast.

But let me add that it was the treason of Thebes that allowed him to do so. Thebes opened her gates, and worse, fed the Medes. So when his advance guard swept down the road they were given fodder and water for their mounts and food and wine for the troopers. Even a day's hesitation by Thebes would have saved much, slowed the storm, held back the lightning.

In fact, Simonides, my cousin, had his own fight on the road, and his brother Ajax lost his life less than five stades from where we had our fight. Except that Simonides, who had grown to manhood in Thebes, said the men who attacked him were Thebans in a motley collection of false Persian clothes. I believe it. Thebes always hated Plataea, and they were quick to attack us. Certainly we know that it was Thebes who asked the Great King to reduce our town to rubble.

But I get ahead of myself.

I could see we had to retreat. I hoped that we had helped Alcaeus. His noble son had taken three bad wounds, any one of which would have been crippling – I hoped it was not in vain. But I couldn't venture farther down that road, and in fact I had Hipponax sounding his horn, over and over, to gather the more impetuous oarsmen back. I found Moire and told him to get the men together on the road – I wanted to lie down and go to sleep. How often has that not been the case, friends? You just want to rest for a little, but the world and the gods and your enemies will not have it.

I pulled the boys – who were about to become officers – and Moire into a huddle while the men formed. The oar-masters made passable taxiarchoi. I wished I had Seckla.

I wished I had Ka and his Nubians. Archers – by Apollo, archers are worth their weight in gold.

However, as the women of Plataea say, if wishes were barley cakes, beggars would eat like kings. I had four hundred and fifty oarsmen, all hard men. We had donkeys and mules and food for three days and a lot of experience in war.

I started by stripping the shrine. The old Hero has always been a friend of mine, and a favourite, and I've given him many a libation of wine, aye, and blood, too. Styges and Idomeneus had stored grain there, in big pithoi jars set into the floors of the barn I'd built them, and wine, and we took it all, or burned it. I told my men to gather downed branches and pile them over the old entrance to the tomb – you can't loot what you don't see. We set fire to the huts ourselves and I took the old window of horn that some donor in the past had made – very well – for Calchus, and I put it in the tomb before we closed it up.

Perhaps I'm not fully explaining, as some of you look so puzzled. The shrine was the centre of our military training for Plataea. We stored food and a few weapons there and we were determined that none of this would aid the enemy. And it was an act of piety, as well, hiding the shrine, denying it to the foe. Besides, we knew it was time to build new sheds. Some of them were pretty foul.

In the middle of all this activity, Onisandros, one of the junior oar-masters, came to me and saluted.

'I was thinking, Navarch. We could . . .' he grinned, 'chop up them dead Saka. Show 'em what we think of 'em.'

I nodded. 'No,' I said.

My feelings must have shown in my face, because Onisandros – a good man – stepped back. 'Oh – pardon me, Lord!'

I shook my head. 'Listen up!' I called, and all the men nearest me fell silent, or stopped dragging branches, or arranging the Saka bodies. And Teucer – the only man who was dead, although a dozen were wounded – they were burying him inside the sanctuary wall.

The best we could do, under the circumstances.

Anyway – most of them turned to me. There was the usual hum – some men will never shut up, and I am one of them, I confess it.

'We will not desecrate the dead. Why? Because we're Greek! By Poseidon, men! Do you want to be as guilty of impiety as the Medes? Let them burn in Hades for their sacrilege. We will win this war *because* we are the better men, because we are above such petty things. I know you are angry. I am angry too. My brother-in-law – his head cut off, his body maimed by cowards – lies in the sand at Thermopylae, exposed by the Persians like a criminal. I am angry – but for my part, I wouldn't do that to a dog.'

Well – something like that. Thank the gods I'd had time to think about it. And I'd already decided I wouldn't allow such shit before I was exhausted and angry and lost Teucer's son.

I still blame myself for that. We didn't need to fight on the road at all – just run. Not one of my better days. And you'll note that when I stopped at the tomb to try and save Idomeneus, I wrecked the ambush's chance of a real victory.

Well, I can't regret that.

But what I'm getting at in this story is that one of the worst parts of leading men in war – and women, too – is that you make mistakes, people die or are maimed, and then *you have to go right on leading them*. You want to lie down and sleep, or murder some prisoners, or perhaps just take your own life in shame – and I have known all these moments, friends. The black despair after combat – the abyss, some of us called it then.

But they are all looking at you, waiting for you to give an order, when all you really want to do is cry. Or die.

More wine, here.

Where was I?

Ah – my huddle – Moire and Hipponax and Hector. I told them my plan in some detail. I sent Hector with the fastest runners to go up the trail ten stades and set an ambush. I told Hipponax that he'd be next and that, no matter what happened, he'd be taking the next group of oarsmen another ten stades, to the shoulder of the mountain overlooking Eleutherae and there he'd set another ambush. And that the two of them, each with twenty men, would play leapfrog with the column.

This is how you retreat – with a sting in the tail. Men pursuing quickly become careless. There is some part of the human animal that believes that running forward is winning and running backwards is losing, and perhaps this is even true, but in a well-conducted retreat you can use this against your enemy. I learned all this from Aristides, and some more of it from Brasidas.

Oh, how I missed him, too. I felt a fool for leaving him at the ships.

At any rate, as soon as our plans were made, Hector chose his men and led them off at a run. We loaded the last of the grain on the pack animals.

I got my own, lighter, aspis off my pack mule, replaced its weight with grain, and placed myself at the very back of the column with my picked men. My little mare was going to have an easy time of it for a few hours.

I gave the boys a ten-minute head start and then we marched.

All that time – maybe an hour we were at the shrine, with the sun getting higher in the sky – I worried that the Saka would come straight back at us. If they had, we'd have made a fight, but it would have been ugly.

Once we were moving, though, we were in better shape. A moving column funnels enemy action to the back. It is hard even for cavalry to surround marching infantry, in bad ground. Out on the steppes or on the sands of some open desert I suppose it would be terrible for the hoplites, but in the woods, we could walk almost as fast as they, when we were on a road and they had to infiltrate through the big old trees and rocks of Cithaeron's lower slopes.

Be that as it may, we didn't see a man or horse for two hours. We passed through our first ambush and they joined our column, then Hipponax led his men away at a run to form the next one. Tired oarsmen being forced to run half the day in their looted panoplies glared at me with death in their eyes, but I was used to making them row all day and I smiled and shouted words of encouragement, as the Spartans do – 'Well run, Empedocles! You look like a god, Onisandros!' – and we continued. When the sun was high in the sky we took an hour's rest, with *skope* on all the high points, watching for the enemy. Just when I was picking the sausage skin out of my teeth, Kassander, one of the older oarsmen in a good leather spolas dyed bright red, called me from the rock above the road.

'Ari! Cavalry!'

'Arm!' I shouted. We were resting in our ranks – a very basic precaution I'd learned at Marathon – and we got to our feet and got our aspides on our arms before the sound of hoof beats was clear.

'Drink water!' I shouted. It is amazing how fast fatigue and black depression falls away when you can hear your foe advancing.

Obediently, men drank from their canteens and leather water bottles, handing them round to the awkward sods who had none, and then, at my wave, Onisandros got the baggage animals moving.

I was between Alexandros, one of my marines, and Sitalkes, another. I had Styges at my back and all ten of the men who blocked the road were in full panoply. In fact, I'd put on my arm and thigh guards since the last halt. I wasn't going to eat any more splinters. They hurt.

The Saka were cautious. They came on slowly, stopped as soon as they saw us across the road, and they loosed arrows. My best aspis began to take hits.

The next hour was like a long, brutal fencing match. Between shafts, we'd back step – when we went around a curve in the road, we'd run, our ears cocked for the rush of hooves, but the Saka were too cautious, and we'd gain a hundred paces and halt, breathe.

sometimes only to run again. Sometimes they'd come on.

After an hour of this, which included one all-out charge – of course we caught no one, but we surprised them and made them run – as I say, after an hour, my legs were made of rubber and I couldn't have hurt a Saka if he'd laid down under the edge of my xiphos.

Then we switched with Moire and his ten. He was as wily as I and his ten were faster than we had been. I had to admit, watching them from the massed safety of the column, that his ten-fleet oarsmen in light armour were better at the whole game – until a Saka arrow took a man in his shin, where he had no greave. He went down, and the Saka were on him in a moment, shooting down into his body. A few began loosing light shafts at our column, but the gods had allowed our baggage animals around the next turn and the shafts only rattled around off of shields.

The road was steep. We were only making ten stades an hour and I knew we were running out of daylight and we couldn't deal with a night on the mountain with the Saka.

I told Styges what I had in mind and I ran off along the column. I wasn't running very well and I had to stop – often. Not my best day.

But I got to the head of the column and then I ran, still in full panoply with my aspis on my arm. I ran along the road for what seemed like an eternity, worried about what was behind me and afraid that I'd lost contact with my ambushing force . . .

'Pater!'

Hipponax was on the grassy slope above me. He came out.

'Perfect,' I said. It was. To the left, the road fell away in a cliff that gave a magnificent view of Boeotia – the first one a traveller coming from Attica saw. Above us there were some volcanic rocks and some stubby olive trees, but the slope was gentle enough to a man to run down, and steep enough for a few rocks to be rolled.

'I need you to stay hidden until the enemy is well past you,' I said. 'We can't just frighten them. We need to kill a few and break contact.'

My son pointed proudly at his hillside. It was true – I couldn't see a man.

'What if they try to ride up the hill?' I asked. But that was rhetorical.

I ran back to the column. Now, on the return run, I had to worry that they'd been savaged in my absence. Losing Teucer loomed again. I thought of Antigonus and Leonidas, their bodies shamed by barbarians.

Philosophers are always praising the solitary life, but I don't recommend too much reflection for the captain. It can be dark in there.

At any rate, they were all still alive. I ran back to the column and immediately sent the twenty men in the front to join Hipponax – all Hector's men, and Hector too. There wasn't going to be another ambush. We were almost at the height of the pass and after that we'd be descending into Attica, the valley would widen, and the Saka would have every advantage.

I ran forward – or back, depending on your point of view – to my rearguard, and then I just walked and breathed for a while.

But there are some things you have to do yourself. I couldn't send a message to make sure the ambush was ready.

That never works.

When I could breathe well, I took my men forward and relieved Moire.

By my reckoning, we were about three stades from the ambush. The ground was slowly opening to the left as we faced into Boeotia. The ground was beginning to drop away to the right.

We practised a feint charge that Brasidas taught and all of us knew it, so I put all twenty-two of us in one block and we backed around a corner and then charged. We went forward *exactly* fifty paces and then turned and ran.

They broke away from us, loosing shafts. But they were wary, and their shafts were few. They'd been on us for hours and I suspected they were tired of wasting shafts on fully armoured men with big shields.

But we'd only chased them about thirty of our fifty paces when some of them began to turn outward onto the rising ground to our left, to envelop us. Of course we broke, all together, and ran back; and then, after perhaps a ten-pace pause, we could hear hoof beats behind us.

Well – it was like running the hoplitodromos with your life on the line and I began to fall behind, because I'm no longer that fast, thanks to various wounds. And a lot of armour, I confess it.

But we passed the bend in the road, the last bend before the ambush, without losing a man. Now we had two stades to go and the road climbed away slightly. The cavalry above us on the hillside were suddenly confronted with a narrow gorge and had to come down, and they were their own roadblock for a few long strides, interfering with the rush of our pursuers.

My feet pounded the road. I was last by five strides – I, who had once been the best among an army of Greeks.

Another stride. Another.

It was like running at the Persians in the pass above Sardis, except that I was now running away.

But there are some things you cannot ask your men to do, and one of them is to be the bait in an ambush.

The last hundred strides to the next turn in the road looked very long.

But the last fifty didn't look so bad, and my feet had wings of fear as I heard the hoof beats. The ground shook. An arrow went into my plume, and another shattered on my thorax, and made me stumble – perhaps twenty strides from the turn, and I was the only target they had. All my men had made the turn. I hoped there was a formed body waiting there, a hundred oarsmen waiting—

I tripped, and fell sprawling. My aspis didn't break my arm, thank the gods, but I rolled over it the way Istes used to, more by Tyche's blessing than any plan of my own. My knees were lacerated, and before I could breathe, there were hooves all around me.

A horse struck me as I tried to rise and I fell again, this time pulling my aspis over me as Calchus taught.

Above me in the dust a Saka leaned down and shot straight down. The arrow struck my aspis near the rim and went six fingers through and pricked my thigh. Another man put his bow over the back of his head as he rode by and shot down into me, and his arrow exploded on the oak and bronze of my aspis's rim. They were so close that I could see their eyes, the sweat on their foreheads. They guided their horses with their knees and they were already concerned about the men around the bend. The man who put the arrow into my thigh had a golden torque and a red leather jacket painted magnificently in tiny patterns; the other man had bright blue eyes ...

All that between one beat of my heart and another.

They came against the shield wall and it held. For a moment – perhaps three of my terrified heartbeats – it was othismos, the crossing of the spears. But light horsemen, no matter how powerful their archery, are no match for hoplites, even well-armed oarsmen, in a confined space.

The line pushed them back. Men were calling my name.

I was lying in a forest of horse legs, and I could see nothing.

I had the sense to lie still.

The line pushed again – there were horns on the hillside.

Many of the Saka had spears and they were wielding them overarm, trying to reach the men behind the shields. They pressed forward, and the men and horses pressed into them from behind.

More horns, and more; the low braying, like wolves calling, or dogs sounding from one house to another on an autumn evening when the moon is rising. A sweet sound to any hunting man.

My son's horn.

They charged. I didn't see it.

The forest of horse legs began to shift. And then the melee exploded outward.

In fact, only one Saka went over the cliff in the first moments, no matter how the song tells it. The poor bastard was on the far left of the fight, or perhaps he thought himself too clever and tried to put his horse among the rocks, and then he was gone over the edge, with a stade or two to fall to the plains of Boeotia far below.

The rest of the Saka turned like a shoal of fish to run – and Hipponax and Hector struck them in the side. The road was not wide. Panicked horses turned and went over the cliff. This time, no more than four or five, but it was, I confess, spectacular and horrible and there is good reason we all remember it.

One horse scrabbled with its back legs on the brink and screamed, and then the rider in the golden torque was gone.

I was back on my feet by then, in the heart of my oarsmen, and my wounds were forgotten for a moment. I went forward, but I never bloodied my spear. We almost pushed our own front rank over the brink in our eagerness, and men were screaming for all of us to stop moving—

We had six prisoners. They were brave men – and one woman – but they were terrified of the cliff.

We hadn't lost a man. That is important, when you take captives, especially – I'm sorry to say it – a woman. We made them dismount and we took their horses.

By my command, we let them go. We let them see the first signs of our making camp and we pushed them away down the hill.

But the baggage train had never stopped moving, and now the rest of the column – exhausted, but triumphant – walked away. We were not marching any more, but we moved down the pass into Attica as the sun sank to the west, out over Corinth somewhere. It gets dark early on that road, because of the loom of Cithaeron, but I kept them at it until full darkness. And then by moonlight, two more brutal hours down that road with many a stubbed toe and many a curse, until we saw the tower of Oinoe rising in the darkness, lit silver by the moon.

I let them collapse on their arms and sleep. But at first light we were up, with no food and no fires, and we stumbled forward with some very upset pack animals and some very unhappy horses.

I suppose that the Saka lost perhaps twenty men in those fights, maybe as many as thirty, including wounded. But that was enough. We broke contact, which of course, meant to them, as old and wily campaigners themselves, that they'd have to endure another ambush just to make contact again. They chose to let us go.

A sailor can tell you the most surprising things about another ship in a single glance from almost over the horizon. A sloppy sail or a well-set one, the bow a little down in the water from poor loading, or a crisp entry because a ship is loaded well; the flash of distant oars can show you a ragged crew or a tight one. And in war it is the same.

The Saka were brave and very professional, but I learned a great deal about Xerxes' army in those hours. The Saka were not particularly motivated. They didn't press us as hard as they would have if, for example, we'd raided their camp. I have reason to know. In fact, they were almost desultory in their pursuit, as if they had better things to do. And it is worth noting that all their cousins were looting helpless Boeotia while they were getting killed, which must have seemed unfair.

But I found it hopeful that the elite of Xerxes' army, with the possible exception of the Immortals and the noble cavalry, were so unambitious. Just possibly, they'd lost interest in the contest when Masistius went down, but he must have been re-horsed soon enough.

We did have some bodies to strip, and the Saka wore a great deal of gold. We took it and put it on the wagons and I saw to it that we took all their bows and all their arrows, too.

At any rate, the sun rose over Attica and it was empty. My whole body hurt like dull fire, like I'd lain on my anvil and pounded myself all day with a hammer. My hip was scored by the arrow that had come through my aspis and my head had a laceration where another arrow had passed between the crest box and the helmet, damaging both without penetrating either, and my arm had several punctures, all of them red and angry, and of course I'd lost two fingers on my left hand and my hand was puffy and swollen—

Idomeneus was still stretched overt the back of a horse, breathing like a man snoring in a bad sleep. Alcaeus's son awoke from his stupor to scream in pain and we had to rig a different mode of travel for him. He'd been stabbed twice with spears, once to the bone in the thigh and once through the back of the shoulder under the wing of his corselet; sheer bad luck.

I didn't want to lose either of them.

I confess I pushed my oarsmen across the plain of Attica like a madman. We ate garlic sausage from our bags as we walked and we kept moving. It was to my advantage that they were oarsmen, used to extreme performance, and not mere hoplites. Aristides would spit to hear me speak such blasphemy, because aristocrats are supposed to believe that the thetes class will always betray them and cannot be trusted in extremes, but my experience is the opposite – rich men will sell their city while the poor will fight on the walls to the last drop of their blood. After all, unlike the rich, they have nowhere else to go.

And of course, they are used to working hard. My oarsmen were magnificent, in a grumbling, angry, bitter, cynical way.

Leon, one of the oldest oarsmen, a man who had some special tie to me, for all he affected to despise me, was one of the best. He'd been aboard *Storm Cutter*, the first of the name, in the storm that had earned her the right to be called so. He'd been there when we killed most of the Phoenicians and later when we survived the hardest manoeuvre I've ever done in a storm. He lacked the voice or the poise to be an oar-master, but he was a big brute with a ready tongue, and he always seemed to end up with me, no matter how many times he collected his silver and went away to open a taverna.

He'd spent most of the last five years aboard Paramanos's ships, but now he'd taken citizenship in Plataea and here he was swaggering his way across Attica.

'Careful he doesn't get you lost,' he said aloud to a mate, cocking an eye at me. '*Lord Arimnestos* has been known to take a few long ways to get home, eh, *lord*?' He laughed his big laugh.

Men muttered about the lack of rations and the fatigue, but Leon shouted, 'What's our hurry, Navarch? We're running from the fucking Medes so that other Medes can kill us, eh?'

I jogged over alongside him.

'I notice you're still alive,' I said.

'Not for long,' he said. But he grinned at me.

Where the road splits for Megara and Eleusis I halted them and let them rest in the olive grove. We fetched water from a well. The owner wasn't there to ask. No one was there. It was *wrong*, somehow, to ride through villages with no people, or with one sad dog.

The sad dog was at the crossroads. He was a fine tall brute with a brindle hide, not a farmer's animal but a hunting dog like those my friend Philip of Thrace raised, or Lykon of Corinth, my sister's favourite. I fed him and he took the food with considerable dignity for a dog and looked at me that way that good dogs do. As if to say, *I trust you, man. Are you worthy of my trust?*

I have never been a great man for dogs or cats. But that dog – he was alone. He had known better days, and he deserved better than dignified starvation in a small town in a deserted Attica – or being killed by Persians for food.

I pulled the rope out of the lining of my good aspis and made a quick collar to hold him, but from the moment I fed him, he showed little inclination to run. He just wanted more sausage. I fed him most of what I had, noting that I seemed very hot for a man who had only walked a few stades, and that my left hand was bright red, which worried me.

But the grumbling was quite loud, so I wandered in among the oarsmen. 'We must have taken four or five mina of gold,' I said. 'Tonight on the beach of Salamis, we'll divide it in shares. I'd be surprised if every man didn't get a daric.'

I suppose I could have given them a speech about saving Greece, but usually a little loot is better.

Or perhaps I'm just an old pirate.

We had to climb the low ridge that towers above the beach at Eleusis, and we were too strung out. I was conscious that we could meet Persian cavalry going in any direction at that point; they could be behind us, ahead of us, all around us. So I sent mounted men racing to the highest point, closer to Athens, and I ordered men to pick up their spears and shields when I saw two of the prodromoi galloping back to me.

But I smelled it before they reported on it.

'Attica is on fire!' they said.

And it was true. The Persians and the Medes must have struck the southern slopes of Mount Parnes that very morning, because we hadn't seen anything from the top of the pass. From the ridge, though, we could see smoke to the north and east, as far as the eye could see. And we could smell it, too.

My new dog sat and howled.

I patted his head and gave him some sausage, which quieted him. Much like the oarsmen with Saka gold, come to think of it.

Before darkness fell, a pair of tubby tuna boats came and took forty of my people across to the Salamis side, where Harpagos and Seckla were waiting. As soon as they knew we were there, they got the hulls in the water with only the top decks manned, and skimmed across.

We saw them coming – five ships under a third of their oarsmen, and we knew they were for us. We'd only been gone from them a week, but it was like a homecoming. For most of the oarsmen it was more of a homecoming than going to an empty Plataea. We put the oarsmen into the ships, packed the top decks with terrified donkeys – not a story I'll tell, but also not an experience I'd willingly repeat – got the horses aboard one of the tuna boats, and made it to Salamis before the Great Sickle rose into the heavens. Brasidas had made a tight camp, with sentries, and we landed like champions, stern first, and waded ashore with our menagerie of stock to find a hot dinner and fresh bread waiting.

Eugenios moved into my tent without a backward glance and for the rest of the war my food was hot and my dishes were clean. Styges served out the former slaves to Giannis, commanding *Black Raven*, who was the shortest-handed.

I'd missed a week of meetings, councils and officers' calls. Fighting the Persians seemed like a worthwhile way to spend my time.

I was just lying on a pile of straw that Eugenios had produced and had my favourite silver cup in my hand, full of good wine, when Themistocles appeared out of the starlit darkness like a god in some play. Probably a comedy about men's folly. At his shoulder was his slave – we all assumed he was a slave – Siccinius. We'd all met him, and he was rumoured to be the Athenian's lover, although Themistocles was not a man to be kept to just one lover, or even just one kind of lover. At any rate, Siccinius was a handsome man, a Phrygian who had been enslaved in war, an educated man. Siccinius went wherever his master went.

'Where the fuck have you been?' he asked. Then, before I could sputter, he said, 'Thank Hermes you've made a safe return. The Corinthians insisted you were gone for ever – gone to Hermione.'

He nodded to Brasidas. 'But this worthy man swore you would return, and none of us has ever met an apostate Spartan.'

'I am a Plataean,' Brasidas said.

Home, sweet home.

I followed Themistocles and his pais up the beach and over the next shoulder of land, a high outcropping. There, on the spur of rock that divides the beaches, is a small temple, and half a dozen tents. As it turned out, it was where Eurybiades had set his tent, and with him, a dozen Spartan messes, Themistocles, and some other wealthy Athenians. Sometime I'll tell you about Themistocles' tent, which was beautiful.

It was inspiring just to stand there, between the two main beaches. Oh, Salamis has many beaches – dozens if not hundreds. But it has three huge beaches that face Attica, and another at the base of a long finger that points right at Athens. The Aeginians had that beach, as it was closest to their home island, to our south, but the Athenians' ships filled the other three, with the Spartans. The Corinthians were farther west, on the same beach as my daughter's school in exile. From Eurybiades' camp, you could see the campfires stretching away east and west.

We were a mighty fleet.

Eurybiades embraced me, which was an honour in itself. I told a little of our journey and produced some of the gold, lest some nay-sayer like Adeimantus of Corinth say I'd invented the whole thing, but he was gracious, which suggested to me that he was up to something.

On the other hand, they were all still there, which I took as a very favourable sign indeed. It had seemed possible in my darker hours that we would come to find no one but Athenians on the beaches.

'So Boeotia has fallen,' Eurybiades said. He frowned.

'In Plataea, they say that Thebes gave more than earth and water,' I said. 'In Plataea, men are saying they opened their gates and fed the Persian cavalry.'

Eurybiades stood straight. 'May the Gods curse them,' he said, the strongest thing I think I ever heard a Spartan say.

Themistocles looked out over the bay. 'And now they are burning Attica,' he said.

I nodded. 'Thebes will do what she can to protect her towns,' I said. 'So if they want loot, they won't lose much time on Plataea.' I smiled, still, in my heart, a cocky boy. 'Perhaps we taught them to be careful crossing Cithaeron, though.'

'And what word from the isthmus?' Adeimantus asked, as eagerly as any. These men were starved for news, and I noticed that Cimon was not among them.

I hoped he was still at sea, keeping watch on the enemy fleet.

'My lord, no word, beyond that the wall is being built and we were invited – that is, the Plataeans – to send our goods there.' I nodded pleasantly. 'My town's phalanx went to join the allied army.'

Adeimantus nodded. 'So ... the League is waiting at Corinth. No reason for us to linger here, then. Let's move the fleet to where the army is.'

This had the ring of an old argument and I knew I'd been used.

Themistocles said, 'We were told that the League army would march, if not to save Boeotia, then to help defend Attica,' he said.

'A foolish dream,' Adeimantus said. 'Which I told you days ago. Attica is indefensible. You are lost. Let us take the fleet and save the rest of Greece.'

Themistocles was clearly tired of all this, and yet in those days of his greatness he did not give way to anger. 'If you go to the beaches of Corinth,' he said, 'you will go without the fleet of Athens.'

A man I knew very little, although he commanded thirty ships and had fought brilliantly the last day at Artemisium, stood forth. He had beautiful white hair that flowed like a horse's mane down his back, and muscles like Heracles. His name was Polycritus of Aegina, son of Crius. He was one of many heroes in our fleet, and men listened when he spoke.

He smiled at Themistocles – a smile of the purest dislike, almost hate. And he laughed, as men will when they laugh at themselves. His lips curled, anyway. 'It pains me like bad milk in my stomach to agree with Themistocles, or indeed with any man of Athens,' he said. 'But Adeimantus, if you take the so-called "Allied Fleet" to Corinth, you take no Aeginian ships, no Megaran ships, no ships of Naxos or any of the islands. While we stand here, we cover our homes. If we follow you to Corinth, our homes are open to rape and sack.'

Adeimantus shrugged. 'While we wait on these beaches, our homes are undefended.'

Themistocles shook his head vehemently, but his tone was measured. 'That is *not* true. While we stand here, the Persians cannot pass us. The beaches of Salamis face in every direction and we can, if we must, be the hub of a wheel – we can move from beach to beach around the island as the Persians try to pass us.'

Adeimantus smiled in triumph. 'So – you would fight in open water to keep the Persian fleet from moving west? So your argument about fighting at Corinth is a lie – you can fight there as easily as here. Better, with one secure flank.'

Polycritus shrugged as if he didn't care. 'If you fall back on Corinth, we will not be with you.'

Adeimantus looked at the Peloponnesian trierarchs standing with him. 'So be it. Go over to the Medes like the soft Ionians you are. We will defend the isthmus.'

Themistocles shook his head in wonder at the man's stupidity. And truly, my friends, I have to say that sometimes it is painful to listen to the self-delusion of men who should know better. Aye, and women too, though men excel at it.

'With your sixty ships?' he asked. 'Your sixty ships that we have protected in every fight because you cannot row well or keep in line?'

'You *lie*,' Adeimantus said. 'My ships keep the best order. My ships are the finest. I have rowers who cannot question my orders, proper captains of gentle birth, and years of victory behind us.'

'Name one,' Themistocles said. 'None against Athens, I guess.' He made a lewd gesture, indicating broadly what the Persians would do to the Corinthians. Many of the assembled Athenian trierarchs laughed. I noted that one of them was Cleitus, a member of the Alcmaeonid family and a pillar of the conservatives. Laughing with Themistocles. War does make for strange alliances. I caught his eye. He didn't avoid mine. We neither smiled nor spat. It was a little like seeing a woman you used to love with her new husband. Bah – no, that's a false allegory, because that sight might give me pleasure, and Cleitus *never* gave me pleasure.

'Athens didn't even *have* a fleet until a few years ago!' Adeimantus complained, with some accuracy. 'You just tell your stupid lies. In a few days, you will be *nothing*.'

'At least I will not be a Corinthian,' Themistocles shot back.

Eurybiades' face never changed. His eyes did catch mine, for a moment.

I smiled. I knew Spartans better than most men, by then. A year with Brasidas and Bulis and Sparthius had taught me a good deal. The old Spartan prince was letting them talk because, to a Spartan, most Greeks talk far too much but do too little.

I moved to stand by him. He put a hand on my shoulder in greeting and managed a small smile.

He was under enormous pressure and mostly he bore it with grace. I suspected that he wanted to kill Adeimantus with his bare hands, and possibly Themistocles into the bargain. I mostly agreed with the Athenian democrat, but he had the most annoying, patronising, intellectually superior tone that won him no friends among fighting men, even when he had himself fought very well at Artemisium. He always had to demonstrate that he was the smartest man in any assembly and his very demonstrations could make you doubt him. How could a man with so many merits need so much applause?

And just then he began a speech with the words, 'In Athens ...'

Now, friends, I love Athens, but many back then did not – aye, and many hate her today. Athens is not a mellow old nobleman like Sparta, but a brash, pushy vendor hawking sweets at the top of her lungs and willing to show a bit of breast to get you to buy. Let us be frank: there is a lot not to like.

So whenever Themistocles started a speech with the words, 'In Athens', he was busy making enemies.

Perhaps the problem, obvious to those of us from the small poleis, and invisible to the mighty, was that when Themistocles talked, he talked for his Athenian audience, and when Adeimantus talked, he talked for his Corinthian audience, and neither was actually speaking to the other.

'Where is Cimon?' I asked the navarch.

His eyes narrowed. 'Not here,' he said in his Laconian way. And then, ignoring Themistocles, he turned to me.

'I am concerned that he has been rash,' he said.

Speaking to Spartans is like visiting the oracles – you have to interpret what they say, because they use as few words as they can.

Eurybiades didn't look at me, but he spoke carefully, as if I was a slightly slow but well-beloved child. 'Cimon spoke of "commerce raiding",' he admitted.

First I'd heard of it. Commerce raiding always appeals to me.

In fact, if anyone had asked me – and no one had since a memorable night at the Olympics – I would have said that we should make a whole war of attacking their commerce. With the nearly four hundred ships we had on the beaches of Salamis and a few more coming in every day, we could have made it impossible for the Great King to even *assemble* a fleet.

Also, my rowers were eating my fortune every day, and my town was being sacked by the Persians.

'Shall I go and fetch him home?' I said as sweetly as possible.

Eurybiades had not been born yesterday, or even the day before. He looked at me levelly, the way my father used to when I said I could go to town by myself. 'Yes,' he said.

Anything was better than listening to Themistocles talk, or Adeimantus shout.

Dawn, and we were off the beach. I took only *Lydia* so as not to make a stir, and her hull was dry and clean from six days in the warm early autumn sun. A dry hull is, next to a good shipwright and good wood, the most important thing in a ship. I'd left Seckla in charge and he'd turned her over, stripped away all the repairs we'd made in the last year and replaced them with the new wood and professional shipwrights that Athens offered to all the Allies. Then he'd dried the hull for three days in the sun and only then caulked her tight again and coated the now dry hull with shining black pitch, finished with her original scarlet stripe along the oar-ports. Her sails were clean and dry and all her cordage was clean and recently coiled down.

Lydia was, as I have said before, a half-decked trireme with a standing mainmast. This is now popular in all the western parts of the Inner Sea but it was rarer then, favoured by pirates and by the cities of Magna Graecia, where I learned of it. The standing mainmast was braced by the deck and two strong beams, which meant more sail could be made in a stronger wind, the boom of the sail could be braced further round, and the ship itself could point a little closer to the wind. None of that was, to be honest, all that important, although it would have been had I wanted to sail outside the pillars of Heracles again. What mattered most was that the sails were always available, day and night, and that we could use them almost to the very point of battle.

The rig has bad points too. You can still lose your mast over the side when you ram. That's a serious problem and a risk every time, because when you lay a seaborne ambush, that standing pole can give you away to a sharp-eyed lookout. On the other hand, our mast had a small basket like a bird's nest, forty feet above the waves, where our lookout could stand. Perhaps worst for a sailor on the Inner Sea is that in the event of a big storm, you cannot simply bring your mast down on deck and a high wind puts an incredible pressure on even a bare pole.

Oarsmen love them, though. They don't have to work so hard.

The deck allowed me to have more marines and more deck crew as well as some archers – every pirate's dream.

I mention all this now because, thanks to Seckla's tireless work – well, and everyone else who stayed behind – our five ships were in a magnificent material state of readiness, and when I rowed away into the dawn the other ships were completing the same process. Many of the Athenian ships were doing the same, and even the Peloponnesian ships, a few of them anyway. *Lydia* was in as pretty a state as she'd ever been, at least since she was launched.

The other major factor in handling a warship besides her design, the quality of her wood, and how dry her hull is, is the men in the hull. As we rowed off the beach at Salamis, I think I had the best crew I had ever had. Listen to my ship list, thugater. I had Seckla and Leukas as helmsmen, both brilliant sailors, both able to command a ship. I had Onisandros as our oar-master, the best lungs in the fleet, and Brasidas commanding my marines.

And what marines! Idomeneus, another man who could command his own ship, and Styges; Sitalkes the Thracian and Alexandros, a brilliant hoplite in magnificent equipment, Hector my sometime hypaspist and Hipponax my son, and Achilles, my cousin. I'll take a moment to say that Achilles had fought in the actions against the Saka, neither badly nor brilliantly. He tried to be a sullen loner, but Brasidas and Idomeneus wouldn't let him. The Cretan and the Spartan were rivals, but only in the best way, and they competed to bring Achilles up to our standard.

I was short by two marines. Teucer, son of Teucer, was dead, and Antimenides, son of Alcaeus, was on the beach with the doctors, badly wounded.

Oh, and what of Idomeneus, you ask? On the beach of Eleusis, when they took him down from his horse, he woke, spat in the sand, and demanded water. He drank pints of it, and more that night at Salamis, and he was with us the next morning – with a headache like the hangover after the feast of Dionysus and no more. I have had my share of fortune in war, but I have never been more surprised to see a man survive a wound then Idomeneus in the fight at Leithos's shrine.

But marines do not power a ship, my friends. That is down to oars-men. I won't name them all – I probably couldn't, but that morning I knew all their names. They were a homogeneous body, had been together for more than a year without a pause, and although we had a few new men and a few awkward sods, everyone was in top shape and most men were well fed and believed in what we were doing.

Especially after we served out the Saka gold.

Leon was the oldest and had the biggest mouth. But he was a man who could row through the whole of a storm and still make a foul joke to the man on the next bench. Giorgos and Nicolas had rowed for me for years and both were capable of being officers when required – they commanded rowing divisions. Sikli, a leering monster from Sicily; Kineas, a handsome young man from Massalia who was tired of fishing and never wanted to go back; and Kassander – and a hundred and seventy more. They had made, every one of them, enough gold to buy a farm. More than seventy of them actually owned property in Plataea, a couple enough to qualify as hoplites.

But oarsmen and sailors do not easily come to wealth. They spend freely, on wine, on lotus flowers, on poppy juice and hemp seeds and women and men and jewellery and tattoos and cats and dogs and monkeys and pretty knives and any other blessed thing that enters their heads. Why?

Men who use the sea know that life is sweet – and can be short. What use the farm, when your mouth fills with the salt water that will drown you? Why save? The next storm may be your last.

And if you spend all today's gold, and you do not die, then perhaps another fat Egyptian merchant will appear through your oarlock tomorrow, eh?

Bah. I should have been a philosopher instead of a pirate.

Finally, we had Ka, and Nemet, and Ithy, and Di and Pye. They were Nubians – actual Nubians. Men called Seckla Nubian but he was from some outlandish place further east, or so he claimed. Anyway, they were from south of Egypt, and they were professional archers. They'd been slaves, and Egyptian soldiers, and then slaves again. They were as talkative as Spartans. I think Ka liked me, but I know he fairly worshipped Seckla. The five of them were expert archers and all improved by having the captured Saka bows, with which they'd been shooting since dawn.

We got *Lydia* off the beach well enough. And when we were skimming across the Bay of Salamis with little wind and almost no waves, she handled as sweetly as I've ever known her. There were some men up on the headland of Cynosura, and they cheered us. They were erecting a lookout tower. I thought of my daughter, and we swept on.

But as soon as we were abreast of Phaleron, where a dozen merchant ships were loading the last refugees and all the naval stores that could be rescued from Athens military port, I turned two points to starboard and put the coast over my left shoulder, and we continued at a good pace. The wind was wrong for sailing, but by noon it came under our quarter off the hot fields of Attica. We couldn't see any burning from the seaward, or smell it. But we ran up the mainsail and braced the boom hard, and the rowers sat back and drank water and cursed the sea.

In truth, it was a beautiful day and the breeze was, if not perfect, certainly enough. We ran along at about the pace a strong man walks, watching the coast, which I kept about ten stades distant, with a boy up at the masthead in a huge straw hat. We sent him water from time to time.

We had the sea to ourselves, which came as no surprise. As the afternoon wore on, I cheated the helm more and more to seaward until we lost the coast altogether in the late afternoon haze.

A few benches forward of the helmsman's bench, Leon's deep voice spoke up from under the half-deck like a disembodied god. 'Poseidon's dick,' he said. 'Here we go out of sight of land, and off into the deep green.'

Men around him laughed.

I smiled.

We landed, a little late for my taste, but the western sky was still orange, on the island of Kea about a parasang south of Cape Sounion. I half-expected to find Cimon there, on that very beach, because it made a fine position from which to watch the coast of Attica and retreat to the open sea if something went wrong. In the morning we put a tower on the headland made of fir trees and dried our hull while we had a big meal. It had been a long pull and a longer sail. The peasants were happy enough to see us and to sell us some sheep, which we consumed after making an appropriate sacrifice in a nice little temple to the Sea God. But despite our sacrifices, the breeze came against us at the height of the sun and in the afternoon we had a heavy rain. Our tents were all back on the beach at Salamis, so we were wet.

We built big fires and slept soundly, then woke to stiff muscles and a beautiful day, and launched into the light surf. There was no sign of yesterday's foul weather, and the wind was a stiff southerly with a little hint of sand in it.

I ran north to Chalkis, but with the wind so strong from the south, I didn't dare risk being embayed. That is, it's not that the waters off Marathon are really a bay, but the narrows at Chalkis are so narrow that a few Persian ships could snap us up, and I needed to watch my back. So we sailed – pure, sweet sailing without toughing a halyard or a line – from Kea north to the southern tip of Euboea, and then we rowed back west, carefully, with the masthead manned and many an invocation to the Sea God. We didn't see anyone, except a pair of Euboean fishing boats. We ran them down and bought all their catch, transforming their terror into wonder. Which was good fun.

We ate their fish on the beach of a little volcanic island in the gulf opposite Marathon, which I estimated was hull down and due west about two parasangs. That little islet was sent by the gods. There was a small village of very poor people, who nonetheless had some store of grain and dry fish to sell us, and from their peak we could see right across the gulf and all the way north to Chalkis, or near enough. The gods gave us a clear day on our fourth day from Salamis. Now we could see smoke over Attica, but no Cimon and no enemy fleet.

Now I cursed that I hadn't brought another vessel. I had the perfect watching post, unless the Persians had decided to go the other way around Euboea, and even then we'd see them as they passed across the southern end of the gulf.

I wasn't too worried about Cimon, who had ten ships and could handle himself. In fact, he was probably the best ship-killer alive at the time, very much his father's son. My only fear for him was that he might try some doomed action, like holding the narrows at Chalkis with ten ships.

I needn't have worried. Or rather, I knew him all too well.

The next morning, the fifth, we saw nothing all morning and we dried our hull, but around the height of the sun the lookout way above us on the mountain signalled with a piece of bright bronze that he saw something.

I went and climbed the mountain myself.

From the top of Megalos, as the locals called the islet, the Gulf of Marathon was like a big Spartan lambda, or an inverse V. The point at the top was the narrows of Chalkis. The opening at the bottom was the Aegean. The left arm was the coast of Marathon and the right arm was the coast of Euboea.

Attica was afire. You could smell it, forty stades away and more, and see the smudges of grey and black.

But what interested us was in the water. Up at the edge of our vision, where the land and water seemed to meet in the noontime haze, there was rhythmic flashing.

For once, there was no hurry. They were half a day away, at least. So I sent for wine and lay in the shade of the little grass shelter we'd built, and watched.

The longer I watched, the more I became convinced that I was looking at Cimon's ships, and the Persians – actually, Ionians – pressing them hard.

But then I'd tell myself another story: that I was seeing a Persian advance guard in front of the Persian fleet.

Aye, but you really can identify some things a great way off, just as you know the silhouette and the movements of an old friend so far away you could never see their face – just the set of the shoulders tell you everything. Yes?

I was sure that one of the lead ships was *Ajax*.

I'd known that ship through three major refits and almost twenty years.

Of course, our strong southerly wind had stayed on, so Cimon – if that was him – was rowing into the teeth of it.

As they came down the coast of Attica, I could see it better. There were nine ships out in front, and two dozen coming behind. My eyes were already too old to pick so many out of the sun dazzle, but Hector and Achilles seemed to be able to look into the very eye of the sun and pick out details, and Leukas claimed to see that the lead ship was red.

Ajax.

Cimon was in trouble. Or, at worst, I was wrong, and that was the Ionian vanguard of the Great King's fleet. Either way, my hull was dry and my crew superb, and I was pretty sure I could outrun any ship on the sea.

'Let's go,' I said. We went down the mountain in a sliding stumble and it was a miracle no one broke their ankles.

I remember cursing, because we looked like idiots or untrained slaves coming off the beach. Too eager, I suppose, but we caught crabs, our hill slewed right and left and the strong southerly almost pushed the head around and broached us too – in calm water.

Suitably humbled, we managed to get moving west, across the gulf.

An hour of rowing and everyone was calmer, and my name was being cursed, which was fine. We were rowing at a fast cruise and the wind was no help, but Seckla had the ship and he was doing his best to keep the rowers together and the wake straight. The marines were armed, and Ka and his ebony archers were all over the ship – Nemet, the smallest man, was in the bird's nest, naked but for his bow and two quivers. All the Nubians had acquired very Athenian tawed thoraxes and helmets. Ka's was magnificent, a capture from Artemisium, a bronze helmet made to look like a lion's head, with ostrich plumes. It was outlandish, but a seven-foot tall black archer can look as outlandish as he pleases.

Nemet was calling down to the deck what he saw.

'Red ship, boss. Sure eno'!' he called.

Then, 'That's *Ajax* and astern of him is *Dawn* and *Golden Nike.*' Remember, we'd all been together many times.

'Point at them!' I shouted up to the masthead, several frustrating times, as my words were carried away in the freshening wind. But after some antics not to be repeated, Nemet got my intention and pointed his bow staff almost due west.

We rowed on. I didn't want to use a sail, which would give us away to even a lubberly lookout. It seemed reasonable – I've seen it before – that the pursuers wouldn't notice us.

For a little while.

I summoned all my officers amidships. 'Here is what I plan,' I said. 'We sweep in, go to ramming speed and try to break up the pursuers.'

Leukas narrowed his eyes. 'If we come in from the flank, the second ship will have *us* in the flank.'

'We oar-rake, nip some steering oars, and go past,' I said. 'Then we turn end for end, raise the mainsail and run as fast as we can – north by east.' I nodded over the side at the water. 'There's a gap between the Ionians and the main fleet. We run through it.'

Leukas shook his head. 'You are still a madman,' he said. 'But it certainly sounds like fun.'

Seckla nodded, seeing it.

Brasidas looked disappointed. Perhaps he thought we were going to go hull to hull with the whole Persian fleet.

'Just keep their marines off our decks,' I said. 'Ka, kill the helmsmen. Onisandros, get some fire pots on deck.'

He made a face. Sailors hate fire, even as a weapon used against others. But we had a small firebox in the bows, lined in brick and sand, for making hot wine when we spent the night at sea, and other pirate tricks, and he put ten fire pots into it with their oiled wicks hanging free.

Hector closed my bronze thorax after I popped my greaves on my legs. I remember that it took me two tries to get my left greave on, because my left side hurt and I lacked the fingers to get the best grip on the damned thing.

By the time Hector pushed the pins through their keyholes in the thorax, the Persian fleet was hull up and visible in the sunlight.

Poseidon's Spear, there were so many of them!

They were spread over the Gulf of Marathon like athletes in a long race. The Ionians, the best sailors, were in the lead, and then there was a gap, and then the rest of the divisions in an untidy muddle trailing away to the narrows in the north beyond the edge of sight. A thousand ships?

I confess that for a moment, I couldn't breathe.

There was Cimon, though, plain as the nose on your face and ten stades away. There was his younger brother in *Dawn* and a few other old pirates I knew. Just for a moment, I imagined I could see Agios there, on the stern of *Ajax*. In fact, he'd died at Marathon, but my eyes filled with tears anyway.

Anyway.

We were well north of *Ajax* already.

Someone on the Ionian ships saw us. Well, it's the law of the sea – if you can see him, he can see you. My rowers were perfect and the sails were laid to the boom amidships and ready to raise, and every archer had an arrow on his bow. The marines were sitting on the deck, not forward in the boarding box but sitting where they had some cover and where movement wouldn't throw off the rowing.

There was a flash, and another flash, from the Ionians and three ships – beautiful ships, with long, elegant lines and Tyrian red in their sails – turned out of their race or their pursuit, and came for us.

Remember, we'd already been fighting these men all summer. I knew the ships almost immediately. The lead ship was from Ephesus and had the half-moon of Artemis on her bow, and so did the third ship. The middle ship was bigger, higher out of the water, and bright vermilion. I suspected it was Damasithymus of Calynda, in Caria. The Carians had been against us in the early days of the Ionian War, and then our allies, and now that the Great King had conquered them again – well, there they were. The 'Red King' was one of their most famous fighters, by sea and by land.

They wore a lot of armour and they had the reputation of carrying the very best marines. But I didn't spend much time looking at the red ship, because any ship from Ephesus interested me. I'd never been close to the Ionians in the fighting at Artemisium.

But the nearer trireme had to be Archilogos. He had the sign of the logos on his sail. His stern curve was painted in a livid and expensive blue, the colour of the house in which I grew up.

I walked aft to Seckla. The three ships had lost way in the turn and now their oars beat the water to bring them to ramming speed.

Archilogos – if it was he – had made the turn last and was behind the other two. The rightmost, or most northerly ship, was in front, so that the three made an echeloned line. We were running head-on for Archilogos.

'I want you to stay on this track as long as you can – but I want you to oar-rake the lead vessel on her north side,' I said.

That would mean a dangerous yaw to starboard at ramming seed. But *Lydia* did such stuff as routine, or so we bragged.

Seckla grinned. 'Good,' he said.

He gave the signal to Onisandros and we went to ramming speed. Seckla made a motion with both hands and every oar stopped at the height of the pull—

Seckla leaned into his turn, and I pulled the port oar to help him let go. His foot slapped the wood and the oars dipped together—

Poseidon, they were good! And now Onisandros *increased* the stroke past ramming speed.

We shot ahead. Seckla gave the signal, Onisandros barked, and all the oars lifted and stopped – and we turned back to our original course, almost due west. Perhaps we had turned a point further south ...

The northmost adversary – the other Ephesian – struggled to match our manoeuvre. They were at ramming speed and most ships don't manoeuvre at all at that speed. But the helmsman saw the danger and flicked his oars to move his beak, and oarsmen, un-warned, lost the stroke or missed the water – it happens. On deck, a marine fell flat.

Their oar loom began to fall apart, still rowing, as one or two failures spread. This was pure inexperience.

Ka gave a shrill cry and arrows began to connect the two ships like invisible ropes tipped in bronze. Either the Ionians had no archers or they didn't trust their bows.

We were almost bow to bow. Our ship was cocked just a little off their path, like a swordsman attacking off line.

Onisandros roared 'In!' and every oar came across the catwalks. I was up on the half-deck, and safe, but any sailor unlucky enough to be on the amidships walk forward was likely to get beaten to death by oar shafts.

But we'd done all this before, hadn't we, my lovelies?

Their oar-master never said a word. He was dead on the deck and black blood flowed from his throat with the arrow Ka had sent him. And because he was dead, their oars lay on the water when we struck, and their whole ship seemed to scream as the long poles were broken by our bow and our port-side cathead, and the shipboard end of every oar struck its rower with all the strength of our ship.

Above me, Nemet shot and shot, straight down into their exposed decks. At my side, Ka emptied a whole quiver of Saka arrows as we passed.

The Ionian fell off in the direction of her now missing oars and as soon as she lost way the south wind took her and spun her like a top.

It was then that I had the idea of how to make this even better. It was too late to employ it right there, but I sent Hector to find a light rope, a grappling hook and an axe.

I was just looking over the port-side bulwark from laying the coil of rope down when I saw him.

My first boyhood enemy. The man who gave up Briseis. Diomedes of Ephesus. He had three of our arrows in his aspis and he'd managed to protect his helmsman – until that moment, when Nemet, high above, feathered the man through the top of his shoulder, and the arrow went in almost to the fletching, and the helmsman – just a few oar lengths from me – died before his head touched the deck. Ka put another arrow into his aspis – one of the last in his quiver.

He looked at us.

'Diomedes, you cur!' I roared. 'How is Aphrodite!' I had once roped him to the pillars of the temple of Aphrodite. Well, he tried to have me killed. You all know the story!

I could see the blood rush to his face as he recognised me, and then we were gone, Onisandros was calling and the oars were coming out.

Diomedes' ship kept turning because no one had told his starboard side rowers to stop rowing.

So his bow fell afoul of the red trireme's bow and the Red King, as we'd called him at Artemisium, had to pull in his oars and turn sharply to port himself. Archilogos, also trying to line up on us, now almost fell afoul of the Carian ship and had to pull in his own oars and turn away to port, losing us out of the melee altogether.

I laughed. For a moment, I was the king of the sea.

But we hadn't yet accomplished a thing, except a sort of sea-jest.

But the collisions gave me a new option. I turned to Seckla.

'Turn to port,' I said.

He nodded, and before Onisandros even had our oars back in the water, we were turning – a shallow, easy turn, because there was no enemy that could touch us. We passed Archilogos's ship, flank to flank, half a stade out, and I waved as I passed and forbade my archers to shoot.

I could see him – my boyhood friend – standing on his command deck. Even as I passed, he tilted the helmet back off his head.

So he knew I wouldn't shoot.

But then he lifted his helmet – a beautiful Corinthian with hinged cheek plates – and waved. I waved back.

Then he shouted something and a heavy arrow punched into the face of my aspis.

And then his ship was falling away astern as my rowers pushed us forward. We were now heading south and west.

Now I was behind the leading Ionian ships that were pursuing Cimon and presenting them a dreadful tactical problem.

But that southerly wind was, if anything, rising, and turning our bow into it was a labour. The oarsmen had stopped curing to save their breath, but they were tired. Not dead tired – that was a long way off. But tired.

However, the Ionians – and Cimon – had been pulling into the teeth of that wind all day.

We rowed a stade, and then another.

And another.

All the Ionians edged away from me.

You have to picture this – here, I'll do it in almonds – no, too sticky. Like this, then. Cimon's ten ships are fleeing from a thousand. Thirty of them are far out in the lead, but of those only a dozen are swift enough to be right on him and three of those turned out of line to stop me. So there are nine ships left, all rowing as hard as they can to catch Cimon. But now I'm between the nine and their fellows, and I'm faster than they, and my rowers are far fresher.

Of course they edged away.

I let Nemet have all the arrows. He was higher, and despite the sway of the mast I knew he could drop arrows into the oar benches of the Ionians. Onisandros and Seckla and Leukas, who took the helm somewhere in this part, raised the stroke to being firmly faster than the Ionian stroke. And our hull was drier and better built to start.

We began to pull in on the last of the nine Ionians like fisherman landing a big tuna. Nemet began to loose arrows. Shooting into the wind – at an angle, no less – was tricky.

But when he got one clear of the enemy stern, the result was immediate. Oars went every which way on the port side and the ship fell off to port and we passed them, my other archers all shooting three or four shafts as we did so. We left them five oar lengths to our starboard side and swept on.

We began to catch the second ship of nine. But he simply turned away towards the coast of Attica. We passed him in a flash of oars and Ka dropped a well-shot arrow into the command station but we didn't linger to see its effect.

This was intoxicating, like fine wine after a great day.

Seckla shook his head. 'How long can we continue?' he asked. 'Surely they'll all turn on us?'

I laughed. 'More fool they, if they do!' I said.

And then ... they turned.

But it wasn't the Ionians that turned.

It was Cimon. His ships seemed to come around by magic. It was close, but because all the Ionians had cheated their helms to starboard, they'd lost the angle that would give them immediate raking rams, and so Cimon's ships slowed and spun end for end.

The Ionians were not our equals, but they were good sailors. They scattered like whitefish when the tuna attack them. And they went in almost every direction.

One slim trireme chose badly and turned towards us. He misjudged his turn. I looked over my shoulder at the big red trireme and Archilogos.

Archi was too far away to get his ram in my hull.

'Take him,' I said to Leukas. 'Marines!'

He got his oars in and managed to retrieve his turn, but he'd lost too much way and our beak hit his cathead and splintered it, pushing his bow deep in the water. It bounced back out of the water like a leaping fish and then our bow scraped down his side and our grapples flew and Brasidas was over the side. I ran along my own half-deck until I liked the distance and then leapt.

It was over before my feet were on his catwalk. They were Aeolians of Lesvos, from Eressos, and they wanted no part of the Great King. When Brasidas killed their trierarch, the rest of the men surrendered and some cheered.

'Greece!' called a rower.

I leaned down into the oar decks. 'Will you row for Greece?' I roared. They were pressed men – always an error in a sea fight – and among the top-deck rowers were men who knew me and one or two I remembered from happier days.

I kept my marines aboard. I was too old to take chances on trust.

I waved to Leukas and summoned Seckla to take the helm. The Lesbian helmsman protested, but I ordered him to sit down on the deck and put Seckla into the steering rig, and then Cimon – a Cimon with a bad sunburn and dark circles under his eyes – was calling from under my lee.

We bellowed back and forth like fishwives. But when he understood, we all turned broadside on to the rising waves, something we didn't think the Ionians would attempt, and we ran east.

Ran is probably the wrong word. We crept east for a few stades and then we raised sail and ran north and east, and then, when we felt safe, at the edge of darkness, we lowered our sails and rowed along the coast of Euboea. We landed on the first good beach we could find and lit no fires. It was a long, bad night.

But as Cimon said, while drinking my wine, it was not a night he'd expected to live to see.

As soon as there was enough light to navigate, we got off the beach, unfed, and rowed south. That was a hard morning, and fifteen stades rowing into that damned south wind without food used up my poor Ionians.

But by noon, in lowering skies and rising seas, I got them all onto the beaches below Megalos and we landed with two thousand hungry men.

There are many ways people supported the cause of Greek freedom. That village on Megalos didn't supply a single row boat for the fleet, but by Heracles and Demeter, they fed every man that day, and again the next morning – a whole winter's worth of salt fish and sheep and goats, consumed in a day. Bless them. When we piled back into our ships, every man had enough food in him to row home to Salamis and enough wine to have made the night before passable.

The Persian fleet stayed the night on the beaches at Makri and Marathon – there must have been officers who remembered their last adventure there. Certainly Archilogos had been at Marathon. And they waited there – it's a fine anchorage – until their supply ships caught them up.

I wish I could say that Cimon and I caught all their supplies emerging from the narrows and carried them off, but our crews were tired and Cimon was disheartened by ten days of raids and ambushes that had lost him a ship and gained him very little. He had made captures and lost them again; he had sunk a pair of merchantmen, but suspected they'd been empty, already unloaded.

Sometimes it does seem that Tyche and Ares are the same god.

The seventh day out from Salamis came up in a red dawn of wrath and we stayed on our beaches, ate our barley soup and mutton, and drank the last of the wine. My Lesbian crew were unsure of their status, somewhere between volunteers and prisoners, and they murmured. I spent the day sitting with them and I wished I had Harpagos or Herk or any of my other Aeolian friends – living or dead. It was, besides them, a very *Athenian* beach.

What I mean by that, my honeys, is that the Athenians, despite everything, or perhaps because of it, were growing rather more than less cocky and self-assured. I had just had a cup of wine with Theognis, the helmsman of the *Naiad*, our capture. He seemed a little too eager – there was something about him I didn't quite like, but then, I've never been a captive on a potentially hostile beach, trying to plead my loyalty to my new masters.

As usual, I digress. Cimon came, wrapped in a himation that was never going to grace a party in Athens or any other city that prized cleanliness. His timing was perfect – I was just rising from my folding seat and Eugenios had just picked up the stool and slapped it closed.

'Walk with me,' I said.

Cimon grinned. It was the phrase his father had used when he had matters of import – and usually, crime – to impart.

I laughed. 'No, I didn't mean it like that,' I said.

Cimon looked back at the Lesbians. 'I sometimes find it difficult to believe that we tried to fight a war on their behalf.'

I nodded. 'I love Eressos,' I said. 'But there is a soft-handed entitlement to them.' I shrugged. 'On the other hand, I don't have a Persian garrison in the citadel of my city.' I paused, as if struck. 'Oh, by Zeus! I do!' I slapped my forehead in disgust.

Cimon smiled, and looked like his father. 'By now, no doubt I do, too.' He looked back at the Aeolians. 'Let's be fair, the Lesbians fought like lions at Lade.'

I looked back at them too. 'I wonder . . .'

Cimon raised an eyebrow.

'Just the thoughts of an old man,' I said. 'Have you ever thought that courage erodes, little by little, fight by fight? Yesterday, when I had to leap from my ship to theirs . . .' I looked away in embarrassment. 'I hesitated. In fact, I find it gets harder and harder to find that spirit – the daimon.'

Cimon nodded and spread his hands. 'What can I say? My father loved you, but he thought you Ares-mad, a war child. If he were here, he might say you were . . . more a man and less a madman.' He met my eye and gave me a surprisingly gentle smile. 'I now fear *every* time I leap.' After this admission, he looked away.

We were silent a long time.

'But yes – age – life is sweet,' he spoke softly.

'Eualcides – do you remember him? The Euboean?'

'My father spoke of him. I never met him. A famous hero.' Cimon nodded.

'He said the same about running.'

We didn't need to say more.

The waves pounded the beach and the rain began; I wished I had my himation.

I remembered why I had started this hare.

'I only meant to say that perhaps the Aeolians are, as a race, like men – brave men – whose courage has been tried too often, and now they are shattered. They fought brilliantly at Lade – and got beaten. They fought like lions in defence of their island – and they were massacred, and their women sold as slaves. Perhaps they have been beaten too often.'

'Perhaps their bravest few are dead. The Killers of Men.' Cimon shrugged. 'I owe you for yesterday. I don't know if we'd have made it or not.'

I shrugged. 'I will remember it fondly for many years to come,' I said. 'After we beat the Persians.'

'By Poseidon and Ajax my ancestor,' Cimon said. 'You are a slap of cold seawater on my depression. You think we can win?'

I bobbed my head back and forth – really, not my most attractive habit, but I do. Hah! You laugh. I laugh too.

'Of course we can win!' I said, with more eagerness than the prior conversation might have led him to expect.

'I want to believe,' Cimon said. 'Please convince me.' He sat against a rock, a reasonably dry rock, under the cliff. I looked up at a pair of boulders that seemed to be held in place by nothing but the hands of the gods and thought that if the gods intended two of the best trierarchs of the Greek fleet to die here, then that was that. I snuggled in beside him.

'You bring any wine?' he asked. He winked at Eugenios, who stood in the light rain. 'Oh, by all the gods, Eugenios, fetch us some wine and I'll give you a share of the shelter.'

Eugenios smiled. Slaves are seldom spoken to directly by men like Cimon, members of the old nobility. But in that month, in that year, we were all in the fight together and such things mattered less. I had virtually forgotten that Eugenios was a slave and that thought struck me with some guilt. I, who have been a slave twice, knew that while I might forget, he would *never* forget.

He ran off. 'I should free him,' I said.

'He's rowing for you and he's your steward?' Cimon laughed. 'Too valuable to be freed. Want to sell him? I could use a steward who could also row.'

Sometimes Cimon could be a rich fool, like anyone.

'The Persians,' I said.

'Yes. I love your confidence. But I don't share it. I spent eight days running and fighting, running and fighting. I left little messages in all the harbours along Boeotia, all the cliff faces, inviting the Ionians to come over to us. So did Themistocles, along the Euboean shore. Not one of them changed sides. You know what I saw every day, every god-cursed day? More ships join the Great King's fleet. Thirty, the first day. Thirty!' He shook his head.

Eugenios came trotting back. It came into my head then: something for the gods, something about Greek freedom, something about who we were and what we were fighting for.

He had my old canteen – a piece of ceramic with the feet broken off, missing a side-lug, that had been dropped on a dozen decks and never split. It didn't look like much, but I loved it.

I poured a libation onto the rain-drenched sand and it looked like blood. 'To Zeus, the god of kings and princes and free men, and to you, Eugenios, who I make a free man with this libation to the gods. I sacrifice this man's slavery that Greece may be free.'

I drank and handed the canteen to Cimon. He straightened up. 'Arimnestos, you are—' he laughed. 'To Eugenios, the very prince of stewards. To your freedom. And to Poseidon, Earth Shaker, Lord of Stallions and the Sea, witness his freedom, and give Athens fair winds.'

He handed the canteen to Eugenios, who drank it and burst into tears. 'I was born free,' he admitted. 'Indeed – oh, bless you, my lord.'

'I'll see to it you are made a citizen of Plataea if we survive all this.' I was gruff. I had not expected hard-eyed Eugenios, terror of my slaves and lord of my household, to weep.

I think that, in truth, I hate slavery. Oh, I have a phalanx of slaves, do I not? But I free them, too. Some men are better and some are worse, that much I acknowledge. But enough better to own another?

I've *been* a slave.

Eugenios wouldn't snuggle into the cleft with us. His ideas of social station were stronger than Cimon's. Mock if you will.

I stepped out into the blowing spray and rain, and threw my chiton over my arm like a boy training to be an orator. 'Hear me, oh Cimon,' I said.

He laughed and drank my wine.

'First, before I deliver my argument, let us set the course of our own judging. Are there, on all the seas, any two men who have faced the Persians and the Phoenicians and the Egyptians more often than we?' I asked.

'My father,' he said. 'Miltiades. And perhaps that prig Aristides. And your friend Diodorus of Massalia, for all that I loathe him.'

'Better than we? Or merely the same,' I asked. 'Your father I allow.'

'Then I shan't quibble,' Cimon, son of Miltiades, said with a smile. 'We have faced them most often.'

'And does that not make us, in the matter of fighting the Persians at sea, the wisest?' I raised a hand to forestall argument. 'If perhaps we had been beaten often, I'd confess that the frequency of our fighting was worthless, but you and I have more often than not triumphed.'

Cimon nodded. 'You want me to agree, and of course I do. But I'm sure that Pythagoras would debate with you whether the frequency of our contact or even our triumph had anything to do with wisdom.'

'He might, but let's remember that he was against eating bacon and beware,' I said, and Cimon roared.

'You have missed your calling, my friend. You should go stand in the agora and preach like a sophist.' He winked at Eugenios.

I was play-acting, mostly to raise his humour. 'Very well then, I'll pass on the agora, which today is probably full of Persian Immortals uncaring of my heights of wisdom, and we'll agree that you and I are as fit to judge the capability of the Great King's fleet as any two men.'

Cimon laughed again. 'I have that sinking feeling I get when I listen to Aristides make a speech in which he wins every point but makes all the undecided men hate him, and our party,' he said.

'Very well, then. Here is why we will defeat the Great King's fleet,' I said. 'First, and simplest, because we have done so already, not once but twice.'

Cimon bit his lip. 'But they have replaced their losses and then some.'

'Have they replaced their hearts?' I asked. 'By your own admission you kept the sea eight days with ten ships facing all of them – and they only managed to take one of yours while you sank, crippled or captured five.'

He shrugged. 'So? What is five ships among a thousand?'

'Answer me this, doubter! If one single Ionian ship had come into our beaches at Artemisium and offered a fight or tried a raid, how many ships would have launched and fought her?'

He winced. 'A hundred.'

'Yet you went right in off their beaches,' I said. 'They are afraid.'

Cimon shrugged. 'I want to believe you.'

'The Ionians are probably the weakest part of their fleet,' I asserted.

Cimon shook his head. 'The best and worst,' he said. 'There are fine captains and ships among them. Don't go beak to beak with the Queen of Halicarnassus – Artemisia.' He stroked his beard. 'There's a woman with a fine helmsman. They say she's Xerxes' Greek mistress. I'm not sure.'

'But the ship we took yesterday?' I asked.

'Not very good,' he admitted.

'Yet it was *leading* the chase for your ships, while the Phoenicians and the Egyptians – who have every reason to hate the Great King – lagged well back in the narrows.' I waved at the Lesbians, sitting disconsolately in the rain. 'What am I to make of that?'

Cimon laughed. 'You are persuasive,' he said, laughing. He almost sounded ... guilty.

'My last piece of evidence requires only that you believe me,' I said. 'Yesterday, when I came out of the morning sun into their flank, I saw them cringe.'

'You took everyone by surprise,' he said.

'First, most of their ships, more then twenty ships, turned a point or two *away*,' I said. 'Then, when three of their ships turned out of the general chase, the rest used the time they bought to get closer to the coast. None of them was trained well enough to manoeuvre at close range against me, and in fact all their hulls are wet through and slow.' I grinned like the wolf I am at times. 'I had them in speed, in tactics, in rowing quality, *and they knew it*. They were like boys facing men. *And that was their best.*'

Cimon was smiling steadily now. 'I'd forgotten how you can be, Plataean,' he said.

'And last is a matter of tactica,' I said. 'The number of ships means nothing. We saw this at Lade, even. Confess it; you defeat the first line and the rest run. It is always this way. The Phoenicians distrust the Ionians and loathe the Egyptians. The Egyptians want to defeat the Great King and be independent. Every Ionian ship has men on board, oarsmen *and* marines, who were our comrades at Lade.'

'By Poseidon, Arimnestos, you make me feel as if it is the Great King who is to be pitied, not the Athenians!' Cimon crossed his arms.

'Say rather: the Greeks,' I said. 'You Athenians have taken to forgetting, in your desperate hubris, that you have allies.'

He winced. 'We will never forget Plataea,' he said.

'In this case, the ally I would remember is Aegina,' I said. 'They have almost fifty ships available and they have decided to fight.' I deflated myself. 'Even if the Peloponnesians run.'

I'm not sure that I changed Cimon's mind. I know I made him feel better.

But Poseidon sent us a better sign. Well – first I think that I should say that my elation was not just from the combat and the deed of the day before. Archilogos had waved at me.

You smile. I sound like one of you girls, delighted that the handsomest boy waved? No. Archilogos was the friend of my childhood and he had been my foe for many years. I had sworn never to do him harm and such oaths have power. This was the first time he had offered me anything but violence in return and I was irrationally cheered. I replayed the moment over and over, trying to test it for more or less meaning. Had he actually waved? Was he merely pointing me out to his archers?

Come to think of it, thugater, you are correct, I *am* sounding like a blushing maiden. But I loved him. The weight and injustice of his hate lay heavy on me. So I took his wave as a sign. I took the whole encounter as a sign. I was no longer despondent. In an hour of manoeuvre and combat I had allowed myself to be convinced, completely, that we had the upper hand, regardless of the numbers.

And then, on the ninth day out from Salamis, the sun was rising on a glorious day. The wind had lowered after sunset and the rain had stopped, and when I rose to piss in the night the stars were out and we had a gentle westerly.

We rose in the darkness and warmed ourselves at our fires and ate re-warmed mutton stew and some oysters. There was no wine. I got up on a rock and addressed the oarsmen, which I now did almost every morning.

'Today we should get back to Salamis,' I said. 'It'll be rowing all the way. And the Persian fleet is just over there.' I waved at the distant dark coast of Attica, as the eastern sky behind me began to lighten. 'But you are all better men than they. Just row. Fear nothing. If they come at us we can always turn south.'

Men nodded. They grinned and laughed and muttered darkly – and in that moment I loved them.

I had decided to send Seckla and Brasidas and twenty of my rowers to the Lesbian ship, and I had promoted six men from the oar decks to the rank of marines under Alexandros.

Brasidas hopped up on a rock and held up a wax tablet. 'I am given to understand that the following men have the great fortune to have been promoted to being marines,' he called. He read out six names. 'To welcome all of them to our ranks, *all* marines can meet me in full panoply for a little run and a little dance.' He didn't grin. Spartans didn't punctuate their unspoken threats with grins. They just said things and did them.

All through the crowd of oarsmen there was backslapping and

good-natured cursing as the lucky six – perhaps feeling less fortunate – hurried to find their helmets.

I walked down in my own panoply. Perhaps it was penance for the day before, but I felt I needed to exercise. And Eugenios, perhaps because of his new freedom, had polished my whole kit so that the bronze shone like gold. I sparkled in the firelight and the rising sun.

So did Brasidas, and we began to exercise, first in simple stretches and then in a run up the beach to the headland and back, sprinting all the way.

Oh, for youth. I was last – last! And the new marines laughed at me. In a good-natured way. Naturally, I hated the lot of them.

And then we began to dance the Pyrrhiche. I probably forget to say everything important, but by that time, thanks to my time with the Spartans and Brasidas joining us, we had more than a dozen dances. In fact, sometimes when only the veterans did them, we improvised, adding elements, or took turns in a dance game where one of us would lead and the others would imitate the leader's motions: thrusts, cuts, throws. Armed and unarmed, swords and spears and shields, drawing and sheathing, footwork . . .

But the first dance was still the old dance of the spear from Plataea, with some Spartan modification, and we began to teach it. Many oarsmen knew it and some did it every morning, hoping to be promoted, but none knew it in the detail with which Brasidas preached it. Now the worm turned; the biters were bit and Brasidas and I pointed out any small errors – phalanxes of them – to our new marines.

One man, Polydorus, shook his head. 'What does it matter whether I turn my foot or not?' he whined.

Brasidas didn't smile or frown. He merely paused. 'It only matters,' he said, 'if you would rather live, than die.'

'Ouch,' muttered Sitalkes.

Cimon emerged out of the murk of the early morning with young Pericles at his shoulder. He swirled his cloak to get my attention and I trotted over to him.

Pericles nodded at the new marines. 'You train them,' he said, 'as if training can make a man into a gentleman.'

'Young man, the Spartans, held as the noblest of all the Greeks, train relentlessly, and so do you.' I shrugged.

'When this is over, we are going to be in debt to our oarsmen,' Cimon said. He was looking out to sea.

'When we faced the Medes at Marathon, your father used the little men to shame the hoplites,' I said. 'Are you *more* of an aristocrat than your father?'

'What in the name of Pluton is that?' Cimon said. My stinging remark was blown away on the west wind. Pericles heard it and raised an eyebrow

I saw it too. The flash of oars, coming from the north-east.

'Poseidon's dick,' Cimon said. 'ALARM!' he roared.

We were off the beach faster than a boy drops his chiton for a run. Cimon's *Ajax* was first off and that annoyed me, but I was trying to help Seckla get his less-than-piratical Aeolians into their places while my own *Lydia*, in the very peak of training, waited for orders.

There were three ships. They were spread over a wide swathe of the ocean, as if not really together. And because of the sun rising in the east behind us, our hulls were black against the black rock of the coast, an old pirate's trick, and they didn't see us for a long time.

Farther out there was a line of ships, perhaps sixty, but they were hull down, just a flash of oars on the horizon.

Then things grew more complicated.

The closest enemy ship turned towards Cimon's *Ajax* and ran right at her. But they ran something up to their masthead and they didn't take down their mast, which almost any trireme did before combat.

I was still on the beach, virtually the last man on it, chivvying the Aeolian oarsmen into their ship. Watching the drama at sea play out, my heart in my mouth, desperate to get aboard *Lydia*. *Naiad* got under way and began to turn end for end.

Well out from *Ajax* the enemy ship turned her bow towards the beach, laying her vulnerable flank open to *Ajax's* ram and folding in her oars like a bird preparing for a rough night at sea.

Ajax turned in a flash of oars – a beautiful display of seamanship – took in her oars and lay longside to longside. But no grapples flew.

I ran into the shallow water in my armour – how poor Eugenios must have cursed me – and got over the side. *Lydia* was hovering in the shallow water just over the first drop-off of the beach – another fine art of rowing – and the moment Leukas roared 'on board' the oars all dipped and we were away like a sea eagle.

The other two enemy scouts were running, but Cimon's brother in *Salamis* was faster. He had everything in his favour – better rowers, better rested, with a drier ship.

And he dared run the fleeing enemy down, in full view of their oncoming fleet. There were sixty ships bearing down on us.

Of course, they all had their masts down. Even though the west wind was at their backs, they were rowing.

Because they were afraid of us.

But Metiochus was not afraid of them, and while *Lydia* left the beach and ran upwind under oars to where Cimon and his capture lay, Metiochus caught the fleeing trireme and rammed it in the stern. You seldom see it, even though it is the dream shot of oared combat. But his ram caught her right under the curve of the swan's neck, and although we could neither see nor hear because we were a dozen stades away, she sank.

Metiochus turned and came back, seeming to skim the water like a bird of prey.

Cimon's capture had, in fact, come right up and raised a branch of laurel. She was from Naxos, crewed with various survivors of the storms of three weeks before, and the crew had voted to change sides.

Leukas lay us alongside *Ajax* as prettily as a kore dances at Brauron, and I jumped from helm to helm.

Cimon's helmsman laughed. 'They're all over there,' he said. 'Tell 'is lordship that if we don't want to join the Persians, we need to get underway.'

I jumped again, onto the deck of the Naxian ship, *Poseidon*. She was a fine vessel – a decked trireme, a heavy ship built on the latest Phoenician lines, capable of carrying cargo or fighting. A little slow for running away, though.

I grabbed Cimon's arm. He was mobbed by excited Greeks – Euboeans and Ionians. Being a heavy ship, they had more than twenty marines. They also had a pair of Persian captives – two men assigned to the ship by their admiral, Ariabignes.

'They just sailed up and joined us!' Cimon shouted.

'Your helmsman wants to get out of here,' I shouted. 'So do I.'

Cimon grinned. 'This is a sign. From Poseidon.' He slapped my back. 'You were right!'

I pointed over the Naxian ship's starboard bulwark. 'There is a Persian squadron *right there.*' I waved. 'Can we help Poseidon help us by not fighting them all ourselves?'

Cimon shook his head. 'I feel the power,' he said.

'Feel it when you have two hundred brothers at your back,' I said. 'Sixty to ten is long odds.'

Cimon laughed. 'Sixty to twelve is only five to one,' he said. But he shook his head rapidly, indicating he was only leading me on. 'I agree. Let's go.'

He left his marines aboard, however, like the practical old pirate he was, and he took half the Naxian's marines as hostages. He made it sound like guest-hosting in the most noble and ancient way and the Naxians – well, the Ionians, really – leapt to the *Ajax* with a will, delighted to be invited aboard.

We all put our oars in the water. By then the oncoming Persian squadron, all Phoenicians, were ten stades away.

I had time to see young Pericles in an animated conversation with one of the Ionian marines, a boy only a little older, maybe eighteen.

Then I jumped back to *Lydia* and we turned south.

By a good chance, Cimon had scrawled his usual message inviting the Ionians to desert on the rocks above our beach and that's what the Phoenicians found when they went inshore. They didn't really bother to chase us. In fact, as we rowed due south, I wondered if they'd make a blunder. If they raced after us, a dozen ships well manned, we might have snapped up their lead ships, especially as I had a sailing rig.

But they did not. They chose to be cautious and, in truth, their ships were the very antithesis of the ships for a long chase; they were heavy and slow and damp.

We put them over the horizon in two hours and then turned west at a flash of Cimon's shield, a loose line abreast to a long, straggling column, but we were old shipmates and we knew the signals. We neatened up the line as we rowed, only one deck at a time to rest the oarsmen. Just in case. It wasn't just the Phoenicians who were cautious.

But we made good time. The west wind was gentle, barely rippling the water. We had started the morning with a victory and that put great heart into the men.

But for all that, the west wind *was* against us, and by mid-afternoon it was clear we would not make Salamis. We'd come too far west to make Andros and night was coming.

Cimon and I had the same thought – to find the narrow beach two bays west of Sounion. But we were cautious; just short of the bay we went in lone in *Lydia* and Alexandros and four mariners swam ashore, naked. They ran up the beach and climbed the ridge behind.

We hovered, the sun sank, and our oarsmen cursed.

Alexandros ran back down the sand and did a little dance, the agreed 'all clear' signal.

We landed. It was tight; it required all our seamanship and, to be honest, a great many blasphemies and some splintered wood to get us all ashore. The last ship in, Metiochus's *Salamis,* was beached between two big rocks and no sane trierarch would ever have put a ship there.

Not to mention that we had neither food nor wine.

We put all our marines together in a body under Brasidas and sent them inland to fetch any forage that could be managed, with two hundred oarsmen to carry it and all our archers as a covering force. Cimon and I went as volunteers and it was as scary as campaigning in a foreign land. North, we could see fires burning unchecked on the ridges and mountains towards Brauron and Marathon. East, the mountains toward Athens were afire.

Aside from Persians and their slaves, Attica was empty. There wasn't much food. We found some olives and some grain and, not far from the beach, we found a village that had chosen not to evacuate.

We found it by the busy cries of sea birds and ravens, feasting. We came into the town at sunset, the sky red as blood at our backs, and to my best guess the poor peasants had tried to send a delegation to offer earth and water to the invaders. At least, that's what it looked like – a tumble of amphorae meant for water, all broken, and two big red clods of Attic earth, dyed redder and browner by the blood of the two young girls who had carried them.

They had died hard. I will not say more ... Bah! I remember one young girl had her eyes open, and the whites were still clear, as only young eyes can be, and I hesitated to touch her, to close them, as if I might hurt her. And the sound of the flies everywhere – they assault your senses with a buzz that warns you not to look ... too late.

There were bodies throughout the village, a village which was more like the sheds of a big farm or a small estate, really just a crossroads. There was a small shrine, with a middle-aged woman dead across it as deliberate desecration, and six houses, all smouldering, with men lying in the road in fly-swarmed sticky puddles and the smell of cooking flesh to tell us where the rest of the people must have been.

They were, at least most of them, slaves. And the Persians – or Medes or Saka or Egyptians or perhaps even other Greeks – had used them and killed them.

All of us were moved. It was impossible to look on it and not hate. I have seldom hated the Persians. The Persians of my youth were great men. But this was like the rape of a whole land. Done apurpose.

Brasidas stood looking at the two young girls who had carried the earth and water. His face ... moved. The muscles of his jaw leaped up and down like a ship on the sea and tears came to his eyes. This, from a Spartan.

'This is despicable,' he said.

Ka glanced at the high ridge to the north. I'm going to guess that he had seen more atrocities than I. It is trite to say, but Heraclitus has the right of it: killing in the heat of battle is a very different animal from killing a couple of maidens in a village, much less raping and killing the entire village. A village of slaves. By the rules of war, the Medes might have rounded them all up and carried them away, the same way they took the bronze statues or the silver coins they found.

But they massacred them.

At any rate, Ka said, 'They are close. The blood is still wet and red.'

Brasidas dropped his shield and spear. He lifted one of the dead girls and carried her, tenderly, to the place where the village shrine was. Hard by it was a small graveyard.

He never gave an order, and neither did Cimon or I, but men found picks and a damaged shovel.

Ka shook his head. 'They are close,' he said.

I mastered myself, although the smell of the dead, the burned people in the houses, was in my nose and lingers there to this day. Darkness was coming down fast.

We put out a dozen watchers in the hills around the crossroads and gave them horns. Ka took the archers and hid them along the northern branch of the road.

Two oarsmen broke into the smouldering barn and found that there was food: sausages, and wine jars. The Medes hadn't even looted. They had merely killed.

When the work of burying the dead, all forty or more of them, was well advanced, I sent half the hoplites back to the ships with Cimon. I was worried that the Medes would attack the ships. I was in a black place and nothing made much sense to me. I slept a little and dreamed of the boy whose soul I sent down to Hades with a sharp knife one dark night on a battlefield in Asia ...

When I awoke, Ka had a hand over my mouth.

'They come,' he said.

Who knows why they came back. Really, I want them to have been the same men, but perhaps they were another patrol, another group. I can only assume that they smelled our smoke, or saw movement in a valley that should have been dead.

They were careless, riding abroad in the first hour of the day, spread across the northern fields in a long line of perhaps sixty horsemen with more coming on the road.

I had perhaps forty hoplites and a dozen archers. And Brasidas, of course.

They came across the fields at first light and up the road.

We killed all of them we could reach. It was an ambush and there was nothing worthy about the fighting. Nothing I will tell you. We threw our spears into their horses and Ka and his archers dropped them until they broke.

It is what came after of which I will speak.

There were three men taken. All had their horses killed under them.

I wanted to kill them. In fact, the idea that occurred to me was to bury them alive with the corpses of the town they'd massacred.

Or perhaps another group massacred them.

I did not speak to them. One – the youngest – pleaded for his life, to the embarrassment of the other two. They simply waited to be killed.

The marines watched them with a hollow-eyed rage that told them everything.

Ka and his archers went out into the fields to collect their arrows. Only Ka looked at me and shook his head, and made a little noise in his throat.

I would like to say that my urge to destroy these three, to humiliate them and then kill them in their despair, that my urge was defeated by the sayings of my master, Heraclitus, or what I had learned in Sicily about myself and about violence. But in that hour I was merely rage.

The sparkling, gleaming whites of a young corpse's eyes. The corpse should have been alive.

Bah! I tell this badly. I was in a sort of shock and I wanted blood.

Brasidas walked up to me. His face was ... horrible.

'We,' he said thickly. The word took him effort. 'We should let these animals go, before we lower ourselves to what they are.'

It was not at all what I expected him to say.

Will you believe me if I say that the two of us stood still and yet seemed to have trouble breathing?

We made it back to the boats. We had lost one man in the fighting, if cutting down surprised men in an ambush can be called fighting. We boarded our ships, a sullen mass of angry, disheartened men. Many of the oarsmen and even a few marines glowered at me.

I was beginning to breathe. I prayed to Lord Apollo that I had done right, because everything in me screamed that those three Medes should have been killed. But we had, in fact, let them go, and the discipline of the marines had held, although I could tell that Brasidas and I were virtually alone.

But there, on the white sand of the beach, young Pericles came and put his hand on my shoulder. 'That was brave,' he said.

Behind him was the Ionian I had seen him talking to on the day the Naxian ship came over to us.

Pericles smiled his too-hard smile. 'Anaxagoras of Clazomenae,' he said in introduction. 'Son of Laertes.'

The young man bowed. 'Lord Istes spoke highly of you, sir,' he said. 'But releasing the barbarians was an act of pure arete.'

I tried to smile, but very little came to my face. In fact, rather than feeling flattered, I felt nothing. Have you ever lost someone you loved? Mother, father, sister? You know that between weeping and recovery there is a time when you feel ... nothing. No desire for sex, no desire for war. Nothing.

I was in that place. I felt nothing. My disdain for their youthful arrogance was but a distant echo of my true feeling.

The Ionian man would have said more, but Cimon, close behind him, had better skills in reading me and pushed him along brusquely. 'Best get aboard your ship, boys,' he said. He used an offensive word – pais, the same word we use for a juvenile or a slave.

Pericles flashed him a look of undisguised, adolescent anger.

Cimon met his look steadily. 'Feel free to go back to your precious father,' he said.

I didn't understand the reference. I had, by then, been living and fighting alongside the scions of the Athenian noble families for more than fifteen years, but I still barely understood them.

94

At any rate, we got our ships to sea. It was a pretty day, utterly at odds with the revulsion I felt – that we all felt.

Seckla told me later that Brasidas threw his sword into the sea.

Salamis was crowded and had begun to develop the same smell as the vale of Olympus during the games – part cooking, part sacrifices, part men's piss. But the place was *alive*, perhaps more thoroughly alive than Attica usually was, because of the crowds. I got my ships ashore and there was almost a quarrel over beaching our Ionian capture, because space on the beaches was at a premium. But Seckla worked a miracle of humble negotiation and convinced one of Xanthippus's trierarchs to float and re-ground his vessel and so we all had room.

When I saw my people ashore and into their tents – it was excellent to have a pre-built camp and food ready to be served, and I pitied Cimon's oarsmen, competing with every man in Athens for bread – I walked across the beach to find Xanthippus. I knew of him – oh, I had no doubt shared wine with him somewhere, but I didn't know him well.

By the time I reached him, his young son was there, speaking in his usual slightly high-pitched, calm, clear voice, an almost unnatural voice for a man so young. He had the young Ionian by him.

He summoned me under an awning with a wave of his hand and a pair of Thracian slaves hurried to place a stool for me and put a cup of wine in my hand. Xanthippus was a big man, with a broad face and heavy muscles. He had the sandy fair hair common in his family and he had humour, which many rich men lack. I knew him as a friend and sometimes ally of Themistocles.

'Arimnestos of Plataea. My son sings your praises. My wife – a member of the Alcmaeonidae! – sings me your praises.' He nodded.

I returned his nod. 'I have come only to thank you for giving me room to beach my spare ship.'

'Spare!' Xanthippus laughed. 'Ah, you are a shame on us, Plataean. You mean, the Ionian ship you took in the very teeth of the Great King's fleet!'

What does one say? I love praise all too well, and praise from a navarch as famous as Xanthippus was praise indeed. But it was laid too thick.

'How do we do here?' I asked, waving my wine familiarly. 'In council?'

Xanthippus barked a mirthless laugh. 'Oh, the Corinthians loathe

Themistocles. It might be better for us if we had young Cimon represent us, or best of all, Aristides.'

'He is in exile,' I said, probably a little too quickly.

'I know he's your friend, for all he's the leader of our opposition,' Xanthippus said.

Through all this, the two young men stood silently. They had not been offered wine.

'Your son served with distinction,' I said. It was true, and besides, I've never known a man displeased by praise heaped on his child.

'Cimon was kind enough to say the same. For myself, I'm still trying to understand why my son would go to sea with a pirate in a fleet of oligarchs rather than his own father.' His bluff face filled with colour.

He was *actually* angry, not merely pretending.

'Can't you let men praise me for once, Father, and not you?' Pericles said.

'Can't you tell the difference between a man who fights for his country and a killer who fights to steal other men's gold?' Xanthippus shot back.

Well. I rose to my feet and put my cup in the hands of a slave.

Xanthippus turned. 'Please – I apologise for my rudeness and my son's. A family quarrel is the most embarrassing thing in which to be caught.'

I managed a smile. 'I too have children,' I said. 'Truly, I have another errand and sought only to thank you.'

Xanthippus turned on his son. 'You have humiliated me in front of a man of consequence. Go to your tent and leave this effeminate Ionian to his own devices.'

These were not words I'd choose to speak to my own child, in front of witnesses or even alone. In a few sentences, Xanthippus, who had a fine reputation as a sailor, had given me the impression of a hollow man: a man for whom appearances mattered more than anything.

Pericles stood his ground. 'He is not effeminate; really, Father, that's a foolish insult, more suited to a man my age than yours. And if anyone here is offensive, it is you. Oligarchs and pirates? You have, in effect, just insulted your own guest. Few men are more frequently called pirates than our well-beloved Arimnestos of Plataea.'

He was deadly, with his calm voice, pitched not for beauty but for ease of hearing. You have to imagine that Pericles told his father and every oarsman within a hundred paces that he was a fool.

I thought perhaps Xanthippus would explode.

And then a woman appeared. She was no kore, but a mature woman of my own age or a year or two older, strong and tall. She wore a fine blue chiton pinned in gold and her feet were bare for walking on sand, which gave her a touch of informality. She'd thrown a woman's himation over her chiton for decency. Athenian noblewomen did go out in public, then, but Salamis had made life even more informal. You cannot live on a beach and piss in a common latrine without a certain breakdown of the barriers of class.

I had never seen her, but one look at her and I knew she was of the Alcmaeonidae. She had Cleitus's black brows and high forehead and his arrogance stamped around her mouth. But where Xanthippus's arrogance rested on the soft sand of fear – fear of his status, I'd guess – Agariste's arrogance rested on the bedrock of wealth, position and a solid belief in her own worth.

She flashed me a very private smile. It was all the apology I was ever to receive for the embarrassment of being privy to the family quarrel, but it was well done. Then her head turned – gracefully.

'My dear husband,' she said. 'Of course our guest is anxious to depart! His daughter is over the ridge with the girls from Brauron. My niece says she is a very accomplished dancer.'

Her *only* acknowledgement of the difficulties of the scene, besides her presence, of course, was a single look at her son, Pericles. Their eyes met and she just lifted one eyebrow.

What she said in that lifted eyebrow I could read, as clearly as if my own mother had done it. *'Really? Must you provoke your father in front of a famous guest who might be accounted an enemy of our clan?'* All this in one eyebrow.

And Pericles, the blue blood of all blue bloods, the scion of the very Alcmaeonidae who I had worked so hard to defeat politically on several occasions – I hope you are all staying awake – bowed to his mother. 'I have not seen my cousin Heliodora in weeks,' he said, with a respectful nod to me. 'Perhaps I might accompany the mighty lord of Plataea.'

'I'm not sure that *mighty* and *Plataea* can be said together in a sentence,' I allowed. 'My father was a bronze-smith.'

That was very definitely the wrong thing to say. Even Pericles winced.

However, I was already on my feet and I'd had enough of them.

'Thanks again for the space to beach my ship,' I said.

'It was nothing,' Xanthippus said, somehow suggesting the opposite.

It is remarkable how you can make an enemy of a man merely by being present when he's made to look weak by his son and his wife.

I smiled at Agariste, who met my eyes with her own. Most women in those days dropped their eyes when a man looked at them and I've said before that I always preferred those who did not. Her eyes were not 'interested'. Merely – annoyed. As I passed her, she said, 'Yet even Cleitus says you are a son of Heracles.'

I nodded, and kept going. I just wanted clear of their family quarrel. I left Pericles to his mother but he slipped away.

Pericles followed me back to my own ships, with his Ionian at his heels. The other man, Anaxagoras, I mean, was tall, handsome, and graceful. I had Eugenios give them both wine while I changed from a bloodstained rag of a chiton in which I should never have been seen in public to a better garment. Eugenios clucked over me and, as a consequence, I strode down to the water's edge and flung myself in. There was some good-natured cheering – many men were bathing – and I swam up and down. When I came back to the sand, a pair of my oarsmen poured a heavy jug of fresh water over me and I took a towel and dried myself and then strigiled carefully with good oil. Life was simply better with Eugenios close at hand: the clean bronze strigil, the fine oil, the oil bottle clean and well kept …

Well, there's more to life than blood and war. I needed to be clean.

Hector and Hipponax joined me in swimming and cleaning. As we left the water I saw Brasidas and most of the marines go in. It had been a dirty business. Does seawater make you clean?

Cleaner, at any rate. Blood sticks to you. So does fatigue and pain. I had a feeling in my pectoral muscles, the deep ache caused by fighting in a bronze thorax, and the fatigue in my upper arms from too many sword blows, too many spear casts. I could no longer count the number of fights I'd been in since the first day at Artemisium, but by that day and that hour I had been in the longest sustained campaign of my life. It was as bad as the siege of Miletus. I was tired, and behind fatigue towered the black clouds of low spirits and disillusion like a storm coming in from the sea. Or in this case, from the land. I knew it affected every man and every woman; the danger, the stress, and the rising smoke over Attica that showed the complete mastery of our foe over our homes. Our world was dying, whether we were Athenians or Plataeans. It set us apart from the Corinthians and the men of the Peloponnese.

I only mention this because as I towelled myself and strigiled with oil, I was in the process of admitting that my joints and my hands and my ankles and my torso ached in a way that they had not ached at Lade, and I knew that I was no longer young. The smoke of Attica was not worse than the knowledge that sweet youth was no longer mine, that I could no longer drink all night, fight all day, and then do it again and feel better. Instead – instead, despite victory and fortune, I felt tired, old, and beaten. And if I felt that way, I had little difficulty in imagining how my people felt.

I confess that all these thoughts were the matter of a few beats of my heart. It takes longer to tell than the occurrence. But the knowledge that your youth is gone is alike a little death. I had learned much about myself from Heraclitus, from Pythagoras and his daughter, from Lydia and the way I treated her, from war and slavery and Euphonia and Aristides and Seckla and a hundred other men and women. But in that moment something changed.

The only outward show I made was to put on a fine chiton with embroidery and summon my two young lads to do the same. Pericles and Anaxagoras were both there. The four of them were ... amicable. They were still sparring, but having shared a battle and a sea voyage, they were comrades.

'I've changed my mind,' I said. 'We will collect Euphonia and then walk to the temple and make sacrifice.'

This seemed to suit my four young men. Now that I put my mind to it, they were already very clean and smelled of perfumed oil, and while I put on a very god piece of cloth I had time to notice that they were already well dressed.

I can be slow. Pericles was visiting his cousin, after all.

We walked over the headland. There were sentries in the improvised tower, a pair of marines off the *Storm Cutter* and two older girls from Brauron. I took a moment to take my two marines aside and explain to them, in plain terms, what might befall them if *anything* happened to the Brauron girls.

I'm pleased to say that I left them impressed with my powers of discernment. And other powers.

When we came to the tent camp of the priestesses, I asked to meet with Hippolyta, the High Priestess of Artemis. She was unavailable

– in fact, she was performing sacrifices on behalf of the fleet – but one of her sisters came to meet me, a mature woman of my own age or perhaps older who was wearing a man's chitoniskos, a very short garment indeed. She was tanned and brown and had muscles on her muscles, so to speak.

'You do not require our permission to visit your daughter,' she said cheerfully.

'My lady, I want to speak about the guard tower,' I said, pointing at the high rocky point.

She took offence immediately. 'We were here first,' she said. 'We do not need help from your men to watch for the Persians.'

I nodded. 'Yes, my lady, yet I would be a poor commander if I trusted anyone – *anyone* – with the security of my ships.' I held up my hand. 'I'm not suggesting you give up the duty – which you have earned the right to hold!'

That got a hesitant smile.

'I wonder if we couldn't have two towers – one watching north and the other south.' I smiled. 'Because my people will serve best if I help them to avoid temptation.'

She blushed. And laughed a sweet, free laugh. 'I think perhaps you may have a point, courteously rendered.'

'I will order a second post built, closer to my beach, watching north,' I said. 'And then perhaps we might tell our people that they should speak to each other's posts at the beginning and end of each watch ... and no more.'

She nodded. 'I think I can approve this plan without any further discussion. Thanks for coming over!'

'Now I wish to see my daughter. Dancing?'

The priestess laughed. 'There is naught to do on this beach' she said. 'We have a great deal of dancing.'

'Don't you all use bows?' I asked.

'We don't have enough bows,' she said. 'They were collected and didn't make it here. Much of our temple furniture and equipment was sent to safety in the Peloponnese or to the other side of the island.'

'How many bows would make this better?' I asked.

'Hmm,' she said. 'Six, I think.'

I liked her. I had to work to avoid looking at her long, naked legs, but inside her handsome body was a fine brain and she thought rapidly and made decisions well. I thought the same as I'd thought among the Keltoi and again with the Spartans. Women, left to themselves, are very different from women carefully trained to be weak.

'I think I can find you six bows,' I said. 'I'll certainly try.'

'I have girls who can draw a man's bow,' she said, 'but not so many, either. We need some lighter bows.'

I shrugged. 'Somewhere on this island are some Attic refugees who brought hunting bows,' I said.

She smiled. 'It must be fine to be a man, and famous,' she said. She said this with no bitterness at all, but in those days, for a woman to roam about asking even the most innocent of questions would have been unthinkable.

Much less a woman in a chitoniskos.

'I'll take you to your daughter,' my priestess said. 'I was dancing myself.'

So we walked down to the hard-packed sand at the edge of the sea, where forty girls and young women were practising an elaborate festival dance, one of the bear dances, I believe, although ordinarily no man is allowed to see.

We no sooner emerged from the welter of tents than I knew why the four young men were so finely dressed. There were *girls*. Of course!

What a fool you can be, to forget your own youth.

The four of them immediately launched into a display of sullen boredom, as if, having spent ridiculous care dressing and oiling themselves, and gone to extra effort to be brought along, they now wanted me to believe that they didn't want to be there.

In the meantime, forty very young women in very short chitons were vividly aware that four handsome young men were standing watching their dance.

Even now I roll my eyes. There are excellent reasons to train the young separately. One is that it's so painful to watch them together.

Girls preened and hid and shrieked and giggled and pointed at each other, while my boys pretended indifference and then attempted to casually look to see if anyone was paying attention to them.

Now, I noticed that neither Iris nor Heliodora seemed interested in my young men; in fact, the pair of them continued to work on a figure. Their discipline, and their form, probably did them more credit than a storm of giggles and blushes might have, but in plain fact my young men were soliciting their attention and they were *not* giving it.

I find it delightful, my daughter, that *this* portion of my story reduces you to laughter. Perhaps, unlike stories of ship fights and sword duels, this part seems like something you have experienced yourself?

At any rate, they danced, and as they danced, I could see Cleitus in Heliodora. He was handsome, however much I hated him, and his daughter was not beautiful, but pretty – at least until she started dancing, and then she was with the gods. And Hipponax was gone, lost to Eros, a slave to Aphrodite, and too young to know what to do about it.

Thankfully for all of us, Despoina Thiale, the dance mistress, came over. She didn't grin, but her strong face showed more amusement than resentment. 'You'll have to take the young men away or I'll have nothing to show for my day,' she said.

But Pericles grinned and exchanged kisses with her.

'My great-aunt,' he said. Of course, they were all related, all the eupatridae. The well-born.

Anaxagoras bore Thiale's scrutiny well and clasped her hand as if she was a man.

'You are my nephew's new friend?' she asked.

The Ionian showed very little on his face. He merely bowed his head with dignity, more dignity than Hector and Hipponax had ever shown, I promise you. 'I value Pericles,' he said.

'You have a fine bearing for a man so young,' Thiale said. 'Like a Laconian.'

Among Athenian aristocrats, this would pass for a compliment.

The Ionian bowed again. 'I find that displays of emotion are a waste of effort,' he said.

Thiale laughed. 'How ... rare.'

I lost the next few exchanges as my own daughter came running across the sand and embraced me – a powerful clasp from a girl already taller by a finger than when I'd last seen her.

'The dance is even more complicated,' she said. 'I'm *actually* leading my line. I wasn't *actually* the leader, but I understood the tempo better than the other girls, and Despoina Thiale said that I could be the leader, and then—'

I kissed her. 'Hello!' I said in greeting.

She hugged me again. 'Hello, Pater,' she said. She laughed. 'But I need to tell you—'

'Sweet, we're going over the headland to the temple to make sacrifice and I thought that you might like to come,' I said.

'May I bring my friend?' she asked. She indicated another girl – there is a certain sameness to girls – smaller by a head, but also thin and agile and full of smiles. 'She's Ariadne and her parents have gone to Corinth for a few days and we're *best* friends and—'

I smiled at Thiale. 'May I have my daughter and her friend for a few hours?' I asked.

Thiale laughed. 'Would you like fifteen or twenty more?' she said.

We walked to the old temple – more than six stades, in fact, and the girls had no trouble keeping up. In fact, they climbed rocks and ran down ravines and righted a turtle that had turned upside down and was grilling in the sun then they poured water on him because they were sure he was parched. I don't think he appreciated them but I was happy to have my canteen returned to me.

Unbroken.

I had Eugenios purchase a fine, fat black ram and I sacrificed it to Apollo. My prayers and thoughts were about the end of youth, but my prayer was for the salvation of Attica and victory over the barbarians.

When the sacrifice was over, and the priest poured water over my blade, Pericles bowed. 'That was very elegant,' he said.

Anaxagoras, who, until that moment had seemed to me to be a self-important prig, also allowed himself a smile. 'Very impressive,' he said. 'I would like to learn how to do that.'

'Pater says you have to learn to draw the sword before you can use it,' my daughter said.

There is something funny and very alarming about hearing your views repeated – verbatim – by a ten-year-old. 'He practises drawing every morning. He says that just as every sacrifice is an offering to the gods, so is the skill you display in making the kill.'

'I do?' I asked.

'You do,' Euphonia said, with the hint of a sneer.

Eugenios was trying to get my attention, and I needed to escape. I went over to him.

'That was perhaps the most expensive sacrificial animal in history,' he said. 'Forty drachma.'

I shook my head. 'That will only get worse,' I said.

He nodded.

*

We walked back, while I explained – without, I hope, too much pomposity – my thoughts on drawing and cutting with the sword, and what I had learned from the Spartan exercises, their version of Pyrrhiche, and the like.

Anaxagoras looked at me as if I might be human, after all. That was interesting.

'These are profound thoughts,' he said. Little knowing what a patronising thing that was to say. 'You are a philosopher of the sword.'

'Hmm,' I said, too polite to openly disagree. Or agree.

He paused and looked at me with his too-serious young face. 'I have offended you, I think,' he said.

I shrugged. Hipponax laughed.

Euphonia said something to her friends and both girls shrieked with laughter. Anaxagoras frowned.

She poked Hipponax. 'Do you want to talk to her, Hip?' she asked.

Her friend blushed and looked away, embarrassed at my daughter's temerity.

'Who?' he asked.

Hector was always faster on his feet and he smiled and knelt by my daughter. 'Hipponax wished a secret assignation with your friend here,' he said. 'He's madly in love with the way she giggles, and the way her feet are dirty—'

Euphonia's friend all but expired in laughter. It is good to be ten years old, still immune to the darts of Eros but aware of their effect on others and find it all funny. Rather like middle age.

Hipponax didn't like being teased and he expressed himself by tipping his friend over.

Hector shot to his feet, indignant. 'This is my *best* chiton!' he said.

'You can buy another,' Hipponax said.

'We're not all rich aristocrats,' Hector said.

Hipponax laughed, suddenly more mature than I'd expected. 'I'm the son of a fisherman's wife,' he said, looking at me.

Pericles winced.

'You are slumming,' I said to the young man.

'I thought he was your son?' Pericles said.

I nodded. 'He is my son. I recognise him – he is in every way mine.'

Pericles let go a breath he had held. 'I'm sorry,' he said. 'But my cousin does fancy him. She's marriageable, and my mother—' suddenly the wily Pericles was just another adolescent boy.

'Your mother?' I asked.

'My mother favours the match,' he said.

'Match?' I asked softly. We were speaking quietly. Hipponax and Hector had made up and Anaxagoras had shown himself more than a windbag by helping clean Hector's chiton and his chlamys as we walked.

'My mother – pardon me – says that your quarrel with Cleitus is foolish and helps to divide the eupatridae when they should be united,' he said.

I probably growled in my throat. 'He killed *my* mother,' I said.

Pericles showed some of the power he would later display all too often. 'He did not,' Pericles said. 'He supported your cousin in making private war on you, in revenge for your use of humiliation and violence in a political matter.'

'I—' I began.

'Compared to the actions of the Great King, your argument with Cleitus is of little importance,' he said, as if he was my own age and not seventeen or whatever he was that summer.

He, too, had a great deal of dignity. And he was right.

He shrugged. 'If Jocasta was here, my mother would have it all arranged,' he said. 'Sorry – among the women, Jocasta is treated as your, hmm, patroness.' He looked away. 'As you inconveniently have no wife.' He looked at me. 'Actually, my mother initially suggested that we get Heliodora as *your* wife.'

'She could be my daughter!' I shot at him.

He shrugged. 'When my mother gets the bit in her political teeth,' he said, apologetically. 'I convinced her that your Hipponax would do as well.'

'When?' I asked. 'We were at sea—'

'Oh, today,' he said breezily.

The speed of the transmission of information from woman to woman on Salamis made the Great King's spies and the priests of Apollo look like amateurs.

'But they've only just met!' I said.

Pericles, like most Athenian gentlemen, didn't seem to think it mattered. 'They've seen each other and they like what they see,' he pronounced, as if he was not, in fact, a year younger than my son.

We might have gone on in that vein, and who knows what might have happened, but we'd been inland on the main road to the town and we were coming to the broad gravel road down to the beach that the Brauron girls used, and the moon was rising in a later afternoons sky and we heard cries. Because of the ridge, we hadn't been able to see the sea for several stades, but as we came to the top we were looking down into the bay and across into Attica as the sun set to the left, over by Megara.

Both of the beaches we could see and almost every foot of the ridge were packed with people, and they were wailing. Men stood with their arms raised to the gods, and women tore their hair and their outer chitons and wept.

Over Attica, smoke was rising. We had to look to see what all the fuss was about, but when we saw!

The Acropolis was afire.

It must just have happened as we crossed the ridge from the temple of Apollo. While Pericles spoke to me of his mother's marriage plots, Persian soldiers were climbing the rock of the ancient temples of Athens, her sacred precinct.

They broke in, and massacred the garrison.

We couldn't hear that.

But we saw the flames as they rose in the clear evening air. The temples of Athens were burning and women lamented as if their children were lost. Screams rent the air as if the Persians were among us.

'Keep walking,' I ordered.

It was horrible.

I can't describe the terrible fascination that ruin has for the eye. It was an awesome sight – the flames shooting hundreds of feet into the air above the Acropolis, which, even twenty stades away, rose so far above the plain that on most days you could see the roof of the temple clearly, and even the glint of gold from the old Erectheion that was.

But that night, they burned like a torch. An immense torch, as if a titan's fist had broken through the thin crust of earth and raised it aloft to illuminate the world.

The flames went so high that they reflected in the ocean. Dry cedar and other valuable woods, ivory and gold – all were being consumed, along with three hundred people and all the treasures and sacred objects of a mighty and ancient city.

We walked down the road into an evening lit by horror. Eventually we found ourselves on the beach, still watching the Acropolis burn, with all of the women of Brauron and all the girls. By then the High

Priestess was back, standing erect despite her seventy years, watching her city burn.

As we came up, one of the younger priestesses said something, apparently suggesting that the girls should not be allowed to watch.

'No,' the High Priestess said. 'No, let them watch. They will be the mothers of the generation that avenges us. Let them see what the Great King has done, and remember.' Ferocity growled in her voice. 'I, for one, will never forget this night. I pray we will never make peace. I ask Artemis, under her own moon, to help us to bring fire to their temples, even to Persepolis and his other cities.' She raised her arms and, for a moment, we could see the massive fire raging between them, almost like a crown on her head, so perfectly was she placed in front of me, and a chill swept me. A god heard her plea, or took her oath – I was there.

My daughter and her friend clutched my knees and wept, and many other women wept, but some stood dry-eyed.

By chance, or perhaps by purpose, Heliodora was standing close to us as the fire burned down, and she stood with her friend Iris – dry-eyed.

Hipponax stepped up close to her, as if moved by some external force, as if pulled by a rope, against his will.

She looked at him: a flick of the eyes, and then a movement of her head as she appreciated who it was standing close to her.

'You do not weep for Athens?' my son asked her.

Not bad, I thought.

'I don't want to bear sons to avenge Athens,' Heliodora said. 'I want to fight the Persians *myself.*'

I was close enough to hear every word, hidden by chance and the way we all stood, and I felt like an intruder. At the same time I could see her face, and his. In a moment, it struck me that perhaps they *should* wed. There was something remarkable to see the two of them, or perhaps this is an old story repeated many times.

And when she made this pronouncement, I feared for how my sometimes desperately immature son would respond. Derision? Mockery?

'I could get you aboard a ship,' my son said.

It was a terrible idea. But it was a wonderful, heartfelt reply.

'You could?' she asked. 'I could row all day!'

I did nothing. What a terrible mistake. And yet, so glorious.

*

We stood and watched until our hips ached and our feet hurt.

It was so terrible that we couldn't walk away.

Eventually, the fires burned down. Girls took other girls to bed, and the priestesses moved among them.

I can say that I was never more than a few arms' lengths from my son, but I must have missed something. And when we walked back to our camp, Pericles looked sombre, Anaxagoras kept looking back, and Hector wouldn't meet my eye.

'Who is Iris?' I asked.

Pericles made a dismissive gesture, mostly lost in the dark. 'My cousin's friend. She's nobody; a Thracian or perhaps Macedonian.'

'She is not nobody!' Hector said hotly.

'Boys,' I said. We were at the guard towers above the bay and a stream of sparks shot into the air over the Acropolis as something enormous collapsed.

We walked down into our own camp silently.

That was the night Athens fell to the Persians.

The next morning, I was unable to sleep in – the usual reasons – and I went up the beach, pissed into the thin belt of bushes and vines, and then went for a run. The beach was not tidy and I had to stay along the water and run into the surf around the bow of every ship. It was a difficult run.

I needed a difficult run. I came back, watching the column of black smoke still rising from the Acropolis, and then I ran into the sea and swam.

Hector was waiting for me on the beach, with a towel.

'I need to talk to you,' he said.

Well, he'd brought oil and a strigil and there was almost no one awake. 'I am at your service.'

'Am I a gentleman?' he asked.

I almost cut myself with my strigil. But ... these are real questions. 'Yes,' I said.

'Was Anarchos my father?' he asked.

His face was a frozen mask. 'Yes,' I said slowly. 'That is, I believe so.'

'A criminal,' he said bitterly.

'Pfft,' I said, or something equally annoying.

'He was! Seckla says he was a terrible man who broke people to his will, ran prostitutes ...' He was going to cry.

'Hector,' I said. I took him in my arms. I was still big enough to prevent him from getting away. 'Hector, shut up.'

'No!' he swore. 'You—'

'Shut up, Hector,' I insisted. 'Your father did some terrible things, and some good things, like most men.'

'He got me on some slave and sent me to you as a debt payment!' he shouted.

An oarsman popped his head out of his tent.

Well, that was one interpretation, sure.

I think that Anarchos, wily as Odysseus, even at the end of his life, sent me his son as a penance and a reward, a threat and a promise. I had given it some thought, but not enough; I wasn't prepared for this.

But then, who is?

'I think that you were his only son and he loved you, in his way,' I said.

'He was a criminal!' Hector shouted.

I wished for – of all people! – Jocasta. She would know how to deal with this.

'What brings this on just now?' I asked. I thought I'd try humour. 'As we're about to try conclusions with the Persians, you thought—'

'No, you shut up!' he said. 'I'm nobody!'

'Don't make me hurt you,' I said, because he was struggling with me. 'You are *not* nobody. You are a citizen of Plataea and you have a full share of everything we take. You are a hoplite, a man of valour. You are a man we can count on, on any deck, on any field.'

He didn't relax all at once. But there was a sea change and his arms moved a fraction.

And then, as suddenly as a storm coming and blowing away, he let go of me, gathered the towel, and walked away, as if he was still my pais and he had chores to do.

I suppose that at some remove I should have expected it, but I hadn't. To me, he was my second son. He had been with me almost five years by then. He'd been to sea with and without me, and the sea is not for weaklings.

It turned out that there was a great deal I didn't know, but that's always true, isn't it?

That evening there was a command meeting. It was widely attended; the best attended in many days.

The Peloponnesians were anxious to sail.

Eurybiades gave a set of sacrifices, which, I'll add, he did beautifully, like any Spartan gentleman, and then he invited the Corinthians to speak.

Adeimantus was the orator. He stood forth and I had a moment: because, by chance, Cleitus was standing across the slope from Adeimantus and both were together in my vision. I thought of what Pericles had said about our quarrel, and how it divided the best men, and I considered how much more I hated Adeimantus for what I still view as his treason and how merely habitual my hatred for Cleitus was.

'It is time to call a vote,' Adeimantus said. 'Let all the cities of the alliance vote whether we can leave for the isthmus.'

Themistocles laughed. 'How do we vote, Adeimantus – one vote for every city, or perhaps by the number of ships we provide?'

Adeimantus turned and looked at Themistocles with contempt. 'You don't even *have* a city. Your city is destroyed. Your gods are thrown down.' He gestured exactly as one does in dismissing a slave. 'You are not even Athenians any more. Wait, and we will tell you what we, who *have* cities, have decided.'

Adeimantus had misjudged. The Spartan trierarchs were appalled; to mock a man for the loss of his city would, under most circumstances, be considered low, but this was terrible, a deliberate insult, hubris committed with forethought.

In fact, even a few of the Corinthians winced.

Themistocles judged the audience like the professional politician he was and responded. He didn't laugh or frown or curse. He was mild.

'As long as we have two hundred warships, we have the largest city in Greece,' he said.

And by implication, of course, he suggested that, unlike their cities, his could go where it pleased. It was, in fact, the most brilliant speech I ever heard: short, to the point, but redolent with other meanings.

And yet, when I think back now, what did he mean? Fully? Now that all is exposed, what was his thinking that fateful night, when the fate of Greece teetered on a razor's edge?

He carried them, for that night, because Adeimantus had been a fool.

★

The next morning, the Persian fleet worked its way onto the beaches below Athens, the beaches of Phaleron. They were not opposite us, but north of us and we were spared the vision of their great fleet blackening the sea, but from the northern headlands of Salamis it was easy enough to see them, a near-endless stream of warships landing in ordered chaos on the beaches of Phaleron.

Cimon put to sea in his own *Ajax* and hovered off the southern edge of their fleet, openly challenging them to single-ship combat, but they stayed on their beaches.

Cimon tells me he counted seven hundred and eleven ships. I have heard counts over a thousand and counts as few as five hundred and fifty, and I'm no help. But I tend to believe Cimon. He had the time, and the view.

The Persian fleet was very careful in its movements. It was odd that they outnumbered us at least two to one and yet they were behaving so cautiously. Of course, their Persian officers had no doubt spent days looking at the scrawled messages we'd left them, inviting the Ionians to come join us, or to betray their Persians in mid-battle. And they'd lost the last few encounters.

Late that afternoon, while I was practising on my own beach with Brasidas and Hipponax and Hector, Pericles and Anaxagoras – a well-trained man for all his quiet arrogance – a dozen ships came in from the south. They came up the Bay of Salamis in fine style and my daughter raced over with three of her friends, including Heliodora, to tell us there was a fleet coming. That created a stir, I promise you. With the Great King's fleet closing all the passages to the north, an attack from the south loomed as a very real possibility and I ordered my hulls into the water. I ran – mostly not – up the headland and climbed the Brauron tower.

I didn't know the ships. But there was something about them that appeared Greek; whether the slight outward slant of the cutwaters or the style of the rowing, but I was sure they were Peloponnesian ships. As they came closer, we could see that the lead ship displayed a dozen shields, all those of Spartiates, and men began to cheer.

I don't usually cheer for Sparta, but more ships are always welcome, aren't they?

But all the beaches to the north were packed. We had the Corinthians and the Spartans on the beaches to the south, and the only beach not covered in ships was the Brauron beach. I ran down like a boy and into the midst of another dance practice. I bowed low to the High Priestess, as if she was the Great King himself, and begged her permission for men and ships to land on her beach.

She made me wait long enough to let me know that she *could* refuse, and then she acquiesced graciously. Seckla was still close enough inshore to summon and I dropped my chiton – in front of a hundred virgins! – and swam out to him, and Leukas hauled me aboard and *Lydia* turned south.

We closed with the lead Spartan ship as quickly as the telling of it, and they all lay to, resting their oarsmen in the gruelling sun, and I leaped again – naked, damn it – onto the helm-deck of the lead ship.

There was Bulis, unchanged by the year we'd been apart. Until I saw him I assumed that he had died with his king. But there he was, and there was Sparthius in full armour. They both embraced me.

'Naked!' Bulis said – a long speech, for him.

We all laughed.

'The beaches are crowded,' I said. 'I've found you a berth, just there by the headland with the two towers. Those are my ships on the other beach.'

Sparthius nodded. 'Good. Very good.'

He motioned to the helmsman and orders were given.

I'd never been on a Spartan warship and it was interesting. There were fewer shouted orders than on one of my ships; everything seemed to happen with the gravity of ritual, and yet ... everything happened. As an example, given the rather rough nature of the beaches at Salamis, sailors on the small foredeck – almost a castle – began raising a stone anchor and fitting it to a wooden stock in the bow. Then they fitted a pair of lighter stones to the anchor cable. It was a very seamanlike operation, but there were no orders given from the command deck, and the oar-master almost didn't know the anchor was being prepared.

I was impressed, yet at the same time, I admit to having reservations. The cacophony of my command deck, with shouted orders repeated in all directions, meant that every crew station knew what was being done. In a storm, the helmsman still knew what was happening forward. But the Spartan way was very ... intimidating.

Fancy that.

Regardless, we landed prettily, and I took my Spartiate friends to meet the High Priestess. I'm happy to say that Eugenios was waiting with a clean chiton and a fine himation – now that *is* service. I emerged from the waves like a king, or at least a well-waited on prince, and took my Spartans to their audience, where, of course, they behaved perfectly. It was delightful to see Sparthius, all his front teeth lost in some long-ago encounter, as big as a house and as dangerous as a lion, impressing this tiny but determined old woman with his perfect manners.

She, in turn, was delighted to meet them, and she did as much – or more – than any Athenian I had seen to convince these two men that she, at least, valued them and the alliance for which they stood, and when the trierarchs and helmsmen of the other ships came up to be blessed she spoke to each one, Spartan and Corinthian, with a light in her eye that made them smile. She really was a fine women and her dignity was not so immense that she could not laugh.

I heard that laugh, and another with her, and I turned and found myself looking at Lykon, son of Antinor, who had stood with me at my wedding, and who I accounted among my best friends. He had once been a man so handsome as to be pretty, and much whispered about, but a boar hunt on our mountain had gotten him a scar on his face that turned a feminine beauty into a masculine one.

I waited as he chatted with the High Priestess, and yet our eyes met and we both smiled and years fell away behind me. Lykon and I had been friends before the Medes landed at Marathon – when my lovely wife Euphonia still walked the earth. In fact, back when she was as young as Heliodora ...

When he was done speaking to the priestess I swept him into a crushing embrace and he crushed me right back. And then another pair of arms encircled me, and I had to laugh through tears. Lykon's nearly inseparable friend Philip, son of Sophokles. His grandfather had been a king in Thrace, but he was as Greek as me. At least as Greek – and much richer.

Actually, I wasn't certain of that. Even with Athens in flames and Plataea the same, I was probably a fairly rich man. When you stop counting, you have reached some level.

Hippolyta was beaming at me and I bowed. But behind her was Aristides. I didn't get to him in the press of men because Hippolyta took my hand. Hers was old and very delicate, but surprisingly strong.

'Such lovely young men,' she said. 'Please make clear that they are to keep their distance from my girls.'

A bucket of cold water on our reunion. But Hippolyta was correct, of course, and I understood that I had made myself their guarantor in her eyes. So I collected the trierarchs and Bulis introduced me.

'This is Arimnestos of Plataea. I have fought beside him.'

They were immediately silent. Hah! Praise indeed, eh?

I pointed out the young women of Brauron and how they were trained, and I managed to include the names of a few fathers – including my own. Men smiled, but not like wolves.

'We will make arrangements,' Bulis said. He nodded sharply.

Two thousand young oarsmen and hoplites in their physical prime. Somehow, they all kept their hands and their mouths to themselves and they went, unmolested, to bathe in the sea or perform their dances between the black hulls of the Greek ships. We all managed, somehow, as if the presence of so many beautiful maidens was an everyday occurrence. Perhaps it was, in Sparta. But it certainly kept our minds off the Persians.

The coming of Lykon and Aristides and Philip marked the end of my black days and the introduction of busy visiting among the ships. I had a symposium on the sand, with proper couches – kline – loaned by Brauron in exchange for all the spare bows I found in a few visits along the beaches. Aristides was there, and Cimon, and Aeschylus and Phrynicus too, and Philip and Lykon and Brasidas, Bulis and Sparthius. The Spartans almost spoiled my little party by bringing another young man, Callicrates, one of the most beautiful men I had ever seen, tall and heavily muscled. He was a little older than Anaxagoras. Pericles was too young for a symposium, but not too young to fight, and he didn't miss an opportunity to mention that to his father or mother. Xanthippus, his father, refused the invitation for him, and declined to come himself, so we had an empty couch space and the beautiful Spartan lay down by the stolid Ionian.

We had fish, of course, and some very nice squid. Listen, if you must feast with the richest men in the Greek world, Eugenios is the man to have at your side, like Idomeneus in a fight. Yes, Idomeneus was there as well, sharing his couch with Styges and throwing food at Lykon.

When we were done eating, conversation turned to the war. I cannot, to be honest, remember everything that men said, although most of it was worthy of thought. Callicrates declined to speak, and Anaxagoras spoke very well, prompting Bulis, who was on my couch at the time, to suggest that between the Ionian's head and the Spartan's body, we had the makings of a god.

Well, it was funny at the time, I promise you.

Phrynicus was just explaining to the Spartans and Corinthians how Aristides had come to be exiled and how all the exiles had been formally invited back when Bulis said in my ear, 'I have a message from Queen Gorgo.'

Gorgo was a widow. I had not really considered that Gorgo was as much a widow as Penelope, but I had seen the depth of her bond with her husband. What can I say that I have not said other nights? Leonidas was more exactly like a god than any other man I have met.

Despite which I had a human urge to go to Sparta and see if his widow desired comfort. Bah! Perhaps I am too honest for you. But men are not simple animals – or rather, sometimes we are, are we not?

'I am to tell you that Artaphernes is dying or already dead.' Bulis had not met the Persian satrap. But he certainly knew of him.

The words went through me like fire.

Gorgo was not the only beautiful woman to be made a widow that autumn. Briseis's husband – my friend and sometime patron – Artaphernes, the Satrap of Phrygia.

His death meant that Briseis was free. Briseis was many things – and I will confess that by the standards of Greek womanhood, she was a terrible woman, an adulteress and a shameless user of her body for political ends. Like a man, in fact.

But she was, in her way, absolutely honourable. She had promised me, a year and more before, that when Artaphernes died, she was to marry me. I had prepared a house for her, a house that now lay in ashes. But there could be other houses.

At the time, Artaphernes had himself asked me to come for her when he was dead. His son by another woman, also called Artaphernes, hated her for displacing his own mother. And so it goes: politics and marriage are deeply intertwined, with the Persians as with the Greeks.

His death also meant that the last voice of reason on the Persian side was silenced. That probably meant little, for he had been left behind when Mardonius, his political enemy, marched to triumph in the west.

It made me wonder if Artaphernes had been directly in contact with Gorgo. Certainly she was in contact with the exiled Spartan king, Demaratus.

All the busy plotters. It occurred to me then that Briseis and Gorgo might be very good friends, or deadly rivals. For a moment I thought of what it would be like to introduce Briseis to Jocasta ...

'You are as tense a boy in his first fight,' Bulis said. 'This is important news, I take it. I also have this for you.'

What he handed me was a needle case, the sort any poor free woman has, a thing made of wood. This one was agreeable; the turning was excellent, and the lid locked to the base with a little click. But I could buy one in any agora for a drachma or less.

Inside were several fine bronze needles, worth far more than the case. In fact, they were a rich woman's needles. I was a bronze-smith and I knew how to make a needle, although not as fine as these. These were masterpieces, with long, tapered eyes in a shaft that had been narrowed throughout its length by patient filing with tiny files, themselves carefully made. One of these needles was worth ten or fifteen drachma, almost a month's pay for an oarsman.

They said *Briseis* as clearly as a signature.

I dumped them out in my palm. Lykon came and sat on my couch just at that moment.

'Those are fine!' he said. 'Thinking of taking up embroidery?'

We all laughed and I dropped the needles, point first, back into the case. And in doing so, I felt the secret.

I excused myself to order more wine and found Eugenios, and after passing my redundant request (when did Eugenios need an coaching on a symposium?), I passed into my tent. I used an eating pick to reach into the needle case and there, sure enough, I found a single leaf of papyrus. I sent a Thracian slave for vinegar. I was so impatient I could not go back to the party.

The boy came back at a run. He had a small amphora of our own Plataean vinegar, made of our own grapes, pale and watery though it is. I brushed it on the papyrus.

Just for a moment, one word appeared, before the liquid ruined the papyrus leaf. Just for a moment the word burned at me, brown on white.

'Come.'

I wish that I could claim credit for the brilliant plan to scout the Persian-held beaches that was concocted that night, but as it was, for as long as a runner takes to run the stadion, I considered summoning Seckla and Leukas and all my people and taking *Lydia* to sea.

It was not my patriotism that saved me, I must tell you. In that moment, I had fought the Persian unceasingly for fifteen years and I owed the alliance nothing. Even with all my friends right there on the beach, I felt pulled to leave immediately.

But thirty-five is a little different from seventeen, and one thing I knew was that the whole Persian fleet lay on the beaches of Phaleron, blocking the only good exit form the Bay of Salamis. Even if I rowed west and went south around the island, I would have to pass in full view of their fleet, or risk some very complicated blue-water navigation at the edge of autumn.

I knew I could do it.

I knew that it would be more noble to help defeat the Medes first.

But by Poseidon and Heracles my ancestor, I burned to get my hull in the water and sail to her that instant. That is what I felt for your mother, child. Perhaps she never launched a thousand ships – although I'd say that, in aggregate, she probably did – but that night, she nearly launched one.

Instead, I returned to my friends and my couch next to Bulis, and discovered that in my absence they'd decided to have a look into Phaleron and tease the Great King's fleet. It was Cimon's plan, but I thought it had some of the madness of Idomeneus and they were all excited. I poured them one more bowl of wine well-mixed with water and sent them to bed as soon as they explained to me that we were all putting to sea before the sun rose.

Aristides lingered with the two Spartans. 'It's the same as the days before Marathon,' he said.

'And Lade,' I noted. 'This war has seen many defeats and almost as many barren victories.'

Aristides shook his head. 'The word on the beaches to the south is that the Peloponnesian allies are threatening to cut and run for the isthmus,' he said.

'Not the Spartans!' I spat.

Bulis reached out and touched my arm, silently.

Aristides shook his head. 'Led by the Corinthians,' he said. 'I truly hope this raid gets us the favour of the gods.' He shrugged.

We all went to bed.

Rosy-fingered dawn had not yet risen in her charming dishabille to touch the horizon when my oarsmen put *Lydia*'s bow into the waves. Salamis Bay is a tricky piece of water; the breeze brought a heavy chop from the south as we weathered the long point men now call the Dog's Grave – you know that story?

Eh? Well, Themistocles had ordered that all domestic animals be left in Attica to starve. He set the example, leaving a beautiful hunting dog to die. The dog supposedly followed him down to the water's edge and then, after some howling, swam after the great man's ship. Themistocles hardened his heart – not hard for him, I suspect – and rowed on, but the dog followed, swimming all the way across the bay to the long point of Salamis that seems to aim like an accusing hand at the harbour of Piraeus. Themistocles landed his ship and the dog swam up, utterly faithful, got itself up on the point: and then died. I heard the story a dozen times that week, as an example of bad omens and how untrustworthy Themistocles was. In fact, most families brought their dogs, and even a few cats. The Themistocles I knew would have told all the Athenians to leave their pets and then bribed someone else to carry his. I'm not sure I believe the story, even now, but that point is still called the 'Dog's Grave'.

We could smell the burning over Attica. We could smell a carrion smell from slaughtered animals and a spicy smell, and over it all that sharp tang that we perceive after a fire.

We put six ships to sea. Aristides was there in his *Athena Nike* with Demetrios at the helm, and I had *Lydia*. Astern of us in a short column of twos were Bulis and Sparthius in their Lacedaemonian *Ares*, with Cimon in *Ajax* and Philip and Lykon in Corinthian ships. It was a deliberate attempt to involve the whole fleet and I know, without being told, that Themistocles and Cimon hoped to provoke a general action.

We were also the fastest ships available, at various points of sailing and rowing.

Or perhaps that's an excuse. We were six ships whose men and trierarchs trusted each other. Good ships, aye, and good oarsmen, were thick on the beaches that autumn, but trust was as thinly spread as good Olbian caviar at a poor man's party.

So as we weathered the long point, passing the island of Psyttaleia to our port side. The island cut off any view of Piraeus and kept the Persians around Athens from watching our movements. As soon as we entered the straits between Cynosura, the Dog's Grave, and the island of Psyttaleia we felt the chop; it hit us for the first time, broadside on. It wasn't so bad at first, because of the loom of the main island, but once we were in the open ocean, it was quite a swell.

Good fortune and years of following Cimon and his father around the sea caused me to watch him as he passed the gap, and I saw that he put his helm over and turned south as soon as he weathered the point. I assumed he was being cautious about the placement of the Persians, but when it was my turn and I felt the first wave and we took water amidships because our sides were so low, I too turned sharply to the south, so that the morning waves came at my protected bow. On this side of the cape we could see, quite close to us, the ships of Aegina on their beaches. We waved and called in Greek to prevent an accident, and rowed south into the wind with every oarsman cursing. There's another small island almost due west of Psyttaleia, and if it has a name I don't know it, but we passed between it and Psyttaleia in water so shallow I had Seckla in the bow throwing a lead.

Dawn was just staining the skies. The south wind moderated as the sun rose and in an hour, as the rowers cursed and the hoplites began to cook their sausages back on the beaches, we passed the promontory of Piraeus and opened the Bay of Phaleron – you know what that phrase means, honey? When you are close in with the land, sailing or rowing, the land all looks about the same and a headland can completely hide a small harbour, a bay, or an inlet. As you pass along the land, you may pass a headland, and then, all of a sudden, a 'hole' opens in the coast and you can see into the bay, the same way that you cannot see into the garden until you pass the first pillar there and get a peak through the door – see?

So we opened the bay.

And in it, on the beaches there, were all the ships in the world, or so it seemed. I had Seckla to do the counting – he was always a good counter, and the man doing the counting needs to have no other work. It's hard enough, when all the enemy ships are black, and all about the same size and far away.

We bore down on them. We'd been crawling west by south under oars, but now that morning was coming, a land breeze rose off Attica, a breeze full of ash. We rowed into it, but all six of us had our main sails laid along on our decks or half-decks.

No one seemed to be stirring on shore.

We rowed in. I found the promontory at Munychia, just south of Athens itself, and aimed at it, to come up the windward side of the enemy fleet, which filled every beach from the rocky tumble at the sea edge by Munychia all the way over to Phaleron herself, a good nine stades. They filled those beaches, west to east, as solidly as tuna fill the Bosporus in the spring.

By my estimate, if every ship beached at two oars' lengths from the next, the minimum safe distance to get a fleet off the beach, then there could be about one hundred ships to every stade, or nine hundred enemy ships. They were not all triremes, either; they had more pentekonters and small fry than we did, but there were also some enormous ships among them, including a great trireme of Phoenician make, high-sided and as big as any two of our ships, which sat right in the centre of the great curving beach.

It was an awe-inspiring sight; a larger fleet than the enemy had at Artemisium. It was both more, and less, impressive than their fleet at sea. It was certainly better ordered than their anchorages and landing beaches had been in Thessaly.

We rowed nearer the land. We were merely cruising; a slow, steady pace with only two banks of oars rowing, so that we moved only twenty-five stades an hour or so.

After about as much time as it takes an orator to deliver a speech, we were coming up on the west end of their beach. We were close enough to hear men calling out. Seckla was in the bow and he waved and shouted in his African tongue and in Phoenician.

We turned east and followed Cimon along the edge of the beach, so close in we might have thrown fire into the ships. Cimon's daring plan was that we would imitate a newly arrived squadron looking for a landing place while we crept along, bold as a Piraeus waterfront girl, and counted our enemies.

We made it a third of the way around the Bay of Phaleron before they smoked us. But when they did, forty ships came off the beach all together, from every compass point. It happened so quickly that we passed from stealth to terror in two beats of the heart. The water was suddenly so full of enemies that it seemed as if we were blood poured into an ocean full of sharks.

The ships nearest me were Egyptian – excellent ships with highly trained crews who nonetheless hated the Great King as much as I did and perhaps more. Egypt had only recently revolted and the revolt had been suppressed savagely. The Egyptians were among the first in the water, but they approached cautiously, giving my ship time to turn end for end. As soon as my bow was pointed at the open sea and I had the wind behind me, I motioned at Leukas and he put the mainsail onto the yard in record speed while the oarsmen pulled us hard to the south.

To my port side, over to the west, lay *Athena Nike*. Aristides made his turn and then, by ill-luck, fouled something, and it took him precious heartbeats to free his ram-bow. He had a crowd of Ionians coming up on *his* port side, and he had to turn towards me to escape being boarded even as his ship finally leapt into motion.

I found myself gnawing on one of my fingers. A dreadful habit, but the tension of watching that race – if it can be called a race when no one is yet moving at full speed – was more than I could bear. *Athena Nike* was slowly moving east and south, but the Ionians were pulling closer with every stroke.

I took a breath and looked to my starboard side. There were my two Corinthians, about two stades away and already setting their sails. Tyche had decreed that the Ionians on the western beaches were the slowest of all to guess who we were, and the ships of Miletus and Mycale and Ephesus were the last off their beach, so that Lykos and Philip pulled effortlessly away.

Leaving me with some empty ocean under my starboard side.

I beckoned to Seckla and got him between the steering oars and gave him a notion of my intentions and then ran down the half-deck to the platform amidships. The sail was set to the yard, but I shouted to Leukas to keep it all on deck, something easier in a trihemiolia than in a trireme, I promise you, because you have a deck under your feet and room to spread the sail without fouling the rowers.

'Prepare to turn to starboard,' I said. I held up my right hand to make sure I did not give the wrong order. I have been known to mix left and right at inconvenient times. I remember because I stared at my right hand and breathed to make sure I called the correct direction.

Right under my bare feet, a rower looked up – Sikli. He grinned.

'Five minutes rowing and you're done for the day,' I said.

He grunted and men around him laughed. Always a good sign.

'Hard to starboard,' I roared.

I saw Sikli dip his oar and *push,* holding the blade steady against the whole impulse of the ship, as did every starboard-side rower, and as the blades bit, the ship turned. It turned very rapidly, losing momentum as it turned, so that the bow went from pointing due south very quickly to east, and then more slowly around to north, the port-side rowers still pulling. The ship heeled a long way, and as we went broadside on to the now northern wind we took on some water through the lowest tier of oar-ports.

I watched my pursuers.

This was going to be close, even by my standards.

I was delighted to see the Egyptians hesitate as I went bow on to them, offering combat. While a dozen of them had exploded off the beach, there were only two in range. The rest were trailing away to the north, rather like the Carthaginians when we caught the tin fleet.

Ka and his lads began to loft arrows into the lead Egyptian even as Brasidas stepped forward with half a dozen marines and provided them with shields from behind which they could shoot. This is one of the few innovations for which I can really claim credit, and even then it's really an idea I had while looking at a piece of Assyrian art north of Babylon. The Assyrians, apparently, had shield men to cover their archers. It was a good idea. May Apollo, Lord of the Silver Bow, accept my words of praise that the idea never, apparently, entered the heads of the Persians.

But I wander from my point. Ka hated Egyptians more than Persians or Phoenicians; his people, I gather, were always at feud with them about something. At any rate, all of his archers, who were usually quiet, dignified men, were suddenly voluble, shouting insults, screaming down the wind and loosing shaft after shaft.

I didn't see any sign that they hit anything. Perhaps they did, or perhaps their shouts and curses had some effect – perhaps one of their gods was listening. At any rate, both Egyptians turned west, declining the engagement.

The archers went mad, cheering, and the marines joined them. You would not have thought fifteen men could make so much noise. Most of the deck crew roared, as well.

All I could see was two Egyptian captains with no more reason to love Persia and the Great King than I had myself. Perhaps less.

At any rate, I tapped my spear butt against the deck. 'Prepare to turn to starboard!' I called again. I leaned over to Onisandros, raised my spear, and pointed it at the three Ionian triremes pursuing Aristides.

He nodded.

'Hard to starboard!' I called, and the ship began to swing, the same rotation as before, so that, having started with our head due south, and passed to the west and north, we now began to slant away east. I ran back up the tilted deck as the marines and archers sat down to avoid overbalancing. Seckla had the steering oars and was leaning forward like a warhorse in a chariot harness.

He needed no order from me. He had known all along what I intended.

I have said before, I think, that a fight at sea, all fights, at that, begin as slowly as the gentle fall of new snow, and then gather momentum as the ships close, so that not only does everything seem to go faster, but the speed of engagement, of orders, of your very heart, all seem to rush towards a climax as the ships near. I'm sure a sophist like Anaxagoras would make something of the idea, but to me it is like a play that begins with the chorus singing about some seemingly unimportant bit of myth, but by the end you are weeping your eyes out as Oedipus hurtles toward his ruin . . .

Anyway.

Between them, the hundred and eighty rowers, the oar-master and my helmsman brought our bow dead on line and a little ahead of Aristides' ship. We were at least three stades away.

Even as we watched, the lead Ionian, a ship of Halicarnassus, may I add – you know this story, young man? Hah. Well, here's my side of it. The lead Ionian was a ship's length aft of Aristides' magnificent *Athena Nike* and something was slowing the rowers on his ship. Usually it was one of the best of all the Athenians vessels, but today the ship was sluggish.

In fact, Aristides was taking on water from a badly damaged bow.

The Ionian was coming up on him fast.

We were hurtling into the Ionian's flank much, much faster. But we were farther away.

It was like a problem in arithmetic and geometry, except that *everything* was variable. The wind was fickle, the waves slowed the ships, the oarsmen were getting tired and sometimes you just have to guess.

The lead Ionian slapped his ram into Aristides' stern. It wasn't a very hard hit, but *Athena Nike* yawed and seemed to skid.

Ka stood in my bow and began to shoot. He was shooting from the bow platform into the amidships of the enemy, and the Ionians were high-sided compared to any but Phoenicians, so that it took great skill and Tyche to drop a shaft in among the benches.

But broadside on gave Ka and his four archers the best opportunity and they loosed shafts at a great rate. The Persians aboard the lead Ionian returned shaft for shaft.

The second Ionian tried to turn towards us. But the now northerly wind caught him and accelerated his turn, so that he was pushed downwind. A well-built trieres has almost no keel – if you build one with any keel at all, the way I'd built *Lydia*, you began to wear it away every time you ran the ship up a beach.

The newly designed ships were unhandy with the wind abeam. That was interesting.

I didn't think of any of that as we hurtled like Poseidon's spear towards the lead Ionian, who had lost way ramming Aristides' stern.

Aristides complicated matters by turning to starboard. The lead Ionian wasn't going fast, but she was fast enough to overshoot *Athena Nike* before she made her own turn, so that now, as Seckla followed the action by a long, curving turn to starboard to bring us back round the circle to due north, we were *behind* the enemy ships, and they lay almost across our course.

Astern, about forty ships were coming on as fast as their oarsmen would pull them.

I could not stop for a ramming attack, or a boarding action. Even an oar-rake would conceivably slow me too much.

Aristides was raising his mainsail.

The nearest Ionian was locked in an archery duel with my ship, and the further vessel was trying to get a grapnel aboard Aristides.

I looked all the way around the horizon, but Poseidon was not coming to the rescue.

But in the bow Ka was screaming his war cry. One of his men lay dead, two shafts in his corpse, but the other three were loosing at an incredible tempo as we closed the distance. Now we were less than half a stade, coming up on the Ionian from behind and at an oblique angle that cramped his archers. That is, *would* have cramped his archers, but Ka and his lads had put them all down. Now they were flaying the helm and the oarsmen and the deck crew. It is, as I've said before, incredible what a handful of archers can do when they have no opposition – four or five arrows a minute, all aimed, at a close range, from four men.

So they did it, not I. The Ionian fell off, oars in confusion. As we passed his stern, Ka ran down the length of our ship from the bow, loosing a shaft every few paces – truly, a magnificent feat of arms. When he reached the stern, he leaped high on the curved gunwale of the swan's neck and loosed a final shaft into his stricken victim.

The Ionian was scarcely damaged, but bad luck and a long, thin trail of blood from her oar decks suggested she'd lost too many starboard-side oarsmen and now she was turning to starboard against the pull of their dead hands on oars stranded in the water.

The original pursuer, the former lead ship, had a superb helmsman. Even as Pye, our tallest archer, loosed his first shaft at the new adversary, he turned downwind even as Seckla jinked for the stern rake.

Onisandros was more awake to the crisis than I. 'Oars in starboard side!' he roared. Leukas joined him.

The oars were coming in.

Ka was loosing. He was standing by the helmsman's rail and I raised the aspis I'd taken from a sailor so that my raven flashed in the morning sun. The rail, just near the stern, had few supports and no bulwark, and Ka knelt suddenly so that I had to lean over him with the shield.

An arrow slammed into it. The shaft exploded and sprayed us both with splinters of cane.

Oars came in. All this in two or three heartbeats.

Another arrow slammed into my aspis, then skidded off the face and up into my helmet, knocking my head back.

Another screamed into the face of my aspis. My left hand *burned* as a shaft went *through* the front face and into my antelabe, the bronze head pressed against my hand.

We began to pass down the length of the enemy ship. We were moving faster, and both vessels were now coasting. We were perhaps a man's height apart, gunwale to gunwale.

It was *terrifying*.

The Persians on the enemy deck were higher. They were noblemen in scale armour – men like my friend Cyrus, bred from birth to shoot straight and tell the truth.

But they were all together in a huddle in the stern because of the Ionian's design with high sides and only a catwalk amidships.

I'm guessing they'd never faced a trihemiolia before. My half-deck was perfect for archery, and the low bulwarks nonetheless provided some cover.

It was the grimmest archery duel I have ever witnessed, made more chilling because I could cover my archer but I could do nothing to strike at the enemy. When you are shot at without the means to reply, you are in a different position from a man facing mere combat.

We passed the length of that ship in perhaps five breaths. In that time, I don't think I breathed at all.

This is what I saw.

A Persian leaned out over his stern to shoot down into our amidships. He killed an oarsman but, luckily, the man's oar was in.

Ka killed the Persian, putting an arrow into the man's back.

Pye, the tallest of the Nubians, shot almost straight up into a second Persian and hit him and the man collapsed back, but a third Persian drove an arrow down into Pye's neck, killing him instantly. Ka's second arrow caught the third Persian, again in the back, and then we were helm to helm for a moment – side by side, the two ships not quite colliding, all the oars in on both sides.

Ka and the Persian loosed together, ten feet apart. The arrow went through my aspis, splinters exploded off the inside, and Ka went down, his face all blood. The arrow went into the top of my thigh, but I wear leg armour and it did not penetrate the bronze.

I threw my spear.

A woman knocked it down.

There was no hiding that she was a woman. She was tall and strong and she wore a fine thorax of bronze that had been fitted perfectly to her very obvious woman's breasts. I had never seen such a thing.

I had the sense to get my aspis up as we blew past her, which was as well, because she threw my spear back at me. I batted the spear down onto the deck with my aspis. My left hand hurt, but the rest of me was intact.

It was one of my best spears. No need to drop it into the ocean.

Then we were past them. I looked back around the swan of the stern, heedless of the arrows that might have flown, but there were none. She *was* a woman, a tall woman in a plumed helmet, and she was pushing her way into the steering oars where the oarsman had apparently been killed, and then I lost her behind the curve of the swan as she began to scream orders in Greek.

Artemisia, Queen of Halicarnassus. I'm sure you know all about her. Well, there she was, the most bloodthirsty of the Great King's captains. But we'd cleared her deck of archers and we'd killed her helmsman, which had a curious result I'll share with you later.

For the immediate future, she yawed suddenly to the north to avoid our grapnels – we weren't, in fact, throwing any. Hipponax had a Persian arrow through his aspis and his left bicep and Brasidas was cutting the head off and pushing it through. Achilles, son of

Simonides, was down, with blood all over the deck, and three of my oarsmen were dead or maimed; as vicious an exchange as I've ever seen.

I looked down at Ka. To my joy, he was plucking splinters out of his face. One was through both cheeks. But he had not lost an eye and he was far from dead.

Close abeam, Aristides was turning back into the open sea, due south. He had the wind in his great mainsail and he had some sort of temporary steering oar out, a normal pulling oar tied to the rail. Together, the two sufficed to bring his head round, and the wind on the sail and the long side of his ship gave him considerable speed.

I saw his stern, crowded with men packed close like a tub of new-caught sardines. I knew then what must have happened: he was raising his bow by pushing the stern down, and that meant he'd opened a seam.

Poseidon!

That was the longest hour I'd known in some years. We ran south on the wind and Leukas got our sail, laid ready to the spar, up the mainmast in record time, and followed Aristides across the Saronic Gulf. Behind us, the Great King's ships fell behind, but as we sailed south the northern horizon became *filled* with the Great King's ships. They were still pouring off the beaches, and we watched Artemisia abandon the chase and turn west, and even saw the rest of her Ionian squadron close around her before we sunk them over the rim of the world. The whole Persian fleet was off the beaches and moving.

Leukas watched with me, under his hand. He shook his head. 'They can't all be coming for us,' he said.

Odd, given the way they'd refused engagement, but the Egyptians stayed with us longest, and there were a fair number of them. But as the sun reached its highest point in the sky, the Egyptians also turned west. We gradually left them behind.

But, best we could make out in the sunny autumn haze, the whole Persian fleet was forming an enormous line at the mouth of the Bay of Salamis and we were off their left or port-side flank. Only when we left them all over the horizon did we turn west across the seas, which by then, just after midday, even though every one of us felt as if it had been a month since morning, were calm and gentle.

Aristides and all his crew bailed as if the Furies were aboard them. I could do little more than hang off his starboard rail and hope to save what could be saved.

I won't repeat a dozen frustrating shouted conversations, but eventually we understood that he could not point any nearer the wind than due west – and that he was running for Aegina before his ship sunk under him.

It looked to me as if the Persians were forming for a fight. It was an afternoon of anguish, for over the horizon to the north the Great King's fleet was offering battle to the league. Would they fight? By Poseidon, I was missing the great contest!

But Aristides, that prig, some might say, was the best man I knew.

We prepared what we could to lighten ship suddenly. *Lydia* had a dozen contrivances to make her a better ship – one of them was a small bricked-in hearth forward of the boat-sail mast, and we prepared to heave that over the side, as well as armour, weapons, and spares. If Aristides foundered, he'd have two hundred men desperate for life in the water – veteran men, and our friends, too.

Aside from preparing for disaster, there was little we could do but watch and fret and speculate about what was happening to the north. I looked at my son's wound, but Brasidas had done a thorough job and he'd even come up with honey to put in the bloody slit. My boy behaved well – his head was high and he swore he was ready to fight again. Hector hovered about and looked miserable.

We'd run Attica under the horizon long before, lost the last Egyptian, and there was a high, blue sky almost without clouds, and we were alone on an empty ocean just a parasang from the largest fleet in history.

West we ran, and west, losing our northing as the world's wind blew us farther south despite our best efforts. But along toward early afternoon, we sighted Aegina, and as the day began to wane we got *Athena Nike* on one of that island's beaches, bow first, as gently as could be managed. As soon as the sail came down, Aristides' magnificent ship began to take water, so that for a heart-stopping moment we thought we might lose her before we got her bow on the beach. Both our crews went ashore and dragged the *Nike* up the gravel.

Aristides shook his head in sadness – and perhaps awe.

His ram was gone, the bronze sunk in the depths of the ocean. He'd struck a floating log, perhaps some great tree ripped up by Poseidon's wrath and sent far out to sea, and the blow had ripped away the ram, and somehow, by luck, one of the bow's planks had been crushed *inward* with such force as to wedge it into the framing of the bow, so that the ship didn't fill and sink instantly.

One by one, all his marines and oarsmen came and touched the bow.

Many raised their arms to heaven, faced the sea, and sang the hymn to Poseidon.

Aristides chose to remain on Aegina. We'd been seen coming in and he had access to some of the best shipwrights in the world to repair his beloved warship. After several embraces I took my own ship back toward Salamis. It was late afternoon. I was – desperate.

I admit that I considered, once again, taking *Lydia* down the Saronic Gulf and out into the open ocean and running for Ephesus. At Aegina, the war seemed far removed from our concerns. The Persian fleet was over the horizon, and they would never catch us, never even pursue us. I had waited my whole life, or so it felt, for Briseis, and now she waited perhaps as little as five days' sailing away, with a fair wind.

But to do so seemed like desertion. Or perhaps I wasn't sure what I wanted. Perhaps, after all those years of waiting, the achievement of my desire was ... frightening. Does this surprise you? And yet, I was no longer the blood-mad boy I had once been. What would Achilles have been, if he had lived? Thetis offered him a long, happy life, or a brief life and immortal fame and I often think of Achilles. What would he have been, in his long, happy life? A bronze-smith in sunny Achaea? A prince of a happy realm, with his Briseis making babies and supporting him, ruling by his side, performing the dances of the goddess?

No man is simple, and desire is as complex as anything else. So is duty.

And at the same time that I could consider deserting the cause of Greece for my woman, I could also be distraught at the notion that I was missing the greatest sea fight in history. Oh, Poseidon, my heart beat faint to think I was missing it! I roamed the deck of my *Lydia* like a lion stalking prey, up and down the deck, and my sailors stayed clear of me.

Did I want Briseis? Did I want the undying glory of the great battle? Did I want a peaceful, happy life?

I wanted them all!

We came in through the mouth of the bay at the islands and there were no wrecks. The Aeginian ships were snug on their beaches, and there wasn't a Persian to be seen.

We landed at the very edge of darkness. It wasn't hard; there were so many fires lit along the beaches of Salamis that the navigation was, if anything, easier rather than harder, and many willing hands came down to the water's edge to help warp *Lydia* ashore.

I landed my ship at Salamis.

Pericles came down to fetch me from the tedious business of getting my ship ashore. *Lydia* was landed, but she needed to be hauled clear of the water and dried so that her fine, light hull caught the full sun in the morning, and she had a small leak forward.

The things you remember! I can tell you almost anything about that ship, and yet, when I close my eyes, I cannot see my Lydia's face very clearly; really, just a soft pale smudge of memory. But every splintered oar shaft and every bubble in her hull's pitch is marked on my brain. That ship was more my lover than her namesake, I suspect. But ...

Pericles came down wearing a himation that made him look even younger than he was.

'Eurybiades has summoned all the trierarchs,' the boy said. 'Cimon is speaking even now.'

I picked up a spear – a little affectation, I admit, as no one carries a spear to a council any more but me – and walked up the sand. I remember my calf muscles hurting and my ankles complaining – too little exercise, and too much time sitting at campfires or standing on the half-deck.

It was a long walk, up over the first headland and along to the temple; long enough for me to consider that I was wearing an old chiton meant only to keep my armour off my naked skin, and a chlamys that had begun life as a fine shade of dark blue and now resembled the sky on a late autumn day; there was some blue in it, but not much, and the rest was a sort of muddy pale grey with a great deal of sea-salt and some spots of pine pitch. It was, in fact, the fine chlamys I'd purchased with my earnings on Sicily, at Syracusa, when I was first courting Lydia. Lydia was suddenly much in my thoughts.

In fact, that walk was ... dark. Too much fighting can have this effect on any man, and I had reached my limit. My fingers burned on my left hand – isn't it odd how a new injury seems to aggravate the old ones? The stumps of my missing fingers were livid and they throbbed in the darkness because of the new wound from the Persian arrow, a wound so inconsiderable that in youth I might never have mentioned it. Facing the Persian arrows had been exhausting and I have no idea why. The entire experience had lasted less than a minute, but I was stumbling on the sandy road and near weeping with the sullen darkness that often infected me after a fight.

Well.

Ahead of me in the darkness, a hundred men or more were gathered on the steps of the temple. They were surrounded by torchlight, as if a festival was going on, and in the clear air I saw the ruddy light before I saw the temple. I could smell the scent of pines and the reek of ash from Attica, and the sound of men's voices stirred me somehow.

I stopped and looked up at the stars. I remember this very well – that surge of pure emotion, as I felt ... something. It is difficult to describe, but my loss emptied a little, and my sense of the rightness of the world returned, looking at the stars. Some men see the gods in the stars, and others see the rational turning of the creation of the gods. Sometimes I see only the points of light by which a man navigates the deep at night and a sailor knows that everywhere you go, the stars change. Think on that. The stars change.

Bah! Enough of my musings. I only mean that when I strode up to the council, I was in an odd place in my head. I will not say I had seen a god, but I would not be surprised if one had been at my shoulder.

By chance, Themistocles had just spoken, and men were honouring his words with silence. I know now that Cimon had spoken about the might of the enemy fleet, and Themistocles had laid out the reasons why we had to fight. Adcimantus waited. He was a fair orator and he knew that to speak too soon would be to lose his audience.

But when he started, he had no mercy.

'Themistocles, perhaps what you say is good for Athens.' He smiled. 'Good for your people, rather. Athens is *gone*.' He looked around allowing the import of that statement to sink in. 'But if the enemy has nine *hundred* ships, if all our fighting at Artemisium has only served to make them *stronger*, I say it is time to retreat. You saw them today! They filled the horizon and they offered battle! By all the might of Poseidon, do you really expect us to face that? You have threatened us with desertion; you say, if we retreat, you and the Aeginians will sail away and found new cities in Magna Graecia.' The Corinthian spread his arms. 'Go, then. Betray Greece. We – the

Achaeans, the men of Pelops – we are the real Greeks, anyway. We will hold at the isthmus. Even if Xerxes passes the wall, he will never take the Acrocorinth, never take Sparta, never survive the long march to reach Olympia. Who knows if the Great King will even pursue us? He promised to punish Athens, and he has done so.' Adeimantus nodded. 'Join us and retreat to the isthmus. When the Great King retreats, *then* perhaps you can found new cities, or creep back to the ruins of Athens. But I can tell you that we, the men of Pelops, are leaving. It would be foolish to stay, so far from the army.'

'Where is the army?' I asked. It was the first many men knew that I was there.

Adeimantus looked puzzled. 'How would I know?'

I looked around and caught Lykon's eye. 'Was there an army at the isthmus when you left?' I called loudly.

Lykon shook his head vehemently. 'No, Arimnestos,' he called. 'No army. Corinth has not even raised its phalanx yet. Men are still travelling home from the Olympics.'

There was bitter laughter.

'Listen, Adeimantus,' I said. 'I am the polemarch of Green Plataea, and my city is already destroyed, and yet I am here. Eurybiades swore that an army of the League would protect Boeotia, but no army came. Plataea, Hisiae, Thespiae – all burned. Attica is burning, and Corinth has not yet raised their phalanx.' I put a hand to my beard, as if in puzzlement.

'The only way the League can even resist right now is at sea. If we lose at sea, as has been said over and over, the Great King's fleet will land wherever they please – from the vale of Olympia to the fields of Argos. And Adeimantus, we all know you speak only to inflame the men of the Peloponnese. I will not ask why you seek to persuade men to desert us. You claim that Athens threatens desertion while you yourself declare that you will desert! Black is white, and sophistry is the order of the day, I guess.' I laughed. Men laughed with me. 'But don't take us for fools, Adeimantus. You say that only you Achaeans are Greeks? Not Alcaeus? Not Sappho? Not Hipponax? You mean that the men of Boeotia are not Greek? Hesiod is not Greek? Or do you mean that mighty Homer was not Greek?' I spat. 'You are a fool. I speak only for my few Plataeans, but I say – run away. This is men's work, and when we have defeated the Great King, we will mock you until you die of shame.'

He drew his sword – there, in the temple precinct.

I stood with my arms by my sides.

Eurybiades stepped between us, and the look he gave me was hard – a look of disappointment and even hatred.

'I expected better of you, Plataean,' he said. 'High words and personal insult are not the way to sway a council.'

I made myself exhale. 'Are they not? I am only a Boeotian bumpkin. I only emulate my teachers.' I pointed to Adeimantus.

Men laughed, but the Spartan navarch was not amused. 'We cannot fight at odds of worse than three to one,' he said.

Themistocles held his head high. 'We can!' he said.

Cimon pushed forward. 'We can,' he insisted. 'I can tell you how we can do it. By Poseidon, gentlemen, numbers mean nothing in narrow waters, you saw that at Artemisium. They *fear* us. Today we outfaced them with six ships against their nine hundred. Ask Arimnestos. We interfered with their launching – with six ships. They do not speak the same languages and half of them hate Persia more than we do. By the *GODS*! You beat them at Artemisium! Why do you fear them now!'

'And you lost the man of justice, Aristides,' Adeimantus spat. 'Very convenient for your democrat here, who sent his worthy opponent to die.'

'Aristides and his ship survived the encounter by the will of the gods,' I shouted. 'Even now his ship is beached on the north coast of Aegina, a few hours' rowing away.'

Adeimantus shook his head. 'You are the democrat's slave and will say anything for him,' he spat. 'But I say this: even if we fight this battle, even if we win, it is a foolish victory. A victory of rowers and slaves! What will we be then, when the hoplites are not men of valour, but the little men are? They will rise and take our cities and drive them to extinction for their own petty pleasures. That is what this man wants. Themistocles the democrat wants this war won by his little petty men so that he can be like a god among them. And if Aristides was here he would agree with me.'

Themistocles all but exploded. 'You – you!' he roared. 'You would rather be a slave of the Great King than see the little men do their share to earn victory? Where are your precious hoplites, Corinthian? Your noble Spartiates and the aristocrats of Thebes and Thespiae *failed*. King Leonidas *died*. Now the fate of Greece is in the hands of the oarsmen, the little men, and they will save us!'

Eurybiades pulled the hem of his cloak over his head. As a Spartan he was insulted, desperately insulted, by Themistocles' last words. He walked, alone, to the altar.

I had time to think of the irony of it all, that in fact, Aristides *did* agree with Adeimantus about the role of the hoplites. And that Leonidas, had he been alive, would have agreed with Themistocles. They formed their conspiracy to save Greece on the notion that it would have many ugly turns and twists. Leonidas had a clear view of the end, I think.

I had time to think these thoughts, and then Eurybiades turned, a grave figure, tall and strong, full of dignity.

'We will retreat to the isthmus,' he said. 'It was always my intention. And without unity, we will only die here for nothing.'

Adeimantus grinned.

'Adeimantus has ordered all the Corinthian ships to gather on the western beaches,' Lykon said. We were at Themistocles' fire, in front of his pavilion, the beautiful tent that had got him in so much trouble after the last Olympics, where the Spartans won the chariot race with a little help from the Athenians. Themistocles' tent was remarkable; dyed blue and red, with woven edges, internal hangings, toggles to hold the walls, it really was a thing of beauty. It was also probably very comfortable to live in. The problem was that it was much more lavish than the tents used by, say, the King of Sparta or the priests of Apollo, and so it was much remarked on.

But he had good slaves and wine, and many stools – very elegant stools. Siccinius, Themistocles' steward, poured us wine. Xanthippus was there, and Cimon, and some of the other Athenians; Idomeneus was there, and Lykon, but none of the Spartans.

Themistocles sat back and blew out through his cheeks. 'Aristides truly is alive?' he asked.

He was a man who lived in such an artificial world that he assumed the rest of us lied as easily as he did himself. Well.

I nodded. 'He is alive. I'm sure he'll come tomorrow.'

Themistocles shook his head. 'I was a fool to speak ill of the King of Sparta, whom I too loved,' he said.

Cimon nodded. 'Yes,' he said. 'You lost Eurybiades there.'

Themistocles all but glowed in the firelight and his eyes were wide – almost mad. 'I'll go to him and reason with him,' he said. He leapt to his feet and all but ran into the darkness.

Well, as I said, their tents were close together on the headland.

I sipped my wine and thought, or rethought, many of the thoughts I've just related to you. Undying fame. Briseis. My house in Plataea. My son and my daughter, my future and the battle.

Siccinius paused by me and poured. 'May I ask my lord a question?' he asked.

Sycophantic slaves are annoying, but think of how hard it is to be them, eh? I have been. To always get the right tone – does this one want slavish manners or straight talk? How about this one?

I tried not to snap at him. 'Speak up,' I said, or something equally surly. No man enjoys having his deep thoughts interrupted by a slave.

'Do you truly speak Persian?' he asked.

'I do,' I answered, in that language.

'As do I,' Siccinius said. 'You led the embassy of the Greeks to Susa, did you not?'

I was suddenly suspicious of this man, and suspicious that Themistocles had a Persian-speaking slave.

Listen – Themistocles never wanted anything but his own glory. There were men among us who whispered that he would be perfectly content to lead the Athenian fleet into exile, because he would be the chief of it, and the lord of the new city. If you have been listening all these nights, you know that I think that most of the Athenians – certainly the whole current crop, Pericles included – would sell their own mothers to lord it as tyrant of Athens.

At any rate, before I could question the man further, Themistocles returned from Eurybiades.

'He refused to listen to me,' he said.

Cimon moaned.

Themistocles pounded one fist into his other hand. 'By the gods,' he swore, 'there must be another way.'

Cimon looked up. 'It is the curse of the gods on the Greeks,' he said. 'We can never be as one. We compete against each other in all things and we hate each other. We cannot unite.'

'Think of Lade,' I said. 'We would have won there and saved *all* this fighting, had only the men of Samos not betrayed us.'

'Think how often we were betrayed during the fighting in Ionia,' Cimon said. 'By my ancestor Ajax, my father was a pirate, but he kept his word better than many lords.'

Themistocles looked at me across the fire. 'The Persians use our petty quarrels against us,' he said. 'And there is always Persian gold to help the cause of treason. It is part of their way of conquering and holding an empire.' He was speaking aloud, but he was thinking – I could see it.

So could Cimon.

'You aren't proposing we sell ourselves to the Persians,' he asked. His voice was light, but I could hear the steel in it.

Themistocles shot to his feet. 'By Zeus, lord of kings and free men, I propose the very thing – and tonight, at that.'

There is a point at which a mad, bad plan is merely a good, if daring, plan. It is a tribute to our desperation that when Themistocles outlined his notion, there was almost no argument.

My part in the plan was simple. And I knew the way, and I had a triakonter on my part of the beach, ready for sea.

Walking back over the headland, Xanthippus laughed bitterly. 'Is this how we have to behave to do what is *right*?' he asked. 'By Poseidon, I hate the Spartans.'

It was dark, but not yet late, and there were people at most of the fires, eating and drinking. The whole of the beaches of Salamis had something of the air of a desperate festival.

We walked together, mostly in silence. Xanthippus had decided that he didn't like me, and yet he craved company. We were about to do a reckless thing that could dishonour us all. I could tell he had little stomach for it and I, in turn, didn't like him much either, but we were allies.

War is complicated.

At his tents, we stopped. 'Let me offer you a cup of wine,' he said, with poor grace. He didn't really want to offer one to me, I could tell, and I didn't want his wine anyway.

'No,' I said. I had a mission, and I would need most of the dark part of night to accomplish it. 'My thanks, Xanthippus,' I said, although I owed him no thanks.

'Is that the Plataean, my dear?' called a woman's voice from the darkness.

'Please keep your voice down, my dear,' Xanthippus said to the tent.

Agariste appeared from the tent door. 'Arimnestos,' she said, taking my hand. 'What a pleasure to see you.'

'He is on an urgent errand and can scarcely linger,' her husband shot back.

Agariste waved a ladylike hand and a beautiful young Thracian girl appeared – dark hair piled on her head and a tattoo of a horse inside her wrist that touched me. The Thracian girl smiled and poured me wine – wine I didn't need – and like the Thracian woman, it was unwatered and very strong.

A stool was placed behind me.

'I really must be away,' I said.

Agariste nodded. 'Of course, but this will only take a moment,' she said. 'Hipponax is your son?'

'Of course!' I said.

'But you have no wife,' she went on.

'My wife died,' I said.

'Euphonia – yes. A most elegant and well-bred young woman. We were all surprised when she chose you.'

Well, what do you say to that?

But Agariste smiled in the near darkness. 'I understand her better now, perhaps,' she said. 'Jocasta speaks very highly of you. Very highly indeed.'

I shook my head, far more confused by one Athenian oligarchic matron than by all the manoeuvres of the Persian fleet. 'Jocasta?' I asked.

She looked at me, her eyes narrowed. 'The lady wife of Aristides?' she said, her voice rising.

'Of course,' I said, feeling slow.

'She is here, now,' Agariste said. She smiled at her husband, but it was only to make him feel as if he was included in the conversation.

I really had no idea where all this was going. I rose to my feet and gave the Thracian girl my cup. Really, it was just an excuse to look at her.

She wasn't looking at me, either. There's age for you.

'We have decided that it is time for you and Cleitus to end this foolish quarrel,' Agariste said.

'Of course,' I answered. I smiled. 'I really must go. I have a duty to perform. Perhaps your husband can explain.'

'Well!' she said. She also rose to her feet. 'I shan't keep a guest who is so very anxious to leave, but really!'

Xanthippus accompanied me a few steps into the darkness. 'I apologise for my wife,' he began.

'Please!' I said. 'Please explain to her why I must go – I think she sees me as some sort of barbarian.'

I thought it was possible that Xanthippus, for all his democratic politics, also saw me as a bore and a bumpkin. Or as a notorious killer with a very thin veneer of manners.

Most of the time, that's a fine reputation to have.

I slipped away, kicked off my sandals, and ran across the beach to my ships.

Leukas was the best small-boat handler. We chose thirty oarsmen, the best men, and I took Ka. A well-shot arrow might save us, but no amount of sword work was going to save anyone. It probably took us an hour to get that little triakonter to sea.

We ran west along the beaches to the headland and there we picked up Siccinius. He was waiting on the beach with Themistocles, and they embraced, and then Themistocles came aboard for a moment and clasped my hand. We unstepped the mast and while we waited we muffled every oar, which made them heavier but almost completely silent.

Then the great man stepped ashore and we put our bow towards Piraeus and rowed. It was not a long row. We stayed close to the island of Psyttaleia for as long as we could and then we pulled almost due east into the harbour mouth. It was terrible and dark; and very strange to enter a mighty harbour with no people. It had the feeling of a trap.

We were very cautious, and it took us an hour to find a landing spot.

Siccinius was shaking with nerves. I went ashore with him.

'I can do this,' I said. Except that I could not, because half the court and all the major Persians knew me. It was a daft notion: the Great King would probably recognise me.

'No,' he said. 'No, they'll know who I come from.'

That was enigmatic and perhaps a little scary.

'I could go with you,' I said.

He paused. He was a brave man, going to do a terrible thing that was almost certain to get him killed. I had all the time in the world to make him feel better about it.

He looked at me. 'What I don't understand,' he said slowly, 'is why a man of your reputation would do this.'

I knew my role. 'I agree with your master,' I said. 'It is better this way.'

Siccinius let go a breath. 'I was born a free man,' he said. 'If it were me, I'd die fighting the Great King rather than face again the life of a slave.'

I really admired him, but the man I was playing needed to feign disgust and impatience. 'We'll see when you have carried our message,' I said.

'I'm ready,' he allowed.

I walked a few paces with him.

'If this succeeds,' I said, 'I'll see to it that you are freed.'

He paused. 'You have a great reputation as a freer of slaves,' he said. His voice was – better. 'Thank you. I would love to be free. Even if my freedom comes at such a price.'

He walked off into the darkness.

What he carried was a message from Themistocles to the Great King.

The message was wholly accurate. On four sheets of wax, Themistocles laid out, in my crisp Persian, the dissent and despair of the Greek fleet. He told the Great King the whole of the truth – that the fleet would break up the next night, in the dark of the moon, and run for the isthmus.

Themistocles offered to lead the whole of the Athenian and Aeginian contingents to change sides if the Great King would accept Athens and Aegina as allies and friends.

And I had agreed to it.

Within an hour, Siccinius was back, frightened and angry. 'I can't find anything but military posts,' he said. 'I'll simply be taken and enslaved or killed.'

This had, I confess, always seemed to me to be the weakest part of the plan, getting Siccinius to the Great King.

Let me explain – I see your confusion.

We didn't know where the Great King was camped. That may sound as if we were blind, but Attica is vast and the King's army, despite its size, was not so large. We knew from spies and refugees that Mardonius had led some cavalry as far west as Megara and we knew that Masistius had another body of cavalry north, by Marathon, probably to reap the symbolic victory there. But the Great King himself had watched the destruction of the Acropolis and then moved north, or so we thought. No one knew. We didn't think he was with the fleet. One of Xerxes' few real errors in the whole of his campaign in Greece was to treat his fleet as auxiliary to his forces instead of as a major contributor.

I hadn't expected to have to work hard to betray the Hellenic world, but now it seemed that I would.

I went ashore again, hung a sword over my shoulder, put on a heavier chlamys borrowed from Giannis, and waved to Brasidas.

Brasidas came ashore. He looked at me by the starlight, his face almost formless.

'What are we doing here?' he asked.

It was past midnight and we had until the darkness lifted to deliver the slave to the Great King.

'We need to get this man to the Great King,' I said. 'You speak Persian; I speak Persian. You know the former Spartan King; I know the Great King. If we tell the guards that we intend to betray the Greek fleet, we will be believed.'

Brasidas fingered his beard. 'And do we?' he asked in his Laconic manner.

By which he meant *Do we indeed intend to betray the Greek fleet?*

It can be difficult to be a commander. The process of command – the habit of requiring obedience instead of discussion – can erode a man's finer sentiments and his judgement, too. In addition, or perhaps first, the position of command settles a yoke of responsibility on the commander, so that he must make decisions that will cause pain and death and he must accept the consequence.

Yet, when leading Greeks, who almost to a man seek the undying glory of Achilles, it is seldom a moral question. You take them where they can fight, and they fight.

But in this matter, only I knew the truth. We had deliberately kept Siccinius from the truth – a slave will invariably betray a secret, if he feels he can derive advantage from it. Did I have the right to keep Brasidas from the truth? Brasidas, who had sacrificed a year of his life to raise rebellion in Babylon? Who had left his mess and his country because he felt that the Kings had made a dishonourable decision about Demaratus?

I leaned very close. I said, *'No. Trust me.'*

The Spartan nodded. 'So,' he said. That was all.

What I am telling here is that, when you come to the point, there is no substitute for the absolute trust of your people, and you can only earn that by working to keep it every day. Seckla and I have a number of jokes about the Long War: about where and when it was won and lost; sometimes we say that we won the Long War with a load of tin from Alba, and sometimes we think that we changed the world on a beach in Syracusa. But one of the pivotal moments of the war was when Brasidas accepted, with a single question, that mission.

We weren't even quiet. The three of us walked up the main street from Piraeus, deserted but for a pair of dogs who followed us. I confess that I fed them – they were so sad, so abandoned by their people. They seemed to me to embody the spirits of the household gods of Attica.

At the old temple of Demeter, the Persians had a guard post just at the base of the steps, right on the road. As I had hoped, it was a large post and manned entirely by cavalrymen.

I stepped up boldly. 'Hello!' I called out in Persian. 'Gentlemen, I need an escort!'

They sprang to arms with the guilty alacrity of men who have been playing knucklebones while on duty. We were surrounded and stripped of our weapons, but not manhandled.

'I would like to speak to an officer,' I said.

'Silence, slave,' snapped one of the Persian cavalrymen. He slapped me with his riding whip – not particularly hard, but it stung me all the way to my soul, and I thought, *this may be the stupidest thing I've ever done.*

'We have a message for the Great King,' I said, and got hit again.

Brasidas grunted.

Siccinius was silent.

One of the Persians put a hand on my tormentor's shoulder. 'We were told to watch out for traitors,' he said.

'Balls, we were told to watch for spies. Greeks are all liars anyway,' my guard said.

Brasidas shot me a look, which suggested to me that he thought it was time to try and break away.

Looking at them, I didn't think so. They were alert, and I had reason to know that the Persian elite cavalry were among the best soldiers in the world. Two of them had their bows strung and arrows on their bows, their thumbs cocked round the string in their strange draw.

I gave Brasidas the smallest of head shakes.

Siccinius summoned his courage. 'I come from the Lord Themistocles,' he said.

I think my guard was one of those who simply like to hit people; he had that look to him, and his riding whip shot out and caught Siccinius in the face, but the smaller guard caught his arm.

'Don't be an arse, Archarnes!' he said. He stepped between us. 'Who sent you?' he asked.

'Lord Themistocles,' I said.

'He's lying,' said the bully. 'He's only saying that because the other Greek said it. Split them up, beat the crap out of them, and we'll get some answers.'

'Ask yourself why we all speak Persian, then,' I spat. My upper lip was split and already throbbing from the whip blow.

My 'friend' raised his whip again, his face flushed in the torchlight. But the smaller man stayed between us.

'He insulted me,' raged the bully.

'Shut up, Archarnes!' said the smaller Persian. He went to the steps of the temple, picked up a horn, and blew it.

Almost instantly there were two answering horns. He blew again – a long call.

Archarnes came over and kicked me in the shin. As I started to fall, he struck me again with his whip.

'Never take that tone with a Persian, slave,' he said.

I lay on the ground and thought of how I'd kill him.

If I ever got free.

Hoof beats heralded the next phase. An officer came, had a whispered conference with the smaller cavalryman and nodded sharply.

'Which one claims to be from Themistocles?' he asked. He butchered the name, but to be fair, the Greeks were not so good at Persian names, either.

'They all do,' spat Archarnes.

'Then I'll take them all,' said the officer. He chose four cavalrymen from the troop at the guard post and they roped the three of us together and took us up the hill towards Athens.

At a run.

They were all mounted on fine horses and we were running at the ends of ropes. I fell once and hot pain went through my knee. Siccinius fell several times and was dragged a bit. Brasidas simply ran. If I had been a Persian, I'd have identified him immediately as the most dangerous man among us.

To be honest, I was cold, and afraid. I knew we'd made a terrible error. I would greatly have preferred to die fighting than this humiliation, and I had wounded fingers, a bad cut on one leg, and months of constant fighting, poor sleep, and endless fatigue. I was not at my most heroic. As we ran up that hill, my breath burning in my lungs, I cursed Themistocles for a fool.

And myself as well. It always hurts most when you have no one to blame but yourself.

At the Piraeus Gates of Athens there is a small temple of Nike and an even smaller temple of Aphrodite; really just a statue in a niche. But the temple of Nike was the headquarters of the guard, with fifty horses tied outside and a substantial number of slaves and messengers attached, even in the middle of the second watch of the night.

We were questioned as soon as we were brought into the torchlight of the headquarters, and those were cursory questions. I could tell that neither of the junior officers barking at us cared a whit for our answers. Then we were taken out of the headquarters, past the city walls, and put into a house   it had, in fact, been a brothel. I knew the neighbourhood well enough. The house was full of prisoners, mostly very old men.

There was a woman who had been raped so often she could not speak.

There were two male children who were completely silent, their faces closed.

Bah! I shan't say more. No army is composed of priests and philosophers, but this was grim even by the standards of Ionian piracy. Someone had beaten one of the old men until his nose was smashed flat and his skull broken, yet he was alive.

We three, despite our bruises, were the healthiest people in that house. Siccinius, who was growing on me as a man, found the covered well, and the three of us raised water and took it to all the battered people who would accept it.

I looked down into the well's cistern and glanced at Brasidas.

He nodded.

We could jump into the cistern and, with a little luck, escape. Many of the houses in this quarter shared common cisterns – big commercial establishments had them cut back into the hillside.

Or we'd drown in the darkness.

Siccinius was trying to coax the woman to take water when the guards returned. There were four of them, and they simply opened the door and shouted for us in Persian.

'All three Greeks who speak the tongue!' a man called. 'If I have to come and find you, you won't like it.'

I remember, again, locking eyes with Brasidas. I wasn't sure whether to be pleased they'd come for us, or terrified.

We left the house. I suppose I thought we'd be brought back after questioning.

They marched us back to the small temple outside the gate, and there was an officer, sitting in torchlight on a good chair, no doubt stolen out of a home.

I knew him immediately, of course. It was Cyrus, the friend of my youth.

It's not so remarkable, either. When last I'd seen him he had been a commander of one hundred. He'd held important positions under Artaphernes, too – he'd been captain of Sardis for a while. And I knew that Artaphernes' son of the same name had led a thousand cavalrymen of Lydia to join the Great King; I'd had to assume my old friend would be in the field.

Nonetheless, it was a shock to see him and I confess I was immediately at a loss as to how to proceed. Friends, guest friendship, duty, honour, truth and lies.

But I may have a touch of the wits of wily Odysseus, because after a moment's terror, I bowed like a nobleman, one hand to the floor of the temple.

'Lord Cyrus,' I said in my good camp Persian.

He had not recognised me until then, and who would, with a split lip already puffy and some other lacerations, in an old brown cloak and a fair amount of blood?

But he rose. 'Arimnestos!' he said. Then he was suddenly cautious.

He sat. 'What are you doing here?' he asked harshly.

He looked at Brasidas.

I swear before the gods, in that moment he saw through the whole of our plot.

But Siccinius stepped forward, brave when it counted. 'My lord, I come from Themistocles the Athenian with a report for the Great King, and an offer of a tremendous service that my lord would like to offer the King.'

Siccinius had been forced to give his wax tablet to the first guards but he saw it lying in front of Cyrus and he waved at it. 'My lord has written—' he began.

Cyrus rose, his face closed. He did not meet my eye. 'Have these men watched closely, but not harmed,' he snapped at a guard. 'These are very dangerous men, and very important to the Great King.'

Damn him!

All the guards stepped a little away from us. The cavalryman nearest me looked at Brasidas, smiled, licked his lips and loosened his akinakes, his short sword, in his belt. He used his thumb, pushing against the throat of the scabbard, to loosen the blade – a man of skill.

Now that they were warned, they no longer treated us as slaves. Which meant that our options for escape were nearly nil.

'Lord Cyrus tells me you can all ride. Is this true?' a soldier asked.

We all agreed, and received mounts.

'Where are we going?' I asked.

'To see the Great King himself,' the soldier replied. 'And the gods have mercy on your poor spirits.'

Irony is present in all the affairs of gods and men. That night's irony lay in the location of the Great King.

He was living in Aristides' house.

When you think of it, it makes perfect sense; it was one of the finest houses in Athens and located well away from the centre, over past the Pnyx in a walled compound with its own stable. Few Athenians had what was, in essence, a small farm in the heart of the city, and fewer still had such a fine garden.

But it seemed very odd indeed to be taken in total darkness through Aristides' outer hall. It was all well lit – the Great King, apparently, had been awakened.

A eunuch took charge of us. He was tall and clear-skinned, with the kind of tanned skin and lush dark hair that makes Babylonians so beautiful. His voice was low and deep and resonant – he'd have made a fine orator.

Eunuchs only keep their boyish voices if you cut their stones away while they're boys, honey. Cut them older and they're just angry men.

While the guards watched us with arrows on their bows, the eunuch instructed us on how to greet the king. It didn't matter, as it turned out – as soon as we were taken into the garden, soldiers of the Immortals slammed us to the ground.

A foot was placed on the middle of my back and a spear point placed in the hollow at the base of the back of my skull where the neck meets it. It was very sharp.

I could see nothing but Siccinius. I couldn't even see Brasidas, and I despaired; I wished I had told Themistocles to go himself (which had occurred to me). You know why I didn't?

I didn't really trust him.

'The Great King bids you speak,' said a voice. It wasn't someone I knew.

Nor was the voice directed at us.

I heard Cyrus. I should have expected that he would be there. I suppose that I should have expected what he would say, but I was shocked.

'Great King, King over Kings, Lord of Lords, these three miserable Greeks are nothing. They are a bold ruse by your enemies to attempt to pull a hood over your eyes. I can't even guess to what lengths the Greeks would go, or what foolishness they intend. I can only say that I know two of these men, and they are lying.'

I knew Xerxes' voice as soon as he spoke.

'Cyrus, captain of Artaphernes of Sardis, are you not?' he asked. His voice was careful and controlled, and yet I swear he hinted that as a captain of Artaphernes, who had been against the war, he was not fully to be trusted.

'I have that honour,' Cyrus replied.

Xerxes cleared his throat. 'Bring me a cup of wine with honey,' he said. 'Tell me what message they bring?'

By the Lord of the Silver Bow and my ancestor Heracles, I'd have given a year of my life to be able to see. I thought the next voice might be Mardonius, although we'd been told he was south and west by Megara.

'They bring an offer of fealty, King of Kings, from that rascal Themistocles.' The voice was smooth, cultured, deeply Persian, and held the kind of malicious humour that delighted the oriental mind. 'The slave on the left is Siccinius, Great King. Him we have seen before.'

Even in that moment of terror and apprehension, I noted that the Great King had seen Siccinius before.

For the first time it dawned on me that I had been used. That Themistocles might be a traitor and he was actually telling the Great King the truth – he was betraying the fleet.

Zeus, god of free men, protect me, I thought.

'The man on the right is a Spartan soldier who fought against you, Great King, in the war in Babylon. He fled and survived, but he is utterly your enemy.' This from Cyrus, my so-called friend. Perhaps he didn't mention me to protect me.

Brasidas shocked me, even in that state. 'You lie,' he said clearly. 'Send for your ally Demaratus, King of Sparta, and ask him who I am.'

Cyrus took a step and was stopped by the Immortals. 'I do not lie!' he said. 'These are dangerous men who intend no good thing for you, Great King!'

'Be silent,' Xerxes said. 'I have been told repeatedly that Athens would have traitors. I have also sent for Hippias.'

There is something horrifying about lying on a mosaic floor for long minutes, a spear in your neck and your hands bound. It was cold, and it was, in its own way, agonising.

I thought of Hippias, whose lustful advances I had avoided when I had been a slave as a boy. He'd been a loathsome worm then.

Hate can help you, in despair. I hated Hippias as a traitor, as a tyrant, and as a fat, ugly man, and that hate buoyed me up. It's not pretty to say – better that I had been suffused with a desire for glory, or love for Briseis, but in all that time on the cold floor I never thought once of Briseis.

And then he came, fatter, uglier, and more perfumed than I remembered. He was like a caricature of himself. I saw him as he passed across the area of wall my eyes could see.

He made the full proskinesis on the floor and then rose, his fat arse an embarrassment to all Greeks.

'How may I serve the Great King?' he asked.

Mardonius spoke again. 'Demaratus has been tested many times and found loyal,' he said. 'He predicted that men of Sparta would come to him. Let us send for him as well.'

Xerxes nodded and pointed at an Immortal. I assume he ran – certainly it seemed no time at all before I heard the deposed Spartan king's voice.

'Great King?' he asked, without much formality. Unlike the worm, Hippias, he didn't abase himself, but merely bowed deeply, one hand to the floor, like a Persian nobleman.

'Unpick this riddle for me,' Xerxes said. 'Here is your man, Brasidas, with a suspicious character and a slave. The slave claims to offer me the allegiance of Themistocles the Athenian. The other two are guarantors of this pact, or perhaps offered to me as hostages.'

'Or it is a trick—' Cyrus took a breath.

Xerxes all but patted Hippias like a dog. 'This slave comes to me from Themistocles. He brought this letter. Read it and tell me what you think?'

Hippias took the tablets and read them. It took him a long time; I don't think his Persian was very good. Demaratus read the letter in half the time.

'I think his offer is genuine,' the old tyrant said, delighted. 'I told you men would come over to you when they saw how powerless they were!'

Xerxes chuckled. 'You promised me they would throw flowers when I entered Athens, and that men would demand that you be restored to power,' he said with Persian honesty. 'I have not seen any flowers, and there was no one left in Attica to demand your restoration, so I'm delighted that in this, at least, you are correct.'

'Great King, if they had not driven the common people into the ships with whips, there would have been cheering crowds to greet your arrival.' Hippias spoke unctuously, the way one would speak to Zeus, if Zeus came to earth.

Demaratus grunted.

'You disagree?' Xerxes asked.

Demaratus made some noise. I couldn't see him, but I'm going to guess he gave a Laconian shrug. 'If the offer were genuine, surely Themistocles would have come in person? I did.'

Cyrus's voice rose. 'Great King, I beg permission to speak.'

Xerxes made a noise in his throat. 'Speak, then.'

'Great King, all these Greeks are liars. They do not see lying as a sin, the way we do. This Themistocles – what can he gain by betraying his own fleet?' Cyrus paused and then threw me to the wolves. 'Great King, the man in the centre is Arimnestos the Plataean, who was their ambassador at Persepolis. You remember him? Can we imagine him as a traitor?'

Xerxes chuckled. 'Is it he, indeed? Well, some of his arrogance has been rubbed off him, anyway. Arimnestos, not so stiff-necked now, are you? Speak, Plataean. Speak well for your life. What do you here?'

'Great King, you have burned my city. I have come to save what I can,' I said.

'You have come to serve me?' Xerxes asked.

'Great King, ask Cyrus – indeed, ask Artaphernes how often he has asked me to command his ships or his soldiers. I have never been an enemy to his house, or yours, Great King. Or why do you think the Greeks chose me as ambassador?'

Xerxes coughed. 'Cyrus? What say you to that?'

Cyrus paused. 'It could be as he says,' he admitted slowly. 'In which case I will owe him a great apology. But ask him only this, Great King. Ask him to swear an oath to the gods to be your slave.'

Xerxes laughed aloud. 'Cyrus, you are to be commended for your caution, but you have said yourself that Greeks are great liars and one oath more or less will not keep them from plummeting into the great darkness. These men speak our tongue but have no idea how *men* should behave. Siccinius? What does your master bid me do?'

Siccinius spoke up. 'Great King, my master bids you do what you would have done anyway – attack! In the dark of the moon, bring your forces into the Bay of Salamis so that the Greeks are surrounded on every side, and then fall on them in the dawn. My master will lead the ships of Athens over to you – he will change sides, and the League will collapse. He asks only that now that you have fulfilled your vow to destroy the temples of Athens that you will allow him to restore them.'

'Him, or some other of my choice,' Xerxes said. I had raised my head from the floor when I spoke, and now I saw Xerxes cast an affectionate look at Hippias, the sort of look a man gives his favourite dog.

For a Great King, Xerxes was a very fragile man. Even from the miserable cold of Aristides' best mosaic floor, I could see that he *needed* the Greeks to be coming over to his side. His intimates had promised him triumph. Men like Hippias had insisted that the miserable Greeks longed for his enlightened rule.

Every man desires to be the hero in his own epic, thugater. Even the Great King. And he was more the victim of his own desires than most.

And if you want to lie to a man, promise him what he most desires. Think, if you will, of the horse the Achaeans sent to the Trojans as *tribute*, a sort of huge trophy of victory. The Trojans desired nothing more than to have won.

Siccinius, greatly daring, went on. 'My master bids you set up your throne where you can see the Bay of Salamis,' he said. 'To watch and truly see how he conducts himself, and what reward he deserves.'

I thought he'd overplayed our hand, myself. Perhaps it *was* best to send a slave – a slave understands how obsequiously a master wants to hear his dreams laid out. I would not have dared.

Xerxes sighed with satisfaction. 'What a beautiful notion,' he said.

I managed to see Mardonius out of the corner of my eye. He was staring at me and Cyrus was whispering to him.

Damn Cyrus and his honesty.

'When does my new servant Themistocles think I should attack?' Xerxes asked.

'Tomorrow night, which is the dark of the moon,' Siccinius said. 'There is no better night for your fleet to surround the beaches of the Greeks.' He paused. 'And my master will need time to prepare. He needs to know by morning. We ... lost much time with your guards.'

Mardonius laughed. 'Slave, you expect that we will send you *back?*'

Siccinius spoke again. 'If you want Athens to defect to you, Great King, we will all three have to be sent back. I am but the herald: these two men are greater than I, and were sent as proof for me. They are Themistocles' friends.'

At first I thought he'd spoken in our favour. In retrospect, though, it sounded as if he'd offered us as hostages.

Mardonius shook his head and I was slammed back to the floor and lost sight of him. 'I say no!' he said with some force. 'Let this Themistocles do as he will; we will surround and shatter this little fleet regardless.'

But Xerxes had the bit in his teeth. 'Be calm, Mardonius. Gentle yourself. If we defeat this fleet, a fleet which has beaten mine twice, if we defeat it, we will have to fight the survivors again, and perhaps again and again. But if the Athenians and the Aeginians change sides, their League will be no more and every one of their little towns will make peace. I know it. I feel this in my bones.'

Demaratus agreed. 'Great King, in this I agree. The defection of Athens would finish the League. Even the Spartans would have to sue for peace. Whereas – I speak only as a soldier – as long as their fleet exists somewhere, it forces you to a long and expensive land campaign. Sparta will not be beaten easily.'

Mardonius laughed. 'Demaratus, you vastly exaggerate the power and importance of a tiny state with no real power, because it was once yours. We defeated the Spartans at the Hot Gates and killed their king. They are nothing.'

Hippias spoke up. He saw a change in his fortunes – Athen's treason meant his own restoration, perhaps. 'Trust this man, Great King. You have little to lose; as Great Mardonius says, your fleet will win anyway.'

The lickspittle knew he'd get some of the credit, too.

'Send the slave back, then, and leave the Spartan and the Plataean as hostages.' Mardonius's suggestion made far too much sense. I began to suspect I was going to die for Greece.

The worst of it was that I no longer trusted Siccinius or Themistocles, for all that the slave had done his level best to have us returned.

Xerxes nodded. 'That is reasonable,' he said.

I raised my head and was not killed. 'Great King,' I said. 'I beg leave to speak.'

'Now you *are* more polite,' he said. 'Speak.'

'Great King, many Spartans, and many other ships, will follow Themistocles, if we are there. If we are not – if you keep Brasidas, who leads the party of men who support the exiles – the Spartans will fight. I too command ships, and they will fight.' I was making things up as fast as I could.

Mardonius laughed. 'Let them fight – the whole Plataean fleet!' he mocked. 'How many ships? None? One?'

'Or perhaps they will all sail away,' I said. 'Tomorrow morning when I do not return.'

'That is a small risk I will accept,' the Great King said. 'Take the Spartan and the Boeotian and throw them in the storehouse. If Themistocles does as he promises, they will be released with honours. If not, I will have them dragged to death by chariots.' He smiled.

Siccinius was taken away. He did not protest again. I don't think he was sorry to leave us behind. After all, he was being led to freedom.

I had never been in Jocasta's storage shed. It was getting light outside and they threw us in, none too gently.

When they were gone, we found some sacking and used it to get warm. And bless Jocasta, there were old blankets, no doubt moth-eaten, and we made ourselves as comfortable as we might on a chilly autumn morning.

It would be hot when day came, but at the very break of day it was cold, and the floor had been cold – and of course, nothing is colder than fear.

Then we sat back to back, for warmth, bundled in old sacking and blankets.

'I am not afraid to die for Greece,' I said.

Brasidas grunted.

'But I am worried that Themistocles is fucking us all,' I said.

Brasidas, who never swore or talked bawdy, stiffened. 'What?' he asked.

I spoke very quietly. 'I worry that I have been used, that Siccinius just did exactly what he appeared to do, that Themistocles used the veil of honesty to pull the wool over our eyes, and that Themistocles will, in fact, attempt to betray the League tomorrow the same way Samos betrayed us at Lade.'

Brasidas grunted.

'And you and I will be seen as traitors to the end of time,' I noted.

Brasidas grunted again. 'That is bad,' he admitted.

I sighed. 'Brasidas, I apologise for bringing you into this.'

He made no comment. After a long while, he said, 'We must escape.'

I suspect I rolled my eyes, even in the darkness.

'Listen, brother,' I said. 'If we escape too early, we ruin the plan – if Themistocles was telling me the truth. And it is, in fact, the only plan that might have a chance of giving us a battle that we still, of course, have to win.'

Yet even as I spoke, I could see a plan shaping in my head.

'But if we escape at nightfall,' I said. I paused and tried to find a stitch in my logic, but the net held. 'If we escape at nightfall, his fleet orders will already be issued and we'll have time to warn the Greeks.'

There was a long pause.

'That's quite good,' Brasidas said. In fact, he chuckled. 'I see it. By arriving, we force Themistocles to behave as if he meant to fight for the League all along.' For Brasidas this was a long speech. He was deeply amused.

'Perhaps he did,' I said.

We were both silent for a while.

Brasidas laughed aloud. 'Gods, you Athenians,' he said.

'I'm a Plataean,' I said.

'Oh, so am I,' Brasidas said, and laughed again, as long and hard as I'd ever heard him laugh.

*

To say that the day that followed was long does not do it justice. I am not a man given over to worry, but that day my whole existence seemed to have been focused down to a nested set of tensions, rather the way that Empedocles' glass focused the rays of the sun into a beam of light and heat. I feared Themistocles was a traitor and yet I simultaneously feared that Siccinius had not reached the Greek fleet. I feared that the Greek League might already have fallen apart, the Corinthians rowing away to the isthmus, and yet I feared that Adeimantus was pouring more poison into the ears of the council. I had time, between naps, to consider the possibility that Themistocles and Adeimantus were allies in treason – an idea that I could not make hold water.

In fact, if they were both traitors, they did it in a typically Greek and fractious way, each man striving to be the one who delivered the League to the Great King.

But surely Themistocles was *not* a traitor? He was the architect of the naval strategy and the originator of the League, with Gorgo and Leonidas and to a lesser extent Aristides. It made no sense that, having built an alliance and a fleet that seemed capable of resisting the Great King to the bitter end, he should betray his own creation.

And yet ... and yet. I have said before, other nights, that I sometimes think that courage is a limited thing; that a man can squander it while young, and then one day find the reservoir empty. Indeed, I observe as I get older that my muscles will no longer respond the way they once would; that even if I train every day, I am more likely to injure something than to become massively strong. I suspect that it might be the same with courage. I think perhaps men can reach a state where they have wrung their courage dry, and then, when they need it, it is no longer there – or no longer there in the abundance that it had formerly been.

And make no mistake, my friends, the creation of an alliance requires immense personal courage – the courage and the confidence to recognise the needs of others, articulate them, and subsume your own needs to cement the good of the whole. When, for example, Athens allowed Sparta to win the chariot race at the Olympics – if that is in fact what happened – Themistocles and Aristides were putting the needs of their allies above their own needs.

But when I thought about it on that long and hot day in early autumn – I had nothing to do but think, and that can be a curse to a man – Themistocles had given unstintingly, and failed. He had surrendered command of the allied fleet, when by any calculation it should have been his. He had recalled the conservative exiles, when by rights it was obvious that his policy had been the correct one. Despite these and other sacrifices, the Greeks had not triumphed at Artemisium – or if we had, it was to no avail. And now, on the beaches of Salamis, it was increasingly obvious that the Greek fleet would splinter as it had at Lade and in other summers.

Was it not possible that at some point, perhaps after Artemisium, when I had observed him to be shattered, almost unable to think, that he gave up? Or perhaps when we all saw the fires raging over his beloved Athens – did he then admit defeat? Was it the serpent Adeimantus, with his assertion that the destruction of Athens robbed Athenians of their right to vote or speak because they had no city?

Was all this the imagining of a fevered, anxious mind, and even now Themistocles was preparing a master stroke?

Perhaps most annoying to me on that endless day was that Brasidas simply slept, the bastard.

I should have trusted my friends more.

Brasidas awoke in mid-afternoon when the guards were changed and brought us water. Our new guards were not Persians or Medes but Sakje, the steppe nomads of the far east, beyond the Euxine sea. There were four of them, and they walked badly – their very legs seemed formed to grasp the back of a horse and they walked with a rollicking gait, like sailors too long at sea.

They did not speak Greek and they didn't seem to speak Persian; one of them struck me with his whip when I tried to ask for food.

They were extremely careful of us. They had clearly been told that we were dangerous men. But as the afternoon wore away, a Mede came and spoke to them in their own tongue. He wore a great deal of gold and was quite tall. The four of them grunted and put arrows on their bows, and the new man came and summoned us out into the yard. We were allowed water to wash and slaves brought us towels to dry ourselves, and fresh wool chitons from Aristides' clothes press. I rather fancied the one I received, with a magnificent flame pattern on the hems, a tribute, I suspected, to Jocasta's skill.

Then we were taken back to the courtyard of the house, where Xerxes sat enthroned. Around the margins of the garden, in among the pillared portico, stood a dozen men and one woman. I knew the woman – or rather, given her presence and her aura of authority, I knew she must be the same Artemisia who had returned my thrown spear. There stood the Phoenician commander, Tetramnestos, who some Greeks called the 'King of Sidon'. There stood Ariabignes, son of Darius and brother of Xerxes, commander of their whole fleet. He stood close by Tetramnestos, as if they were brothers. Theomestor, son of Androdamas, a Samian, one of the traitors who helped the Great King beat us at Lade, stood by Artemisia, with another man who I knew better than all the others – Diomedes of Ephesus.

Men like to say of such and such that their blood ran cold, but so, as I watched him, did I feel his eyes come to me, and so, as our eyes locked, did the hairs on my neck begin to stand as if I was in bitter cold water.

Behind me stood four Sakje with their bows slightly bent and arrows on them, and in front of me, a garden full of my enemies.

And there, over by Ariaramnes – a man I had met as a boy, a friend of Artaphernes and a member of his faction – stood Hippias, the broad smile of a merchant selling used goods stamped on his greasy face, and close by them, the deposed King of Sparta, Demaratus, who looked as if he'd eaten a bad egg.

When we entered the courtyard, most of the men there fell silent. Mardonius continued speaking to the Great King in a low tone, and Artemisia looked at me and kept talking. She had a low, pleasant voice, deeper than many men's and not less feminine for it. She was speaking to Diomedes of Ephesus, and her last words before she was shushed to silence were 'beat us like a drum'.

And then they all looked at us.

Demaratus winced and looked away and I saw my fate sealed. And Diomedes grinned at me.

Without being pushed by the Sakje, I made my obeisance to the Great King, exactly as I had done at Persepolis, with one hand on the ground. No one pushed me down into proskynesis.

Xerxes made no reaction and I didn't know whether to rise unbidden or stay in this uncomfortable posture. I was sure he meant me to be uncomfortable, but I held it. I was, after all, supposed to be a willing conspirator, not an arrogant Greek.

Mardonius continued speaking in a low voice. I caught only a little of what he said for he spoke quietly and quickly. He said 'captains' and he said 'council' and he went on with real animation about altars.

Of course, I could not see him.

Eventually, Xerxes must have bored of his harangue.

'Rise, Arimnestos. Be at ease.' I rose. 'And your Spartan, who is, I believe, dear to my good friend Demaratus.'

Brasidas rose.

Demaratus bowed his head. 'My thanks, Great King.'

Xerxes nodded civilly enough to me, as one gentleman might to another in the street.

'Mardonius and Ariabignes thought that we should question you about the Greek fleet before my captains discussed tonight,' the Great King said.

I bowed. 'Ask me anything,' I said with as much panache as I could manage.

Xerxes shook his head. 'No. *Tell* me everything, Plataean.'

I looked around, surprised by the quality of hate focused at me. Perhaps I am dispassionate when I make war; certainly, I have made a business of it sometimes, and I feel little hate and even some compassion for my victims – once they are beaten. But Diomedes bared his teeth, almost in a snarl – fair enough, since I tried to turn him into a temple prostitute once, his hate did not surprise me, but the look on Ariabignes' face was remarkable: a rictus of anger. And Mardonius's brows were furrowed, his mouth set, as if we were about to go sword to sword, edge to edge.

I had no friends there.

And I was supposed to act the part of the traitor?

I thought of Odysseus. It is hard, forcing your mind when men hate you. When your cause appears hopeless. Or, just possibly, my mind focused well *because* my cause was hopeless.

'It is a better fleet than yours, Great King,' I said.

With that, the anger on faces was translated to hisses and mutterings, with the sole exception of a woman's laugh, which cut through the other sounds like a sword through spider web.

Artemisia was laughing.

'Tell us what is so funny,' Xerxes said, somewhat pettishly.

Artemisia was apparently without fear – or at least, without fear of the Great King. She gave the slight shrug of a modest woman and cast her eyes down. 'I thought this Boeotian bumpkin you all described was a great liar,' she said. Then she chuckled, a lovely sound. 'I find instead that he tells the truth, and thus I suspect he may be what he claims.'

'You think the Greek fleet is greater than ours? These rebels?' Xerxes asked. It's worth noting here that to the Persians, we were all rebels against the authority of the Great King. Xerxes turned to me. 'How many ships in your fleet?' he asked.

I met his eye. 'Almost four hundred trieres,' I said. 'Some pente-konters and triakonters, too.'

Xerxes sat back and clasped the arms of what had once been Jocasta's favourite chair. I could not tell whether he was genuinely relieved or mocking relief, as if what I had said had no worth.

'My fleet is more than twice the size,' Xerxes said. 'So I have little to fear.'

'If that were so,' I asked, 'we would not be having this conversa-tion, mighty king. But as it is, your fleet has lost to the League's fleet twice, and never beaten it.'

'He lies in everything he says,' Ariabignes said. 'Their fleet is fewer than three hundred trieres, and it has never beaten the fleet of the Empire.'

I met Xerxes' eyes and held them. 'I would guess that your slaves have chosen not to trumpet their defeats to you,' I said.

'Silence him!' Mardonius said. 'This is no turncoat, but one of their partisans.'

A spear was placed at my neck and I was kicked hard in the back of my knees and I fell. A man's foot was placed in my back and I felt the point of his spear.

The only sound was that of Artemisia laughing.

I could see Xerxes' feet and I could see under his chair. It was the oddest view of the room, and I remember thinking that Jocasta had the cleanest floors in Greece. And that I was going to die in the midst of public humiliation. And be thought a traitor.

In fact, I was so terrified, so very sure that this was death, that I had few coherent thoughts at all, and so there was room in the temple of my head for the cleanliness of the floor. I lay and waited for death, Artemisia laughed, and I looked at Xerxes' very clean feet.

He adjusted his position, drawing his feet together under him.

'What defeats, Greek?' he asked. 'Let him speak.'

'Great King,' I began. I had passed the point of no return. I was going to die and I had to see if I could help my comrades a little, sow some dissension, and goad him to the fight.

If Themistocles was not a traitor . . .

But I couldn't see Cimon or Ameinias of Pallene, or Eumenes of Anagyrus simply following Themistocles blindly into treason, or so I hoped.

'If you were to ride to Phaleron and review your fleet,' I said, 'you might find it smaller than you imagine, Great King.'

'He lies!' Mardonius and Ariabignes said together.

'And if you were to count all the Greek captures on the beach, you might count them with the fingers of one hand,' I added. In fact, they had captured almost thirty ships at Artemisium, but I knew he was unlikely to go and count. 'If you were to climb Mount Aigeleos and look across the bay to Salamis, you might count the Greek ships on their beaches for yourself, and you might count the captures there – Phoenicians and Ionians.' I couldn't shrug, but I tried to sound derisive. It's not easy with a man's foot in your back and a spear tip pricking you in the cheek.

'He lies!' spat the King of Sidon.

'He says nothing but the truth,' Artemisia said.

'What does a woman know of war?' spat Mardonius. 'Keep your words to yourself if you have nothing reasonable to say, woman.'

'I know the difference between victory and defeat,' the woman said. 'Which is apparently beyond you.'

Silence reigned. I lay on the floor for the second time in two days and tried not to think.

Finally, the Great King sighed. 'You did not break the Greeks at Artemisium?' he asked.

Ariabignes was a son of Darius by a different mother than Xerxes, which made him both a blood relative and just possibly a competitor. He certainly showed fear. 'We would have, given another day,' he said. His tone betrayed him.

'In another day you would have had no fleet,' I said. 'And I will be honest if others are not. Had we had another day at Artemisium, I would not be here!' I remember every word – note that I spoke nothing but the truth, and yet . . .

'Let the lady of Halicarnassus speak,' Xerxes said.

She came and stood not far from me. She was dressed in women's clothes, not armour, and she was tall, taller than most men, and well muscled, and had copper-red hair, whether by artifice or nature I know not. She stood where I could see her. 'I think the Greek exaggerates,' she said. 'But only by a day or two. Great King, we have not beaten these Greeks. I am your majesty's loyal slave and I promise you that the Greeks are masters of your fleet at sea.'

'Silence,' Xerxes said to the rising protests. 'Why?'

Artemisia didn't shuffle or hesitate. 'You have many poor

trierarchs,' she said. 'The Phoenicians are afraid to take further losses and it makes them cautious. The Egyptians hate you. Your only reliable ships are the Ionians, and your own Persians seem to hate us. These divisions mean that each contingent succeeds or fails alone.'

Well. Just then, I loved her. And she was saying what I had suspected; indeed, what I had observed.

'Ship for ship, we are better sailors than most of theirs, and any ship of Sidon can beat any Greek in a race or probably any other contest. But my father used to tell me that what made the Greeks mighty and made the hoplites great was that no one fighter had to be particularly skilled, but only the whole of all the hoplites needed to know the way to fight as a group. And this is what I observe with the Greeks – they fight in answer to a single will, as horses yoked together to a chariot, whereas your ships fight the way foals race, each according to his own will. Is this not humorous, Great King? Your will rules all of us, and yet your fleet is leaderless; the Greeks are all democrats and little men, and yet their fleet acts according to a single will. Worse, because of their cohesion, they pack in close and make the sea battle into a land battle. They put more marines on their decks than many of your ships, and the lack of manoeuvre in close tells to their advantage, as we are the better seamen.'

Silence.

The woman had silenced a dozen men, all tried warriors. Of course, what she said was true – and damningly accurate.

Xerxes leaned forward and put his chin in his hand. 'What do you recommend, Artemisia?'

She looked down at me. 'If you can take the Greek fleet by treachery, do so. Their captains are as superior to yours as men are superior to women in matters of war.'

I remember laying there and thinking, *but you are a woman, and the wisest captain here.*

'Is that all your advice?' Mardonius asked, his voice silky. It seemed to me that he wanted the woman's destruction and saw her walking straight into the Great King's bad graces.

She looked at him, her head high. 'Break the Greeks with time and money and avoid another contest at sea or by land. Every fight makes them look better, puffs up their sense of their own importance, brings them allies and admiration – little Greece contending with the might of the Great King? Whereas, with time and gold, you can let their natural fractiousness rule them and their league will collapse, then you can impose any peace you want.'

'A woman's advice!' Mardonius said with deep contempt. 'Stay in the bedroom where you belong, comb your hair and speak not concerning things beyond your babies and your hand mirror. The Great King needs to show his power and crush these maggots so that other men know his might. That is how a man thinks.'

Artemisia let half her mouth smile. 'No, Mardonius. That is how *you* think. I am a woman and I have born babies, with more pain than you will ever know in battle. And I say unto you – you squander the children born of women and yet your way will fail against the Greeks; I protect the children of women, and yet my way will bring triumph for the Great King and for the Empire.'

She spoke like Athena herself and I wondered: in the Poet there are moments when gods and goddesses take the mouths of mortals. My heart soared, because I could see that Athena had already pronounced the Great King's doom, and yet, as the gods love to show mortals their folly, the Parthenos spoke, herself, through this woman, giving him the best possible advice. Even I, listening to her, approved. She was more dangerous than Mardonius. I think it is lucky for Greece that she was almost forty years old, her face lined with laughter and life. She was attractive enough for her age, but not much younger than Xerxes' mother. Had she been twenty and beautiful ...

But she was not.

Xerxes' sandals moved again and I looked up in time to see him smile. He put out a hand and placed it on the elbow of Mardonius. 'She speaks well, and from love of me,' he said. 'You believe the Plataean?' he asked.

She looked at me. In one enigmatic half smile I saw how little I fooled her. She was *wise*.

But she bowed her head. 'I believe he tells the truth,' she said.

Diomedes spoke up. 'He was at sea, fighting us, just a few days ago!' he said. 'He is our enemy!'

Xerxes looked around the room. 'Is this true?'

I spoke up. 'It is but three days since I threw a spear at this lady,' I said.

Xerxes laughed. 'Ah!' he said.

Mardonius looked at me. 'Let me give him to the Immortals. They will beat the truth from him.'

Diomedes said, 'Great King, give him to me. I have promised that this man, who was once a slave, would meet a vile death. I will wring from him anything he has to say that will serve you.'

Apparently, men at Xerxes' court demanded deaths of other men all the time, because the Great King ignored them as if they were small boys. 'Three days ago you threw a spear at one of my captains in a sea fight,' he said. 'Today you kiss my slipper. Why?'

I thought of Themistocles. 'Because three days ago I still believed that the westerners, the men of the Peloponnese, would fight; now I think that they will abandon us – perhaps they already have. So I agreed with Themistocles to make a different offer to you, and have peace.'

'You sell them to me?' Xerxes asked.

I raised my head more, and looked at him. 'No,' I said. 'They will betray themselves and you will take them.' It was the sort of defensive *they did it to themselves* crap I'd heard from other traitors.

'I think perhaps my cousin and my brother are mistaken in you,' Xerxes said. 'Take him outside where he cannot hear us. I will decide his fate later.'

I was pulled ungently to my feet and pushed out of the room. Diomedes stopped us under the portico by the simple expedient of standing in the way of my Sakje guards.

'Doru,' he said, almost caressing me with his voice, 'I will buy you from the Great King. Rest assured that I will.' He pursed his lips and leaned towards me. 'I will have you raped by my slaves, do you hear me? And then I'll feed your polluted corpse to pigs. That is what I promise you, Doru.'

As he spoke, the veneer of his urbanity peeled away and his spittle flecked my face, as hot as his hatred.

I'd like to say that I met his eyes calmly and snapped some retort – I've thought of many over the years – but age has granted me a little honesty, and I have to say that his words made me afraid – to die in so much shame, and be thought a traitor too?

But I managed to keep my head high. I made as if his words puzzled me, and the Sakje pushed me along.

'You are dead and defiled even now, Greek!' he shouted.

One of the Sakje said something to the other, and they both grunted.

As soon as we were clear of the main building, Brasidas flicked his eyes at me. 'Old friend?' he asked.

I was shaken, and trying hard not to show it. 'Yes,' I said.

'No talk!' the larger of the two Sakje said.

The next two hours were unmemorable, except that they were miserable. The Sakje didn't leave us, and did not allow us to talk. We could see and hear nothing of what went on inside Aristides' house, and we simply sat. I think I remember Brasidas going outside with one of the guards and relieving himself.

A troop of Immortals arrived up the back road that servants used for deliveries in happier times and began to replace the guards around the perimeter of the small estate. They did it with a great deal of talking and even some argument.

After they were done, an officer went into the house, and then the captains began to emerge. Each had a tail of one or two men, and it was ... instructive ... to observe them from so far that their comments could not be heard and they were, themselves, merely a sort of mime. They postured a fair amount, once all their flunkies were gathered. I wondered if I looked like this from a distance, if this was merely an ugly part of command. Perhaps this was what the vaunted Spartan discipline avoided.

I saw Diomedes gather a pair of hoplites, both in full armour, and by full I mean head-to-toe bronze, the kind I wore for serious fighting. He put his arms around them both like a port-side gang boss in Syracusa, and he spoke to them briefly, and then he came among the cook's garden – it filled the back of the house, and all these memories are touched with the scent of oregano.... Anyway, Diomedes came along the edge of the garden and walked up to the summer house and looked in. He called out to one of the Immortals who was still on guard, and the man pointed his spear at the shed.

Diomedes and his two soldiers came towards us. The Immortal headed back towards the alley behind the estate. The Great King was going, and taking his guards with him.

Diomedes would have no witnesses.

In Persian, I said to the older of the two Sakje men, 'This man is my enemy and means me harm.'

He looked at him, tilted his head to one side for a moment, and then shrugged.

I repeated myself, more slowly. This time I pointed at Diomedes for effect.

Diomedes stopped outside the shed door. It was propped open by a piece of wood – the axle of a chariot, I believe.

'Take him,' he said. He pointed to the two hoplites.

One began to push in.

I stepped back, and the older Sakje man raised his bow, drew it, and put the arrow in Diomedes' face. He said something. It was in his own barbaric tongue. Then, in Greek, he said, 'Away! Go!'

Diomedes had counted on force and effrontery. 'Just give him to me,' he said.

The younger Sakje put a bone whistle between his teeth and blew. Both hoplites froze.

Diomedes suddenly had a dagger in his hand. He didn't turn it on the Sakje, but suddenly thrust at me, holding the dagger like a sword.

I got both hands on his wrist, thumbs up. He leaned against me, pushing at the blade, and got my back against the shed wall.

But I got the arm against the shed wall and my body across it, and in one twist I had the dagger. I tossed it to Brasidas even as the rest of the Sakje wrenched open the door.

Diomedes raised his hands. He smiled at the five barbarians. 'Just a misunderstanding,' he said. He looked at me. 'I'll come back with enough marines to take care of the riff-raff,' he said. 'And then – oh, how I have longed for this, slave boy.'

He was going to say more, but the Sakje were angry and they all waved their bows. Two men drew again and put their arrowheads close to the Ionian hoplites' faces.

Diomedes walked away.

Brasidas and I tried to tell them of the danger for as long as it takes to put new tiles on a roof and perhaps longer. The sun began to set and the five Sakje pushed us back into our shed and slammed the door. Then they began a furious debate outside.

I had not been alone with Brasidas in hours. He showed me the dagger he'd concealed – the Sakje had either never seen it or lost track.

'We have to go now,' he said carefully. 'I use the dagger. You run.'

He was right, of course. First, he was, if only marginally, the better man with a weapon. With almost any weapon except a bow, or with no weapon at all. And second, we both knew that I was the one who needed to make it to the fleet – not Brasidas.

That didn't make it any better.

'I want—' I said. I'll never know what I wanted to say. I wasn't sure then, and I still don't know.

There was a sharp grunt and a low shriek outside, and then shouting, and then a bellow of rage.

I looked out.

Three of the Sakje were face down in the dust at the edge of Jocasta's garden with arrows in them, and the leader was kneeling with his back to me and aiming his bow.

Sometimes, to see is to act. I slammed my shoulder into the door and it flew open. It hadn't been locked or attached, but merely held with a bit of wood that turned on a copper nail. The door slapped into the Sakje leader and he went over and I was on him.

Because his bow arm – his left – was outflung, he fell that way, and I got my left arm in under his and around it in a joint lock then I pinned his arm back. He had to give it to me or have it broken, and I used it to put him face down. He tried to spin out, and he tried to get a leg between my legs.

I got my left hand on his neck when he tried to roll flat and kneed him hard in the guts when he tried to curl to me. Even as his free fist slammed into my left thigh – an agony of simple pain – mine went into his groin, and he was done.

The fifth man was nowhere to be seen. Brasidas came out warily, marked me, and came forward, knife out and ready. He knelt by my assailant. I put a hand on his wrist. Elation was stealing over me – I could see that the arrows were Ka's and his friends.

No need to kill the Sakje.

Before I could explain all this to Brasidas, Ka was dropping out of one of the olive trees. He loped towards us, head low, almost inhuman he was so low to the ground.

I grabbed his hand, right hand to right hand, and he surprised me by leaning in and embracing me, touching his forehead to mine.

'One got away,' he said.

'Allow this one to live,' I said.

Ka shrugged. He produced a rope, well decorated with pale blue glass beads and bright wool thread. He often wore it – I'd never seen him use it and I'd assumed it was a zone or belt. In fact, it turned out to be a rope for tying prisoners.

The Sakje man simply watched us, his eyes blank.

Ka pushed a gag made of a dead man's loincloth deep into the old Sakje's mouth. The man almost choked.

Ka nodded regretfully.

'Too soon, his friend find him, eh?' Ka said. 'Faster to kill.'

I shrugged. 'Perhaps,' I said.

We were gone in less time than it would take a man to sing a hymn, over the back wall, and along the back of the houses.

I am not sure I've ever been happier. No, I lie. I have been happier once or twice, and if you remain, I'll tell you about these good times, too. But by the gods, friends, I all but flew over the ground.

I was so sure I'd had it. Sure I was a dead man – shamed, degraded, and my memory blackened for ever. Pluton and Tyche, gods of good fortune, hear me: to this day, I praise you for my release.

The night was dark and silent. I had never known Athens so silent. There were fires on the Acropolis – there were troops there, apparently – and men were camped north of the city. But in among the estates of the rich, and the small rows of hovels and simple wattle houses where slaves and freed men lived, there was only silence. Dogs barked, angry, starving dogs, left by their masters. There were more rats than I'd ever seen in Athens and they moved constantly, drawing the eye.

I suppose we might have gone into Aristides' home and looked for the sword I'd been wearing, or my rings, or my clothes – or some secret writing of the Medes that would betray all their plans, but honestly, friends, all I wanted was *away*.

When we were well clear of the house, we worked our way along the edge of the cliff under the Pnyx. Then, using the Acropolis as a guide, we moved south. Ithy and Nemet joined us when we passed the Pnyx and crossed the open ground to the edge of the Keramiki. Then we ran, with me the slowest, constantly lagging. The Africans ran like champions and Brasidas ran – well, like a Spartan.

It took us three hours to work our way west and south, past the long walls, and onto the Megara road – the road to Eleusis that many called the Sacred Way.

It was full night when we came to the edge of the beach. There was a row boat, a light shell built for six oarsmen, and every spot was manned, bless them all, by good oarsmen off my ship. *Lydia* herself was just off the beach and we were aboard her ten minutes later and on the beaches of Salamis before another hour passed.

When we were all aboard, the lights of the Persian camps just visible on our left and the fires on the beach visible on the right, I turned to Seckla at the helm. 'How did you find me?' I asked him.

He shrugged. 'Ka followed you,' he said.

I looked at Ka.

Ka shrugged. 'This Siccinius,' he said. And shrugged. 'We don't trust him. So I follow you – yas. Yas!'

I do not, in fact, know what 'yas' means, but it is said for emphasis like 'heh', except more so.

'Last night you go to guard post? I follow. See you talk, move past temple. When Parsi and Medes move you, I follow.'

'Bless you, Ka.' I hugged him.

He laughed. 'Hah! It was easy – yas. Easier then hunting antelope, by *far*.' He smiled.

'You knew that was Aristides' house?' I said.

Ka frowned. 'I know Aristides,' he said. 'His house?'

Of course Ka had never been to his house. Who takes his head archer to parties?

Me, that's who. I was going to take Ka anywhere he wanted to go for a long time.

'You saved my life,' I said.

'And mine,' Brasidas said.

Ka smiled. 'I did, yas!' He grinned.

Seckla picked up the tale. 'Late last night he came back to the pentekonter. He told us what happened.' Seckla leaned over and spoke very quietly indeed. 'You know that the Medes let Siccinius go?'

'I know,' I said.

'They escorted him right to the guard posts,' he said. 'Ka stayed on him all the way and gave him the fright of his life as soon as he had him alone.'

I thought about that.

'I rowed him back to his master. He only told us that the Medes kept you as hostages. He said he tried to save you.' He looked at me in the darkness. We were lit by two oil lanterns in the stern and it was difficult to read a face.

I shrugged. 'He tried, as much as a slave tried to save anyone,' I said.

Brasidas raised an eyebrow, a very un-Spartan gesture he'd learned from us, I suspect. I think he had already decided at that point that Themistocles was a traitor. I wasn't sure.

I wasn't sure, but the evidence was building.

We landed on the Athenian beach, as close to the tents of the commanders as we could, although ships were all but wedged in there.

Seckla put our stern between two rocks and I hopped down, dry-shod, with Brasidas. Even from the beach we could hear that the 'council' was over-full. The murmur of voices and the shouts cut the dark air like Persian arrows, and they were so loud that the gulls that roosted on the point complained, which might have been the voice of the gods, for all I know.

We climbed the headlands into a melee of oratory.

One of the Peloponnesian trierarchs was talking, saying he had his ships laden and he was leaving in the morning, no matter what the council decided.

I looked for Themistocles, and found him near the speaker's rostrum, standing with Eurybiades. He wore the slight smile of the superior man.

I continued to watch him while first Phrynicus reviled the Corinthians as traitors – not, perhaps, the most politic speech, but Phrynicus, much as I love him, was a hothead. In fact, his heat made him the greatest playwright of his day. But he offended some waverers, and the Peloponnesians began to shout at the Athenians that they were a conquered people.

Still Themistocles smiled to himself. If anything, he looked bored, his eyes moving from one man to the next as if savouring their reactions.

I was careful to remain hidden.

Eumenes of Anagyrus spoke up, repeating, in effect, what other Athenians and Aeginians had said – that if the fleet broke up, the Great King would win.

Adeimantus watched Themistocles.

It was, by then, very late indeed. The oarsmen were, one hoped, asleep. But here were two hundred captains, bellowing like fishwives, screeching, and twice there were blows given.

For perhaps the hundredth time that autumn, I considered leaving. My town was already burned. I had property in Massalia, and I could trade tin and marry a buxom Keltoi girl or keep five for my pleasure.

But I wanted two things. I wanted to beat the Great King, because he had humiliated me, and because he meant to humiliate Greece, and because, to be honest, I was a man of Marathon and I had tasted the fruit of the gods in that victory and I wanted it again. And because I wanted Briseis, and she had called me to her, and the road to her lay through the Great King's fleet.

And I had escaped. They had had me, the Persians and Medes. My escape seemed to me a sign from Heracles, my ancestor, that I should fight. By Zeus, I have always taken omens as signs I should fight, I confess it. But why free me to die an empty death, or flee to some forgotten grave in Gaul?

So the real question was how to make sure that the fleet fought and didn't run. I knew that it came down to men – a few men. Really, it came down to two men – Adeimantus and Themistocles. Perhaps Eurybiades, but I thought him both sound and just. Adeimantus I thought a traitor, although I never heard a word from Mardonius or any of the Medes to suggest that he was. But he had just sixty triremes.

Themistocles – was he a traitor? Or was he playing *both* sides for his own profit? Did he, in fact, even have a plan?

I made my decision. It depended on Eurybiades. I suppose it says something about me, and the situation, that when the dice were thrown, I trusted a Spartan. I said a few words to Brasidas and the Spartan nodded and went off to my right, into the crowd.

I walked around the outside of the council fire and moved cautiously through the crowd of Athenian captains behind the great man. Ameinias of Pallene recognised me, as did Cleitus. Both started.

I pulled my chlamys over my head. Ameinias shrugged.

Cleitus stepped closer. He was tense; his entire body conveyed his tension, so that my body reacted as if he was about to attack me. I didn't believe he would, but such were our feelings for each other.

'Where have you been?' he hissed, an odd greeting from a sworn enemy. And in this case, 'sworn enemy' is not an empty phrase. He had sworn my death to Olympian Zeus. 'Everyone is looking for you!'

That told me a great deal. It told me, unless Cleitus was lying, that Themistocles had kept my capture a secret. To cover his own treason?

I still don't know.

'I need to get to Themistocles,' I said. 'Victory and death depend on it.'

Hate is akin to love, all the poets say it. Men who truly hate, men who have gone word to word and sword to sword, can know each other like lovers, or be as ignorant as fools. These are the only ways to hate, and Cleitus and I knew each other so well ... He looked into my eyes by firelight and then he turned without a word and began shoving men out of my way.

Just at that moment, I forgot that he was the engine of my mother's death and saw that he put Greece before his enmity.

Then I followed him. He burrowed through the retainers, the captains, the desperate men. Off to the left, I saw Siccinius and he saw me, despite my filthy chiton and the chlamys over my head like a beaten slave. His eyes grew wide and he started for his master.

But he was too late. And Cleitus, as if he was my partner and not my adversary, stepped past Themistocles, blocking his view of the council and forcing him to turn by the sort of pressure you exert when you put a hand in a man's face and make him be silent without speaking.

Themistocles turned and saw me. His expression flickered. In that moment, I tried to read him – and failed. There was no open hostility, no guile, no obvious guilt.

Just that flicker of change, as if, for a moment, he was several different men.

Quietly, I spoke to him, leaning my head close. 'My friend,' I said, 'I have just come from the Great King. We can talk here, if you like, or in private.'

Cleitus couldn't help but hear the words 'Great King'. Again, our eyes met. What passed then?

Both of us made decisions, that's what passed.

Themistocles sighed. 'Always I am at your service, brave Arimnestos,' he said. 'Let us hold a private parley.'

I took his hand like a maiden leading a man to a dance, and I would not let go of it. I pulled him free of the crowd, and when men began to follow, Cleitus – Cleitus! – bade them go back to the council.

But Cleitus himself followed us under an old oak tree by the sacred well. There was a stone bench there and I sat. Themistocles sat. Cleitus leaned against the tree.

'Your plan is working perfectly,' I said. 'Even now, the Great King's ships are loading their rowers. They are on the way.'

Cleitus folded his arms, but his right hand was close to the hilt of the small, Spartan-style xiphos he wore under his left arm.

'My plan?' Themistocles asked.

'Your plan to force the Greek fleet to fight by luring the Persians into the bay,' I said. 'In an hour, they will be at sea.'

The skin around Cleitus's eyes tightened. Crow's feet appeared at the corners of his eyes. He was a brilliant man – I think he understood *everything*.

Themistocles sat very still. 'What – how – how do you know?' he asked.

'Brasidas and I have just escaped from the Great King,' I said. 'We escorted a certain slave to the Great King himself, and he took us prisoners. Hostages.'

'I knew nothing of this!' he said suddenly. He was lying, and it was a foolish lie, but Themistocles was such an able politician and so contemptuous of other men's minds that he thought – and perhaps he was right – that anything my friends said after the fact would be forgotten.

I shrugged. 'It is true. Not a few hours ago, I lay on my face before the Great King while his commanders discussed their attack and a spear was pressed into my neck.'

'This is – incredible!' Themistocles said.

I almost hit him.

His hands were shaking.

Let me pause here, on the edge of saving Greece, and say again: I think he was as guilty as an adulterer caught in the act. So why not expose him?

Think about it. If I exposed him, who would fight? The Athenians would shatter instantly into pro- and anti-Themistoklean factions. What? You think the democrats and the oarsmen would convict him out of hand? You must be joking. Facts? There were no facts. It was all intuition and supposition. Heraclitus did not train me to think for nothing. The only hope for Greece was to pretend that Themistocles had all along planned to force the Greek fleet to fight. Perhaps it was even true.

Perhaps he intended the Greek fleet to cut and run – into the closing jaws of the Persians. Perhaps he imagined that the Corinthians and Peloponnesians would be caught and destroyed piecemeal, leaving Athens and Aegina in a powerful bargaining position and making his position tenable.

It makes my head hurt.

'The Persians will be at sea any moment,' I said. 'It's time to reveal this to the fleet, so that we can prepare. To fight.'

Themistocles allowed his eyes to meet mine. He was searching me. I knew, just the way a girl knows when a man is looking at her breasts and not into her eyes. He wanted to know what I knew.

Cleitus tugged at his beard. 'Reveal what?' he asked.

Themistocles stiffened, and then rose to his feet. 'I have a plan to save Greece,' he said portentously.

Well, whatever else might have been true, from that moment he bent his will to save Greece.

The gods play a role in most affairs of men, so it will not surprise you that they had some part in that night. The first was probably my rescue by Ka, but the most vital was to come. We were walking back to the council, which was still loud. My friend Lykon was speaking, promising the men of Athens that Adeimantus did not speak for all Corinthians. We were twenty paces from the firelight, near the outer ring of listeners where men stood to piss against the trees and slaves waited with wine skins. Out of the darkness came Aristides.

'Themistocles,' he said.

'Aristides,' the democrat answered.

If I wanted to know what Cleitus and I looked like when speaking to one another, here it was – a tableau of mutual antipathy. Yet they had worked together from the first for the liberation of Greece. If I was correct, Themistocles had changed his mind or given up. But Aristides had not.

'We are surrounded,' Aristides said. 'Do you know?'

'Surrounded?' Themistocles asked.

Aristides nodded. Behind him, two of his slaves held torches. 'I left my *Nike* back on Aegina,' he said. 'I came with a pair of Aeginian triremes carrying sacred statues of their gods. Aeginian fishing boats reported to us after sunset.' He looked around. Cleitus stepped closer, and other men began to gather; Cimon was there, and Xanthippus too. It was Aristides' voice gathering them, his friends and his enemies too.

'The entire Persian fleet is at sea,' he said. 'The beaches at Phaleron must be empty. We came through the Egyptians. We were challenged repeatedly, but one of my oarsmen speaks Egyptian and Persian as well.' He shrugged.

Themistocles gave a false laugh. 'Ah, Aristides, we may be adversaries, but you are the man to appreciate my cleverness. I have brought the Persians.'

'You?' Aristides asked.

'I sent for them,' Themistocles joked. He looked at me. 'Ask Arimnestos.'

Oh, he was clever. Aristides would never believe I was involved in a treason plot. Themistocles had just played me – again.

I could not allow myself to care. This was for everything. 'Now we have to fight,' I said.

Themistocles took Aristides by the hand. 'You saw the Medes?'

'Medes, Persians, Phoenicians and Egyptians, and far too many Greeks,' Aristides said.

Themistocles pumped his hand. 'You must tell the council. No one will believe me. But all know how you hate me – you will be believed.'

'Say rather that I will be believed because I do not make a habit of telling lies,' Aristides said. It was true and false, too – Greeks have a foolish habit of believing men that they would like to be telling the truth, rather than those they know to be honest.

Themistocles winced but did not let go of my friend's hand.

Cleitus came up behind me, and very softly said, 'What in the name of black Tartarus is going on?' he growled.

'We're saving Greece from the barbarians,' I said.

Cleitus laughed. 'Not the first time,' he said.

I roared with laughter. Men turned, and saw me laughing, and before the gods, I embraced the bastard. 'Too right, mate,' I said.

He returned the embrace and Aristides smiled in the torchlight.

'If those two can be at peace,' he said, 'I will make peace with you. And it is only the truth, after all. Take me to the council.'

So it was that Themistocles, the arch-democrat, led Aristides the Just, the priggish, snobbish arch-conservative and my best friend, to the rostra in front of three hundred captains. It was deep in the night.

Themistocles pointed to the man standing ready to speak.

'There is my nemesis, Aristides, returned from exile to speak to the captains,' he said. 'Pay heed, and know that I support his every word.'

Aristides looked around. His eye met mine, and then passed over – he was never a man to wink. He was silent for long enough that men coughed and the silence became edgy.

'The Persian fleet is already at sea,' he said softly. 'They are all around us. They have ships on the beaches opposite us to the north, and they have sent a squadron to close the western passages to the isthmus.'

Now the silence was absolute.

'There is no longer a choice to be made,' he said. 'I will argue nothing. Unless you choose to submit and be slaves, we must fight.'

The silence stayed, and then a babble began, the usual Greek game of finding whose fault it must have been, might have been. It rose all about us, and then Eurybiades struck the speaker's rostra with his staff – I remember the sound like a thunderbolt.

'Are you children?' he asked.

He was going to say more, and Themistocles stepped past him into the firelight. 'I have a plan,' he began.

'Silence, or I strike,' Eurybiades said, raising his stick. He was angry, as any commander would have been.

'Strike, but only listen,' Themistocles begged. He actually *bent his knee* like a beggar requesting alms.

Zeus, it was a masterful performance.

There stood the Spartan, stick raised, and there the Athenian knelt before him in supplication.

'Speak,' growled the Spartan.

Themistocles leapt to his feet. 'The Persians think this is a land battle,' he said. 'They think that having their right overmatch our left will lead them to collapse us. They imagine that we will fight with our lines spread east to west. They don't know the waters, and their ships will have been at sea all night, their hulls damp, men tired. *We can win.*'

Say what you will – and I have – once he was committed, he was brilliant. I saw it immediately. Other men had to be convinced; some had to hear the whole thing two or three times, and all the while Eurybiades was sending the lesser men to bed, and ordering heralds to wake the rowers an hour before sunrise.

It was not in any way my plan, although in its relation I knew that my words had played a part. Certainly Themistocles planned to use the dawn chop and the breeze, but his notion that we could form the trap by backing water, despite having inflicted two defeats this way at Artemisium, was entirely his own. He told them that the Great King expected the treason of whole bodies of Greeks and thus would expect us to flee.

Well. I still had an eye on the Corinthians.

But it was a good plan, simple enough, with the flexibility so that if the weather went our way, he'd make use of it, and if the day was calm, we had alternatives.

Aristides, without a ship, as his beautiful *Athena Nike* was still being repaired, added a wrinkle. We had far more hoplites than we could fit on ships. Aristides was given command of all the hoplites left on Salamis. He said he would attempt to take the two islets in the middle of the straits. Neither is very considerable, but the larger is big enough for a thousand men to stand in formation and archers on that island would be able to wreck our centre. We gave him all the pentekonter and all the fishing boats.

In fact, once the decision was made to fight, we moved along at a great rate. I want to say that it was Eurybiades who decided to fight. He never called for another vote. Perhaps he thought it was obvious or perhaps he was tired of oratory. I know I was.

We trudged back to our camp and I laid out my panoply and woke two of my slaves to shine it. I planned to wear the whole thing – shin guards and thigh guards and arm guards and everything. To shine like a god. Because in war, these things matter.

And then I rolled in my cloak and went to sleep without another thought.

Part II

The Razor's Edge

When all Greece was balanced on the razor's edge
we protected her with our souls, and here we lie

Cenotaph to the dead of Salamis

I woke from a dream so erotic that I might have been on the point of an indiscretion, and pondered what the gods meant by sending me a dream of making love to Jocasta, for whom I had infinite respect but towards whom I had never felt the least attraction. But my waking mind found the notion humorous, and I rolled out of my cloak looking more like a satyr than a man and threw myself into the sea. I dried myself with my linens in the darkness and woke Seckla, and all around me men blew life into campfires.

I sent Hipponax up the ridge to see what could be seen from our watchtowers, and I walked along the beach until I was sure that the Athenians were in motion. Xanthippus was civil enough and already in his armour, while I was still naked and my hair wet from my swim, but I felt better for it, and better still when Hector put a horn cup of mulled wine in my hand.

The first kiss of dawn touched the sky and I put on my best chiton, milk-white wool with purple stripes and red embroidery, ravens and stars. Then I put on the leather straps that went around my ankles to protect them from the slap of the greaves against my instep, and then I snapped the greaves over my shins, cursing the way they cut into every old wound and new scratch from my last outing. Hector knelt behind me and buckled them on, and then he put armour on my left thigh – the thigh most likely to be hit. Sometimes I wear armour on both, but usually I do not.

Then he hinged open my beautiful bronze thorax that Anaxicles had hammered out of new bronze back in Syracusa, what seemed like many years before. He closed it and slid the pins shut, slipped the arm guard on my right forearm and the shoulder guard on my right shoulder. No man needs a guard on his left shoulder or forearm – that's what the aspis covers.

Many men were gathered there. It was like a ceremony and a festival, too. I was Achilles being armed, or Ares, or mighty Ajax or Diomedes, or one of the Immortals or the heroes, and the dawn gilded my bronze and made it glow red, as if I'd spilled a fiery immortal blood. Hector brought my helmet and Hipponax, back from his mission and looking furtive for some reason, reported that the Peloponnesians were already arrayed and putting rowers into their ships, and also reported, somewhat unnecessarily, that the Brauron girls were awake and singing hymns. He put my aspis on my arm, and then he and Hector armed together. Brasidas came out of his tent armed, and Idomeneus, who looked more like a god than any, with his perfect body and shining bronze and his old-fashioned high crest nodding like Hector's in Iliad. And Achilles' namesake, my cousin, did us no disgrace, despite his recent wound and his surly ways, but he ran down from the upper beach fully armed, and his bronze also lit up in the new sun.

But against our bronze, most of the rowers were naked, or wore loincloths. But the top-deck rowers on *Lydia* had helmets and thorax of captured Persian linen, stitched tight and hard with embroidery, or quilted, or beautiful leather spolas taken off Ionian ships, or tawed leather yokes made in Athens or Massalia, and spears. A few even sported swords, or axes, or little maces with bronze heads. They watched us arm, as if our bronze plate protected them as well as us – and I like to think it did.

When we were all together, as far as I could see – the marines in neat rows, and Leukas and Onisandros and Polymarchos, standing with Sittonax, the laziest deadly fighter I knew, my old Gaulish friend and my old sparring mate and newest marine – then our ship's dog condescended to join us, running down the beach. He ran to me with a live rabbit still breathing in his mouth. I gentled him, gave him a hug and a long pat and beckoned Hector to give the dog a sausage, which he clearly craved. But the rabbit was from the gods and I slit its throat, as much a mercy as a sacrifice, and opened it over the fire.

'Victory!' I roared, before I had even glanced at its entrails. But the liver was whole and spotless – not all that usual with rabbits, let me tell you. I am no great diviner, but that rabbit was sent by Zeus and told me we would win.

My people cheered and cheered and the men on other ships began to cheer, and the cliff above us echoed hollowly, as if the gods were shouting approval.

One of our Gaulish wine barrels was open and Onisandros was serving a cup of wine to every man. I leapt on it.

'*Lydia!*' I said.

They all froze.

'Listen, brothers!' I called. 'Many times before today, I have heard men argue whether the hoplites or the rowers would save Greece.' I paused.

By the gods, it was quiet.

'I tell you, we will only save Greece together. I tell you, today, any man who pulls an oar against the Medes is my brother, a descendent of Heracles, noble in his birth, free to walk the earth and defy his foes. I say that this is our hour, when the world will decide if indeed we are worthy of that freedom our fathers won. I say that those who die today will go with Hector and Achilles and the dead of Marathon, even if they were born of slaves and were themselves unfree, and those who live today having done their duty will be remembered as long as free men in any country walk under the stars. And as I make every one of you noble sons of Heracles, then every one of you must want nothing better than to die in arms, or live victorious. For I promise you, brothers, I will not leave the field today alive and beaten. If Greece, free, is a dream, I will die today, still dreaming. Will you, my friends, be my brothers?'

Zeus, the noise they made. I was carried away – I was already with the gods and Athena said those words in my ear, yet even as their cheers rang like the voice of Poseidon echoing from the cliffs over my head, I heard a curiously high-pitched cheer from close at hand.

I remembered it later.

Themistocles held one last meeting. I confess that I think the man loved a council, where his particular merits shone forth at their best. Or perhaps he just liked to talk.

It was greater than just a council, because he had there most of the trierarchs and navarchs, but also many of the helmsmen and marines, both captains and famous men. No one was forbidden to attend. The sun was not yet fully in the sky when he made his speech, and Eurybiades did nothing but bid us to hold our places, to back water when ordered and not break the line.

I felt that Eurybiades' speech was more to the point.

But I'll give Themistocles this, he was calm, dignified, and when he said we were assured of victory, he looked the part of a general.

He gathered two dozen commanders as the marines and helmsmen ran for their ships. The morning breeze was stiffening to a wind, and we could see the Persian army marching along the roads opposite us, under the slopes of Mount Aigeleos.

But between us and the Great King's army lay one of the most awesome spectacles I have ever seen. The breeze was stiffening to a wind, but over the Bay of Salamis a morning fog lay. It clung to the water like smoke clings to the sacrifice on the altar, and the Persian fleet, their masts down, was only visible in the same way that a sharp-eyed hunter might spot a herd of deer on a foggy morning: by movement, and by fleeting gaps in the haze.

But even with these disadvantages to sight, from our eminence we could see that the Persians had moved silently past the island Psyttaleia and that the island itself was crawling with Persian troops. They were moving to encircle our beaches – indeed, had almost done so already.

Aristides nodded, tall and godlike in his panoply. 'We'll take the island,' he said.

'Not until I give the signal,' Eurybiades said. 'The Persians want a sea battle like a land battle?' he asked. He didn't smile or grin – that was not the Laconian way. But he exuded a steady confidence. 'I will give them a battle that will remind them what is sea, what is land, and what is merely air.'

Then he ordered the Aeginians to stay fully armed and ready to launch, bows out, on their beaches, covered by Aristides and his hoplites and the Athenian corps of four hundred archers – enough skilled bowman to clear the decks of five ships in a single mighty volley.

'Circumstances have changed, but not so much,' he said. 'Note how far their lead group has advanced,' he said, pointing.

Cimon spoke up. 'Phoenicians,' he said, looking under his hand. 'I'd wager my life on it. Almost to Eleusis.'

'You may have done,' Eurybiades said. 'You, Cimon – and you, Plataean – will take your ships off the beaches and bear away west, as if fleeing. Xanthippus, you will follow them.' He nodded. 'When you see the gold shield flash you will engage, and not before. Every stade you can make on them westward that allows you to turn the battle back to the east will be the better for us.'

Men looked confused. 'You want us to fish-hook to the west and drive back east on your command,' I said.

'Exactly,' he said.

'Lade in reverse,' Cimon said cheerfully. 'We'll remind the Phoenicians of how well they fought there.'

'The Corinthians will face east against the Egyptians, in case they weather the island and approach from the west. I have sacrificed and prayed that they may not, as then the Corinthians will be our reserve.' Eurybiades waited, as there was a babble of complaint. He rode it out with his impassivity. 'You will not advance until I send a pentekonter for you.'

Adeimantus nodded, pleased, I think, to be held back from the fighting.

He looked at Themistocles. The wily Athenian nodded, as if they'd planned the whole talk like a play, each with his part. Perhaps they had. Themistocles, at least, was committed. No one now talked of surrender or flight. Even Adeimantus – I wish to give the slug his due – was armoured, alert, and committed.

'What we must do, in the first minutes of the action, is turn the battle,' he said. He pointed out over the straits.

Below us on the beaches, men were restless. Helmsmen shouted up at us, as if they thought we were not aware of how close the Persians were. It takes strong nerves to talk to your officers in the very face of the enemy, but it also wins battles. Eurybiades was such a man. He seemed as calm as a man about to go hunt hares, or have a walk in his vineyard.

Themistocles went on. 'The Persians intend to fight with their line from east to west,' he said. 'We will turn them and force them to fight with their backs to the straits, and a north-south axis.'

We could see that even as the Persian ships deployed, more ships were passing behind the lead divisions. To my eye it looked as if they'd left themselves too little margin for error, too little rowing room.

And I liked our plan.

I'd heard it in the early hours of the morning. I knew the plan, and I liked it. And I liked that we would start with three of our largest squadrons apparently running west for open water along the coast – deserting. Just as the Persians expected.

'Not until I raise the gold shield,' Eurybiades said.

I nodded, and so did Cimon. I assume the rest of the navarchs nodded as well.

'Let's do this thing,' Eurybiades said.

'Remember,' Themistocles began, but the older Spartan cut him off.

'The time for talking is done,' he said, mildly enough. 'Now, we fight.'

As we walked away, Adeimantus remarked, as if to the air, 'The old Spartan knows who he can trust! The Corinthians have the place of honour, in reserve – the balance of the battle.'

Cimon ignored him.

I managed a smile. 'You know, Adeimantus, I have been in forty or so fights, and no one has ever once suggested that I be in reserve.'

He flushed, Cimon laughed, and several men patted me on the back.

I do get in a good thing from time to time.

The fog still lay over the bay, although it was burning off. The sea smelled beautiful and the breeze was almost a wind – more wind, in fact, than any captain wanted for a sea fight. It made our launching off the beaches tricky, to say the least, catching us broadside the moment the bow anchor-stones came in and threatening every ship with being laid broadside in a light surf. But we didn't have any trierarchs – or helmsmen – so inexperienced.

We launched well enough, but we were ragged getting into formation and Xanthippus's helmsman cursed Seckla like a man buying a bad horse in the agora, and his imprecations carried across the water. Strangely, we could hear the Persians, too, even with the thigh-high waves – nothing for a sailor to fear, but unusual in the bay.

My ships came off the beach. I only had four, *Lydia* included: Harpagos in *Storm Cutter*, Moire in *Amastris,* Giannis and Megakles in *Black Raven. Athena Nike* lay useless, her bows stove in, on the beach of Aegina to the south. My other ships were now crewed by Athenian citizens and not Plataeans. Ah, I lie. I had five – *Naiad* of Mithymna, my capture turned 'free Greek'. I left Theognis as the helmsman, but I sent away half of his marines, and replaced them with young Pericles, with his father's permission, and Anaxagoras, and a captain, a Spartiate provided by Bulis, named Philokles. It was the only ship with an 'allied' crew; I added twenty of my Plataean rowers and took twenty men of Lesvos aboard *Lydia.* But I still didn't trust *Naiad* in the first line, and I told Harpagos and Moire to keep eyes on her. Had Aristides not taken command of the hoplites, I'd have offered him the command.

But four ships or five, it wasn't the sort of fight where I was needed to tell my captains what to do. My duty was simple: to follow Cimon, to row as far west as I could manage; and then to obey the signal.

There's something every sailor and every oarsman loves about duplicity. Perhaps it is the touch of the criminal in every man, but all our lives we're told to avoid duplicity, to be honest – and then, when you are told that it is your duty to act a part and deceive your enemies, it can be great fun. I promise you, as our ragged line, a column of triremes three wide and thirty or more ships long, raced west under oars, I heard an oarsman grunt 'We'll be at the isthmus in no time, mates!' and another pretend to weep from fear. It was not, perhaps, good enough for Dionysus and Aeschylus, but I promise you that our ill-kept column that scattered over a third of the bay to the west would have convinced anyone we were fleeing in panic.

The problem was that the Persians couldn't see us very well. They could *hear* that something was up, but they couldn't see.

We kept rowing west, along the beaches of Salamis. The Corinthians were off, now – I passed Lykon, just coming off the beach, and I waved. The bay was full of men I knew. But visibility was a stade or a little more, and while I could see Cimon on his helm-deck just ahead, I couldn't be positive that the ship two behind me was Ameinias of Pallene in *Parthenos,* although I was fairly sure.

Every stade gained of westering was good.

Behind us, someone began to sing the paean. I've heard dozens of suggestions – some say it was the Athenians behind us, under Themistocles, some say it was Aristides and the hoplites, and some say it was the Aeginians. It didn't fit with our deceptive plan – in fact, had the Persians only known us, they'd have known when they heard the paean that we meant to fight, and indeed, I heard years later from Artemisia that all the Ionians knew what was up as soon as they heard it.

This too had an effect on the battle, as the Ionians began to deploy out of their columns into their battle lines, facing neither east–west nor north–south, but about halfway between, and opening a large gap between their own westernmost division, led by the ships of Ephesus and Samos, and the Phoenicians who had the vanguard of their fleet and were already level with the town of Eleusis.

What we didn't know yet was that the Great King himself had set his throne on the cliffs below Mount Aigeleos and was watching, and that every contingent in the Persian fleet knew that he was watching. The Phoenicians had been defeated by us several times

– badly handled at Artemisium – and the presence of the Great King stiffened their spines and put them on their honour, if they have any. They were in the lead, the vanguard, and they were determined to be aggressive. After half an hour of listening to the muffled sounds we made with our oars and our shouting getting off our beaches, they heard the paean, and determined to attack. But – and this is important – they were determined to attack in their new manoeuvre, and they came forward in long columns, so that every captain, in turn, could find a hole in our dispositions and break through. This Phoenician tactic – I've spoken of it other nights – was called by us diekplous. The captain of the lead ship looked for an opening – like the break in a dam, or the hole in a bridge – and he shot for it with all his speed, passing through the gap, raking the oars of ships on either side, and then wheeling rapidly into a flank if he could, with his mates crowding in behind.

At Artemisium we'd solved this dilemma two ways. In the first fight we formed a great wheel, our hulls so close that we left them no gap through which to exploit us. And in the second fight we were so practised that by backing water we kept our lines closed, and when we attacked, it was we, not they, who exploited errors in their formation.

I was not a great navarch at Artemisium and even less so at Salamis, but I suspected – and now I am sure – that the greatness of the Phoenician fleet was past, possibly gone in the constant drain of their best captains throughout the long years of the struggle for the Ionian and Aeolian cities. While the Great King triumphed in the Ionian Revolt, Phoenicia suffered in every battle – twenty ships here, forty ships there. I am going to guess that there comes a point in the loss of your best captains when you cannot easily recover all that skill.

It was not that the Phoenicians were bad sailors or fighters. It was merely that they had fallen from being *the best*. But they clung to a set of tactics that had been developed for aggressive, trained trierarchs and superb helmsmen who had long experience of each other and their enemy, and they tried to use it in a choppy sea, against an enemy line they couldn't make out in the fog.

Remember that there was a stiff breeze blowing, although already, an hour after sunrise, it was dying away. Remember that it brought a choppiness to the bay that none of us had really anticipated. And remember that they had been up all night.

I thought all of these things as I listened and watched to my starboard side, to the north. I heard a horn, and another. There was shouting.

Then I saw a sight that burned itself on my eyes like a view of a god. Two images I can summon in the eye of the mind at will – Briseis's naked body the first time I saw her undress in Ephesus, and this.

The morning haze *flashed*.

And then, again. *Flash*.

Flash.

Flash.

It was – unearthly.

And then, suddenly, the flashes were everywhere, like a line of fire when peasants and slaves burn the weeds out of the fields.

And then, Poseidon! – a line of bows began to emerge from the haze – a line of ram bows that seemed to fill the whole of my eye, and the *flash* was the sun shining on their oars, carried into the fog. All the oars moved together on each ship, and there were dozens, hundreds of ships, like a swarm of fireflies at nightfall. *And these were just the leaders of their columns.*

I have never seen anything to match it, except Briseis.

And they were coming at our naked flank, out of the fog, at ramming speed.

Behind me, someone quicker witted or with a better sight line had already turned out of the line, 'fleeing' west.

He had the right notion, whoever he was. We had no sea room to back water, and we might have outrun the Persians to the west, but we couldn't guarantee it.

The man who turned out of the line without orders was Ameinias of Pallene.

Well, I never said I was a Spartan, either. I followed him.

'Hard to starboard! Ramming speed as soon as she's round,' I called.

Seckla nodded. I remember that he used the lean of the ship's hull to spit over the side. The starboard-side rowers reversed benches smoothly, gave two hard strokes, and reversed again. Hah! I had never commanded such a vessel with such men. She was dry and light as air and rowed by Argonauts.

We went round faster than I can tell it. The heads of the Phoenician columns were flying at us out of the fog, but Moire was with me immediately. Harpagos followed me, and Giannis followed Moire, and *Naiad* came after, so we were a compact squadron of five, and when we went, the entire 'western' Athenian division turned, almost as one, column into line, and in pretty good order, with Ameinias leading a compact wedge on the leftmost flank. Cimon in *Ajax* was less than a ship's length behind me, perhaps half a stade to the west, and four of his ships were beyond him, off to the west.

We turned from a mob fleeing west to a line abreast racing north in a few beats of a calm man's heart, and even at ramming speed the trierarchs and the helmsmen were adjusting their places. We were not in three crisp lines, but rather in a series of compact squadrons as helmsmen closed up tight to ships they trusted.

I remember that I paused, waved to Cimon, and then clapped Seckla on the shoulder. He'd already chosen his first target.

I was merely an elderly marine. He smiled, I smiled, and then I was running forward.

From the bow, I could see the backs of my ten marines and my three archers. And I could see the Phoenicians coming down on us. They were flat out, at the full ramming speed you need to get an instant ship-kill. But they were widely spaced because of their columns, and there were curious gaps between ships – just to the east of me, there was a gap two or three stades wide before the rest of the Phoenician fleet, the Ionians, who'd formed a more traditional line, could be seen. The sun was now burning off the haze rapidly.

My heart beat very fast. I shouted.

It was sheer exuberance. They were scattered over the whole bay east of our beaches and their formation was terrible. The night, the breeze and the fog and their own ambition had not been kind. Or rather, the gods had been kind to us.

Only treason, the treason of Lade and every other great battle against the Persians, only treason or lack of will would save them.

Oh, Poseidon, my heart beat like a hammer, and I was under no threat. The opportunity was there, if only we could grasp it.

Ameinias of Pallene's ship was first to strike an enemy. I was very close, maybe a hundred paces away. His helmsman yawed and then turned suddenly back into line, as fast as the stoop of an eagle. He caught the Phoenician a third of the way down the side. The enemy ship had its oars in and the angle was too shallow for Ameinias's beak to bite home, but he jarred the enemy ship, ripped a strip along the side, and grappled.

The Phoenician behind him – second in the column – came forward full speed. Unlike at Artemisium, their files were well closed up, close enough to support each other, but also close enough to be enveloped. The second Phoenician drove for the bow of Ameinias's ship *Parthenos*, turning slightly to the east to get a better angle.

I trusted everything to Harpagos. There was a Phoenician bearing down on me for a bow-to-bow attack from their next column, so I ran back along the catwalk over the forward oars, and back along the half-deck. I was not going to be in time, and running has not been the best of my talents since the wound, so I merely pointed at the other Phoenician, the one running at Ameinias's flank.

Seckla bet with me, on Harpagos saving us, and *Lydia* turned a few degrees, perhaps an eighth of a circle, to point at the place where Seckla guessed that the Phoenician would be, in the time it would take a good man to run the stadion.

I can only describe this in terms of bronzeworking. When you make greaves, with all the intricate curves of the human leg, you can only guess how to hit the metal so that it curves in two ways. You cannot *know*. Seckla had to aim where the Phoenician *might* be, while his flanker came for us, and we trusted Harpagos to take him.

To my port side aft, I heard Harpagos roar an order.

His crew pulled *harder*.

He was at ramming speed, and he got them to *row faster*.

It is hard to describe what happened without some almonds and a big table. But let me try.

We were turning to our starboard side – not far, but enough to become the hypotenuse of a triangle. The Phoenician opposite us kept coming, but had to turn off his intended line, too.

Harpagos, who had been so close behind us that we might have leapt from ship to ship, began to pass us.

Onisandros, at my urging, let the men rest for three strokes. Let me add that only the finest oarsmen can do this. Most ships can only go from a crawl to cruising speed, and from cruising speed to ramming speed, with time for the stroke to change. But a really good ship with rowers and officers long together can stop and start rowing at almost any speed. Remember, friends, that any hesitation by an oarsman can mean death: if he catches a crab at ramming speed, he's going to get his oar shaft in his teeth at least, and he may do the same to other men.

We drifted at top speed for the time it would take a man to leave his house and call to his wife.

Harpagos went straight at the Phoenician who came straight for us.

'Now!' I called.

Onisandros began to pound his spear on the deck.

We shot forward.

'We have to bring in the port-side oars,' Onisandros shouted.

'No! Everything you have!' I roared.

Off to starboard, Ameinias's marines were storming along the narrow catwalk above the Phoenician's rowers.

The Phoenician headed for his flank was so close ...

We slammed into his cathead, and before you could count to five, Harpagos's beak went into the second about fifty paces before his beak slammed into me. Thus, the margin between victory and defeat.

Ameinias's oarsmen were cheering us. Our Phoenician broke in two as our oars came in – we hit him so hard that our ram scraped paint off *Parthenos*.

On my port bow, Harpagos's marines, all men I knew, were going into the third Phoenician. I had no idea how the rest of the battle was going, but within a hundred paces of me we were winning.

Their third ships were coming up, but so were ours, and Cimon led his ships in from the west. The gods – and good fortune, and good planning, and strong rowing, had put us just off their western flank, and now, like sharks closing for the kill, Cimon's veterans came into the flank of the oncoming Phoenician charge and scattered them. They had to turn to meet his attacks, and then we were free. Seckla, without orders from me, turned us back west, where a dozen Phoenicians were going head-to-head with Cimon's ships – and exposing their flanks to us.

It was glorious.

We sank a second ship, catching him flat-footed, trying to face in two directions at once.

We ran down the side of a third, coming up from behind his stern – I can't remember how we lay, or how we got there – it was too fast. The marines leapt before the ships touched, so eager they were, and I followed them, the last man aboard, which felt odd. But I leapt aboard amidships, my old trick, right in among their rowers. I got a foot on each of the beams nearest me and killed the two oarsmen closest and then stabbed up at the catwalk, putting my spear into the legs and feet of the Phoenician marines. I watched Hector go forward like a man ploughing a field, and his spear was like one of the thunderbolts of the Lord of Olympus. He was not a big man like Hipponax, but lithe and so quick that each step forward seemed to baffle his opponents, and he gathered himself so that he seemed to sway side to side like a maiden walking in the marketplace, except that each sway was a deception, and his spear always struck home – left foot forward, right foot forward, a brilliant series of strokes, each delivered with the fastidious precision of a cat and the power of Ares come to earth.

I was so proud.

Behind him came Hipponax, who threw his spear to give Hector room to breathe and got another handed over his shoulder from Brasidas, who was third.

With such marines as these, what need of me?

I contented myself with tripping the men behind the men my Hector was killing, and in a moment – a moment of pure glory – the survivors broke and fled for the false safety of the stern, where they threw down their weapons and begged mercy.

They were lucky they were facing me and Brasidas and men we had trained. There was not much mercy for the Great King's looters and rapists that day, but we gave it, perhaps because our hearts were high and perhaps because we'd stormed their ship without a man lost or a single wound.

I gave the ship to Hector to get it to the Greek beaches, and gave him two sailors to help him. We disarmed the marines and put them to the row benches, and then we were cutting our grapple-ropes and poling off.

Brasidas was the last man off the enemy vessel. He told them in good Persian that if they rose against Hector, we would capture them again and kill every man aboard, with no exceptions.

But that had all taken time. A sea fight, as I have said too often, is an odd corruption of the way a man perceives time. Nothing seems to happen, and everything is, as it were, trapped in honey and slug-gishly crawling, and then everything seems to accelerate, the way a horse goes from a walk to a trot, and a trot to a canter, and then suddenly to a gallop, faster and faster. But then it can slow again, more than a land fight.

I wasn't even winded, and only the very tip of my spear was red.

My armour had not even begun to seem heavy. I went up my main-mast. It was left standing on a trihemiolia, as I have said before, and we had built a little platform amidships, by the mast – only two steps up, like a ladder, but it could give an officer a greater view. I went up it, and then up the pegs we'd set into the mast.

The sun had burned away the last of the fog while we stormed our victim, and now every part of the battle was laid bare to me.

To the west of *Lydia*, who, by the fortune of the last fight, was pointed south and east, were the little islets off the coast of Attica and the slopes of Mount Aigeleos. Locals call them the Pharmacussae and no, I don't know why. I could have struck the nearer with a spear if I'd thrown well. Our original beach was only three stades away, almost due south. We had, I believe, travelled almost six stades west and then come as far back east in our sweep and our first three fights. At least, I think that's what happened.

From my ship, which, together with Cimon's a few oar lengths to the south, was the westernmost of the entire fleet, the straits of Salamis wound away like the point of an arrow towards the Saronic Gulf to the east, and every cup of salt water seemed to have a ship in it. In that hour a man might have walked dry-shod from Salamis to Piraeus on the decks of triremes, there were so many and they were packed so close. The thickest press was away east, near the tip of the Cynosura Peninsula where we had had our meeting just a few hours before. The most open water was around us – in truth, we'd crushed the westernmost Phoenicians and their supports had already fled. A handful of combats continued: just to the north of me, Harpagos's marines were clearing a Phoenician ship from the stern while Moire's marines boarded them from the bow.

Indeed, we were victorious. The western thrust of the Persians was not just broken, but wrecked. But we all knew we had the elite of our fleet. And to the east, all was not well. Or rather, numbers had to tell. The Greek fleet, including every capture and every Ionian who changed sides – and many did in those last days – was still fewer than four hundred vessels, and even that 'few' was a huge number and a mighty fleet. But the Great King could muster, by the account of my friends Cyrus and Darius, both of whom had reason to know, at least six hundred and eighty vessels and now, as the sun rose and the fog burned off, any errors they had made in disposition were revealed, but so was the might of their armada and the presence of the Great King himself. At the moment I climbed my mast he was visible, perhaps three hundred paces from me, a little to the east, sitting on a great golden throne under a canopy of Tyrian purple red that itself was worth the price of a ship, I suspect.

I would like to say that I called out to him, shook my fist, but in truth I could only see the throne, and anyway, I had more important concerns.

To the east, as close as the Great King's throne, was Xanthippus. He had a magnificent ship, touched up with gilt, and easily picked out among his foes. He was already grappled to a heavy Phoenician and the ships that had broken away from us were now making a counter-attack, supported by some Ionians. I took this in faster than I can tell it.

Nearer the beaches of Attica – the north shore – floated the largest warship I'd ever seen. A trieres, yes, but both longer and heavier-built than any other, and with a full deck of wood crowded with men. The upper works were painted red, and some was touched in gold. The ship itself was almost directly under the towering imperial throne.

Someone important was on that ship. It had a distinctly Phoenician look to it, but it was too far away to be certain. It might have been the toy of any of the great Ionian tyrants, or it might have been their grand-admiral's ship. I couldn't be sure.

And to the south and slightly to the west of us, unengaged, lay our Corinthians – heavier ships than ours, with good crews, sitting on their oars. Taking no part.

As I say, I had time only for a long glance, turning from horizon to horizon. Cimon was getting his *Ajax* underway behind me as I completed my scan and let myself down the mast – go ahead, climb in a breastplate and thigh guard and tell me how well you do – and I ran to my own rail by Seckla as Cimon had his rowers fold their wings and his beautiful, unscarred ship came to rest, bow-to-bow, beside mine.

'Like Lade!' he said, his voice full of excitement.

'Better than Lade,' I said. 'The Samos bastards are on the other side!'

We both laughed, but in truth, betrayal haunted us like a spectre at a wedding feast. And both of us had lost so many friends – a whole world – at Lade. Harpagos lost his brother, my best friend. I lost so many friends that even now I drink to them and pour this wine to their shades. And *I did not trust Themistocles*.

I mention this because as we lay on the waves, side by side, Moire and Harpagos came up and formed a line with me and Cimon's squadrons began to fall in as crisply as hoplites going to parade before the gods. The boarding actions had given the oarsmen time to drink down some wine and water, to spit on their hands, to stretch. And winning is a tonic.

One of my youngest, fittest rowers, a fine youngster named Phylakes, rubbed the small of his back and shook his head. 'How many more sprints, Grandfather?' he asked Giorgos, one of the older rowers, who sat close by.

Giorgos laughed and drank wine from a pottery flask. 'You boys!' he shouted. 'This is just the warm-up!'

Men laughed. And with men who can laugh after three ship fights, you can accomplish anything.

I missed Hipponax, though. The marines were stretching and drinking water and my son was not to be seen.

I asked Onisandros, who looked remarkably blank. 'Don't know, lord,' he said, staring off into space. He knew something and wasn't telling me.

I had no time for more questions, because Cimon was beckoning.

'You ever see the signal to start the battle?' he asked.

I shook my head. We both knew this was bad. Eurybiades had in mind a more complicated battle than Themistocles and had wanted to control the pace – the lack of signalling might mean the Spartan was already dead or taken.

'I think we should commit the Corinthians,' Cimon shouted.

'Better you than me,' I shouted back, meaning that Cimon was the man to give orders, and that Adeimantus was more likely to follow the aristocratic Cimon than to follow me, who he'd made a public career of disparaging.

Cimon was silent a moment.

He was looking past me, and I turned. We could see Xanthippus's *Horse Tamer* take a great blow, her oars splintered. The press was growing so close that no trierarch could see every threat.

'Give me the ships we have and you go fetch the Corinthians,' I yelled.

Cimon nodded. 'Go!' he roared. He leaned over his starboard side, opposite me, and shouted something to Eumenes of Anagyrus, who was a powerful aristocrat of Cimon's party, although not a sea wolf. But I saw the man wave his spear at me, and point, and I took that for his acceptance of my lead.

Remember, too, that my ships and Cimon's, alone of all the ships in either fleet, had a signal book, evolved in almost twenty years of piracy and sea war. It did not have many signals, but it had more signals than any other.

I motioned to Seckla, but he was coming out of the steering oars, handing over to Leukas. The Alban nodded. Onisandros needed no orders; so well trained was *Lydia* that the first thud of his spear against the deck brought out the oars without another word. My deck crew was poling off from *Ajax,* careful not to foul oars. It speaks a great deal that Cimon turned on the spot, half his rowers forward and half reversed, and shot away west and south for the Corinthians, even as the rest of us moved cautiously eastward and began to form two lines for battle on my signals – and no two ships collided or even had to deviate to avoid one another.

I had a round dozen warships – even in a battle of a thousand ships, a dozen is a fair force, and an important moment was at hand. The Phoenician counter-attack, straight into the heart of the Athenians, directly under the Great King's eye, was an attempt to restore their 'east-west' line and force the Greeks back on their beaches. The fog was gone, the breeze was gone, and the small advantages we'd de-rived from the wind and fog and the chop of waves in the bay – that was over. Now the Great King and his admirals could see all we did, and the whole sweep of our line, and our plan, if any part of it survived, was laid bare. Fools say the Great King sat on his throne to enjoy the battle the way a god would watch the actions of mere mortals, but the Great King and Mardonius his cousin were far can-nier than that, and a constant stream of imperial messengers came down the hill bearing news of exactly how our fleet moved.

It was a brilliant counterstroke. Twenty Athenian ships were taken or sunk in the blink of an eye, and then the Phoenicians were in among the lesser ships of the Athenian second and third lines, making the breakthrough that we'd robbed them of in the early going, forcing the open-water fight our lesser captains dreaded. You could *see* the Athenian line stretch and sag as trierarchs and helms-men in the back lines tried to manoeuvre, and friends collided with friends. Ships moved backwards – crews backed water for their lives – and other ships, struck hard by rams, recoiled. The noise was like nothing I'd ever heard, because water allows sound to travel more easily than ground – hundreds of thousands of men roaring for the approval of the gods, or screaming for mercy, or both, and the snap of oars, the heavy, crushing thud of the bronze ram at impact, the zip of arrows, the clash of bronze and iron.

I made myself take my time to bring my little squadron into action where it would matter most, and in the best possible order. I considered all my signals, while at the same time I considered what had to be done. It is true that for a fleeting moment the flank of the Phoenicians was vulnerable, but it was very close to the beach, on purpose, and a regiment of Immortals stood there, with arrows to bows. To fight a boarding action in the shallows was to take a heavy risk and to abandon Xanthippus and the Athenians' centre to their dooms.

It is a maxim of many navarchs and strategoi to always make the bold stroke and never reinforce failure and this is, I confess, often true. But in this case, it appeared to me – and there was no one with whom to share my decision – that if Xanthippus and the Athenian centre were not saved, the Persians would restore their line, win a morale advantage, and be able to isolate us to the west and reinforce at will. I could not even have said this then. I had heartbeats to decide and a very limited number of codes to tell my trierarchs what I fancied.

What I decided was that I had a dozen of the finest captains on the waves and I'd let every man go for his own kill. Athens was not a great sea power in those days: many of her ships were officered by cavalrymen, if you take my meaning, and rowed by desperate lower-class men who had never touched an oar before that summer. They had strict rules and manoeuvres, taught over the summer and autumn, by Eurybiades and Themistocles.

But, with a couple of exceptions, the men under my hand were old sea wolves who didn't need formations to kill. We were *in* a formation, a pretty one, sweeping west and a little south.

It was time for us to act like Phoenicians, in fact.

We had a signal from pirate days. We'd used it enough times that I hoped every captain would know it. After battle a pennon from my masthead summoned all the captains to my ship by saying the traditional *'Now we divide the spoils of war.'* But in the midst of an action, against a Carthaginian tin convoy or Egyptian merchants, it meant *'Pick one and take her.'* In effect, it allowed every trierarch to use his head.

Hector usually handled the signals, such as they were, but he was gone with our capture, so I pulled the wicker basket from under

Seckla's bench and found the little red pennon, and put it on the halyard kept for the purpose. We were two hundred paces from where Xanthippus's ship was being taken. His marines were fighting and dying like Olympians or titans, but he had four ships on his one.

I ran my signal up.

I leaned out over the side to Eumenes of Anagyrus, who was not really one of us, and shouted, 'Pick a target and take or kill her! Forget formation!'

He smiled. He raised his arm in the salute Olympic athletes give the judges and shouted an order.

I leaned the other way and got Harpagos's attention, but he'd already seen it. He pointed up, said something to his helmsman, and waved to me with his kopis in his hand. He was smiling, and his face was full of light – that very fire, I think, that Heraclitus thought made us greater than mere men when in battle.

So having formed, we broke apart, like a pack of wolves breaks when they see the deer.

I ran back to Leukas. 'Pick one by Xanthippus and put me where I can board *Horse Tamer*,' I said.

Then I ran forward to the marines. 'Let me past,' I grunted. Hipponax was there – wherever he'd been off to, he was back. He wouldn't meet my eye – the young man personified. He was up to something, and it did not matter in that moment.

Brasidas grinned at me – very un-Laconian. 'Good to have you here.'

'We'll make you a Plataean yet, with all these displays of wild emotion,' I said, but I clapped him on his armoured shoulder and smiled at the men around us.

'We winning, boss?' Achilles, my cousin, asked. As if we were friends.

So we were. 'When we clear the centre,' I began. Then I realised they had no notion what was happening. 'We're going aboard Xanthippus's ship,' I said. 'Clear the Medes off *Horse Tamer* and I promise you we will win. This is it. All or nothing.'

I stood up and an arrow slammed into my aspis. We were close. But the gesture is everything. Men had to know.

I pointed to the golden throne, less than a stade away.

'Want to show the Great King what you think?' I roared. 'He's right there, watching us.'

Arrows came past me. Ka and his pair were using us as cover, shooting carefully. They had their own orders – to kill archers. Every marine with an aspis was a shield, and we practised this.

My marines began to sing the paean – just ten men. But by the gods ... by the gods, my eyes fill with tears to say it, the sailors and the oarsmen took it up. Oh, that moment, and that day.

The paean of Apollo came off my benches and spread to other ships. I have met men from *Horse Tamer* who said that the sound of the paean coming towards them was the sound of salvation, that they joined in who could.

Leukas put our bow into the bow of a Phoenician ship that was grappled alongside. It was a daring, precision strike, and the result was spectacular. We smashed into his bow, our own oars safely in, and we were just a few finger widths to the inside of his bow, so that after the shattering first blow, our ships went between *Horse Tamer* and the enemy ship, popping the grapnels and breaking the ropes, smashing the enemy ship's cathead and heaving it away, oars smashed, rowers injured, and cutting all its marines off from their ship. It wasn't as instantly satisfying as the strikes that sank ships immediately, but it was one of the two or three finest ship-strikes I've ever witnessed.

We boarded *Horse Tamer*. We were long side to long side, stern to stern, and Seckla led the sailors in grappling close and then boarding. Seckla did not wait for me to tell him to go. My big deck gave me the power of carrying more marines and more sailors than most, and as I've said, most of my sailors were better armoured than more people's marines.

We went from our bow into his bow, right into the teeth of an Ionian contingent coming from another ship directly opposite us. The press of ships was amazing – like nothing I've ever seen.

No time to think about it. No time to worry that my own ship was going to be boarded – unavoidable.

I leapt first. I went aspis to aspis with a man as big as me or bigger. He lost his footing in the blood, and down he went.

That one to Ares, and no doing of mine.

Brasidas, despite the terrible footing and the three-sided fight in a densely packed foredeck, got his shield lapped with mine like the veteran he was.

It took the Ionians too long to realise we were not on their side. They were Samians – oh, the delicious revenge on that nest of traitors! I killed three before they fully understood and Brasidas heaved them off the forward gangway, back onto their own ship, and I lost him there. He chose to board into the Ionian ship. You must imagine that Xanthippus's ship had three enemies bow to bow, like limpets stuck to a fish, and the Ionian was one, we were one, and the third was a sleek ship with a red hull.

Again, there was no time to think. Brasidas went forward into the Ionian and Hipponax went with him, and Alexandros and Sitalkes.

Idomeneus was in his old accustomed place at my shoulder. Achilles came with me, and the others.

There was no quarter asked or given. They were under the eyes of their emperor, and we knew we were fighting for everything.

Nor can I pretend to remember every blow. I know my spear broke and instead of going for my sword I hammered away at my opponent, a smaller man, with my butt spike, hitting him again and again, stunning him with my blows until his strong left arm sank. I hit him with the sauroter to his helmet and he staggered, limbs loosed, but I hit him again and his helmet collapsed into his skull, and it too gave way.

I took a wound there – he may have been the one who got me, as he was a canny fighter. It was in my sword arm, and the bronze saved most of it. But not all.

I didn't know. I powered forward down the narrow catwalk. Behind me my people were still singing the paean, which was wonderful, because by the blessing of Poseidon the Athenian rowers by my feet knew I was on their side, and they began to foul the enemy and stabbed up into the catwalk with daggers and javelins, and suddenly the Phoenicians in front of me collapsed. Few survived to run – they were literally pulled down, as if by the tentacles of a monster called oarsmen, except one or two brave men, who stabbed down with their spears and leapt back to gain space to make a stand.

But another ship disgorged its marines into us from *behind* me.

The first I knew was that I could not feel Idomeneus pressing into my back. Long practice taught me to turn if he was gone, and there were plumes, towering plumes, the kind that our forefathers wore, the kind I wore in our first contests, a dozen or more of them, and lots of armour, and red cloth, red paint, red enamel. Very showy.

Idomeneus was adding to their red display. His face was lit by a beautiful, godlike smile, very like the one that Harpagos had worn. His right arm was poised high when I glanced at him, his smile like that of a man who has seen a god or found true joy, as he batted a thrown spear out of the air with his spear shaft, in just a twitch of his hand. His aspis licked out, caught his opponent's, rim to rim, and pulled it aside, and his high right hand shot forward – his spear point went in under his opponent's chin, buried to the base, so that when Idomeneus pulled, his wretched adversary tried to grab the point and was dragged forward; the spear shaft shattered, and Idomeneus used it like a club, as I had earlier, and then threw it overhand at the man behind his current opponent – all this in the time a runner would take two breaths. I couldn't look longer.

I still had men in front of me. I had to be sure of them, and the man who'd backed away now dropped his spear and fell to his knees. His eyes pleaded for life. Behind him, another Phoenician was cut down from behind by a Greek, while a third was almost buried in my sailors.

I *hate* killing prisoners. It is against the will of the gods, against the justice men demand from men, and against the code by which warriors should act.

But I had a shipload of marines coming behind me and I could not leave this man to pick up his spear and attack me. And past me, my friends.

I killed him. I hate that I did, but there were other lives dependent on my actions. Probably he would have stayed in submission – or perhaps the sailors or the oarsman would have finished him. Or perhaps he'd have killed me, then Idomeneus, and then the rest, turning the tide of battle.

It does not matter. It was my choice, between one beat of my heart and the next, the way a man must choose inside the battle haze.

This is why we all despise the war god and his rage. But I did it, and then I turned, leaving remorse for other times, and put my shoulder behind Idomeneus's back, and began to stab underhand with my victim's spear, attacking his opponents in their thighs and feet.

And then he was down. He was standing, fighting like a statue of Poseidon come to life, and then a well-thrown javelin from his open side caught him in the side, under his sword arm. He finished his cut, sending one more foe ahead of him to Hades, and then he fell, with blood spurting far into the rowers' benches – heart's blood.

I got my left foot over him as he fell and squirmed, face down, the spear shaft still in him, and I went shield to shield with his killer. That blow broke mine, the laths of wood that supported the bronze face all cracking in against the layers of rawhide and linen. But his rim cracked and I stepped as far as I dared off to my right with my right foot, the ruin of my shield flapping like a sail in an adverse wind, but his spear stroke, overhand, couldn't penetrate the bronze and raw-hide wreckage as I tabled my shield, gathered my left leg to my right and reached over our locked shields and pounded my point down into the place where the shoulder and neck meet. My spear went in so effortlessly and so far that I lost hold of it, and Idomeneus's killer fell, blood gushing from his mouth, and by the gods, he was in Hades before my friend.

But the marines in red were big, well armed, confident and capable, and the next man came forward undaunted. I was overextended, still amazed at the power of my overhand blow and its success, and he pushed his shoulder into me and knocked me over, and then only Ka saved me, as my adversary grew a black feathered arrow in his chest and fell over Idomeneus and his killer.

There were so many men on Xanthippus's ship by then that it tipped back and forth like a living thing, and I began to wonder if a trireme could capsize from too many men on her fighting deck.

Like some of the newest Athenian ships, the heavy ones, Xanthippus's *Horse Tamer* had a full top deck, so that the rowers sat in their boxes protected from arrows – and so that Xanthippus could carry twenty marines. But all this weight was high, which was bad for stability, and had to be countered with more ballast, which in turn made the ship harder to row and slower. *Storm Cutter* had been a similar ship, in her earliest form, and I confess that the full deck gave an element of protection to the rowers that was lacking when all they had was a canvas screen – and that deck also allowed a series of beams that helped stiffen the hull much better in heavy weather. But against that, the more difficult diekplous tactics of the Phoenicians required a lighter ship with a faster turn. Both fleets had every kind of trireme. Big and small, high and low, every shipwright had to try his hand at the perfect arrangement of rowers and oars, fighting deck and mast space.

When the Athenians built their new navy they made the rational decision to build heavy ships with big decks so that they could domi-nate boarding actions against the lighter, better-rowed ships of their traditional nautical enemy, Aegina. Of course, the sea wolves pre-ferred the lighter, faster ships – and those of us who had fought in the west, off Magna Graecia, had come to prefer the hemiolas, which seemed to me then, and still seem to me, the best compromise of rowing, sailing, heavy hull and fighting platform.

I mention all of this because it is otherwise difficult for you youngsters to imagine that we were twenty feet above the water on a slightly convex deck that shed water and blood to the sides, and the sides had no real bulwarks, but just a narrow 'catch-all' the width of a man's hand. In other words, a man who fell had a tendency to go overboard. My backplate was pressed against the 'catch-all' and my right arm dangled – empty-handed – over the sea.

The red marine towered over me, or so it seemed to me. And there, in utmost vulnerability, I knew him. It was Diomedes.

He recognised me, and just for a moment hesitated – savouring the moment of triumph? Wanting to take me prisoner to torment me? Who knows. His arm was poised for the kill – I was flat on my back in the blood at the deck edge and had no weapon and my aspis was broken and mostly off my arm.

I rolled over the side. It is hard to say exactly why. I think my last thought was to deny my boyhood foe his triumph. Or perhaps I had the sense to take my chance on Poseidon, who had saved me before.

I hit the water before I had time for another thought.

What's that? Yes, sweet, I drowned – went to the Elysian Fields, met Achilles, and was then brought back by beautiful naiads, a dozen of them, who led me to an underwater cave, armed me in fresh armour, and then swam me to the surface.

No.

Impact with the water finished my aspis and wrenched my left shoulder, but I didn't notice it. I was barefoot, and my armour weighted me down, but I had time to catch a breath and I had the wreck of my aspis off my arm in a heartbeat – and then I was swimming. Just for a moment I was deep, under the hull of *Horse Tamer* and looking up at the surface. There were dozens of men in the water, and blood – and sharks. And the hulls of ships as far as the eye could see, projecting down into the water with sunbeams slanting away into the depths.

Poseidon, it was terrifying down there, and the more so as I was afraid I was sinking, and I panicked, thrusting my arms out like a fool. But before I breathed water and gave myself to Poseidon, I made myself take a stroke, and I shot up – I could match my progress against the wreckage – and then I was close enough to the surface to raise my heart, and then I was breathing, the plumes of my helmet a sodden, hairy mess in my face, and I didn't care.

I couldn't rest. I had to keep swimming.

But Pericles and his friend Anaxagoras saved me. *Naiad*, the Lesbian ship, had come in to Xanthippus's stern to put marines into the back of the fight and save the men still fighting around the helm. Anaxagoras had been the first man aboard *Horse Tamer* over the stern, and Pericles saw me go over the side. And saw – still waiting for his turn to go aboard the *Horse Tamer* – that I came to the surface. He grabbed a boarding pike and held it over the side from the marines' box of *Naiad*. I grabbed it, and young Pericles hauled me aboard.

It took two Aeolian oarsmen and Pericles to pull me up the side – I was already spent. I know a man who swam to Salamis from one of the stricken Athenian ships, in his armour, and he deserves much praise for his swimming. I was only in the water for two hundred heartbeats and I was *tired*.

Hah! But I was alive.

I was on one knee on the catwalk for a long time – long enough for twenty more men to die aboard *Horse Tamer*. That fight had become the centre of the maelstrom.

I looked about. Pericles left me to go onto *Horse Tamer*. Even as I discovered my sword was still strapped to my side, and none the worse for a little salt water, I saw that my riposte into the Phoenician counter-attack had sufficed. Hipponax had killed again; his ship was backing water. Cimon's brother was finishing off an Ionian ship that looked familiar, but I could not place her. Megakles and Eumenes were both taking ships.

It was here, and now. The Phoenicians were pouring men into this boarding fight and now there were more than a dozen ships all grappled together, and there were Phoenician marines aboard *Lydia* – I could see Leukas fighting in the stern with his bronze axe. I could see Brasidas's plume two ships away, on board an Ionian which itself had a Phoenician boarding it over the stern, and behind him my son Hipponax's spear went back and forth like a woman working wool on a loom.

Seldom have I had so much of a feeling that the gods were all about me. I drew my good sword – my long xiphos – and leapt down onto the ram of *Naiad* and then cambered up the stern of *Horse Tamer*. Once again, the enemy had pressed the ship's defenders into the stern – there was Seckla, and there Pericles, and there Anaxagoras and beside him Cleitus, of all people, with Xanthippus roaring orders and throwing well-aimed javelins from the helmsman's bench.

I took an aspis off a corpse. it was too heavy for my liking, but there it is, on the wall – Heracles and the Nemean Lion. As if it had been left for me.

I went forward even as Anaxagoras fell.

I got a leg forward, got my right arm well back, and stabbed from very close. I had three opponents, and only then did I realise how badly injured my left shoulder was from the impact with the water when I fell over the side because when my opponent bashed his aspis into mine, the blow ran up my arm to my shoulder like a wound.

But it is when everything is on the line that you show yourself.

Listen, then.

Seckla's long-bladed spear baffled one of my opponents – he turned his head and I stabbed him in the throat-bole with a flip of my wrist, and then I pivoted and swung my sword backhanded. My second opponent was fouled by the falling body of his mate and he allowed himself to be deceived by the reverse my blade made in the air. I struck him full across the face with my blade, which cut the depth of two fingers into his skull, and then, good sword as he was, didn't snap when I tore the blade free.

The third adversary got his spear into my helmet; a good blow, but the helmet held, and although I smelled blood, I got my blade over the top of his shield. I did him no damage, but my point lodged at the base of his bronze crest-box on top of his helmet, and the force of my blow moved his head. Where the head goes, the body follows, and he went backward – and straight over the side.

I found that I was roaring Briseis's name as a war cry. Well, Aphrodite has turned a battle ere now, and on Crete they have a temple to her as Goddess of War. But by *all* the gods I was full of new fire, and perhaps it was Briseis and her own unquenchable spirit, or Aphrodite herself.

Cleitus fell by my side. Anaxagoras was up, pulled to his feet on the bloody deck by Pericles. And down the deck, two oar lengths away, I saw a familiar bulk: Polymarchos, at the head of my marines, pushing towards me, but the Red King's marines and those of my foe Diomedes were fleeing back into the two triremes that lay, beaks in, amidships.

I got a foot over Cleitus and parried away his death blow from a Phoenician. Later, I prayed to my Mater that she not be offended. In the press, he was Athenian – indeed, he was my brother and not my foe, as I had promised all my men.

There must have been fifty men on that deck and another thirty corpses – and Poseidon only knows how many more gone to feed the squid over the sides. That ship was the epicentre of the western end of the battle.

But like a man waking from long illness, or recovering from injury, I felt the lightening of the pressure, roared my war cry, and baffled Cleitus's would-be killer with a heavy blow to his head. He raised his shield and I cut his left thigh to the bone. I remember the delicious satisfaction of that cut.

I put my other leg forward, leaving Cleitus behind me, and Seckla cut a man's hand right off his arm with the sharp edge of his spear-head – his favourite trick, cutting with a spear, which his people apparently did routinely.

And then I was chest to chest with Polymarchos and he grinned evilly.

'You stopped for a bath?' he laughed. 'You look like a puppy someone tried to drown.'

'Better than being dead,' I said. I turned to Cleitus, still trapped on his back in the press, gave him my sticky right hand and got him to his feet.

He didn't say anything. He just stood there for two breaths. When you go down on the deck in a boarding fight, you are very close to becoming a corpse or fish food. I knew – I'd just been there.

But there was no time for talk. He took a spear from someone and we pressed up the deck, finished the last Phoenician marines, who died well, and went over the sides. I led my people back aboard *Lydia*, where Ionian and Phoenician marines were fighting my deck crew and my top-deck rowers. My men were making a fight of it, but rowers are no match for hoplites.

I say my men, but there was one obvious exception – a tiny girl, dwarfed by the bronze men against her, was fighting with a spear. She mystified them, her steps sure, her movements deceptive, and two trained men could not kill her. She gave ground steadily, stabbing when she could, and even as we boarded she turned and leapt into the sea.

I knew her immediately – Cleitus's daughter, Heliodora.

But the tide had turned. An Athenian ship came in behind *Lydia* and put marines over her stern even as we went back aboard over the starboard side, and the Phoenicians collapsed, dead, dying, or in the water before I could get my sword on one.

Then I saw my son.

Hipponax came down the gangway from the bow, at the head of my people who'd followed Brasidas – indeed, the Spartan's plumes were just behind him. He fought like one possessed, or maddened, and his spear point was everywhere, his aspis was a battering ram and a trickster's cloak, and yet he seemed to walk forward unopposed.

Then I knew where the girl had come from, and whose girlish voice had sung the hymn to Apollo.

As soon as my deck was clear, I ran to the side, but Hipponax beat me there – and she was not among those swimming.

Brave soul – to wish to face the Medes. I sent a prayer for her winning, and turned to Leukas, but he had two wounds, and I ordered Seckla gruffly into the oars. Xanthippus was cutting the grapples.

We were winning. But when you are outnumbered two to one, you cannot stop fighting for a local victory. As oarsmen went back to their cushions, I tried to climb my mast – and could not. Something was awry with my left shoulder, and my missing fingers were not helping. I could not climb at all.

I could not see Cimon's *Ajax*, nor any of the ships of his squadron – nor any of the Corinthians.

We had stopped the Phoenician counter-attack, but that was all. The Ionians were backing water toward the straits, unbeaten. The survivors of the Phoenicians were gathered around that red and god-giant ship, and it towered above the others like one ship piled atop a second.

Off to the east there was a great roar, like the sound the crowd makes going to the mysteries at Eleusis – and then again, and then, a third time repeated, and again we heard the paean sung, and then a Laconian cheer, so different from our own.

Xanthippus, who was covered in blood and certainly one of the day's heroes, leaned over from his ship's rowing station. He shouted some words that were lost, and then ' . . . big bastard.'

I assumed he meant he was going for the big Phoenician.

I thought that was the best new attack. So I nodded emphatically.

Seckla was in the steering oars. My son Hipponax was on his knees, weeping.

Oh, rage. Ares and Aphrodite, together.

I pulled him to his feet and I struck him. 'Cease your weeping!'

I shouted. I am ashamed now. I struck my own son, and I said, 'Avenge her first. And then explain to her father why she died, you useless shit.'

He stood and looked at me like a whipped dog.

I struck him again and Seckla and Brasidas dragged me off him. I cannot ever remember being so gripped with rage, and the image of that poor girl, and the bravery of her leap in to the waves – a beautiful defiance.

But there were arrows in the air again, and Ka and Nemet were in the stern, lofting shafts at the Ionians. I was hit in the aspis and the shards of the cane cut my face and woke me from my rage.

But I didn't apologise.

I turned to Seckla. Most of our rowers were in their positions. Onisandros was wounded but on his feet – by Heracles my ancestor, it seemed to me that every man on my deck was wounded, except my son and Brasidas, who seemed to have had godlike powers that day.

Leukas was sitting on the port-side helm bench, bleeding, with Polymarchos, stripped of his aspis, trying to staunch the blood and close the wounds. But elsewhere on the aft deck, surviving sailors were slicing cut cables and serving out new oars to men who'd lost theirs in the fighting. The men moved with decision.

We were still a fighting ship.

'Fetch me alongside the big Phoenician, or ram him if you can,' I said to Seckla. Leukas gave a great cry and fainted.

'Hipponax!' I called. He was standing with Brasidas, head down.

He came slowly, even as the oars came out raggedly and the once nimble *Lydia* gathered way.

He was crying, and he was ashamed.

I dropped my sword on the deck and put my arms around him.

'That was ill-said,' I admitted. 'It was hubris for me to strike you.'

He looked as shocked as if I'd hit him again. 'But you are right, Pater,' he moaned. 'I might as well have killed her myself.'

I held him for a moment. So complex are the weavings of the gods. I knew he would now fight like one with no hope – brilliantly. And perhaps take his death wound, uncaring. Killed, in a strange way, by Cleitus. So we are tied together. Yoked, like oxen in a field.

'No time for tears,' I said gruffly. I might have said – stay, live. But I did not.

'No,' he said. He straightened. 'Only revenge.' He managed a crooked, terrible smile. 'Let me go up the side first,' he said.

Brasidas shook his head.

'Perhaps,' I said. I turned away. I had once been young – how would I have felt if I had caused the death of Briseis? Who was I to tell my son that there would be other loves?

The Ionians deployed well, but now the battle had turned completely along the narrow north-south axis that Themistocles and Eurybiades had wanted. The Phoenician flagship was still closer to the coast of Attica than I liked, almost under the Great King's throne, but the chaos of the fight had put us hard by and Themistocles was going into the remnants of the Phoenicians even as the Laconians – and the Corinthians, although I could not see them – were smashing into the Ionian centre.

And still there were mighty cheers coming from beyond our centre.

As *Lydia* went forward, *Naiad, Storm Cutter* and *Black Raven* joined us. There was a brief pause – the Great King's fleet was collapsing in two directions, back against the coast of Attica for the Phoenicians and westernmost Ionians, and back towards Phaleron for the rest of them. Many ships were simply trapped. Ameinias in his *Parthenos* made another spectacular kill just then, right in the centre, far from us, but under the eyes of the main fleet, and as his doomed adversary broke in half, the Athenian main squadron gave a huge cheer.

There were no cheers from our adversaries. And we knew we were winning. We knew that, after many days of defeat, and some hard fought draws and one victory squandered by the death of brave Leonidas, that now was our hour. Now was our moment. *Now* we were going to win. And yet, no one shirked. It is easy in the hour of victory to turn aside, to feel the weight of your wounds and wait for another man to do the final work and cut the throat of the downed enemy, but no one shirked.

Nothing needed to be said. From the fight at Sardis to this day in the Bay of Salamis, all had been defeat and retreat and now we had men who were willing to give their lives to be sure it was done.

I was one.

The Phoenician squadron under the Great King's throne had to be beaten. It stood off our new flank as the battle turned, and if left unfought, it could change the tide again. And yet ... they had no room to manoeuvre. Indeed, their sterns were almost on the beaches, and the Persian Immortals guarding the Great King were in position to bury us in arrow shafts.

But they had their own crisis, and the flagship suddenly had its oars out and was coming at us, trailing escorts the way a mother duck trails ducklings. It was badly coordinated and to this day I can only assume that the Phoenicians were humiliated that we were going to attack them without any response.

It was a foolish decision, because they came out from under the screen of their archers.

But it was also the closest thing to an open-water engagement that day: a dozen of theirs against about the same of ours. That was when I discovered that Xanthippus was not there. He'd gone to the big fight in the centre.

War is often like tragedy – the Fates walk, and dooms are laid, and what happens often seems either incredible or easily predictable. We had the same number of ships on either side, in that engagement. Our ships had fought two or three or four engagements that day, and most of theirs – the Phoenician reserve – were as fresh as a child waking from sleep.

But Harpagos was still avenging his brother, and his ram had taken the lives of four ships. Moire was just showing the Athenians how good an African helmsman who had once been a slave could be, and he wasn't done with his demonstration. Giannis was close enough to me that I could see his tight-lipped determination, despite the three desperate fights his ship had seen that day, and Megakles – I had never seen him fatigued by the sea.

We were buoyed by Nike. Indeed, to this day, I think of her, and I think of Cleitus's daughter leaping into the waves – later I will tell you why. But it was Nike herself who had us in her hand. We weren't tired.

We were workmen determined to finish the task we'd been set.

Nor were we fools.

I gave no orders. Seckla determined to take one of the outermost Phoenicians and set us to rake her oars. Onisandros, his voice tight with pain, begged the rowers for another burst, and they came on like heroes, so that we went up to ramming speed from very close.

Then it went like a fight between wild dogs in the agora.

Our chosen prey baulked. At ramming speed, her helmsman panicked and yawed well out of line – and like a flash, Onisandros ordered the rowers to slow their stroke and Seckla turned us to port so fast I was thrown onto the deck. *Another* Phoenician flashed past our stern – I hadn't seen him, screened by the first – and we struck the stern quarter of a third as he tried for the ship from Naxos that had come over to us a week before. Ka stood in the stern, loosing arrows into the Phoenician passing our stern, and even as I shouted for a grapple and a spear, Dy put an arrow into the helmsman and he fell forward into his oars. His ship skidded on the waves and came to a stop with half the rowers injured, all her oars going – and Harpagos cut off her stern, his fifth or sixth kill of the day.

We were gathering way again, all our oars out. We hadn't hit our opponent very hard, but he was pulling away with all his might, and none of our grapples had clinched the deal. He backed water into the shallows, and men started leaping over the side – where the Great King's Immortals began to slaughter them.

I didn't have time to watch or laugh – the Phoenician squadron was gone. Half the ships were running east, and the rest were taken or driving their sterns ashore to be butchered by the Great King's bodyguard. I assume he was consumed by rage.

Giannis took his ship against the tall flagship. He handled it brilliantly – feinted a head-to-head collision and then went off, forcing the bigger ship to go to ramming speed for nothing. He passed the behemoth's stern and turned, his archers shooting up into the Persian archers crowding the enemy deck, but in this they were our betters and Giannis took an arrow in his right thigh as he turned and his helmsman was shot down at his side, and two of his marines killed.

But with all of their attention on him, they missed Harpagos, who had cut the stern off one Phoenician like a housewife cutting sausage and then turned, a long, easy turn to port, passed under my bow, and slammed his beak deep into the Phoenician flagship.

Too deep. He struck at a weak place between frames, and his ram went in. Immediately the Persian archers shot down into *his* ship, and the Phoenician marines, from their higher vantage, went to board.

About then, Seckla swept along the enemy flagship's port side – opposite to where Harpagos had holed it – and raked along their trailing oars, killing oarsmen with their own shafts and breaking their oars or ripping them out of the ship like a man pulling the legs off a crab. And as soon as we were broadside to broadside, we went at the red and gold monster.

Her sides were a man's height higher than our aft deck.

No one baulked, but it wasn't like any other boarding action I've ever been in.

Usually you go over onto the enemy deck, sometimes off your

own ram, like a bridge, and sometimes from your own upper deck or catwalk straight aboard the enemies'. It's an art, a dance, not a science.

This time we went in through the rowing frames. Only on a ship so big could it even be done, and it meant we couldn't take spears, and I, for one, left my aspis behind me. Scarcely mattered – my left arm was barely able to function.

As we slowed and our grapples went home – no misses now, because the enemy marines were all on the other deck, watching the wrong ship – Hipponax got to the starboard-side rail, ready to leap.

Bless Brasidas, he simply pulled my son off his feet and flung him to the deck. 'Another day, boy,' he said. He gave my son a smile – a smile I still treasure – and then he leapt for the enemy's side, grabbed the edge of a rowing frame, and flipped over his arms, his feet slamming into the rower.

In truth, most of the rowers we faced couldn't have fought us on their best day, and many were injured by Seckla's oar-rake. But it is no treat going in an oar-port that is only slightly larger than your shoulders in your bronze thorax, which will not compress. I killed the oarsman in my entry port with my sword, and climbed over his dying body to get inboard – and took a spear full force in my back plate. It penetrated, too. Right here. See? About an inch into this muscle.

That motivated me to move faster.

I had no aspis under which to curl and I was cramped in the rowing frame. My opponent was above me. But I rolled over, which hurt my back wound like blazes, and parried with my sword – and got my weak left hand on his spearhead.

He pulled.

That hurt, but I held on, and he pulled me to my feet, mostly. I slammed the spear down and missed.

I scythed my sword across his ankles, and that was the end of the fight for him. Then I climbed out of the top-deck rowing frame. I was not the first man onto the enemy deck. Hipponax and Brasidas were ahead of me – without shields, and fighting against thirty Phoenician marines.

But the difference was that Nike was with us, and not with them. They already knew they were beaten. Even as I counted the odds, Moire's *Amastris* grappled bow to bow. Moire had a gangplank for landing men and animals on open beaches, and he used it here, dropping it across to make a bridge for men with a good sense of balance, but Alexandros ran across the gap and onto the deck, and he had both aspis and spear, and suddenly there were a dozen more like him and then deck crew and top-deck oarsmen.

I wasn't watching. I knew these things must 'be happening, because of the despair of my foes, but they were not eager to die without taking us with them, and we were locked sword to spear, breast to shield. The lack of aspides was terrible, the press was close and Hipponax went down with a wound to his leg, but Brasidas demonstrated why the elite of the Spartans practise for everything. And I confess that I fought hard over my son, too.

A man with sword alone is not without advantages. Nor were we facing a tide of enemies, but merely three or four at a time. Then I had cause to praise Polymarchos for making me learn to cover myself with the sword as well as with the aspis, and to fight the longer weapon with the shorter, and when I covered a spear-thrust, the man was at my mercy in a turn of my hand, nor was my left so weak I couldn't catch a spear and pull a man off balance.

And in that hour, Sittonax, the Gaulish loafer, came into his own. He boarded from Harpagos's vessel, where he'd chosen to be a marine, and he came up the side unseen through the blizzard of arrow shafts with his long Gaulish blade and began to cut his way aft using looping butterfly strokes, both hands on the hilt of the sword, a technique you never see in Greece, and he panicked the men in the stern.

The pressure eased and I caught up a round shield, more like something a peltast would carry than a man's shield, but better, by far, than having my left side naked. It was light and I could hold it, even missing fingers and with my shoulder a wreck, and I pushed forward with Brasidas and Polymarchos himself, who came up through the catwalk onto the fighting deck, followed by Sitalkes, who had somehow managed to fight his way aboard *with* an aspis, a remarkable feat.

We formed a line, and then Alexandros was next to Brasidas and a rear-rank marine handed the Spartan his shield.

Only then did I see the gaping wound in the flesh of the Spartan's left shoulder – I swear by Athena you could see the bone. But he got the aspis onto his shoulder and pressed forward.

I didn't know that Harpagos was dead at the bow of his ship, an arrow in his throat, or that two more Athenians were boarding over the stern, with ladders, incidentally saving Sittonax from certain death as the Great King's brother and his elite warriors turned on one Gaulish madman. Seen from above, I imagine the great Phoenician ship must have looked like a city under siege.

And being stormed.

The marines closed with us one more time. There were arrows, but there was Ka, *sitting* in the crosstrees of my permanent main mast, loosing shaft after shaft into their archers. He was naked, without cover, alone, and yet untouched. This is what I mean by the presence of Nike. Any Persian might have seen him and, with one calm arrow, dropped him.

Instead, he loosed every arrow he'd carried aloft and half of them found flesh. And then we were pressing them back into their own stern – into our allies, coming round the bend of the swan.

Hipponax tried to get past Brasidas and Alexandros tried to get past me. The last moments of the fight for the big trireme … I can't say everything that happened, except that I took a long cut on my right leg, which I think might have been caused by my own people. Hipponax fought like a mad thing – which he was. He had a round target, much like the one I'd picked up, and he used it well, in among the last Phoenician marines. I was afraid for him; for a few heartbeats he was alone.

He battled a spear-thrust aside on his target and wrapped his shield arm around the man's outstretched arms then threw the man, armour, weapons and all, over his hip and over the side of the ship.

The Phoenician to his right swung an axe—

Hipponax pushed forward, took the shaft on his buckler, and Brasidas threw his spear – and killed the man about to kill Hipponax. The shaft broke several of Hipponax's fingers, and he roared – a surprising sound – and went down on one knee from the pain, but Brasidas and I muscled past him.

There was a man standing in gold, head-to-toe gold: gold armour, a golden helmet, with a golden bow in his hand. I knew him to be Ariabignes, Xerxes' brother. But my marines didn't need to know anything but that he was the one covered in gold.

I'd like to say I killed him in single combat, but too many of my friends were there for me to get away with such a lie. *We all killed him.* I got my sword into him, Moire put his spear into the man's eye, Sitalkes and Alexandros, Hipponax and Polymarchos and Achilles my cousin and Sikli the oarsman were all there, and two Athenian marines, Diodorus, son of Eumenes, and Kritias, son of Diogenes, and Sittonax the Gaul, with a cut across his neck that should have been a death wound.

And then a strange silence fell for a moment. Far off, we could hear cheers and, closer, we could see Persian Immortals on the land, loosing arrows into the Athenian triremes under the Phoenicians' stern, although their arrows fell short. Persians were walking into the sea, shaking their fists in their impotence.

I pulled the golden helmet off its dead owner and went to the side. I looked up the hill – the Great King's throne was the closest it had been all day. The sun was high in the sky.

I knew he'd be watching. Where else could his eyes be?

I raised the golden helmet high, gave the Greek battle scream *eleu eleu eleu*, and hurled the golden thing into the sea.

That was not the end of the fight. But it was the end of the part of the fight I saw myself. It was too great a battle for any one man to see, so I'll tell you a little that I know from my friends about what happened elsewhere.

The fog fooled Eurybiades as well as fooling the Phoenicians. He never gave the signal for the attack – nor, in fact, would we ever have seen it for the haze. So much for signals.

In fact, what happened was better than our plan. When the Ionians abandoned their own plan, which I know from captives and even friends who were with them, was to move in long columns along the coast of Attica, west, until they encircled all our beaches, and then to press forward in a milling fight, forcing us right back until they could massacre us in shallow water; when it was clear that we were going to fight, from our paean, the Ionians turned in place, going from three long files of ships headed west to three long ranks headed south, and they met the Peloponnesian ships and some of the Aeginians ram to ram. They beat the first line and pushed the Peloponnesians' ships back.

But we broke the Phoenicians and, in fact, the western flank of the Ionians. The survivors retreated – and hopelessly muddled the Ionian centre, so that it was then vulnerable to the Peloponnesians. Cimon led the Corinthians – late, but we'll leave that go – into the maelstrom of the centre, trusting us to beat the Phoenicians against odds.

And then there were four hundred ships packed into a very small stretch of ocean, and that fight was at least as dense and deadly as the fight we had around *Horse Tamer*. No, I will not tell you that my ships won the day. Every ship in the League won the day. It was all vital: every ram, every marine, every oarsman.

But when we swept Xanthippus's deck clear, he chose to lead his ships back east into the same maelstrom that Cimon had adventured with fifty Corinthians. And at the same time, as we all reckon, though no one can quite tell anyone else for sure, Aristides accomplished a great deed – one of the day's finest. In small boats, and swimming and wading, four hundred hoplites crossed to the shores of Psyttaleia. It should not have been possible. But the Persian garrison was trying to use their bows to support the hard-pressed Cilicians, who were losing steadily to the Aeginians, and suddenly they were taken in the flank by Aristides and the Athenian hoplites. Certainly the Aeginians landed some men on the island and Phrynicus says that they used a captured Phoenician freighter, a tubby thing, to bring the Athenian archer corps to the island without wetting their bows.

The Persians were cut down to a man. And then the Athenian archers began to flay any ship that came within range.

And, finally, the Aeginians on the eastern-facing beaches of Cape Cynosura gave up on waiting for their signal to act as the eastward arm of the trap and attacked out into the channel. Or, according to others, they supported Aristides' attack. I wasn't there. But either way, the retreat of the Cilicians became a rout.

There is tragedy even in victory and the heroes of the Persian retreat were Greeks. The Ionian Greeks, who had been led so ill at Lade, held together, and fought like lions for their ill master. They killed almost as many Athenian ships as they lost themselves; the only Aeginian casualties that day were from Ionians. The Red King's ship sank at least two of ours and perhaps five, although many blamed him for things he could not have done. And Diomedes, his henchman, sank an Aeginian ship at the very moment of victory.

But it was to Artemisia of Halicarnassus that the honour of the day must go. Not only was she the leading Killer of Men for the Great King, but when the Phoenicians broke, she was caught in their rout. It is interesting to me that I must have been within a few ship lengths of her, watching Heliodora leap with dignity into the depths, when she got her ship free of the wreck of their van, and fled east. But when Ameinias of Pallene pursued her, eager to take the Great King's female captain, she escaped by ramming one of her own ships!

Now, I have since heard from men of that region that the ship she rammed was a political enemy of hers; some say it was the Red King, but as you'll hear, I promise you it was not. Others say she was just a wily woman. I raise my cup in respect. It was a trick worthy of Odysseus himself, and when she rammed the Ionian ship – some say a Phoenician – Ameinias naturally assumed she was Athenian and let her go.

Such was that combat; it was in many ways easier to fight the Phoenicians when we could always tell their ships from ours, than Ionians – every ship full of Greeks.

The Ionians fought us as the rest of the Great King's fleet fled. But exhaustion kept us from destroying their fleet utterly. Too many of them made the beaches of Phaleron.

But that was for another day.

I remember standing by Seckla. Brasidas and Hipponax had Leukas out of his armour and to everyone's great relief there was a lot of blood but danger only of infection; he had a bad cut all across one buttock, which makes you all giggle but is, I promise you, not a light matter, and a deep but clean penetration of the back of his left thigh and another in his guts, almost certainly a death blow. Brasidas had a deep cut across the top of his shoulder that bled like mad, and required him to be stitched up like a sail. Sittonax looked as if he'd been decapitated and his head sewn back on – a horrible-looking wound. We were all gathered around Leukas, as his wounds were the worst that were still saveable. Perhaps.

I mention this because Leukas had, for one reason and another, been sure he was to die in the battle, and despite that he'd fought very well – but he was sure that the wounds were mortal, until Brasidas began to wash them.

'Men got behind me,' Leukas said. He was, apparently, afraid we would think he'd turned his back and fled.

'So I see,' Hipponax said politely. He was holding the honey pot in his unbroken right hand and helping Brasidas, who was keeping him busy despite, or perhaps because of, his own pain. I knew that when the despair of battle's end hit him, added to the death of the girl, he would be in a bad place.

Hipponax's hand had swelled up like a melon. But I'm digressing.

Onisandros was not doing as well. The farther he got from the fire of battle, the worse his wound seemed, and I suspected he was slipping away on us. And he was in pain, and pain robs a man of courage. He had two deep stab wounds and a dozen cuts.

His screams were not helping young Kineas, whom Seckla had appointed acting oar-master. Kineas admired Onisandros and wanted to help him and we were trying to get a ship full of wounded men underway.

I think Brasidas wanted me to put him out of his misery, but I was in a black mood – I hadn't liked killing the man who had raised his hands for mercy and as I grew older, the blackness after battle grew worse, not better. And I had been with Onisandros and Leukas too long.

War is a terrible mistress. I have given so many friends into the maw of Ares. And I could not forget that Seckla took a belly wound and lived.

But Onisandros's screams and whimpering were not the trumpets of victory that we deserved and there were twenty other men as badly off or worse, and neither were they silent.

I went to Onisandros's side, and held his hand a while, and my son brought the honey and we anointed him as best as we could.

He screamed.

I could only think of my master, Hipponax, when I found him after the fight at Ephesus, when we stopped the Carians and the Persians broke the other rebels. He'd been in a worse case, and a life of nobility was screamed out in fear and despair.

War is terrible. Let no one doubt it.

I knelt by Onisandros and considered cutting his throat – for his own good. For the good of all. And I decided that the man who was afraid was me and that I needed to be strong and listen to him scream and do what I could for him, and not be afraid of his screams.

But by luck, or the grace of the gods, when we wrapped a clean length of Egyptian linen around his belly, he grew quieter. His eyes fluttered open – and then closed.

He took a few breaths.

'Just remember,' I said to my son, 'that this could as easily be you or I.'

Hipponax was crying.

I stood up, and looked over the sea. Kineas had the oars in the water – about two-thirds of our benches were manned, so that he'd emptied the bottom rowing deck. We were moving steadily, but slowly, because we were towing the great Phoenician trireme we'd taken.

As far as the eye could see to the east there were dead men, floating wrecks – triremes rarely sink when they are hit. Usually they just turn over and float like giant turtles or huge basking sharks.

Wrecks, corpses, and broken oars, a hideous carpet. As with everything else about Salamis, I had never seen anything like it – after Lade, the dead sank and the water hid the horror, but it was as if the Bay of Salamis wanted men to see what they had wrought.

The Great King's throne was gone.

It was late afternoon. Over towards Phaleron the Ionians fought a desperate rearguard action with the Aeginians, who came in like sharks to kill the weakest ships, and harried the Great King's fleet almost to their landing beaches. But around the island of Psyttaleia, the rest of the Greek fleet lay on their oars in an agony of exhaustion and victory.

In a wing beside me rowed Moire, in *Amastris*, with *Naiad* next outboard, followed by *Storm Cutter* with fewer benches manned than I had – Harpagos was dead and his nephew Ion was at the helm, and every marine aboard had died, except Sittonax, and many oarsmen and sailors, too. Then came Giannis and Megakles in *Black Raven*. I'd say we lost almost a quarter of our manpower without losing a single ship – the worst casualties I can remember taking in a sea fight, win or lose, except Lade.

The other Athenians whose ships ended the fight over by the coast of Attica gathered round me and Eumenes of Anagyrus, and we began to move slowly southward. The unwounded marines fished for living men as we rowed, and brought aboard a Persian nobleman and a dozen Ionians. We spared them – everyone had had a surfeit of blood, and men swimming in the water offer no threat.

The Persian was white and pasty from being in the water – he said his ship had been among the first struck. I gave him wine and fresh water and set him by Onisandros, because he was pretty far gone. He'd been in the water a long time.

Touchingly, he knew who I was. So I leaned over him, shading him from the sun, while Brasidas got me out of my armour.

I screamed too.

Blood from the earlier wound to my lower back had dried, making a great scab pressed between the back plate of bronze and my flesh. Brasidas tried to use water to break the scab away, but in his haste he got salt water.

I screamed for some time, I promise you. And no one offered to put me down.

But my recovery was swifter because I'd been wounded – often – and knew that the wound had only gone into fat and muscle. In fact, my wrenching of my left shoulder when I hit the water was to prove the worst wound I took that day, but that's another matter. Age magnifies wounds. Youth, however, fears them.

Eventually – and I swear it took us half the afternoon to cross six stades of water – we were nearing our landing beach, and the beach was full, crowded beyond belief with people. The whole population of Attica was there.

They were cheering and cheering. Xanthippus was just beaching – he came up from the east as we came from the north – and I saw Cleitus with a pang, knowing that the death of his daughter aboard my ship would reignite our feud. That is how men are. Someone must be blamed, and truly, my Hipponax was to blame.

He was by me, and I was glad he was alive. But I was going to make him do this thing.

I pointed at Cleitus's golden head. The man looked magnificent and still had his armour on. I was stripped to a terrible old chiton and my greaves.

'You must tell him,' I said.

Hipponax's eyes were red and his whole face was so puffy that he might have been badly beaten in a boxing match.

His head sank.

'You loved her?' I asked.

'I was going to marry her,' he said. His voice was barely audible for the cheering. 'I thought you knew.'

I admit that in that moment I understood a great many things I'd been told and to which I'd paid no attention in the past month. 'You brought her aboard?' I asked, attempting, and failing, to conceal my anger.

'She demanded it,' he said. 'You didn't know her, Pater. She was like ... a goddess, or a force of nature. She said that if I wanted to wed her, I needed to know that she was of the same – gold as me. That's what she said. That she could row and oar and fight.' He was crying again.

It was excruciating to hear him. I knew her only as the best dancer of the girls, nothing more. But Gorgo might have said the same to Leonidas.

'She claimed it was her bride price ...' He hung his head. 'I knew she could pull the oar. Onisandros helped me.'

I shook my head. But I could imagine Lydia or Briseis or Euphonia making the same demand and I know I'd have smuggled any of them aboard for the ultimate contest. And I had a sense – maybe because of what happened between me and Lydia – of what a woman's life was like. How the horizon began wide and narrowed with marriage to become almost a cage with children in it.

But that didn't assuage my anger, as a father and as a commander.

Anger, fatigue, fear, pain – all close friends. With the black mood that clouds your head after battle, a poisonous gang.

But I was no longer seventeen and I managed to walk away from my son and to help order the landing of the great Phoenician ship. She – he, I suppose, as most Phoenician ships were male – still had most of his rowers aboard with twenty Greek marines watching over them, and I had no intention of letting them be massacred by the crowd, or by Persians or Ionians either.

Brasidas led the unwounded marines ashore, despite his wound. They cheered him and the marines, but he cleared a large space and Xanthippus and his oarsmen pitched in, making space for the Phoenician ship to come ashore. The crowd began to bay for blood like hounds after a hunt, but some of the Priestesses of Athena and of Artemis were there and they silenced the crowd so that we could work the big Phoenician ashore.

We landed well, and the surf was down, and with the help of the priestesses the crowd went from vicious mongrels to willing hands. We got the ship up the beach as if he was made of parchment and a *taxis* of Athenian hoplites, eager to give us help, took the prisoners away, except the Persian, who I kept. Doctors came with a dozen remedies for wounds; one specialised in arrow removal and was very popular, and another had a preparation of vinegar and honey that he used on wounds, which he said averted the arrows of Apollo. The sheer number of helpers lifted my mood – there was even a man setting bones who looked at my son's hand and splinted it carefully, and another who, as I have mentioned, used needle and thread to close the flap of skin on Brasidas's shoulder and then pushed the Gaul down on the beach, knelt by him like a tailor of human flesh, and began on the slash to his neck.

Here is how close Sittonax came to death. While he fought, alone, a Phoenician marine or a Persian came behind him, threw his sword over the Gaul's head, and was just tightening his grip and cutting my friend's throat when an Athenian spear took the would-be killer from behind.

Onisandros and Leukas were taken with the rest of our badly wounded men to the big tents going up all along the streams – all made of our sails. Triremes, for the most part, don't put to sea to fight with their mainmasts or their sails on board. The wood and canvas is heavy and the rowers don't need the extra work. The handful of trihemiolias, like *Lydia*, had standing masts and rigging and made up for the weight in other ways. Suffice it to say we left our sails on the beach – most of us – and they made good tents for the wounded.

And then we had to contend with the adoration of the people of Attica. One of the oddest elements of that wonderful, terrible day is that we fought under the very eyes of our people. I don't think any battle in which I had ever participated so clearly brought home to me the division between a war of justice – the defence of people who would otherwise be made slaves – and a war of injustice like the piracy which I had made for most of my life. To be wrapped in the thanks of thousands, or tens of thousands of people … the blackness of the day evaporated. It was not just me; every man coming off *Lydia* to pull her ashore lifted his head from the weight of pain and blood, saw the welcome prepared him, and smiled. Matrons kissed me while their husbands pumped my hand; little girls held my knees, and boys gazed on me with the devotion given to gods, and such was the favour shown equally to every marine and every oarsman, too, top deck or bottom deck.

Perhaps it was the cheering and the smiles that gave Hipponax the courage to face Cleitus.

I'm thankful that at the last moment, I stripped my sword over my head – lest it be misconstrued – and followed him. I could not leave him to face Cleitus alone. I admit it: I feared Cleitus would cut him down on the spot, and my enemy – I still thought of him as such – was still in his panoply, very much the aristocratic warrior.

I had seen him on the deck of Xanthippus's *Horse Tamer*, but I lost him when he leapt into the shallows to help drag his own ship ashore. And I had other things to which I needed to attend; anyway, I trotted a little although my shoulder burned and caught my son on the wet sand.

'I'll come with you,' I said.

He gave me such a look. So many meanings.

I stayed with him.

We went through the crowd around our own ship – every slap on my back hurt me – and then out of it, and then through the admiring crowd around the capture: '*Did you help take this monster? Was this the Great King's ship? Did you fight in the war, mister?*'

Out the back of that crowd, trailing admirers. I confess that I was proud of my son. He was determined to face the consequences, even while attractive maidens threw themselves at his feet.

We came to the edge of the crowd around *Horse Tamer*. We plunged into the back of the crowd and Hipponax pushed people aside ruthlessly; he was in that hurry of spirit that drives a man to face something terrible and get it over, I imagine. And we trailed a few curses, except that the blood flowing over my left hip and the cuts all over Hipponax's forearms made it obvious we'd fought, and no one cursed us twice.

We pushed forward and I could hear Xanthippus, good Athenian aristocrat as he was, giving a speech. Of course he was giving a speech.

Somewhere, Themistocles was no doubt also giving a speech.

And to be fair, so was Aristides.

That's who they were.

Anyway, suddenly Hipponax slammed to a stop as if he faced a line of Phoenician spear points. I collided with him from behind.

A cry – an odd, barking cry – escaped him.

I pushed past.

There was Cleitus. He stood a few paces from Xanthippus.

And in his arms was Heliodora, his daughter.

Very much alive.

Of course she, a Brauron girl of eight summers' experience, had swum ashore. In fact to this day, she derides us for ever thinking otherwise – eh, honey? I have often been told that I was a great fool, as was her lover, for imagining that a little three-stade swim would even be a challenge.

On that day, however, she tore herself from her father's arms and threw her arms around my bloodstained son, who had been born a fisherman and was now publicly embracing the bluest blood in Athens.

Cleitus looked at me. 'I gather your wastrel son kidnapped my daughter aboard your ship,' he said calmly.

'I gather that your daughter possesses all your arrogance,' I answered.

His eyes met mine. 'By Zeus, imagine our grandchildren,' he said. 'My arrogance and yours, my hubris and yours,' he added.

But he offered me his hand.

By his orders, my mother died.

But she died a hero, after a misspent life. And as I have said before, revenge is mostly for weak men without enough to do. Like tend grapes and bounce babies.

I took his hand.

And there, on a beach in Attica, ended a feud that began in the market below the temple of Hephaestus in Marathon year, or perhaps before that, at the tomb of the Hero in Plataea. I won't pretend it wasn't mentioned again, in drunken anger, several times. I am only a man. But Achilles stood at my back in the fight at Salamis and put Simon's shade to rest, I think, and I took Cleitus's hand in the same spirit.

That was the beginning, for me, of the realisation that we had *won*.

So many defeats and so many wasted victories. But that day in early autumn, as the sun headed for the western mountains, the whole world looked different to me – to all of us, I think. The people of Attica saw hope fleeting by and began to believe they might return to their farms. And I? I saw my son, openly kissing Heliodora, and I thought of Briseis.

Briseis, whose needle case I had carried as a talisman. Who had called for me.

I suppose that I had thought of her earlier, as I had kept my Persian prisoner. I think that as soon as I heard him speak of Cyrus, I thought of how I might use him. And let me add, do him a favour as well.

At any rate, Xanthippus pressed my hand and said some pretty things to his crowd about Plataea and me, and then a cup of wine was pressed into my hand. I remember Hector, all false contrition, telling me of how he'd landed our first capture and then taken part in Aristides' assault on Psyttaleia. He had Heliodora's friend Iris under his cloak, she pretending not to be there and sometimes nuzzling his neck, so that they seemed one creature with two heads. And I remember lying beside Brasidas and listening to an old-style rhapsode sing the Iliad, and then hearing Themistocles make a speech to a great crowd on our beach, by torchlight. I remember Anaxagoras of Clazomenae and young Pericles talking about what the victory would mean, while my daughter, up far past her bedtime, snuggled against me and asked me to tell her what the battle had been like. The stars wheeled overhead and I was on my sixth or seventh bowl of wine when Cimon tugged at my chiton.

'Council,' he said. 'Why aren't you at it?'

So I rose carefully and moved my sleeping daughter into my tent. There was there enacted a brief scene straight from a comedy; Heliodora was in my tent and so was her mother. They were hissing at each other – that's my memory, which both deny. My son, fully dressed, may I add, was reclining on my kline, his hand bound to his side and his eyes a little glazed in the lamplight – by poppy, I think.

I tucked Euphonia into bed beside her brother.

Heliodora thrust out her chin and whispered something very emphatically, and then leaned over and kissed my daughter – ah, I loved her for that, and for her fighting and rowing, now that she'd survived it – and then kissed my son in a very different way, and her mother made a noise of exasperation.

Her mother dragged her away.

Who was I to protest?

I went out into the star-strewn darkness and followed Cimon up the beach.

'You angry at me?' he asked.

I stopped. People believe the oddest things, especially after a fight. 'No,' I said.

He hugged me. 'Good. It took me for ever to get the Corinthians into the fight. Your friend Lykon offered to fight Adeimantus on the spot and he still wouldn't move. And when we did start rowing—' he shrugged. 'You weren't the worst off.'

We both knew what it was like to make those decisions. Life and death for friends and foes, done without time to ponder or weigh.

We walked into the darkness in more perfect understanding than most lovers ever reach.

About halfway to the headland, he said, 'We won.'

I think those were the only words we exchanged.

The council was confused and very loud – what a surprise.

Many of the navarchs were there, but not all. I embraced Lykon and Bulis, delighted that more of my friends had escaped the embrace of death.

Themistocles was talking, but then, he always was.

In fact, he was demanding that we rise in the morning and attack the enemy beaches at Phaleron to finish the job.

He went on and on. In truth, I think he was drunk – drunk on a heady mixture of wine and victory. Well, most of us were. But Themistocles lacked our years of fighting and he had seen the fleet rise and fight again and again at Artemisium. I think he imagined we'd come off our beaches the next morning, fresh as flowers or perhaps tired but capable. And he had a point.

'Make no mistake,' he said. 'What is left of their fleet is still larger than our fleet.'

'No ship that fought today will fight well tomorrow,' I said.

Many men muttered agreement.

Cimon spoke up. 'I had an easy day,' he said, though most of us knew he was lying. 'I'll have a look at their beaches in the morning.'

I nodded. 'I'll go with you,' I said. 'But I'll have to pull the best rowers out of four ships to row *Lydia*.'

I went to bed. Men drank well into the night and the crop of babies born nine months later suggests that drinking was not the evening's only sport. Heh! I can see a pair of you from here.

Born in the summer of Plataea?

But I get ahead of myself.

It was sad and yet delightful to go to sea the next morning as dawn broke. I had Moire as my oar-master and Megakles in the steering oars and Giannis standing with Alexandros as marines. I'd sent young Kineas and old Giorgos to pick the best of the unwounded oarsmen, and many were the drink-fuelled curses that morning. And as we pulled away from the beach to meet up with Cimon I wondered briefly if we'd suddenly find ourselves off Massalia, or coasting along the tall white cliffs of Alba.

'The Argonauts,' I whispered.

Seckla smiled.

I'd like to say we did some great deed, worthy of being sung for ever – and the time was not wasted, as you'll hear – but in fact we made our rendezvous with Cimon's long black *Ajax* and rowed out of the Bay of Salamis against the wind, experiencing a little of what the Persians had felt the day before when the wind had been the other way, and then we pulled across the open water for Phaleron with our sails laid to the battens and ready to raise for the run back. The risk was very small.

And as it proved, the enemy fleet was gathered at the eastern edge of the Phaleron beaches. Of course Cimon wanted to scout them and perhaps even put fire into their ships, and of course I wanted to as well.

But our rowers spoke in loud grumbles and some very slow rowing. So we promised them a quick trip home and contented ourselves with a distant reconnaissance, safely out of bowshot. We could see that Mardonius had moved much of the army down onto the plains above Phaleron, so they clearly feared that we would attack. There was even a stockade, and we could see slaves digging and others bringing up cut olive trees – cutting olive trees, curse them!

But there we were, perhaps ten plethora off the beach, beyond extreme bowshot, anyway. The day was clear, the wind soft and steady, and no one was coming off the beach.

But the bastards were busy. And I could now pick out individual ships – there was the Red King, for example, and there was Artemisia's elegant ship – and there was Archilogos's ship.

If I hadn't seen his trireme, beached bow out and with Briseis's beautiful eyes painted either side of the ram, I might not have noticed. But I stepped up on the platform amidships, wishing my shoulder was good enough to climb, watching Archilogos's ship. Three hulls to the west was Diomedes' ship.

There were men moving around all of them, all the best Ionians.

I looked for as long as a man might speak in the agora to a friend. Then I waved for Seckla's attention. I didn't want to move my eyes and lose my targets.

'Take us in,' I said.

Kineas thumped for the oarsmen, but close by me old Giorgos spat. 'You said, "easy day",' he commented – not to me precisely, which might have been bad for discipline. His head was turned away, as if he was speaking to the air.

'I won't get us in a fight, and I'll serve out good wine with my own hands,' I said quietly.

'And a drachma per man,' old Giorgos said. He shrugged. 'I could be gettin' me dick wet. 'Stead of getting all of me wet, so to speak. Eh? Lord?'

'And a drachma per man. But not paid today, *mate.*' I was not a rich man just then.

He spat over the side and looked along the gangway at one of his own mates.

'Well, then, since yer so agreeable, like,' he said.

And they all started rowing.

We crept for ten strokes and then, at a shouted command, we went for it – straight to a fast speed – faster than a long cruise, anyway. We covered the stade to shore like a good runner and turned end for end even as the first arrows began to fly from the Persian troops on the beach. They were well shot, but passed over us – a dozen went into our canvas screens along the forwards rowers' banks, but not a man was hit, thank all the gods.

In the time we turned, I had confirmed what I suspected.

Then we raised our sails and raced for home and oarsmen came on deck. It was a free day, and after the victory, only a fool or a very bad officer indeed would have forbidden anything to an oarsman, so they came and went, and laughed, and discipline was almost nonexistent. Seckla looked worried and I think Brasidas, whose wounds made him stiff, would have been appalled, but I had some notion of what they'd done the day before and what it took to go out again, and I let men loll on deck, watching the headland reach by – I even let young Kineas and two of his friends try their hands as steering, with Seckla and Megakles giving laconic advice and encouragement. The ship had a festive atmosphere that was marred briefly by the dead washed up like sea wrack after a storm on the Cynosura headland and we had to pull down the sails and row carefully after we struck a submerged wreck and almost lost Megakles over the side.

He looked at me wryly – he was probably the oldest man aboard.

'I think I'm for home,' he said. No preamble, and no argument.

'I need you for one more thing,' I said.

He shrugged. 'Will you give me a boat to take home?'

I nodded. I owed him too much to make conditions.

'Just the triakonter,' he said. 'I'll take her in lieu of my wages and my shares.' He shrugged again. 'What thing, boss?'

I pulled at the knots in my beard. 'I'm going to Ephesus,' I said.

He nodded. 'Course you are.' The men who'd been with me for years knew it all. 'Fighting?'

'I expect,' I admitted.

He shrugged a third time. 'Triakonter?' he asked.

'Yours,' I said. 'And anything else you ask for.'

He laughed. 'You're like a story,' he said. Perhaps the best compliment I've ever been paid.

*

That afternoon we saw Xerxes come down, in person, to the beaches opposite. I didn't see it, but others rowing our guard ships say so. And the Persians began to salvage any wreck close enough to the beach to be pulled ashore. They immediately began to fill the hulls with earth.

You could see all this activity as a smudge of busy, distant ants over by Piraeus.

'He's trying to build a bridge,' Themistocles said. I think there was genuine admiration in his tone.

Aristides sat on his heels – still, I think, exhausted from the day before. 'Can't be done,' he said. 'Insane hubris.'

Themistocles and Eurybiades took the threat seriously, however, and were discussing sending ships and archers to attack the workmen.

Anaxagoras had a different point of view. He was silent for a long time, unusual for him. Then he raised his hand cautiously, like a schoolboy afraid to speak.

Our Spartan navarch was not a fan of the Ionian boy. 'What, youngster? In my home, a ten-year man doesn't speak at all unless invited.' The ten years were in the first phase of manhood – older, in fact, than Anaxagoras.

Anaxagoras nodded. 'That's interesting, sir. But what I wanted to say is – it cannot be done.'

Eurybiades was never very fond of being brought up short, even by men he saw as his peers. 'Oh?' he asked. Spartans see sarcasm as a form of weakness (I think they're wrong) but short answers often betray anger.

'If you would consider,' Anaxagoras said, 'the volume of mythemnoi of earth required to fill a basket that is six stades long and, say, a plethora wide?'

The mythemnos was a volume of grain that Athenians used to measure a man's wealth. In Athens they sell grain by that measure, and many other things. You can put a mythemnos of grain into a basket as big around as two men's arms in a circle and knee-high.

We all tried to do the maths.

'It's millions,' Anaxagoras said, using the Persian word. 'Tens of thousands times tens of thousands of mythemnoi and all that has to be dug and moved and rolled out over the jetty as it forms. Can't be done.'

Aristides was a fair head at arithmetic and I had studied with

Heraclitus and read my Pythagoras, and we looked at each other – and frowned.

'I think he's right,' Aristides said. 'Even if he does talk too much.'

'I agree,' I said.

Themistocles stroked his beard. 'Then why is he doing it?' he asked.

We all passed a bowl of watered wine – Cimon's – and I watched Themistocles and his slave and tried to decide if he'd intended to betray Greece or not. To be honest, it no longer seemed to matter.

It was Eurybiades who spoke. 'He's covering something,' he said. 'He wants us to watch him build that bridge. Or he's run mad with anger, which I hear from Bulis is well within his character.'

Cimon looked at me. 'Someone's boiling to tell a tale,' he said with his usual light mockery. 'Go ahead, Plataean.'

I shrugged. 'We went in close when we scouted their ships,' I said. Eurybiades nodded.

'I went close because there were men moving on the ships – on the Ionian ships.'

'Do you think they mean to fight again?' Eurybiades asked.

'I'm telling this badly,' I admitted. I am often guilty of trying to make a good story of everything, I confess it.

I looked around the fire. 'They were getting masts and sails aboard,' I said.

'By Poseidon!' Eurybiades said. 'They can't mean to fight, then.'

It was just a feeling I had – a feeling that had something to do with my own mission to Ephesus and my fears for it. 'I think the Ionians are running for home,' I said.

Themistocles wore an odd face.

'Perhaps we should stop them,' he said. Even as he said it I could see him considering some other angle. By then, despite our out-and-out victory, I distrusted him all the time. 'We could give chase.'

But it was Cimon who made the lucky guess. 'What if the Great King is running for home?'

'We didn't beat them *that* badly,' the Spartan navarch said.

'We did, though,' Themistocles said. He was picking his teeth and looking out to sea. 'He is a long way from Susa.'

Bulis laughed, by which I took him to mean 'don't I know it,' but Lacedaemonians don't say everything that comes to their minds.

The fire crackled. We all drank some wine and slaves ran and fetched more and I saw a look pass between Themistocles and Siccinius.

'We could run them all down,' he said, with rising excitement. 'We could capture the Great King!'

'In a running fight across a thousand stades of ocean?' I asked. Cimon said almost the same thing, while Aristides crossed his eyes and looked discontented.

Eurybiades looked especially thoughtful. 'We could break the bridge at Hellespont,' he said. 'And trap his army in Europe.'

That stopped us all.

Cimon grinned. 'Now you are talking, sir!' He leapt to his feet. 'I wanted the forward strategy to begin with. This is – beautiful.'

'I'm just thinking aloud,' Eurybiades said primly. 'You Athenians are so hot-headed.'

Themistocles looked troubled. 'And yet that might *not* be the best notion,' he said.

We all looked at him. He'd won a brilliant victory – it was largely his fleet and his plan – and yet we didn't trust him, and he could feel our want of regard and that, in turn, made him more difficult. He fed on adulation, like the gods eat ambrosia and nectar.

He stood up. 'Think!' he said, suggesting we were all fools. I think he really did think that. 'Think! The Great King, trapped in Europe, has no choice but to win or die. He has all Thessaly to provide grain and remounts, and he has Macedon at his back as well. He can fight a long time here and many cities that are with us are also expecting winter to bring an end to the war. Trap the Great King here and we could fight him for ever, as a neighbour.' He looked around. 'Don't you see? If he's panicked, all the better! If he runs, his troops will lose heart.'

'If we took him, we could all be rich,' I said. I admit it – I said it out loud.

Even Cimon glared at me in distaste.

'Oh, you fine gentlemen,' I said. 'Not a one of you doesn't like a ransom?'

'Ransom the Great King?' Eurybiades asked. There it is, friends – a Spartan officer saw the Great King as perhaps the enemy, but still the 'first among equals' of all royalty.

I made a disgusted noise.

So did some of them, although Cimon gave me a slight shake of his head. He meant that I was a fool to say such a thing aloud. And I was.

'No, we must not do such a thing,' Themistocles said.

And he carried the vote. The Corinthians didn't want to give chase and neither did any of the Peloponnesians. The Aeginians, on the other hand, were for immediate pursuit.

I began to make my own plans.

When I went back to camp, I patted our dog – he'd moved in and was as much part of the company as Seckla – and then nabbed Ka. I gave him instructions and he rolled his eyes.

'I fight yesterday too,' he said.

'Then send one of the others,' I said.

He shook his head.

I went to the next beach, where I had heard the Brauron girls would perform the sacred dances they had practised all summer.

That was a beautiful night, if you could ignore the smell rolling off the waves that told of the deaths of many men, and frankly, I could. As a well-known priest of Hephaestus I was invited to lie on one of the few actual couches after the sacrifices – a great honour that night.

Of course they danced brilliantly!

My daughter had, in fact, a very small part, but she did it flawlessly, and she was summoned back by one of the priestesses to take a crown of olive to Iris, who was flawless in her dancing, and another to Heliodora, who really looked like a goddess – she had something that is difficult to describe, something I had seen the day before in the fighting, from my son, from Brasidas, from Harpagos – some inner glow, a smile that was more than confidence. It was as if watching her dance made us all better people and I think that in fact, despite all the competitive crap and the hard words and the anger, it is this that is true arête, the excellence that makes men – and apparently women too – better than they were.

And I smiled to think that this goddess would wed my son, who excelled at temper tantrums and collecting expensive swords – and war. He was going to need to find other talents.

I suppose there might be a version of this story where Hector moped while Hipponax courted but, if anything, Hector moved faster than his sword brother. Or rather – I was there and it seems possible to me that Iris moved faster than Hipponax or Hector. There was a different fire in her and, once lit, I suspect it was not easily quenched. I'll say no more, as she lives yet, and might grace us with her presence!

But the dance was superb. Euphonia would only tease me with how little I remember of what was danced and how; suffice it to say I was entranced. The priestesses were in many ways the best of all – mature, flowing, controlled, like the best athletes. The two priests of Apollo sacrificed. There was a huge crowd – I was lucky to be with the priests – and the roars went on and on. Men began to serve out cooked meat to the crowd and other men brought more animals to sacrifice, and I suspect they killed a hecatomb before the night was through.

The High Priestess came and lay by me after she made the last dance and oversaw the sacrifices. It was a great honour, considering all the powerful men around us on the beach, lying on improvised couches. Themistocles was sitting on a camp stool and Aristides gave up looking for a spot and sat on the end of my straw-stuffed mattress and stuck his legs out in front of him like an oarsman catching a nap, about two heartbeats after the elegant old woman lowered herself with the grace of a maiden.

Thiale nodded to him as he sat. 'Hail to thee, best of the Athenians.'

Aristides' head jerked around, looked down his long nose at her, saw something he liked, and let his tone lighten. 'I am not the best of the Athenians this night. That honour goes to Ameinias of Pallene. My pardon, Lady – I mistook you for one of Arimnestos's friends.'

Thiale looked at me. Then at Aristides. 'I can't say I'm flattered,' she said, and we all laughed. 'But then,' she went on, 'I can't say that I've been on a kline with a man recently, either.'

Priestesses of Artemis were not generally fond of men at all, of course.

'Your girls were superb,' I said.

'Weren't they?' she said brightly, like a much younger woman. She had the face of an old matron, like a ripe apple with a few wrinkles, and twinkling eyes that could be hard as granite, but the legs and feet of a young woman, and her facial expressions were also young: passionate, fluid. 'I think this was a miraculous year, but, I confess, I almost always think so.'

'They will not soon forget dancing the ritual on the beaches of Salamis,' I said.

She nodded. 'Will you, gentlemen? Soon forget? Because, I must tell you, I can be a mean-spirited old woman when I must, and tonight, on this holy night when all the gods are watching, I'm trying to raise funds to rebuild our temple when you have moved the Persians out.'

Of course. In the moment of victory, I had all but forgotten what any true Athenian or Attic farmer knew in his bones – the sea was won, but Attica was still in the hands of the Medes.

Aristides nodded. 'I will find a talent of silver for you, Lady.'

She put a hand to her breast. 'A talent! By my goddess, sir, you are generous.'

'You may have to wait until I have a functioning farm or two to raise it,' Aristides said.

'At least your house is intact,' I joked.

She looked at me.

Hector, who was still a good boy despite his infatuation, appeared by my couch with a pitcher of very good wine and three cups – not a bowl. Upper-class women did not drink from a kalyx, at least, not in Greece when lying with men. He brought little egg-shaped cups such as we use in Boeotia to have a dram when the work is done. Iris appeared as if my magic and held the cups while he poured.

The High Priestess accepted the wine and smiled at Iris.

'Yes,' Iris said.

Some message passed between their eyes.

I put a hand on her arm. 'I too will give a talent of silver, if my ships have survived the last month,' I said. 'If Poseidon, and Artemis and all the gods are kind. It will take me a year.'

She smiled – a smile which lit her face.

I noted that Iris was still standing there, and Hector.

The High Priestess nodded. 'I am acting as mother to Iris,' she said. 'Her father is a famous man – I cannot say his name aloud. Her mother is a Thracian slave.'

'Freed woman,' Iris said. Those two words carried so much content. Iris was tall, beautiful and handsome at the same time, the most athletic of the girls and you could see her Thracian mother in her strength and her oddly light eyes with black rings around the iris. She was one of those people whose intelligence shone forth from her eyes, and the two words she said told me that she accepted her mother's status, and her mother, without bitterness.

The more I looked at her, the more likely it seemed to me that Xanthippus was her father.

'Am I acting as father to Hector?' I asked.

Aristides laughed. It was not like him to laugh at such a time. He rose to his feet. 'My friend,' he said, 'you are in fact acting as his mother – a position we will all be in if we do not re-conquer Attica and get our wives back in our houses. I miss Jocasta.'

'I miss her too,' I admitted. It is hard to talk to a woman who is so close she can smell your breath. But I turned to her. 'My lady, I view Hector as my son.'

She nodded. 'If you had a wife ...' she said.

'I may have one by the end of winter,' I said.

She nodded, and gave a slight smile. 'Very well. May I ask – what age will this wife be?'

I frowned, calculating. 'I believe she is but one year younger than me, my lady.' In that moment my mind had a flash of Briseis, naked in a chlamys, pinned under my body in a garbage-strewn alley in Ephesus when I thought she was my rival and a man.

'Ah,' the High Priestess said, obviously surprised. 'A woman your own age?'

'My first love,' I said.

'The things one learns at feasts,' Aristides said.

I motioned to my friend for peace. I looked at Hector. His face said everything it needed to say.

'My Hector is eligible, free of entanglement, clean of mind and body, and will have a small fortune from me when I die,' I said, 'unless the Medes have it all, of course. And he also has money of his own – shares in our last captures, for example. He is a citizen of Green Plataea.'

'My Iris is not a citizen woman of Athens,' the priestess said. 'But I can promise a fine dowry, and I suspect Athenian citizenship for her husband could be arranged.' She looked at Aristides.

He was still standing, trying hard to pretend he was not there. I knew the look – I had shared it.

But he nodded. 'I suspect that Themistocles will offer citizenship to many of the metics and allies who served in Athenian ships. That would be a just action,' he said primly, 'and young Hector of Syracusa has risked as much as any man here.'

The High Priestess rose as gracefully as she had lain down and kissed Iris on the brow. 'Do you consent to wed her, young man?' she said to Hector.

'Oh – yes!' he said, for once at a loss for words.

She nodded, satisfied. 'Iris, you are one I might have kept to be a priestess. But I think the life of the world is for you.'

Iris smiled, but she was crying. 'My daughters will come to you, Mother.'

Well, by the gods, I cried too.

As soon as the young people went off into the dark to celebrate their engagement, and the High Priestess went away lightly over the sand, Aristides lay full length at my side. 'You are going for Briseis,' he said.

I nodded.

'I can't be party to it,' he said. 'I am needed here.'

I nodded and gave him a small hug, to show that I understood. 'I don't need men,' I said. 'In fact, I have a different role for you – and Jocasta – if you will accept it.'

He nodded.

'Will you winter here or in Hermione?' I asked. Hermione was where many Athenians and almost all of the Plataeans had gone, you'll recall.

'I will go back to Hermione to fetch Jocasta as soon as I understand what our military plans might be,' he said.

'Will you and Jocasta arrange – things – for me in Hermione?' I asked. 'I'll guess that both my sons will wed. And I will wed Briseis. Or, alternatively, I will be dead, and you will see to it that my estate is divided, and that the boys marry.'

Aristides nodded, his eyes on mine. 'Yes,' he said.

'I will be back in a month,' I said.

Later that night, and I was sober and alert and busy choosing crew and talking to men I wanted. I was sitting on a camp stool beside Brasidas. Euphonia was asleep in her bed and Cleitus had sent me a slave asking me to come to his tent for wine. I knew what that conversation would be about, but I put him off with a message of my own.

Ka appeared. He made a sign, which I understood.

I nodded to Brasidas and Polymarchos, who was close by, sober enough, and the three of us hung swords over our shoulders and walked across the sand, through the milling crowds, to where Cleitus was camped, well up the ridge and nearer to Xanthippus. I was welcomed into his temporary home.

I introduced Brasidas and Polymarchos. Cleitus was not just polite, but welcoming, as was his wife. She was small and quick, like a bird – very pretty, and sharp as the kopis under my arm.

She put a hand under my arm. 'I do not think you need to wear a sword to visit my husband ever again,' she said. 'Although when I heard you let my daughter aboard a warship—'

She was not really joking. She was both pleasant and furious at once.

People are not simple, and had I been in her place I believe I might have been the same.

'I did not know,' I said. 'In fact, I should have known – I heard them begin to plan it, and I thought it was all … childish stuff.'

She shook her head. 'Heliodora has never been childish,' she said. 'And what keeps me from grabbing for your sword like Medea is that I know her well enough to know that it must have been her notion and her hand at the tiller.'

Considering that I had previously only known her as the matron pulling her daughter out of my tent – as I say, that could have been a scene in a nasty comedy – I thought that she was both wise and very well-spoken.

I bowed to both of them. 'We are wearing swords for a purpose,' I said. 'Because Cleitus and I are well known to be foes, I would ask him to come with us – armed.' I nodded to Aspasia, Cleitus's wife. 'I am more than willing to discuss wedding terms,' I said. 'But this is a question of the future of Athens and perhaps Greece.'

Cleitus didn't quite trust me. 'May I bring a friend?' he asked carefully.

'Or two,' I said.

He disappeared out his pavilion's back door and returned with a sword and thorax and two large men – marines.

I eyed the fine wine and cheese and round cakes carefully piled by couches, clearly prepared for a nice upper-class wedding discussion, with remorse. 'With luck I'll be back in a few minutes,' I said to Aspasia.

She sighed. 'Is this a sample of our shared family lives?' she asked.

Then we were off across the sand, to the headland.

Cleitus didn't even ask who Ka might be.

Instead, he asked, 'What's this about?'

I looked at him a moment. 'I may be wrong in everything I'm about to say,' I said. 'But I have suspected Themistocles for a month. He is in contact with the Great King and right now, unless we've taken too long, he is preparing to send his slave Siccinius to the King across the bay.'

Cleitus walked on for several paces.

'Shit,' he said.

We surrounded his tent. It was past midnight. I could hear his voice and that of Siccinius. He was drilling Siccinius on what the man should say.

Even now, it's difficult to be *sure*. Is it treason to hedge your bets?

I say yes. I say, when most men cannot build themselves two beds, it is treason to do so.

I had Ka knock on his tent pole and then I went in, followed by Brasidas, Polymarchos, Cleitus and his friends. We were quite a crowd.

'Gentlemen,' Themistocles said. His voice was even, but I heard the catch.

'Themistocles,' I said, 'there is a boat prepared on the beach with two slaves to row it – and you ordered it prepared. You are telling your slave what to say to the Great King – we all heard you. I accuse you of treason.'

'I am used to dealing with small minds incapable of understanding my mind,' he said slowly, as if puzzled and hurt. 'But you are a subtle fox, a man of deep thought, and I expect better of you.' Then he saw Cleitus and he reacted as if in surprise. 'And you, Cleitus,' he said, as if this was even more of a disappointment.

'Treason,' I said.

'There is more to life than sword cuts, spear blows and boarding actions,' he said to me. 'I am working to panic the Great King into a hasty decision.'

'By telling him that you have kept us from launching an assault on the Hellespont,' I said. I'd just heard the bastard drilling his minion on his plan.

'Yes!' he said. 'We need him to run, Arimnestos. Imagine five years of war fought in Attica and Boeotia. Imagine all the olive trees cut, all the farms burned, every house ruined, every temple thrown down.'

'I can imagine all that, and not send messages to the Great King.'

'And yet you have spoken to him three – or is it four, times?' he asked. 'And I have never spoken to him once. Which of us is a traitor? You went to him of your own free will – against our instructions!'

Cleitus looked back and forth. 'I am not this Plataean's greatest friend,' he said, 'but I've never heard anyone sane accuse him of being an ally of the Medes.'

Brasidas nodded. 'Have you informed Eurybiades of your plan to deceive the Great King?' he asked.

The two men locked eyes, and it was Themistocles who flinched.

Brasidas nodded at me. 'Before you make more accusations, Athenian, let me say this. I can speak to Demaratus any time I want. He has long been the Great King's confidante. Shall I ask him how he views you?'

I had brought the former Spartan for muscle. I tended to forget who he was.

It was silent in the tent.

'I play a deep game,' Themistocles said, which made me smile. It was probably true. 'We have been starved for news this whole campaign. Remember the Vale of Tempe! I will not let that happen again.'

And again, I was on the horns of dilemma. Was he lying? I was sure he was.

Or he wasn't.

Gods – or he didn't know himself.

'What news do we gain?' I asked. 'Wait. Will you allow me to speak to your slave?'

Themistocles shrugged. 'Be my guest,' he said wearily.

I took Siccinius outside, to a campfire, and Brasidas came with me, and Ka. Polymarchos stayed with Cleitus, and one of Cleitus's marines, Antiphon, came with us.

Siccinius was shaking. 'I only do what he tells me,' the man said. 'And by Hades, it is killing me with fear. I am a slave – the Great King can have me burned alive, pulled apart by horses. What can you do to me?'

I knelt on one knee by him. He was on a camp stool, and my other friends were close around him. But by arrangement, Ka pulled out his beautiful bronze canteen – loot, I fear, from Artaphernes' trireme – and gave him some wine, good, Chian wine.

'I can make you a citizen of Plataea,' I said. 'I can see to it that you have a shop or a small farm or a school in which to teach children. All you need to do is answer my questions.'

'Hades,' the man said. He sounded miserable.

But he answered all our questions.

Listen, friends, a man like Themistocles can either lie without changing his face, or worse, make himself believe anything he says is true. Such men are as dangerous as mad dogs, even when they lead you to great victories, or perhaps especially then. But Siccinius was really just a bright, brave man of otherwise average merit, enslaved by war and circumstance. Spying had burned away a great deal of his courage, and you must understand: everyone comes to the end of courage. It is one thing to face the spears one day – I have said this before – and another to live in fear *every* day until your whole life is a curse and nothing is real, nothing is good, there are no gods. Blessed father Zeus, friends, if you have not fought a long war, you cannot imagine how dark the bottom of that pit can be.

Eh, lads?

I won't bore you with everything he said. I'll only say that nothing he said damned his master absolutely. Some of it was pretty dark – he'd been ten times to visit Mardonius or the Great King, and he'd made a trip before Artemisium.

But ... many of Themistocles' best notions had been products of Siccinius's spying.

In effect, there was no easy answer. Was Themistocles a traitor?

I was, in fact, no wiser, except that his lover and slave did not think his master was a traitor – thought him, in fact, the architect of the greatest and most complex deception ever planned.

I cannot love Themistocles. But I could not, in honour, find him guilty.

'You go to the Great King tonight?' I asked Siccinius.

'Yes, lord,' the younger man said.

'You know the Lord Cyrus, a soldier?' I asked.

'He that spoke against you?' Siccinius asked.

'I still cannot discern whether you tried for our release or not,' Brasidas said.

'Lord, I did as I was bid, for the good of Greece,' Siccinius said.

Brasidas nodded, rising. 'I will vote to make him a citizen of Plataea,' he said. 'He's a man, if nothing else.' He walked off to the tent of Themistocles.

I took the slave by a shoulder. I reached into my chiton and withdrew, from the fold I'd made, the needle case and handed it to him. I, too, could plot, and make arrangements. 'Give this to Lord Cyrus,' I said. 'I give you my word that it is not treason. He is an old friend.'

He took it.

'Nor is it a poison pill. Read the message yourself, if you must, but give it to him and I will guarantee my eternal gratitude and your freedom.'

He smiled. 'I swear this is my last trip,' he said. Then he looked away. 'I've sworn that since the first trip.'

'May the goddess stand by you,' I said.

I went then and bowed to Themistocles. 'I will neither publicly accuse you nor apologise,' I said. I looked at Cleitus, who nodded. 'I will watch you. If your story proves out – well, you may apply to me and I will praise your subtlety as the greatest since Hermes stole cattle from Lord Apollo. If I catch you in direct treason ...' Again I shrugged. 'I will take some action.'

'But you will tell no one,' Themistocles said. His smile as he said it was, to me, proof, and led me to wonder if Themistocles was enough of a player to have me killed.

'Imagine how long you would last if I told Aristides,' I said.

Themistocles looked away.

I had asked Cleitus because he was not really a member of any party except the eupatridae. He turned his head towards me – trying to read if I was tricking him, I think. But when we had left and were wallowing along the sand of our beach, he paused beyond the firelight.

'What was all that about?' he asked.

'Everyone knows you and I do not see eye to eye,' I said. 'I wanted you to see and hear, so that I had an impartial witness.'

Cleitus winced. 'I've never liked him. A democrat of the most vulgar style. No one will believe me—'

'Aristides would, if it came to that,' I said.

Cleitus paused, and then motioned to his marines to step away.

'This is poison,' he said. 'If men thought that Themistocles was betraying us, our League could collapse.'

'I know,' I said.

'What do you propose to do now?' he asked.

'Go plan my son's wedding,' I said.

Cleitus laughed. 'Well,' he said. 'Probably the best course.'

I awoke with the dawn for the usual reasons and dragged my aching limbs out of my blankets. The morning had a chill to it but the sun rose into a cloudless sky and the wind was from the west. I walked down to the edge of the sea where many men were already about their business. In the bustle, Siccinius bumped into me and, rather cleverly, handed me back the wooden needle case. He bowed, apologised for being clumsy, and went to attend his master while I returned to my tent and read the message in the case.

Greeting, Doru.

My new master, Artaphernes son of Artaphernes, rides in the morning. He is going all the way to Ephesus. He will go very quickly. He will leave my war-brothers and me because he knows we will fight him in this.

He means to kill her and her children.

Doru, I owe my honour to my king. But I will pray that you save her. And I remain your friend.

It was plainly written in Persian, in the new script that the soldiers used. I knew it well enough, and I knew who would have written it – Cyrus. I wondered at it though. Why on earth would young Artaphernes, who'd already, I assumed, been accepted as Satrap, need to kill Briseis? Why would he ride home to do so?

I found Seckla just rising, and visited Leukas, who was still in agony. But not dead. Onisandros, however, was. Seckla had just closed his eyes.

I put a hand on his forehead, and it was already cold. Death is ... death.

I went and knelt by Leukas. He looked terrible – grey instead of fleshy. He was in control of his voice though, and he locked my right hand in a grip of adamant.

'I want to come to sea,' he said.

I knelt by him. 'You're better off here – look at all these pretty girls,' I said with, I confess it, false humour.

Leukas pulled me close. 'I want to die at sea,' he said. 'Clean. Put my body in the water. Float home. Closer to my gods. You owe me, sir. Promise me!'

I gave my oath and Seckla and Brasidas had him taken aboard. We also shipped Harpagos's corpse. I intended to return him to his sister.

We rigged a big awning forward of the helmsman's station and made Leukas as comfortable as we could.

That is, Seckla did. I went and visited the other wounded men. A dozen had died but now the rest would probably make it. That's what I thought at the time – the horrible maths of the butcher's bill. If a man lives a week, he's probably going to make it. Apollo takes a few in the third week, from infection, but if you live even three days your odds are much better.

I thought about Leukas. And about Seckla. About Briseis and Artaphernes and even about Xerxes; and war, and men who inflict war.

And then I moved on. This is one of the hardest aspects of leading men, and women. You cannot stop, not to mourn, not to admit defeat or even to rest on the laurels of a well-won victory. Because people need to be fed and clothed and motivated, and you just cannot stop. Sometimes, when my spirits are low, all I want is sleep, and yet ... there are wounded men to visit, there's the supply list to check, there's Seckla feeling the darkness and needing a friend.

Don't start on the road of leading men unless you plan to finish, or die trying. Because when you accept responsibility for them – by the gods, if you fail, they all fall with you, and on your head be it.

I drink now to my own dead. If you could see them, if, like Odysseus, I might pour out a libation of blood and see them come to drink it, what a crowd there would be in this room, my friends!

Anyway, I asked all the oarsmen to gather on the beach. While they were coming in, many with hard heads and some looking almost green, we heard cheering from the headland and before I had my people together, news had come that the whole of Xerxes' fleet was putting to sea.

I wasn't surprised – they'd been getting their masts and sails aboard the day before – and yet I *was* surprised. These days, when people speak of Salamis, it is as if our big fight won the war. I know better. Until we saw them running, most of us assumed we'd have to fight again. When they ran, they still outnumbered us.

The problem, of course, was that the part of the fleet that had been destroyed was the part most loyal to the Great King, and the part now cutting and running for home was mostly Ionian. They had fought well – many were ships commanded by the Tyrants and their families, who would lose everything if a democratic government arose. But at the same time they had little love for the Persians. And no interest in taking further losses fighting us.

War is complicated because it *is* politics.

I gave up on speaking to my people. We all ran, pell-mell, to the peninsula and looked out over the sea, where hundreds of sails covered the ocean to the east, as far as the eye could make them out – not just triremes, either, but smaller ships, all the Egyptians who'd never been engaged and all the hundreds of merchantmen who had supplied the fleet.

Most of the men saw in that stampede of enemy ships the moment of victory.

Cimon was by me. He grabbed my chiton. 'Look at that!' he said. 'A fortune for any pirate quick enough to snap them up.'

'But we're not to pursue them,' Lykon said.

As events proved, Eurybiades and Themistocles had already decided on the next step. We had a brief conference near the ashes of the altar fire.

Eurybiades didn't need advice. He simply reiterated the ideas put forth the day before as to why we should not race the enemy for the Hellespont.

'But,' he said, 'it would be foolish for us to let them go without any pursuit. If those more eager for freedom see our ships coming behind, some may yet defect.'

That made sense, too. A half-dozen Ionians had defected *before* the battle.

Eurybiades looked around. 'I ask you gentlemen to make one more throw. The weather is fair. Let us pursue them a few days at least.'

Themistocles wouldn't meet my eye, but he waved for attention. 'Nor can we simply give chase,' he said. 'We must be prepared to fight. I would like to put to sea in three columns: the Athenians under Xanthippus, the Corinthians and Peloponnesians under Adeimantus, and the Aeginians under Polycritus.'

Polycritus smiled without mirth. 'I can be off the beaches before the sun rises another finger's width,' he said. 'See that you Athenians keep up.'

Cimon caught me as other men began to race for their ships. 'Let's form together,' he said.

'When Themistocles turns,' I said, 'I'll be going on. All the way to Ephesus.'

Cimon knew why. But he was still hesitant. 'You could find yourself alone in a sea of enemies.'

'Perhaps you'll come too,' I said.

He scratched his beard. 'Prizes,' he said aloud.

And then he turned and ran for his ships.

The squadrons were putting every hull in the water – indeed, the Athenians were fitting out half a dozen captures from the battle, although none of them was fit for sea quite yet. But we had volunteers that morning – hoplites and other middle-class men who offered to pull an oar. I had intended to take only *Lydia*, but it became plain to me that, again, Themistocles was right, traitor or no – we had to be ready to fight again. So I lost an hour putting together crews for all five of my ships. I put Megakles into the ship Hector had taken, with Hector and half a dozen Athenian archers and as many hoplites as marines. We promised the oarsmen their freedom at the right end of the sea if they would row, and they did, at least that day. We renamed the ship, and Hector called her *Iris*, to no one's surprise.

We were not the last ships off the beach, but Xanthippus's *Horse Tamer* was making the turn by the island and preparing to enter the open sea by the time my column was formed, with *Naiad* and *Iris* in the lead where I could watch them, and *Black Raven* and *Amastris* and *Storm Cutter* behind me. There were almost two hundred Athenian ships in four columns, over stades of sea. We rowed from the beaches to Psyttaleia, and there I caught up with Cimon's squadron.

Then we saw the difference between the old sea wolves and the new ships made plain. Eurybiades had done well to train this fleet – better than many I had seen in action – and they could row, they could back water, and they could manoeuvre. But sailing and sea-keeping in a pursuit are very different from keeping a careful line, forming an orb, and backing water. Now the new Athenian ships with their heavier, slower design were struggling, and their deck crews fumbled with raising sail.

Cimon turned out of the column. We had come off the beach as a mob and then made our way through the narrows at Psyttaleia in single file, but now he turned north towards Phaleron and raised his sails in ten beats of a calm man's heart – beautiful seamanship. And every trireme in his squadron followed suit, so that they seemed to blossom like flowers.

We followed his lead. I could hear Hector and Megakles shouting at a new and unwilling crew and I didn't want to pass them, so we lost distance on our leader, but soon enough their boat-sail set, and then their mainsail, and *Naiad* was twice as fast with her good Ionian crew. *Lydia* had the sails on the wood already and they went up like glory, and the three old pirates behind me were as fast, and then we were running along Xanthippus's inboard column, passing ship after ship. Xanthippus waved, or perhaps shook his fist, as we passed – certainly Cleitus looked none too pleased, but if I was going to contribute my part of the wedding, I needed some ready money and there it was, four hours' sailing ahead of me.

It became clear as we ran down on the enemy that they were in no condition to fight. They had almost no formation – indeed, three hours into the morning, I could have snapped up a pair of little merchant tubs, but they weren't worth the bother. The Ionians weren't stopping to protect anything, the Phoenicians had their morale broken, and the Egyptians, although we didn't know it, had been stripped of their marines by Mardonius – Egyptian marines are crack troops and no mistake – and consequently the Egyptians didn't dare try any kind of conclusion with us, but simply ran downwind.

It was glorious.

Cimon and I exchanged just two signals all day, one query from me and his answer that we'd stick together.

But it was heady stuff, to be at sea on a perfect autumn day, not a cloud in the sky, the sea blue, the sky bluer, the wind behind us, the sun warm – running at a fleeing enemy! I wish I could tell you some great event, but it was simply beautiful to go along, to eke every scrap of speed out of the hull, only to have to slow again to avoid over-reaching the slower ships. *Naiad* was a fine ship, but *Iris* had a curve to her hull – a common enough flaw in hasty boatbuilding, or so Vasileos used to tell me – and she sagged off to starboard all the time, keeping Megakles and Hector busy.

Well before evening, I let *Lydia* have her head, and we raced past the ships ahead of us and caught Cimon's *Ajax*. Because of the perfect wind and the oars all being in, Seckla was able to lay me alongside *Ajax* in easy hailing range.

'Are – you – going – to – weather – Cape – Zoster?' I roared.

Cimon vanished for a moment and then reappeared. 'Yes!' he called back. 'Good idea!'

I had my people brail up the corners of my great sail until *Lydia* proceeded at a more sedate pace and we dropped back into our slot in line. The ships were now spread over the seas – we had, for the most part, six or seven ships' lengths between each ship in our column, and half a dozen stades between the columns; indeed, the seaward column was more like a flock of birds. As the day went on, it became obvious that there would be no fight. Our enemies were *running*.

Our course had been south of west all day, past Phaleron and Aegina just visible on the starboard side. In fact, some ships of the seaward column turned due south and camped on Aegina's beaches, but kept on a more westerly course. Cape Zoster protected a set of beaches, the last really good beaches before Sounion, and I promise you, not a man in my ships or Cimon's was eager to return to those beaches.

We had plenty of daylight left. I remember this mostly because what came next surprised me. My head was down, looking after Leukas, who was in great pain despite a draught of poppy from one of the doctors on the beach. All I could do was hold his hand and sacrifice to the gods. I did both. Something bad was happening in his guts.

'Better have a look,' Seckla called. I thought perhaps he was just trying to give me a break – is it horrible to say that spending time with a dying friend is hard on the soul?

But Seckla was not just buying me a minute's reprieve from my conscience. Technically speaking, we didn't have to 'weather' Zoster, because the westerly allowed us to swing past without much course change. But when we were well past we could see a big portion of the enemy fleet – and we *knew* there were no allied ships north of us.

'Ten, fifteen, eighteen, twenty-four,' I counted. I looked back at Seckla. Brasidas came up.

I thought that they were Ionians. I didn't recognise any ships, but they were still many stades ahead of us. The problem was that we were no longer in company with the rest of the allied fleet; they were well over the horizon already, headed for anchorages and beaches on Aegina and the islets.

Cimon gave the signal for us to form line.

We obeyed. But we were under sail, and before the ships came up with him he'd turned further north, so that we formed our line at a narrow angle to the coastline.

After almost an hour of very tense sailing Cimon flashed our signal for taking our sails down and preparing to fight. Naturally this slowed us a good deal, but our oarsmen had had a picnic all day and were happy to get a little exercise, or so the wags phrased it. Still, by the time we had all twenty ships in line, oars out and in good order, the Ionians were *gone*. They didn't stop or slow or threaten. They just ran.

Except the three that were coming towards us with men waving olive branches in the bows.

I didn't know any of them, but we picked one up, and Cimon's ships took the other two. Mine was Chians – that is, men of Chios. The navarch's name was Phayllos and he knew me – knew my ship, in fact.

I was in armour, and so was Brasidas, but I didn't even take an aspis when I leapt from my ship into his. We clasped arms and I was glad for us both that we had not gone ship to ship a few days before – there was no hatred between us, or even anger.

'I don't want to run any more,' he said with a shrug. 'And the Phoenicians didn't play fair this morning with fresh water, so my crew is parched. I have heard you are a fair man and have men of Chios among your people.'

Brasidas looked him over. 'Did you fight at Salamis?' he asked.

Phayllos shrugged. 'We fought, and fought well,' he said.

Brasidas gave me the movement of his eyebrows with which he expressed approval and admiration.

'Are you worth a ransom?' I asked.

'I am, and so is my nephew,' he said. He pulled under his arm a very thin, not very handsome young man in beautiful armour. The fit of the armour almost made the boy – and I use the term carefully – look like a man.

But despite his spotty face and his starveling build, the boy had a certain presence and good manners. He bent his knee. 'It is an honour to be taken captive by the famous Arimnestos of Plataea,' he said.

Brasidas laughed outright. He didn't speak, but his laughter spoke volumes.

'You made no bargain,' I said. 'I could take the two of you and clear your benches over the sides – in pursuit, it's within the laws of war.'

Phayllos was a brave man. He was afraid, but he bore it with nobility. 'Yes,' he said. 'I told the oarsmen and the marines that very thing.'

I nodded. Brasidas did his eyebrow thing again. We were in agreement that these were good men and deserved decent treatment. I'm not saying that, had they been oily or arrogant, we'd have massacred their crews. Merely that honour calls out to honour, and dishonour encourages the same, or so I have often found it.

The time it took us to take those three ships cost us any chance of snapping up any more Ionians. So we turned, left our masts down, and rowed a little north of west onto the beaches by Cape Zoster. We landed early enough, but it was a major chore fetching water from the one creek big enough and deep enough to water us, and there were neither shepherds nor sheep to feed more than three thousand men.

However, we were well prepared, with dried meat and sausage.

I saw to it my own people were fed and then we squandered our reserves on our captives.

Cimon and I had a meeting over garlic sausage and onions and very, very good wine.

'It's like going to a good symposium at a poor man's house,' Cimon joked. 'We spent all our money on the wine!'

'We need some merchants full of supplies. Mine are all running in the Bay of Corinth.' I shrugged.

Cimon nodded. 'What are we going to do with our captures?' he asked.

'Ransom the trierarchs and let the rest go,' I said. 'If we're lenient, we might pick up more and we won't have to fight.'

Cimon chewed a bit of gristle and spat. 'Just what I was thinking. I'm going to be a very poor oligarch, friend. I enjoy this far too much.'

'Stealing money from those too weak to defend it and spending it all on symposia and flute girls?' I chided him. 'You'll be the *perfect* oligarch.'

'You were right, too,' he said. 'We beat the Medes.'

The stars were rising. I could hear Phayllos, who was already friends with Brasidas, laughing his deep laugh.

'I don't want to be Tyrant in Athens,' Cimon said suddenly. 'I don't give a shit. I'm ruined, and my father would be enraged. I want this – for ever. I want to sail and sail, to beat Persia every day, to conquer them and rule a great empire.' He paused. And grinned – self-knowledge is always the best tonic, or so Heraclitus used to say. 'All that on one cup of good wine. I'm sorry, my friend. What do you want?'

'I want Briseis,' I said. Indeed, I felt like a young man, with his first woman before him – and I felt the cold hand of time and fortune on me, too. She might already be dead, with some eunuch's hands round her lovely throat. I had not hurried, or so I told myself when I was honest.

Cimon laughed. 'You are consistent, I'll give you that.'

After a pause, he said, 'I expect we'll get more surrenders tomorrow.'

I sat with my back against a rock, still warm from the sun. 'I can take the Chians home and the Lesbians too. I can use them as cover when I move into Ephesus. If I get ransoms out of them, so much the better.'

Cimon nodded. 'Well, I got two good ones, ten days' pay for all my rowers in each ship.'

I smiled. I knew something Cimon did not know and I had no reason to tell him. I remembered his father all too well. All Cimon had to do was say 'walk with me' and he'd *be* Miltiades come to life.

'So you are content that I keep mine and you keep yours?' I asked.

'Seems simple,' Cimon said.

While we were talking, more allied ships appeared. They were from the northern column, and we had Themistocles with us, and Eurybiades, in an hour. I fed them both sausage and Eurybiades opened an amphora of good Aeolian wine and we sat at a small campfire. Siccinius waited on us.

Probably the most remarkable thing was that as we all settled in to drink, Brasidas came up – and Eurybiades greeted him by name, rising as if Brasidas was one of the peers.

After a hesitation so brief that I think I'm the only one to have noticed it, Brasidas accepted this and saluted Eurybiades as one man does another and then settled comfortably, as if this was not an epochal event in his relations with his former city.

It was a fine fire, and just because I know that Themistocles was a black traitor didn't mean he could not be good company, especially when he was relaxed and victorious. Eurybiades treated him with deference, which he craved. I was polite.

But when the opportunity came, I pounced. I made the face men make when they want to piss, and leaped to my feet. Then I followed Siccinius a few paces into the darkness, to where he and two of my sailors had set a couple of boards over three small rocks and put wine on them for serving – like a crude symposium, in truth.

But I didn't have to chase him. In fact, when he saw me coming, he placed his amphora on the side table, gave orders about mixing the water and the wine, and then beckoned me, and we went around a great boulder – some god or some titan had thrown it there, no doubt – and it was he, not I, who began.

'Will you truly see me a free man?' he asked.

'I will,' I said, not only because I would, but because I knew he had something important to say. Even in the darkness, everything from his posture to his voice betrayed his tension and his emotion.

'The Great King is running for home,' he said. 'He is going overland – with half his army.'

I stroked my beard. 'How do you know?' I said. I raised my hand for silence. 'I mean, do you *know*, or were you simply told?'

'I saw the horses prepared, I heard him order Mardonius into motion, and I heard the orders he gave Artaphernes.'

It was too dark to read his face, but I could guess.

'You know how important Artaphernes is to me,' I said.

'I know he is your enemy,' he said. 'Lord Cyrus could scarcely hide that. And let me say, my lord – I have earned your citizenship. I took a risk, a very real risk, in approaching Lord Cyrus.'

'Really?' I asked as urbanely as I could manage. 'A smart boy like you should have used my request as a cover for his whole mission.'

Silence passed, like time, but heavier.

'What do you want me to say?' he asked.

'I want you to tell me the truth,' I said. 'Did you speak face to face with Cyrus?'

'Yes,' he said.

Most men give themselves away when they lie. It is a simple thing, but liars tell stories and truth-tellers say things like 'yes' and 'no'. Some men are verbose by nature so it is not an absolute law, but it is a good guide.

'And what order did Xerxes give to Artaphernes?' I asked.

'My lord, I can tell you more than that – I can relate to you what conversation Artaphernes had with Diomedes of Ephesus,' he said. 'But then I will require your oath, and some reward, because I will be leaving my own lord.'

I was, in my turn, silent. Just by pairing Artaphernes and Diomedes he made my blood run cold and my heart beat fast. In fact, I didn't really need to know what they said to each other. But the mere idea that they had talked was a terror to me. And the fact that this spy knew my affairs so well that he knew that these two names would affect me meant that, on the one hand, he must be telling the truth, and on the other, than he was appallingly well-informed.

'Freedom, citizenship in Plataea or Thespiae, and a farm and ten talents of silver,' I said. 'But that's all I can ever offer. Be bought, or do not be bought.'

He moved, and I realised that he – as slave – was holding out his hand for a gentleman's hand clasp.

I'd been a slave, and I gave it.

'I give you my word, and my oath to Zeus, Lord of Kings, and Poseidon, my master every day at sea, Horse Tamer and Giant

Killer, that I will give you your full reward, citizenship, ten talents of silver, and a good farm, or I shall be accursed, if you will aid me to your fullest in the recovery of the woman I love and the saving of her children,' I said. I had learned a little about oaths.

'Wow,' he said, or words to that effect. 'Very well, lord. All know you are a man of his word. Here is what I have. Diomedes and Artaphernes are allies in this – they both hate Archilogos and his sister too. Archilogos was to be held as long as possible on the beaches to let Diomedes have the start of him. Artaphernes is racing to Ephesus on the Royal Post, taking the place of the messenger the Great King was sending to Sardis.'

'Heracles!' I swore. 'Artaphernes is putting his revenge on his father's wife over the Great King's commands?'

Siccinius shrugged. 'I find Persians even harder to understand than Greeks,' he admitted. 'But he hates her, and he claims she has humiliated him. He means her to die very badly.'

I didn't need to hear a description.

'But her brother means to save her?' I asked.

Siccinius shrugged. Even in darkness, that gesture is unmistakable. 'You ask me as a spy? I do not know. As a judge of events? I would say that both men fear him. He is one of the most famous warriors in the Great King's forces. They say that, without him, Miletus would still be free, and they say that his ship scored more kills at Artemisium than any other Ionian or Phoenician.'

I laughed. 'That's no surprise,' I said. 'He was always best.'

I admit it – I smiled to think that we were about to be on the same side, to rescue his sister.

Half a world at war, and heaps of dead men, oceans of blood, and the three of us were about to be at the centre.

Sometimes, it is like living in the Iliad.

He told me more, everything he knew about the Great King's plans to abandon Mardonius and run for Susa. I admit it: I doubted what he was telling me as the Xerxes I'd met was far braver than that. I had a hard time imagining any Persian monarch cutting and running on an unbeaten army and a single naval defeat.

But it didn't matter.

Almost nothing mattered but getting to Ephesus.

'One more thing,' he said. 'If my master knew I was telling you this, I'd be dead.'

I nodded. What more could he tell me?

I saw his head move, his unconscious glance to left and right to make sure that we were not overheard. 'Xerxes has lost three brothers and two sons in this campaign,' he said. 'He's putting all the rest of his boys on two of the fleet's fastest ships. They're running for Sardis via Ephesus. Artemisia is taking two of them, and Diomedes the other two.'

I could see – I still see – the hand of the gods in all of it, and like any good tragedy I had been manipulated by my own needs and desires, and only allowed, now, at the last hour, to know what the stakes were, and what my role might be.

I did not dare even allow myself to imagine what fate Artaphernes had in mind for Briseis. It would be horrible, and it would not allow her either dignity or repute. And I knew Diomedes hated her and was weak enough to seek such a horrid revenge.

Perhaps it says something about me that, until that moment, I had never really considered that either man would exact 'revenge', because it's *such* a waste of a strong man's time to do such a thing. But they were both weak men and they needed to hurt something they were strong enough to hurt.

Artemisia was made of different stuff. I wondered if she could be brought to bargain – if she might mislike the killing of another woman. Or perhaps not. Common gender had never stopped me from killing a man.

Let me say one thing more as we head for the finish line in an ugly race. Briseis knew the odds against her – had, in fact, warned me herself. And she was not a poor weak woman who needed my sword arm; that is, she might, but she was the mistress of her own life and her own fate. I knew that, short of outright swordplay, she could probably master Diomedes by politics alone. Artaphernes would be trickier – but I knew she would not go lightly.

I knew that, in the last case, she would kill herself rather than fall into their hands. And that the knife she fell on would be red with the blood of her foes.

But I *wanted her alive*. At my side. And that was going to take the luck of the gods and some serious planning.

The *Royal Post* was as fast as the wind. Diomedes was at sea and had a full day head start.

All this was through my head in an instant.

'I will do as I promised,' I said. 'Find me in Hermione in a month, or in Plataea in a year, and I will do my part.'

'And if you are killed?' he asked.

I laughed. 'Then I will have to bear my own curse,' I said.

In the end, I decided to take all my ships. My people – my oikia, the men who'd been with me for years – they were family, and I was about to tempt the Fates to overthrow me. Indeed, I already had the blackest picture. Diomedes' head start concerned me most of all.

And besides, Moire and Seckla and Hector, Hipponax and Brasidas – there were petty rivalries among them, but they were also united, and they made it plain to me that they were coming. All of them. My clever plan of a single ship slipping unnoticed through the rout of the Ionians was derided. And probably with good reason.

So instead, I led five other ships.

Cimon was bitter and proclaimed that I would take all the good prizes and leave the seas empty. But he promised to cover me with Themistocles.

One thing more you need to understand. From the beaches east of Cape Zoster there are two equally good routes to Ephesus. A good trierarch can hop from Attica to Andros, and from Andros to Chios, and then drop down into Ephesus – there's some blue-water sailing there, but not much, and if you know your landfalls, it's not that difficult. However, autumn was coming on; we were entering the 'season of winds' and ships were lost in autumn. A more cautious trierarch or helmsman would stay in with the land and go along Euboea and then nip past Thessaly and Thrake before turning south, with good beaches and mutton all the way. I've done both, as you may have noted.

But with Briseis's life on the line there was no question that I'd take the more direct, riskier path. And with six ships, the risk was lesser in every way – but mostly because I assumed the Phoenicians, the best mariners if not the best fighters, would take that route home and we were going to be sharing the same waters and perhaps the same beaches. With six ships I felt I could realistically handle any-thing that Ba'al had to offer.

Be that as it may, breakfast was very early. There was no 'cap-tain's council' because my friends presented me with their demands. Moire and Seckla stood in front of the rest, in the dark, and I noticed that for once, Giannis and Brasidas, who were never far from me, were standing with their other friends.

'We're all coming to Ephesus,' Seckla said.

I nodded. 'Very well,' I said.

See? Leadership. Command. Knowing when to follow. Hah! I am only mocking myself. In truth, I was mad as a tanner for a few beats of my heart, merely because they were flouting my wishes, but before a single libation had been spilled, I saw how much easier moving in force would be. Besides, with Phayllos's ship and *Naiad* we had some chance of passing as Ionians ourselves.

Except *Lydia*. With her heavy mainmast and raked boat-sail mast, she was probably the best-known warship on the ocean that year and there was no disguising her. In the end, I decided we could pretend to be a capture if deception was required.

The next hours were so frustrating I could barely restrain myself. I wanted to get into motion, but Cimon restrained me until Themistocles let it be known that we were to continue forward. Again I feel I have to explain – I did not want Themistocles to know I was gone. The risk of betrayal was still real.

So we didn't leave the beach until the sun was fully above the horizon, and those were some of the longest hours of my life, although we all benefited from them by exchanging oarsmen and loading fresh water where we could.

I was determined to make for Megalos, the islet with the perfect beach where I'd waited for Cimon less than a month before. It was a full day's sail and required some luck, but it had the signal advantage that I would appear to be Cimon's vanguard all day, if Themistocles were to watch at all.

Finally, when I was ready to rage at anyone who stood against me – isn't waiting the most frustrating thing, thugater? Finally, we put oarsmen to stations and got her keel off the beach. Themistocles and the rest of the fleet were left behind and my ships – *Lydia, Naiad, Iris, Black Raven, Storm Cutter, and Amastris* – were away, in a loose file led by *Lydia* and Cimon's squadron fell in behind us.

We still had a beautiful wind and when we came to Sounion and turned due west, the wind was perfect, just over the starboard quarter, and *Lydia* began to pull away. Then we began to use all the tricks we'd learned in fifteen years at sea: wetting sails, using rowers leaning out to stiffen the ship, brailing up parts of the sail to get the perfect drive – a warship can drive too deep with her ram when overpressed by sail and sometimes, just to confuse a landsman, a little less sail is a better rig.

But it was noon, the sun high in the sky, and our lookout in the basket high above us called down that he could see two sails to the west. The development was sudden, as it always is at sea. In an hour there were forty enemy ships hull up to the north and west, running for the Euboean channel, and another forty running west and south under sail. Either going for Andros or planning to sail up the eastern shore of Euboea – by the way, not a course I'd have chosen, and the wrecks of fifty of the Great King's ships would show why.

Right before us were a pair of ill-handled merchantmen. The beautiful west wind that had us racing over the seas was not so kind to them and we were making distance on them five to two.

I had Megakles aboard – a precaution in case of a storm – and I waved to Brasidas and then summoned both of them aft.

'There's what we need to make Ephesus,' I said. 'Take either one, collect mutton and grain at Megalos, and no one will starve.'

Brasidas nodded.

I turned to Megakles. But he shook his head.

'Seckla's been to Megalos and I ain't,' he said. 'I'll steer this girl and Seckla can have the tub all day.'

That was sense too. I had the oddest feeling that my friends were taking charge of me, that I was not, strictly speaking, 'in command', but Megakles was correct – Megalos had a tricky beach, especially if he should come in after the sun set, which it did earlier every evening.

We came down on the pair of them like falcons taking rabbits and they did not fight. Since we had to lose way to take them, I let Hector blood his crew by taking the nearer while we took the farther, but he had shouted orders only to take ransoms and strip any valuables and leave them – orders which, as the afternoon lengthened, we watched him disobey.

But the kind wind threw all my calculations out the window, and we were on the beach when the sun was a fine red ball over Attica to the west, and the two round ships were already visible as sails. They came in on sweeps well before darkness fell. We had fires roaring on the beach and a little drama as two triremes appeared and gave them chase – two triremes who proved to be Cimon's and not Ionians.

Hector had picked up a supply ship belonging to Artemisia. He took a fair amount of teasing from my friends about whoring after a prize and getting rich too young, but then he led me aside.

'Summon Phayllos,' he said.

He was so serious I knew he must be in earnest. So I went and fetched Phayllos and his young friend Lygdamis. The Chian trierarch was not pleased to be summoned and his face froze when Hector came up the beach with a small man with a nose like an eagle's beak – the captain of the merchantman.

'Aye,' he said, in Phoenician-accented Greek. 'That's him. The Queen's son. Like I said.'

I had Artemisia's son.

The two ships were full of food and had almost a thousand gold darics in back pay for various Ionian crews. I took it, served out the money instantly as pay to my own oarsmen, and kept the food, packing it all into one hull. Then I graciously put the two crews into the slower of the two ships and let them go without ransom.

In thanks, the Phoenician captain showed me where another thousand gold darics were dangling from an oar-port into the water on a rope. I had never seen that one before.

The gods were with us. I was sailing to redeem my oath, and by Poseidon and my ancestor Heracles, the capture of two fat prizes – useful little ships – and the good west wind made me feel that it *was* possible after all. And – I freely admit it – my friends held me up. It wasn't anything I can describe – no backslapping, very few words.

But they were all there, save Cimon himself and Aristides, and they had other responsibilities.

To cap my good luck, the villagers on the back of the islet sold me most of what was left of their flocks and grain. The Medes had never come near them – that islet was a long row east of the channel, as my oarsmen had cause to know.

We were up before dawn and the hulls were wet as soon as we could see the two rocks that made the beach a hazard. Then we rowed south – not a long row, but far enough to warm up our bodies and give the oarsmen a sense of how lucky they were to have a favourable wind, which today, as if Poseidon and the zephyrs were my personal friends, blew from the north and west to the south and east, wafting us, once we weathered the southern tip of Euboea, almost due west, leaving Andros on our starboard side, and then – with the sun still low in the east – we coasted out into the deep blue and turned south and east, and dolphins came and played by our bows – a huge pod of dolphins that leapt and leapt, playing like people in the waves, so that we knew the gods were with us.

Then I really began to hope. My fertile mind could imagine every horror – torture, rape, degradation – inflicted on her. But my rational head said that she was as brave as a lion and had a cool head, and would not be an easy mark for any man.

The dolphins were a good sign. Indeed, all the auguries that day were favourable, and the birds of the air were from Zeus, and as we passed the east coast of Andros – probably less than sixty sea stades from where Themistocles was even then demanding that the allied fleet lay siege to Andros town – my heart rose again, as it had the day before.

Noon, and I could see the cape at the south end of Andros. As I had expected, the channel between Andros and Tenos had ships, both merchants and triremes, emerging on the wind and spreading their sails. It is a narrow channel, and I came down on them as if I'd planned the ambush for a week.

Six ships – only four warships. Easy pickings. A fortune in ransoms and gold.

We passed across their bows and left them in our wakes, with a new pod of dolphins escorting us. As the sun rolled down the sky we lost the wind against the island and began to row. Our attendant, the captured merchant, went far to leeward on the wind. I missed Megakles, but he was the best ship-handler among us.

We began to pass Tenos. I was going south of my intended track because of the wind. I had a feeling for it, and I wanted to have one more meal on land. But I needed to beat the fastest of the enemy ships across the deep blue. My choices in navigation were severely limited and the knowledge that I was wagering Briseis's life and honour was always with me.

I do not seek your sympathy, but some among you wish to know what it was like for us, then. So let me say – my left hand was still not healed of the loss of fingers, and when I rolled over the side of the trireme in the Bay of Salamis I wrenched my left shoulder, and a day of fighting – again and again – is more wearing that even the blind poet Homer could tell. It was, I think, three or four days since the great battle, and I was only starting to feel like a man, and my moods swung wildly between elation and depression, so that I had to watch my words the way a good shepherd watches his flock, for fear of speaking dung to a friend, or spitting bile on someone I loved. To add to this the burden of a long seaward chase against odds –

I only say this to say that, despite the years and the events, I loved Briseis enough to try. With everything I had.

We made the southern tip of Tenos and the beach there was

empty. We were now south of the track of the fleeing Ionians and we'd made a remarkable passage.

We landed well before sunset. I gathered my people and laid it out for them: we were going into the Deep Blue in the darkness. This had always been my plan, my secret weapon to beat Artemisia and the Red King into Ephesus.

And I wanted them all to eat well first. We slaughtered the sheep and boiled the grain and drank the wine – thin stuff, but infinitely better than no wine at all, I promise you.

No one was grim. Indeed, a day of fair sailing and dolphins made even the superstitious old men like Sikli and Leon pronounce the night crossing of the open ocean to be 'something to remember, boys and no mistake'.

We left Megakles on the beach. He chose the role, and he was most fit for it – to hold tight three days and if we did not return, to bolt for Salamis or Hermione. He still had a day's food for my whole squadron, and that could be our salvation. I had to plan for the escape, too, not just the rescue.

And then we were away, running east into the darkening sky.

I hadn't tried this exact trick before, but it stood to reason, and even Megakles voted for it. My thought was that the rising sun should show us the mountains of Samos at the very least. It is ten parasangs, more or less, from the southern tip of Andros due east to the southern tip of Chios. A day's sail with a perfect wind. Why not a night's? And thus, no worries about navigation with the stars.

Men slept.

I did not.

There is nothing to tell. The rising sun showed me Chios on my port bow, and well it should have – I had a dozen of the best navigators on the ocean with me, and all perfectly willing to tell me if my heading went from their reckoning. We raised Chios in the first dawn and then the race was on.

Full dawn showed me more than Chios.

Away to the north of me, as I turned north on the morning breeze to run up the west coast of Chios while I had a favourable wind, I saw ships coming off the beaches of Chios.

I knew the Red King as soon as there was enough light in the sky, and I was fairly certain that I knew Artemisia.

They were at least a parasang – thirty-six stades – away. But it was no coincidence, if you do your reckoning. They'd had a few hours' jump, and we'd just earned that back running all night on the Great Blue, and now they were under my lee. I had the wind, and the initiative.

Artemisia had the Great King's sons, and six ships – a perfect match for my people, except that we'd just beat them like a drum at Salamis.

I went into the bow with Brasidas and Seckla, leaving Hipponax in the steering oars, where he was almost competent.

I had a great many choices. At the start of an engagement, especially when you are upwind, you have a full range of choices, like the first guest to arrive at a banquet. My views were coloured by the knowledge that my oarsmen were rested but without sleep, and that five of my six ships would be forced to fight with their masts aboard, a useless weight of canvas and wood. My ship was built for it – a different matter.

Against that, whatever Artemisia might want, I suspected her oarsmen's morale would be low, to say the least. Beaten men do not wage battle. And believe it or not, morale is far more important than equipment. Every fight sees dead men in superb armour, but high-hearted people win battles. And my people had had two days of leaping dolphins and fat prizes and other men's gold.

All that was the thought of ten beats of the heart.

I took a sip of wine and handed the clay canteen to Brasidas. He already had his armour on, the bastard.

'I'd be happy to hear your thoughts,' I said. 'Please don't drone on in your usual long-winded way.'

Brasidas looked out over the sea, a thousand sun-dazzles sparkling away in the new sun.

'Fight,' he said. 'But don't forget what you are here for.'

'Sometimes you sound like an oracle,' I said.

He shrugged.

Seckla merely winked. 'Do the thing,' he said.

I went aft and armoured, keeping my own council. I nodded to Seckla, who pointed our bow at the Red King, and we sailed after them in a file, with *Lydia* still in the lead and *Black Raven* tailing, but the trierarchs closed up on me. I never even flashed a signal.

Even with *Lydia* in hand like a restive mare, we were coming down on them rapidly. The Ionians had choices, but they were all bad. They clearly wanted to weather the southern tip of Chios and run for the coast of Samos and an easy reach into the delta of the Kaystros and up to Ephesus, now only half a day's sail or a full day's rowing away. But to weather the headland of Chios at Dotia, they had to come south and east, a little too much into the wind for sailing in a trireme, and that meant rowing. Not quite straight at me, but close as it made little difference.

Or they could run north with the wind on their quarters, but of course then they'd be coming off the beach with their masts in.

In fact, that's the choice they made.

But as we raced forward into the sparkling waves they didn't make much of a job of getting their masts up.

Now we could see them all quite clearly and I no longer thought they had any chance of escape. Nor did my lookout report any other sails.

All of them turned their bows towards me. One ship threw his mast and sail over the side.

Then another.

They were going to fight.

At about six stades, when I could see Artemisia's ship and was *almost* sure that I could see Archilogos's ship hard by the Red King, I reached around my own stern and flashed my aspis in the sun three times. I wished I had a trumpet and a trumpeter, but in those days the skill was almost unknown among Greeks. We used smaller horns to signal, but the sound didn't carry well at sea.

Ships make noise – do you know that, thugater? The oars strike the water – splash! – no matter how well trained the oarsmen. *Pitylos* we call it. The word is the sound. And then the surge of motion as the oarsmen pull the water with the mighty stroke that hurtles the ship forward – we call that *rothios*. These two sounds are like the beating heart of a warship. And then, over all, the sound the bow makes cutting the water – the curl of waves, the sound of the wind over the hull, and the voices of the oarsmen singing, chanting, or merely grunting, depending on the exhaustion of the crew and the needs of the ship.

We took in our sails. My friends – my brothers – folded theirs away even as they came alongside. Our adversaries' hearts must have died within them as our sails came down and we formed line, because training shows.

So does heart.

They came on, but their hearts already weren't in it. The Red King's rowers were good, and so were Artemisia's, and as they came on I became more sure that the third good ship was Archilogos's. But off to the eastern end of their line were two ships with ragged oar strokes and unwilling men.

We were less than five stades apart when the two easternmost ships broke out of the line and ran. East.

Nothing is perfect. On a perfect day, Moire or Harpagos – I missed him already, and his honey-covered corpse was wrapped in linen on my lower catwalk, waiting delivery to his sister – or one of the other old pirates would have left our line and gone for them. But Giannis and Hector had different loyalties. They let the two ships flee, to make sure that we could win the fight.

Good reason, but with their eyes on the wrong prizes, so to speak.

I watched Diomedes run, and my heart filled my throat and I almost vomited.

Choices.

We were two stades from combat. To turn and run east was suicide for all my crew, and yet I considered it. He would run free while we fought. He would have hours of head start, if the fight went as I expected.

After all, the Red King and Artemisia were their best, and Archilogos was no slouch.

I spared the gods my curses.

Instead, I ran into my own bow. With an olive branch. And my line continued forward, rowing a normal stroke, as they bore down on us.

I waved the olive branch like mad, and prayed to Aphrodite, goddess of love, and Poseidon who rules the sea.

Artemisia accepted my olive branch. Diomedes wasn't six stades to the east when I leaped onto her deck, unarmed. Her ships had backed away a stade and I had rowed up alone. It was six to four – no one was fooled, and she must have wanted my offer of peace with all her heart.

Certainly she welcomed me to her deck. She was in armour, and yet she kissed my cheek like Jocasta rising from her loom.

'I confess, I never expected a Greek squadron this far east,' she said. She smiled without flirtation. 'You have the better of me. But I will fight to the death, I'm afraid.'

'You have the Great King's boys,' I said.

She coloured in shock.

'I don't want them,' I said. 'I will allow you and your ships to sail away – north. If you will give me free passage east, after Diomedes.'

She leaned into the tabernacle where her swan stern overhung the steering oars. 'It seems to me that I could just take you and use you as a hostage,' she said. 'After all, you must be worth a pretty ransom. And I will not be taken, Plataean.'

I nodded, and pointed over my shoulder at my own mid-deck, where Brasidas stood with a tall, thin boy. 'Your son, I believe.'

She stared, and for a moment, I thought I'd misplayed and she was going to gut me on the spot, the very lioness deprived of her young that Sappho describes.

'Listen,' I said. 'I love Briseis, daughter of Hipponax, sister to your ally Archilogos. Diomedes means her harm – terrible harm. I appeal to you as a mother and a lover – I will do no harm to Ephesus. I swear it by all the gods. But if I have to fight you, by the same gods I will kill every one of you for delaying me.'

We rocked in the bosom of the ocean and all the Fates and Furies held their breath.

'I want my son!' she said.

'I will release him, and Phayllos, and their ship, unharmed, when I row out of Ephesus.' I confess it – I was making this up as I went. But her alliance would be far more powerful than her avoidance.

She watched me. Her eyes narrowed, and I think perhaps she hated me only for having over-mastered her. She was a great warrior – and none of us likes to lose.

So I decided to treat her the way I'd have treated any other noble foe – to ease her mind.

'There is no surrender involved,' I said quietly. 'I will hold your son as surety, but in the harbour of Ephesus you'll have every hoplite at your beck and call. And you will know – none better – if I take Briseis alive. And I give my word.'

'Greeks lie,' she said.

'Damn it!' I said. My temper was flaring, Diomedes was running east to kill my love and this woman was considering fighting a hopeless sea fight against terrible odds because that's who she was.

Brasidas was too much of a gentleman to actually threaten the boy. But I saw him move, and his helmeted head turned. And I followed his eyes and saw another ship coming up under easy oars – Archilogos, my almost-brother, was coming to talk.

'You will take my son, raid Ephesus, and then run, leaving me a laughing stock,' she said. 'And then you will hold him to ransom half his life. I'd rather just fight and die. And who knows? Perhaps I'll triumph,' she said, and her eyes flared.

I was suddenly tired. All my injuries pained me, and all the fatigue of a four-day chase came down to this moment, and I wanted it to end. This is where men make bad choices. Aye, and women, too.

My beautiful plan was coming to pieces. The threat to kill them all had been foolish, because they could not understand the stakes.

'Do you know what it is like to be a woman and command men?' she asked. 'It means you must win every time.'

'It's not so very different as a man,' I said.

'Nonsense,' she said. 'If *you* free a man, it is mercy. If I do, I'm a soft woman or a whore who pined for him. I cannot afford to be humiliated at all, Plataean.'

Through this exchange the friend of my boyhood was coming aboard, his ship coming alongside, and he stepping from ship to ship as they didn't quite touch. He had good steady oarsmen.

Black Raven began to come forward. My trierarchs were growing restive.

'I will *not* humiliate you,' I said. 'I swear before the gods.'

And then my friend – my enemy – came up the catwalk. His bare feet made no noise and his only greeting was to remove his helmet.

'He swore to save my family,' Archilogos said. His voice was deeper and more beautiful than mine. 'Then he slept with my sister and killed my father.'

'I'm here to *save* your sister, Archilogos! Even as Diomedes sails away to kill her.' I all but spat the words. I wanted his friendship, but his ignorance was about to kill *everything*.

Artemisia looked at Archilogos. He was handsome – beautiful, even – and he had scars on his face and lines at the corner of his mouth. I hadn't seen him from this close in years.

'Does this man love your sister?' she asked.

Archilogos shook his head. 'Oh, I suppose he does,' he said wearily. 'And she him, or so she never ceases to tell me. But I no longer bear the responsibility for her.'

Artemisia was looking at me. 'Give me a hostage,' she said. ·

Archilogos looked at her, and then at me. His bronze armour was magnificent – but not as fine as mine. It was a stupid thing to think in the moment, but there it was.

I turned to him. 'Artaphernes, son of Artaphernes, is even now riding *Royal Post* to Sardis and then Ephesus to order her death. Diomedes is his ally in this – that's why he received two of the Great King's sons to carry on his ship.' I could see, further down the catwalk, two well-dressed Persian youths. 'The other two, no doubt. They mean to kill her.'

'I have disowned her,' Archilogos said. 'She is no sister of mine.'

'That must have been a magnificently empty gesture,' I shot back, 'given whose wife she was.'

Oh, I'm a fool. Always antagonise those you hope to sway by argument. But Archilogos smiled as he had when we were boys, and he acknowledged a fair hit.

'I mean to have her as my wife, Archilogos,' I said. 'By Heracles, my ancestor! The Great King is beaten! The next fleet to come here will come from the west, and it will be Greek. The world is changing, brother!'

I don't know where that came from. We used to call each other 'brother' when we were boys.

He turned his head and looked away.

Artemisia suddenly nodded decisively. 'Well, call me a fool or a fatuous woman, but I believe you. No one could make this up. Give me a hostage.'

'I will give you my own son,' I said.

Seckla met me coming back aboard after I'd seen Hipponax and two marines – all allowed arms – over the side. I returned Phayllos and his companion their arms.

'I will return you to your ship when we leave Ephesus,' I said.

Phayllos smiled. 'She is very persuasive, is she not?'

I wasn't paying attention. Diomedes had a parasang head start.

I had a very good ship, and now, with two signals to my friends, I ran for Ephesus.

From the south end of Chios, it's not a complex voyage into Ephesus, but it has challenges. The coast of Chios runs from the southern point at an angle, from south-west to north-east. My ship was well placed and had the right rig. We raised our sail – indeed, it was laid to the brails – and we were away.

An hour passed and none of us could tell if we were gaining. I was beyond mere spirit. My whole being was in the bow and in the sails.

More to distract myself than to help my friend, I walked back out of the bows and knelt by Leukas. I found myself telling all this – explaining my decisions.

My Briton's eyes opened. I hadn't really been paying enough attention, but he had been breathing fairly well and now his eyes opened. 'Sixth day,' he said. 'I may yet equal Seckla.'

I hadn't even hoped. So much of my spirit was seeking after Briseis that I had wasted no hope and too few prayers on my friend and helmsman. But now my hope soared.

Brasidas came and knelt beside me.

He took Leukas's hand, ran another hand down his side and over his gut.

'No fever,' he said. He shrugged. 'Sometimes the spear point never goes into the gut.' He shrugged.

'Sometimes the gods are kind,' I said.

Brasidas looked at me, rubbed the closed wound on his shoulder, and I think what I read in his eyes was pity. 'Sometimes,' he said.

The sun was three fingers higher in the sky when one of the fleeing ships turned end for end. We were coming up on them rapidly enough to see with the naked eye – our sailing rig was so much better than theirs. Just having the mast permanently anchored into the hull is a powerful tool and the rake of our forward boat-sail mast, which raised the bow very slightly against the downward pressure of the mainmast, gave us a lighter entry and made us faster.

I wondered what Diomedes had promised this poor bastard. His tactics were obvious – if I lowered my mast to face him, I'd lose an hour. No question.

Of course, I didn't have to lower my mast. But Diomedes had never been in the western ocean, and didn't know this rig.

'Seckla?' I asked quietly.

Let me add that half a parasang astern the rest of my friends – aye, and the Red King – were spread over the ocean. Artemisia was close behind me, but Archilogos was closest of all. Moire was just behind him. I had a little concern about betrayal, but more about the loss of time. And ever I had the spectre of Artaphernes riding, riding, and losing no time for adverse winds or grey days or enemies. A good man could ride twenty-four parasangs a day on the Royal Road and he was a renowned horseman and a relative of the king. Athens to the Hellespont was fifty parasangs. From the Hellespont to Ephesus was much less. On the one hand, much of that distance was very rough ground, but on the other, we knew the Great King had built roads as he came.

He should have been in Ephesus the day before, ordering my beloved's humiliation and death.

I am not one to leave things in the hands of the gods, but in this I knew I could do no more than I had done.

Kineas left it late – on purpose – and Seckla forced our last opponent but one into a wide manoeuvre to cut us off as we threatened to merely sail by. He must have thought his sudden turn was a guarantee of victory.

And he must have died in his heart when he saw how fast our mainsail came down. We left the boat-sail set. We were going very fast.

Our rowers grabbed the mid-ship's ropes and lay out to starboard, and Seckla's steering oars bit. One-third of the aft port-side oars went into the water, too – slowing us, and turning us very quickly. Oh, the years of practice in that moment.

And we almost missed.

And as we turned, the deck tilted at an angle I had never experienced and I thought we were going over. I felt the weight change and I feared our mast was taking us down, knocked flat, sideways into the sea. The starboard side rose and rose and every oarsman who could climbed out of his box and threw himself over the deck to the starboard and climbed over the catwalk, and lay out over the starboard rail. A hundred men weigh a great deal.

But what saved us was the impact. Our bow struck their stern. It would have been a glancing blow at a lesser speed, but at our racehorse gallop we sheered off his stern and the resistance – the moment of impact – slowed us.

Grudgingly, *Lydia* righted herself. She did not come up willingly, and for ten heartbeats, it was like watching the last heat at the Olympics, cheering on some beautiful runner who is stride for stride with another – will he win?

And then, with a sudden shake, we were on the level, bobbing like mad, and one of the port-side stern oarsmen lost his oar to the sudden change.

But by then, even though he was pale under his dark skin and looked grey at his own temerity, Seckla was bringing us back on course for Ephesus. Diomedes had sacrificed his consort and now he was only ten stades ahead of us. He was pulling away – of course.

But now our mariners proved their worth again. The readied sail was set back to the mainmast and twenty men raised it with a song. In the distance I could see the opening of the river mouth – the river whose first bend would lead us to magnificent Ephesus and the temple of Artemis shining on the hill of the citadel. It had been years.

I felt the Furies, their wings beating about me to the rush of the wind.

Do you know the feeling you have in the theatre, when you writhe your hips in your desperate wish that Oedipus may make another choice – even though you know that all is written and ordained? When the rhapsode sings the Iliad and you wish that, just this once, Patrocles might live, or Hector triumph?

Well then.

Here we are.

We entered the delta of the Kaystros, passing over the bar under oars, and we were perhaps five stades astern of my enemy. Nor were there warships waiting in the estuary. Indeed, the harbour was empty.

Empty.

One of my many fears in those hours was to find a port packed with enemies, instant allies for Diomedes. But remember, between two hundred hulls to support the bridge over Hellespont and the thousand ships he sent in his navy to Hellas, the Great King stripped the Ionians of their ships and their hoplites.

Diomedes ran.

My crew, Poseidon's blessing on them, shifted us effortlessly from sail to oars. The promontory on the north of the estuary all but killed the wind, and Seckla and I had it to the last breath, with every rested oarsman on his cushion before the sailors raised their hands to lower the sail.

Four stades.

I could see beaches by the town where Aristides had beached the Athenians eighteen years before, when I was still a boy and the world had seemed a sweeter place. I could see the temple of Artemis on the hill and I thought I could see a certain red-tile roof.

Diomedes took no chances, the coward. He ran his warship onto the beach below the town, bow first. He and all his marines were over the side, abandoning hull and rowers to their fates. And I could see his purple-red cloak fluttering as he ran, wallowing in the deep sand at the top of the beach.

Ka loosed an arrow – and then another and another. His archers joined him as soon as they had the range and the running hoplites began to grow arrows in their shields. It was marvellous shooting for the distance.

I could not watch.

I ran to Seckla. 'The piers,' I said. Remember, Seckla had been in and out of Ephesus two years before. He knew the harbour well, although not as well as I. I could not leave my ship and my crew to fall into Persian hands. This had to be touch-and-go: leave me and get into open water to wait conclusions.

That meant the stone pier beyond the breakwater where we could leap ashore and run through the town without crossing a beach. In fact, it was the choice that Diomedes should have made, but he didn't trust his tired rowers and another two stades of channel.

Well. I did.

Seckla governed our turns. I was my own oar-master, and we made the two turns into the inner harbour at the speed of a cantering horse. Risk upon risk upon risk.

But at my feet, Leukas *sat up* against the mainmast.

'Get forward,' he said in his odd accent. 'Get your ... enemy. I will lead the rowers.'

'Poseidon bless you, brother,' I said. The word brother came to my lips often that day, because indeed, they were *all* my brothers in this moment of reckless, tragic insanity.

Leukas used the mast to rise to his feet. But his spear was thumping the deck and all around me oarsmen began to smile.

And I thought – *we're going to do this.*

Leukas's voice should never have carried. But it did – a little higher and weaker than usual, but the port-side oars came in and the starboard checked, and we slipped down the long stone quays, and long before Kineas threw a loop of rope over a stone bollard, I leapt over the side to the rushing stone quay, stumbled and blessed the bronze greave on my knee as it struck the sand on the surface of the stone, and began to run. Brasidas came across behind me and Polymarchos and Achilles and Sitalkes and all the rest. And although I had never run well since my first bad wound, yet it was hard for them to pass me, because Aphrodite and Ares held my arms and I skimmed the earth. And behind me, ten heroes bent on glory.

But after *Lydia* came Archilogos in his magnificent, gilded *Heracles*. He was going to get ashore just behind me.

I have reason to know that it is three hundred and some steps from the top of the beach to the base of the steps to the Great Temple of Artemis. Ephesus is a steep town and I had run up and down the steps of that city all the days of my youth. Three hundred and twenty-six steps, I believe. And the dooryard of Hipponax is at the top, where the city's great aristocrats live just below the temple precinct.

When everything you have ever wanted in the world awaits extinction at the end of your run, you do not stop. You do not rest, or gasp for air. You do not make a humorous aside, or banter, and practise the kind of bravado boys use when they want to fight.

You merely run, the greaves on your legs weighing like oxen tied to your feet. And despite the best armourer in the world, as you climb, the base of the bronze begins to drive into the top of your instep and the sides of your brave bronze thorax begin to restrict the full expansion of your lungs, and your helmet weighs like a young heifer on your neck; your plume seems to have a life of its own, and the sweat pours down your face from the wool and straw that lines your helmet, stinging your eyes and making you blind.

I had not slept one moment the night before. I had new wounds and old, and I was no longer even a little young.

That *I* ran to the top of the town is *not* the miracle. I was in the hands of a god and a goddess.

That *every one* of my marines ran to the top of the town is a miracle. Not for them, the wonder of Briseis. They only knew that this was my desire – and that Brasidas and I led them. It was for this that they had trained. Beside it, the day at Salamis was a pleasure outing.

Wear full armour. Wear it all day, and then, as the sun sets, leap from a moving ship to a stone pier, land, rise, and run four stades up three hundred steps.

And then fight for your life.

I can tell you about that run in detail. But it would be lies. I remember nothing.

No thought entered my sweat-soaked head, and no sight entered my eyes until I was at the top, on the well-remembered path – too narrow for a street – that led to Hipponax's arched front gate, and the mural of Heracles my ancestor that decorated his entryway.

By Heracles – it had all started here, in this house. The Furies were close – all their wings beating like oarsmen pulling together.

I saw the entryway. Standing in the narrow alley was a pair of hoplites and they filled it, just the two of them.

Thoughts came into my head. And for the first time I wondered if she was here at all, or in her house in Sardis.

But Diomedes thought so.

The two men facing us were big and brave.

Brasidas threw his heavy ten-foot spear from three paces out, at a dead run. He was just behind me, and yet he threw over my shoulder. His spear struck the aspis of the left-hand hoplite. The man had his shield on his shoulder as men sometimes do when tired, and thus it had no 'angle' to the spear tip – which struck full force, as if Achilles himself had thrown it. It went in the width of a hand, weight and strength blowing through layers of hide and wood and linen and pitch, and the man screamed as it went into his bicep, perfectly aimed and thrown, and his instinctive movement ripped it back out of the entry wound, the spear bobbed up and down, lashing through muscles in his left arm, and his own spear fouled his mate as I slammed my aspis into his. Achilles my cousin put a spear in the downed man's throat somewhere behind me, or so I've heard since, and I was entering the gate, where two more stood.

Now they both threw their spears together. I had my own spear up high, my thumb back around the shaft and a little cord between my fingers, as is my habit in a ship fight. From this position it is child's play to cover yourself against a thrown spear and both casts went wide – one skimmed off my angled shield and would not bite, and the other clattered against my own spear haft as I rolled it, a turn of the wrist, right to left, a little snap that meant life and not death.

Then I slipped between the right-hand man and the gatepost, placed my aspis against his as I slipped, moving his weight the way the end of his spear-cast led him, overextended, right foot forward and thus without the structure to support his aspis. And high above my head, Heracles in his lion skin looked down on me as my spear point rose a fraction of a finger's width over his aspis and struck almost straight down. He wore a corselet of bronze scale, but my spear went into the muscles of his neck where it met the shoulder, unprotected, under the cheeks of his helmet, and my spear point went far into his body and he was dead before his knees buckled – and my spear leapt back out again, untrammelled by his death.

And I passed my left foot past my right and carried on, leaving the second man, alone, to face Brasidas and Sitalkes.

In the great doorway were two more hoplites, and behind them, two more – a tiny phalanx.

But their spears shook.

No one, my daughter, can watch four of their friends die in twenty heartbeats without a moment of deep doubt and real fear.

I threw my dory when I was half a pace from the faces of their aspides. My spear flew perhaps a single pace and slid between the edges of the man's helmet, deep between his teeth into his throat. I tugged the cord, but it was gone, lodged too far.

The other front ranker lost an entire action being afraid.

I got my hand on my xiphos.

Finally, he struck – a simple, straight blow to the face of my aspis. A wasted blow. If he had been trained by Calchus he would have known what to do when a Killer of Men came and faced him. He and his friends would have set their shields together and put their spear points to my face, and driven me away or let me expend the rage of Ares on their impenetrable shields.

But I was Hector *and* Heracles, and they had no hero to steady them.

My long xiphos came out of my scabbard as if called by Ares. My draw lengthened into a high cover that took my terrified adversary's spear high and then I sprayed his fingers over his companions with a flick of my wrist, and my aspis and my shoulder cast him into his own second rank, a step higher on the marble, and his blood sprayed over his friends.

They reached for me with their spear, but they also stumbled back.

And Brasidas was there.

What evil fate set those men to face me, and to face Brasidas, on the same day and in the same hour?

His sword flew like one of the ravens of Apollo, stooping and rising.

And then – I tell it because it will be difficult to believe – we drove them back from the threshold into the portico, and I have never seen it, before or since, but Brasidas's opponent thrust, pushing forward on his right foot with his spear reversed, and while he went shield to shield with the Spartan, he was wide open to me. I had just covered a heavy, sweeping blow on my shield and I turned and killed Brasidas's opponent with a thrust to the throat – and in that beat of the heart, Brasidas drove over my arm into my man, killing him.

My sword caught in Brasidas's adversary, though. The swell in the 'leaf' of the blade had gone too deep and he took my sword in death. But Ares guided my hand and I took his spear from him as if he had handed it to me.

I ran down the hallway to the women's quarters.

I knew it well.

And as I had imagined it a thousand times that day, there he stood. Diomedes.

Two women dead at his feet, their young corpses piled one atop another like lovers in a tragedy.

I might have wept, but neither dead girl was mine.

He had Briseis by the hair, and he had one of her arms pinned, because it had a long curved knife. His hand held a sword – a kopis such as I had used in my youth. It was red to the hilt and for a long moment I could not tell if her throat was cut or not.

'Stop!' he commended me. 'Or I kill your whore.'

I was still moving forward.

'Kill him, Achilles!' Briseis said.

'Shut up, you bitch!' he said. His grip must have hurt her terribly, but she still had the knife and he could not make her drop it – she was a dancer, fit, and flexible, and the grip that would have broken a man's arm was hurting her terribly, but she still had the knife. And her struggles made him unable to just cut her throat.

His two men were opening the doors to the women's yard beyond. He tried to drag her feet from under her, so that he'd have her arm and the knife, but she moved with fluid grace, despite his grip.

I saw it all, the last act of a tragedy older than me. Before I threw my spear I knew that wherever it lodged, Briseis would be the victor – alive, my bride, or dead, avenged and unbroken. Like it or not . . .

All her will passed to me in one glance of those eyes. When she told me to kill him, she told me all.

I turned my head slightly, as if tracking his henchman, who raised his spear to threaten me.

And then, without looking, I threw. My throw had everything behind it, and my right foot went forward, making me as vulnerable as the man I'd killed a moment before in the portico. And Diomedes' man threw at me.

And all the gods laughed and oaths were fulfilled.

Archilogos's shield snapped forward – and the brother and owner of my youth deflected my death.

And Diomedes stood.

Briseis was on the floor.

Diomedes stood
  because
        my
           spear
               pinned
                   him
                      to
                         the
                           door

Blood fountained over his chest from his throat, and his face distorted against my shaft. His mouth moved like a gaffed tuna, and no sound emerged.

Briseis had fallen to her hands and knees. In truth, my spear ripped along her scalp and blood flowed – but she was *alive*.

As fast as I could reach her side, my people butchered Diomedes' remaining men, and Briseis was raised from the floor – I had one of her hands, and her brother had the other.

'I came as best I could,' I said.

Archilogos looked at me across his sister.

'My hate for you burned hot,' he said. 'But now I find only ashes. Heraclitus, ere he died, told me that you tried to save my father.'

Briseis's eye caught mine. Fear, despair, elation – they left almost no mark on her, and one eyebrow went up despite the blood. Indeed, Archilogos must have been told many times that I had tried to save his father – that I had only killed him in mercy, never in anger. But ... time passes its own messages.

Brasidas said, 'Arimnestos! We must go.'

I looked over my shoulder at him, and then at Briseis and Archilogos. 'Briseis,' I said. 'Come and be my wife.'

Then she smiled, the same smile she always had when she put the knife in.

'I want nothing else, my love,' she said. 'But I must have a moment, or I'll come to you with no dowry.'

'I would take you in your chiton,' I said, or something equally foolish.

Archilogos shook his head. 'She's right, and don't be a romantic fool. All our fortune is in this town. If Artaphernes is coming for us – we need to do some selective removals.' He grinned.

'Archilogos,' I said. 'Artaphernes will kill you. And Xerxes will do nothing to stop him. Come with me and be free.'

Archilogos paused. 'My oarsmen will kill me,' he said.

And he smiled.

'You saved my life,' I said.

He shrugged. 'So help me carry my fortune down to the ships.'

The Wedding

Χορός

ἀλλά, θεοὶ γενέται
κλύετ᾽ εὖ τὸ δίκαιον ἰδόντες·
ἥβᾳ μὴ τέλεον
80δόντες ἔχειν παρ᾽ αἶσαν,
ὕβριν δ᾽ ἑτοίμως στυγοῦντες,
πέλοιτ᾽ ἂν ἔνδικοι γάμοις.
ἔστι δὲ κἀκ πολέμου τειρομένοις
βωμὸς ἀρῆς φυγάσιν
85ῥῦμα, δαιμόνων σέβας.

Chorus

But, gods of our race, hear, and regard with favour the cause of
righteousness; if you refuse youth fulfilment of its arrogant desires, and readily abhor violence, you would be righteous toward
marriage. Even for those who flee hard-pressed from war there is
an altar, a shelter against harm through respect for the powers of
heaven.

Aeschylus, *Suppliant Women*

The trip home had adventures of its own and I will only mention a few. We took food in Ephesus – stripped it from a town still unaware how few we were. In fact, I confess that we stripped Diomedes' palace and left his wife and children destitute – but un-raped and alive. We stripped the house of Hipponax, and took aboard a number of family servants and slaves. And then we sailed into a setting sun and landed a few hours later, after heavy rowing, on the beaches of Chios. Before night fell, Harpagos had gone to his sister, who looked at him dry-eyed.

'He lived longer than I expected,' she said. 'So have you.'

She was never one for soft words.

And when we'd arranged for his funeral pyre, and we walked away, Briseis – her head wrapped in a bandage – took my hand in the darkness.

'She loves you,' Briseis said.

I shook my head. 'I have been the death of her brother, her hus-band and her cousin,' I said. 'She loved me once.'

Briseis shrugged. 'It is no easy thing, being the lover of a hero.'

I lacked the strength to laugh. But I caught her shoulders and kissed her.

'It is no easy thing, to be the lover of Briseis,' I said.

She broke off our kiss. 'Why should it be easy?' she asked. 'Why should anything good be easy?'

And when I tried to be insistent in my advances, she put a hand on my chest and pushed hard.

'Marry me,' she said. 'Until then, no.' She laughed at me, in the darkness. 'Listen, Achilles. My head looks like the Gorgon and my courses are on me, and I have never desired a man more, or less, at the same time. Wait and be a groom so that I may, once more, be a bride. I swear, who has been Aphrodite's tool, that I will never know another man. Indeed, long and long have I awaited this day.'

I knelt. 'Lady, I have a wedding prepared in far Hermione.'

She laughed. 'What barbarous place is that? Is it near Plataea?'

'Oh, my love, Plataea is destroyed by the Great King. Hermione is a town in the Peloponnese that has taken in the survivors.' I could hear my crew, drinking wine on the beach. I didn't like the sound of the wind. The time of storms was upon us – it was late for anyone to sail the ocean.

'And you? Are you now destitute?' she asked.

I sat on a rock and dragged her down beside me. 'Perhaps,' I said. 'I won't really know for weeks and perhaps longer. Until I see how many of my ships survived the autumn.'

She nodded. The moon was high and I could see the signs of age on her face.

Not that I cared.

'I was a fool,' she said. 'I was a fool to aim at worldly power when I might have spent my youth with you.' She looked me in the eye and shrugged. 'But we are what we are. I never wanted home and hearth. I wanted to sail the earth and sea as my brother did.' She shrugged.

'Where are your sons?' I asked her.

She leaned closer to me. A chill wind blew across the sand. 'They went as horsemen with the army, thanks to Artaphernes. My husband, not the viper his son.'

I nodded. I had a hard time imagining that – if they were indeed of my blood – they loved horses.

'I was a fool,' I said. 'To want the life of the spear and ship when I could have been a bronze-smith in a shop, and been happy. But only with you.'

We sat in silence.

'We are not so old,' Briseis said. 'I almost feel I might be beautiful, in the right lighting.'

I laughed. 'Lady of my heart, truly, I never fought better than I fought today. So I am young in the midst of being old, and I invite you to join me. Tomorrow, the aches and pains—'

'Hands off, improvident suitor!' she said, quoting Homer. She leapt up. 'My mother warned me about boys like you,' she said. 'Don't follow me.'

And she walked off into the darkness.

And I drank wine with my people and Archilogos, who I found drinking with Seckla, of all people.

Early the next morning, Harpagos's funeral pyre lit the dawn and we shared wine and poured more on the fire. And as if the fire was a beacon, Artemisia's ships joined us on the beach of Chios one by one – the Red King, and her own swift ship. Archilogos we already had by us.

We met them on the beach. I was crowned with laurel from the funeral, clad only in a himation, without arms, and Brasidas the same. But the rest of our marines – thirty of them, at least – were full armed.

Artemisia was not in armour either. She was dressed like a slightly outlandish matron, in purple and saffron peplos and chlamys, and her clothing was beautifully embroidered, with her magnificent red hair as an ornament, so that one could easily see she was a queen. And she, despite being tall, floated over the sand and didn't seem to stumble or wallow as many of the rest of us did.

Briseis was by me. She was, of course, a priestess of Aphrodite, and Harpagos, like many men of Chios, was a devotee and an initiate, so that Briseis had said the rites and sung the hymns. She was very plainly dressed in a dark chiton, long and slim as a dark flame, with a single stripe of brightest white.

We all came together from our opposite ends of the beach.

I had an olive branch, as did the Red King, for all that he was in full armour and had a sword on.

'I have your son,' I said.

'And I yours,' Artemisia said.

But she was looking at Briseis.

It struck me – in a moment of wonder – that they must know each other, as they were of an age, from the same social class, and from cities not so very far apart.

Briseis laughed. 'Artemisia!' she cried. 'You!'

She turned to me. 'We were at Sappho's school together as girls,' she said.

And the other woman shook her head. 'The circle of the world seems vast,' she said. 'And yet, the compass sometimes seems very small.'

I had her son and his military tutor brought down the beach. 'I release your son and his ship as well,' I said. 'And I have done better than my part of the bargain. I include two sons of Xerxes I found on the beach at Ephesus.'

To be fair, Seckla took them prisoner while Brasidas and I were racing up the hill.

The Queen of Halicarnassus laughed like a man and kissed both my cheeks.

'You are the most honest Greek I have ever met,' she said.

'Foolish, more like,' the Red King said. He had my son Hipponax by the elbow and he gave him a gentle shove. 'I hope, Plataean, when next we meet, that we do not have all these women and children between us.'

I looked at him. His old-fashioned Corinthian helmet gave me little of his face. 'Are we enemies?' I asked. 'Do you owe me some vengeance?'

He laughed. 'No,' he said. 'But men say you are the best warrior of the Greeks. You are too old to hold that title. I will strip it from your dead hand.' He bowed. 'Do not think I do not honour you, Arimnestos of Plataea. But I will be the best spear in the world.'

He nodded, helmet still firmly on his head, turned, and stalked away with a dozen scarlet marines at his back.

As we prepared to leave the beach at Chios, a fishing smack brought us word that Artaphernes, son of Artaphernes, had come into Ephesus with a regiment of Lydian cavalry and found us gone. The fisherman told us that Artaphernes rode his horse into the sea, looking towards Chios, and cursed my name.

It's good for men to know who you are. Powerful enemies show that you haven't wasted your life, don't they?

The next evening found us on the beach at Tenos. Now, you may recall that the ships of Tenos came over to us just before the fight at Salamis and the island had declared for the League of Corinth. So we found Megakles safe and happy enough, with a mountain of food ready to serve out to my oarsmen.

We half-emptied the hull and ate ourselves to repletion, and then weathered a nasty day of squall after squall to pass up the west coast of Andros where we could see much of the League fleet on the beach.

I had no temptation to land and place myself at Themistocles' service. Listen – he may have been the greatest of the Greeks, or a traitor. But I could not trust him, and it was clear to me that, having beaten the Great King, he would now go from hubris to hubris.

I wanted no part in the loot of Andros. The island was poor sand anyway. But Moire and Harpagos's nephew Ion felt differently, and I saluted them and sent them on their way to join the League fleet. *Naiad* surprised us by declaring that they would winter with the Greek fleet, if we could feed them, and we could.

And Briseis had moved to her brother's ship. To say I burned for her is not to do justice.

My dreams were dark, though I had Briseis, and Archilogos warmed to me, day by day. Leukas was alive, and far from dead.

I should have been with the gods – the victory, the pursuit, the accomplishment of the dream of a lifetime.

Instead, for the whole of the voyage home, I was haunted by the dreams of the past, the deaths of those I'd loved and hated. I think I feared more on the voyage home than the voyage out. A day of dark skies and low squalls all but unmanned me, so sure was I that the gods would now take from me what they had briefly granted.

That is, all too often, the way of the gods. Is it not?

Megalos, again. The last time that autumn, and my squadron limped in after a long day skirmishing with Poseidon's winds. No man sang or drank wine on the beach that day – we fell into dreamless sleep, too tired to do more than pour libations and fall on straw. And in the morning, sore from days of rowing, we pointed our bows straight into a strong wind – and pulled.

But towards the hour when a man goes to the agora to see his friends, the winds relented of their torments and we got a light breeze from the north – cold as a woman's refusal, but gentle enough that we chose to raise sail and run slantwise, south by west, across it. And gentle as that wind was, it lasted the day and saw us to Aegina – and the next dawn it waited for us, and wafted us, without another thought of ugly death, across the Aegean Sea to Hermione.

And there, in that lovely town which rises over a promontory with beaches facing two ways, like a proper port, I saw *Athena Nike* beached, high above the water. And somehow, seeing Aristides' ship there, I knew that now I could cease to worry, at least for a little while.

We were a tired crew of Argonauts when, ship-by-ship, we landed on that beach. It seemed a third of the fleet was there: Cimon's *Ajax* and a dozen others I knew, and even Xanthippus's *Horse Tamer*. But we landed, and from pride I landed last, allowing each of my captains to pick his place and run his stern up the beach. It was smartly done and quite a crowd gathered. They cheered, by the gods – cheer on cheer carrying out over the water, especially when they saw Archilogos's ship, which of course they assumed was a capture.

And there was Aristides – and there Jocasta. There Penelope. There was Hermogenes, smiling as if he'd just won the laurel in a contest, and Styges and Teucer and a dozen other Plataeans. There was Hector, and, further along the beach, Cleitus, with his wife and daughter, and my own steward, Eugenios, and my daughter Euphonia.

Many times in my life, coming home has had its own perils. Or I have brought the perils home with me.

But in Hermione, which was temporarily Plataea too, and Athens as well, I landed to the cheers of my kin and friends. I leaped over the stern to the beach, and Simonides my cousin embraced Achilles his brother – and then embraced me.

I pulled away to lift my arms. Above me, Briseis looked over my head at a thousand people or more.

She smiled and looked down at me. And jumped into my arms with the trust of many years, and I put her on the sand without, I hope, a grunt.

By my shoulder, Jocasta said, 'And this is Briseis, I make little doubt.'

I had long wondered how she might greet the woman of my dreams, who was so much her opposite – so much more like Gorgo of Sparta.

She folded her in an embrace. 'Are you marrying him?' she asked.

Briseis's eyes were too bright for a mortal woman, and her look at me held too much meaning for words. 'I cannot resist him,' she said.

Jocasta took her hand. 'Then we have a great deal to do,' she said.

And my daughter came. She looked at Briseis – and took her hand and kissed it.

And my Briseis, hard as steel, burst into tears.

A few paces away Hipponax leapt from the stern of Moire's ship. He reached for Heliodora, but she swayed like a reed and ran.

Despite his armour, he gave chase.

They were both laughing.

Hector's Iris stood at the back of the crowd shyly. I think she wondered if he really wanted her – if, indeed, he meant the promise he'd made. I can read men, and sometimes women, and I saw her there, and the look in her eyes.

But Hector was a much greater man than his father Anarchos, and he stood on the stern of his ship, his armour burning in the sun, until he saw her. And then he leaped into the shallows and ran at her as if he was charging a line of Median spearmen.

And then she laughed from joy, and we were home.

Leukas was the last man off the ship. He didn't leap, and a dozen of us competed to help him onto the sand.

He knelt and kissed the beach. 'I never expected to reach here alive,' he admitted.

Brasidas nodded. 'Me neither,' he said. 'This is not the ending I had imagined for any of us.'

Styges had to hear of Idomeneus's end – and had to weep. Many other wives came down to that beach, hoping against hope, and were disappointed. No homecoming of warriors is unmarred by this reality, but our losses might have been so much the worse – I had to content myself with that. Because amidst my happiness I was aware that I had achieved fame, victory, and the woman I loved by the shields and spears of my friends, and I had left many of them face down in the sands of time. They did not haunt me every day, but they certainly had, the last week before landing. Briseis may have brought her own dowry of silver and gold, but her bride price was paid in spears, bronze, iron and blood.

And Brasidas. I think that night he was very close to the edge.

We had a house – Eugenios had it prepared, and it was small, but so was Hermione. It had a bridal chamber, and I slept on a mat on the floor so as not to ruin the beauty of the place before the big day. But it had a beautiful garden, and that night – a few days before my wedding – I sat with Brasidas, a cup of wine, and the stars of autumn. I confess, men are difficult beasts. I wanted to be celebrating victory with Aristides, and bathing in Jocasta's good cheer, and dandling my daughter on my knee – and watching Briseis.

But I was drinking in the darkness with Brasidas, because he was my friend, and he was in pain.

'I thought I'd be dead,' he said suddenly. It was such an uncharacteristic thing for him to say.

I shook my head.

'Xerxes is beaten and I am alive,' Brasidas said. He drank again, and I realised that, for the first time since I had known him, he was drunk.

I sat back – we were sitting, not reclining. The house had but one kline, and that had a special purpose.

'Xerxes is not beaten,' I said. 'If I understand Aristides, Mardonius has withdrawn to Thessaly, but he'll be back.'

'Xerxes has run away,' Brasidas said thickly. 'Leonidas is dead. Demaratus will never return.' His dark eyes were like spears in the starlight. 'I will never be avenged.'

I didn't know what he was avenging, and it didn't seem the time to ask.

'Revenge is for fools,' I said. 'Take a wife and be happy.'

Brasidas laughed. It was not hollow, or bitter, but real mirth. 'Arimnestos,' he said. 'Of all men, can you see *me* with a farm and wife?'

'Yes,' I said with perfect honesty. 'We are Greeks, not Medes. We have more music than the song of the spear and the hymn of woeful Ares. There is another loom beside the beat of spear on spear, or oar on oar.'

Brasidas's head snapped round. 'You know,' he said after a sip of wine, 'only you could say that. Killer of Men. Spear of the West. You have the world fame, and yet you are a bronze-smith and a farmer.'

I raised my cup and poured a libation to my own dead – those I'd slain, and those who'd followed me and died.

'Listen, Brasidas,' I said. 'Every oarsman at Salamis carried a spear. No man is the "Spear of the West", and every man, every thetes with his cushion, is a Killer of Men. This is not Sparta. And in time – I'm sorry – but Sparta's dream of war will have to change.'

Brasidas stared long into the darkness. So much darkness. I knew it was there.

Then he raised his head. 'Perhaps I must truly become a Plataean,' he said.

And several amphorae later, he said, 'Do you think the Queen of Halicarnassus is single?'

We laughed, and I knew he would live. He had been to the edge and walked away.

That's how it is. I hope none of the rest of you ever see that darkness. But if you do – find a friend. It is a like a fight: and fights are better fought in the phalanx than alone.

I spent the next day trying to find a chariot.

Hah! It's the turn of all the kore – the maidens – to know what I'm talking about. After nights of sailing tackle, ship design, aspides and swords, finally, I've reached something that interests my own thugater.

Ouch!

You will give your husband-to-be quite an image of yourself, my dear, if you show so much temper in public.

In good families, at least in Attica and in Plataea, you need a chariot for a wedding.

Hermione is a small town – a very pretty one, but small – and not much given to display. But eventually a chariot was found and Hermogenes and Styges and Tiraesias and I scandalised the whole town by stripping naked, taking over a forge and a wood shop, and rebuilding the ruin of a chariot from the wheels to the pole. I don't think the little vehicle had been used in fifty years. The tyres were leather and the wheels had broken spokes, and the body had long since fallen to tatters.

We worked while a rhapsode from Thespiae told us the Iliad, and it wasn't work, it was holiday. Our Plataean silversmith melted down some old jewellery of mine to make decorations and a pair of leather workers made headstalls and reins while Cimon, perhaps the best cavalryman in Athens, went across the ridge to buy me a pair of colts that men said were the prettiest in Attica. Jocasta came in with Penelope and Euphonia several times an hour to ask my opinion on some things about which I knew nothing, like flowers. I don't think, in a thousand questions, that I gave a satisfactory answer to more than ten.

But they were planning my wedding, and they needed my permission.

Archilogos had a house, arranged by Eugenios, who, like the genius he was, had assumed my raid would be successful, and had further assumed that my bride would wish a traditional wedding. May all the gods bless you, Eugenios!

Now the manner of a wedding among the aristocratic classes is this: first, there is a proclamation of engagement. For many people, and this is true throughout Attica and even Boeotia, the engagement *is* the wedding, and many a baby born in the best families can count back its nine months to the night of the parents' engagement. But it is a familial ceremony, and often done in the bride's home, although sometimes the groom's. The wedding itself, on the other hand, marks the day that the woman goes to live in the man's house, and is a much more public, riotous, and wine-soaked affair.

My first wedding, to Euphonia, my beloved honey-haired girl, had included both the engagement and the wedding, but the final acts of the wedding had been somewhat lacklustre, as she had come over the mountains to Plataea and her family had not followed.

As an aside, her father, Aleitus, was in Hermione and asked, with his beautiful manners, to be included in the wedding, as family. And of course, weddings were supposed to be for young people, not old men like me. I was about to turn thirty-six. Briseis was one year younger, an old matron of thirty-five with two grown sons.

So I asked Aleitus to take the place of my father, and I asked Simonides and his boys to stand with me, alongside my friends.

I need to mention that in one ceremony, I was to wed Briseis, Hector was to wed Iris, and Hipponax to wed Heliodora. I told my boys that they had to find their own chariots.

Well.

I remember little of that week in Hermione, except that it was beautiful. There were tears – we had a ceremony of remembrance for many who fell at Salamis, including Idomeneus. But for the most part, we had happy work and the memory of a great victory; we, as a people, had survived hardship, and we were unbowed. My ships rode at anchor or were overturned on the beach, and in fact, after we'd forged bronze tyres and sweated them over new-cut wheels (made by a professional, let me add) and cut and painted a magnificent Tyrian-dyed cover for the cab of the chariot, and gilded it, and reassembled the whole – after we'd done all that, and then repeated our triumph for Hector and for Hipponax – of course I helped them with their chariots! – then we bought a cargo of pinewood from Arcadia and we built ship sheds on the promontory below the temple and set our fighting ships to dry.

On Hermoú, the day of the week named for Hermes, patron of the city, we went to the temple of Poseidon on the headland. The engyesis was a major event. Cleitus spoke at length, praising me – how he enjoyed that – and my son Hipponax. And Xanthippus – I must give the man his due – stood up for his daughter like a gentleman, and his wife Agariste, who quite clearly disapproved of whatever union had begot Iris, nonetheless did her proud, with linens and wools, a loom, and a fine wagonload of household goods. Xanthippus spoke eloquently about the need to rebuild in the aftermath of the war and that the rebuilding was beginning even then, in exile, in the Peloponnese.

Aleitus, representing my father, and Simonides, gave speeches welcoming their family into ours, so to speak. Simonides even went so far as to make a joke about the destruction of our cities, and the houses to which these brides would be carried.

Men laughed. That's how confident we had become that we would triumph. It was funny: we were exiles, and our cities destroyed, our temples all thrown down. Our ships outside on the beaches of Pron and on the waves – our wooden walls – were all the fortune any of us had.

The girls, Iris and Heliodora, both fifteen, and Briseis, at thirty-five still the most beautiful – wore veils of fine Egyptian linen in pure white and never pulled them back, although they were flimsy enough to see through. Briseis wore a fine chiton of dark blue, with a woven edge in a startling Persian pattern in red, white, and black, and she wore a chlamys across her shoulders leaving only the fine linen of her chiton exposed on one breast – an unheard of innovation in Hermione, I can tell you, and while the younger girls wore their peploi more modestly, every woman present was watching Briseis. Her Ionian fashion was both exotic and enticing and dignified. Nor did she wear the crown of a kore, but instead wore the headpiece of a priestess of Aphrodite.

Heliodora, probably the richest girl, wore the plainest chiton in wool, with a magnificent embroidered border that I had no doubt she had done herself. She was that sort of person.

Iris wore a vivid red peplos that had cost Xanthippus a fortune, because he was *that* sort of person. And libations were poured, hymns to Poseidon sung, and the girls went back to 'their' homes in a torchlit procession. All the women followed them – by prior arrangement they all shared a beautiful house overlooking the agora for that one night – and all the women went to a single party, while all the men went to the home of Aristides, which was 'my' house for the evening, and that of Hipponax and Hector.

Very little was done the next day. I'll leave you to imagine what kind of party we had – we, the victors of Salamis, with a whole town to supply our wine. It was there, on a kline with my 'father' Aleitus, that I heard the story, from him and from Aristides, of the storming of Psyttaleia, and a dozen other tales of the fighting that day.

But the next day more ships entered the little harbour, and still more landed at Thermisia and on the beaches of Troezen north of us. Themistocles had taken Andros, or driven them to capitulate, or made a face-saving gesture towards victory (no one could quite tell me) and the sailing season was well and truly past. Winter was coming on.

But the returning sailors, who included my friend Lykon of Corinth, and Ion and Moire, had news. They had scouted all the way to Skiathos opposite Thessaly, and Mardonius had taken Larissa, ejected its inhabitants despite their status as 'allies' and was wintering his horses in the green fields of the north.

It sobered us. At first blush many men had been sure that the whole Persian host was fleeing and our work was done. But in fact, as Lykon attested, already Persian ambassadors were going out to every city, demanding earth and water before the next onslaught.

We were far from despair, but we were thoughtful.

On the day given to Aphrodite, in the last week of Pyanepsion, Gorgo came. Now, in truth, Sparta is not so very far from Hermione, as the city had cause to know all too well a hundred years before, but I had not expected her, a new widow, to come. And yet, when you consider how very hard she had worked for the League ... and between Troezen and Hermione, we had most of the League's captains.

Pyanepsion! I've become an Athenian. And well I might – I'd been voted a citizen after Marathon; my sons were both made citizens, Iris was allowed to be a citizen by birth (essential if her children were to be citizens), and yet in poor old Boeotia, in Green Plataea of my youth, that late harvest month was called Pamboiotios, and it had some weeks left to run.

Pardon me for once again wandering like a drunken shepherd, but I digress only to come to my point. It was in Hermione that week and that month, and not in Corinth, that the League began to look at the next step in the war.

It was, I think, two days before my wedding. I was fighting my own black mood; I remember asking my daughter if Briseis was well, I was so sure that Apollo or some sly god would snatch her and my happiness from me.

Euphonia put her arms around me. 'She said the best thing,' my daughter said. 'She said she'd always wanted a daughter, and now

she was getting a beautiful, talented girl without the pain of childbirth or the wakeful nights.' Euphonia sat back. She was sitting by
me in the garden of my borrowed house. 'I thought to be offended,
and then I thought that you, too, had me without the pain of bearing
me or hearing me cry as a baby.'

Penelope, who was living in my house, put a cup of wine in my
hand. 'You were the best baby,' she said wistfully. 'My sons were
loud and demanding, and you were always sweet—'

'I pulled your loom over when I was six,' Euphonia said.

There was a brief silence.

'I thought Andronicus did that,' Penelope said with that dangerous tone in her voice.

I remember looking out from the little portico where we were
sitting, and seeing the marvellous stars, thousands and thousands on
a perfect autumn evening. I thought we were going to have a row,
and I was willing myself away.

But Pen just hugged my daughter. 'Well, that loom is ashes now,
my child,' she said. To me, she said, 'Your chosen wife gives more
orders than any woman I've ever met. And spends more time on
her appearance.' She raised a hand to forestall my response. 'Despite
which, she is easy to like. Her clothes are going to cause a scandal in
Athens, I promise you – she all but wears one breast bare! We'll all
have to exercise like Spartans to support them, I do declare.'

Pen, in fact, still had a fine figure, and ran for exercise, but I understood her comment.

'Ionia is different,' I said. 'And she has led a different life from
you.'

Penelope sat and hugged her knees like a much younger woman.
She looked at my daughter.

'Oh, I see! Adult things. I *know* how babies happen!' Euphonia
said. She tossed her head and flounced off. 'Perhaps I should attend
the Queen of Sparta? She always speaks to me as if I am an adult!'

I had grown wise enough as a parent to merely blow her a kiss.

'She asked me,' Penelope said. It was dark in our little porch with
its beautiful columns and the fragrant garden. 'She asked me how
long I would wait to marry again.'

I blinked.

'She said did I really want to sleep alone? And I knew I did not.
Oh, brother, is that treason?' Penelope was suddenly crying and I
wondered, guiltily, if it was my place to comfort those in need just

that week. Brasidas – the strongest man I knew – and now my sister, who, with Jocasta, was my model of strong women.

Yet, using silence to cover my confusion, I had to admit that loyalty to a dead partner could be very cold comfort. 'I think you must do what seems best,' I said.

'That's a cowardly answer,' Penelope spat at me. 'You mean I should do what is right? I'm asking you *what* is right!'

In fact, she was asking my permission to find someone, or to leave off mourning eventually. I knew it. I bit my lip. She was my sister and I confess I saw no reason for her – or any man or woman – to spend what could be a long life, alone or with her sons.

A voice floated out of the darkness. 'My husband told me to find a good man and make strong sons, if he should die.'

That was Gorgo's voice, and she came up the smooth, ancient steps to our little portico. With her were two Thracian women and Bulis – but her being out in the darkness would still have been a scandal in Athens.

In Hermione, though, there were no rules. I won't belabour the point, but we were a nation at war; we knew we were riding the fell beast in a pause between two deadly engagements. Girls and boys flirted and even kissed and their elders winked at it. It was not like the Athens or Plataea of my youth.

We all knew we were living on borrowed time, I think.

At any rate, the Queen of Sparta, widowed in the same hour as my sister, came up the steps, and she and Bulis sat with us. Eugenios came and placed lit oil lamps on small tables, and cakes appeared. And more wine.

But not before Gorgo said her piece.

'I will always see Leonidas as a demigod,' Gorgo said. She neither choked with emotion nor sounded happy. Her voice was neither flat nor full, but almost light in its delivery, like an oracle. 'But I will never compare him to any man who follows him into my bed. What is, is.' She smiled at Penelope, who came and embraced her.

She looked at me. 'We have all missed the Mysteries, have we not?' she asked, by which she meant the Eleusinian Mysteries, which should have been celebrated the week of Salamis. And her statement, 'what is, is' is contained in the Mysteries, although I was not, at that time, an initiate.

Bulis looked at me. I waved, and Eugenios put wine in his hand, and then another cup by the Queen.

My daughter returned, looking smug. Behind her came Jocasta, pink by torchlight with embarrassment and secret joy at being out of her house after dark. And Aristides. And Brasidas joined us and sat close by Gorgo.

'We meet in the darkness like conspirators,' Bulis said.

Gorgo spoke, again like an oracle. 'In the darkness, we can all pretend we were never here,' she said.

Euphonia laughed and almost got sent to bed.

I'd like to say that we then went on to solve the League's problems, but mostly we sat and watched the stars and drank wine.

Jocasta laughed softly. 'I've always wondered what men do at parties.'

Aristides laughed. 'You have? Really, this is quite a bit better than most symposia. For one thing, Eugenios mixes wine better than any host I know, and for another, each of us thinks before we speak.'

Jocasta leaned back so that her head rested on her husband's shoulder. Even then, in the near dark and in the afterglow of a famous victory, Aristides looked shocked that his wife would touch him in public. It's who he was.

'The wine is going to my head,' Jocasta said. 'Tell me, men. Will we defeat the Great King?'

I remember the silence. Far away, a cat yowled. Closer, there was the scent of the fig tree, like cinnamon and honey on the wind that rustled the branches to tell us that winter was coming.

'You know that Mardonius has the army in Thessaly?' I asked.

Gorgo nodded, her profile sharp against the light of one of the oil lamps. 'I know more than that,' she said quietly. 'I know from ... a friend ... that Mardonius, who, according to my source, seeks to be Great King himself, will seek to invade Attica again.'

Jocasta moaned. We all sat up.

'He believes that, even now, Athens can be destroyed so thoroughly that her citizens will disperse or leave the League.' She looked at Aristides. 'And even now there are many in Sparta who speak of holding the isthmian wall at Corinth and leaving Boeotia and Attica to their fate.'

Bulis nodded silently.

'Most of the peers who wanted to save all Greece,' he said, 'died with the King.'

We all sat silently and digested that.

'Tomorrow I will meet Themistocles and escort him to Sparta,'

Gorgo said. 'I hope that he, at least, as one of the architects of the Temple of Nike at Salamis, will help me to convince the ephors to march an army in the spring.'

Brasidas laughed. 'The architect of the Temple of Nike,' he said. 'Why do the Athenians think women cannot be orators? That's a beautiful phrase.'

Jocasta laughed. 'You, Gorgo, were the architect of that victory. Themistocles was merely a stonemason.'

The Spartan queen shook her head. 'Too much praise is like too much wine. I must go to bed. But I will keep Themistocles waiting one more day – if it means I can attend a certain wedding.'

She looked at my daughter – remember, we were guest friends, and my daughter had known her now for some years. 'Sing us something, my child,' she said. 'We are old and silent.'

Jocasta laughed again, she was becoming immodest, by her own lights. 'Yes, what shall we sing?' she asked. 'I thought men sang at these parties.'

Euphonia stood up and sang. But like most very young people, she sang to shock. And her voice was as beautiful as her mother's had been.

θέλουσα δ᾽ αὖ θέλουσαν ἁγνά μ᾽
145ἐπιδέτω Διὸς κόρα,
ἔχουσα σέμν᾽ ἐνώπι᾽ ἀσφαλῶς,
παντὶ δὲ σθένει
διωγμοῖς ἀσχαλῶσ᾽
ἀδμήτας ἀδμήτα
ὀρύσιος γενέσθω,
σπέρμα σεμνᾶς μέγα ματρὸς
εὐνὰς ἀνδρῶν, ἒ ἔ,
ἄγαμον ἀδάματον ἐκφυγεῖν.

And may Zeus's pure daughter, she who holds securely the sacred wall, willingly, meeting my will, look upon me; and, grieved at our pursuit, come with all her might, a virgin to a virgin's aid, to deliver me— That the mighty race of our honourable mother may escape the embrace of man (ah me), unwedded, unvanquished.

Brasidas, who loved my daughter, laughed aloud.

I sat up. 'That is a song *against* marriage,' I said.

My daughter tossed her head. 'It is a song we sing at Brauron, when we are little bears,' she said. 'Some of the priestesses say men have no purpose but to break us and marriage is to women what taming is to horses.'

Gorgo forsook her mourning long enough to laugh her hearty, man's laugh. 'A fine song,' she said. 'I can see she is truly your daughter. But Euphonia, never let any child born of woman tell you that marriage breaks man or woman. Is all Greece stronger, or weaker, for the League we have made against the Persians?'

'Stronger, of course,' shot back my daughter.

'So it is with marriage. Despite a thousand kinds of compromise, the result is stronger than either one was alone.' She rose. Bulis rose with her like a shadow. She leaned over and kissed Jocasta. 'I swear by Aphrodite I will not come as the Queen of Sparta,' she whispered.

'Thanks all the gods,' Jocasta murmured. 'I have enough troubles as it is.'

Anyway, that's all I remember of that evening. I think Gorgo had another meeting with Jocasta, but that's for another story and another night.

And then it was my wedding day.

It was bright and sunny, not quite warm – almost perfect for wearing a heavy himation in public. I had a magnificent one, a length of fabric I'd taken – to be honest, Hector had done the taking – two days after the battle. It had probably been Artemisia's and she had the best taste I knew of, except Briseis. It was Tyrian red, with tasselled ends and gold-tablet woven borders. I didn't have a zone rich enough to wear with it, but Cimon did. It is amazing how, no matter how much you prepare, something is forgotten, and Cimon sent back to 'his' house, first for a zone of gold, and then for sandals – how on earth had I expected to be wed in my military 'Spartan shoes'?

His spare sandals were a rich white, so white I didn't really know that leather could be so white. They had gold tassels and gold laces and, frankly, they looked ridiculous on my feet. Almost every toe I have has been broken, some four or five times. There are parts of me that are handsome still, and back then, at the height of my powers, I was accounted handsome, I think, but never for my feet.

In truth, I think part of getting wed is proving to your soon-to-be wife that you will wear whatever it takes. I wore the sandals and the zone. And as I stepped up into my chariot – alone, symbolically – I ran a fond hand over the bronze tyre of the wheel that I had helped forge.

And all my friends – I mean all of them, all that were living and, I think, a few of my dead – followed my chariot through the steep streets of Hermione, to the house where Archilogos waited. It was by then the edge of evening and the sun was setting red and mighty in the west behind the hills. I have no idea how I spent that day: looking for sandals, apparently. But I remember the light on the ships and the roof of the temple of Poseidon. I remember Aeschylus and Phrynicus becoming shrews as they matched wits against each other; I thought of telling them to be quiet, but I was old enough to realise that they were, in fact, enjoying themselves. And Styges was there, and Tiraesias and Hermogenes and Brasidas and Bulis, and Moire, and Ion who was too young to be one of my friends and was clearly more comfortable with the younger men, my sons.

And there they were, each more beautiful than the last, if I may say it of them. Hector's hair was like a blond flame, long like a Spartan's, and Hipponax, heavier, but strong and calm, with his ringlets oiled and a superb woollen himation that just possibly his bride had made for him. And there with me were most of my marines – Sitalkes was gone to find his wife at Corinth and missed it all – and many oarsmen, too. Kineas strode by one of my chariot wheels like a god and he made me think somehow of Neoptolymos, the friend of my youth, the Cretan.

There were so many men we filled the streets, and three chariots – I tried to take it all in, but Aristides has told me since that he and some of the more formally dressed men were only just leaving their houses because of the press when I was arriving in the courtyard of Archilogos.

We had arranged that each of us would go to our bride's house, pick her up in our chariot and lead a procession of her dowry through the streets to the temple of Poseidon, where we would all make offering and sacrifice, and where, by the courtesy of the town's elders, we were allowed to make a marriage feast inside the precinct, as it was the only area in the town large enough for so many.

And it seemed unreal to me that I was going to wed Briseis in this pretty little town that was not my own, or hers, amid the same men who I led onto enemy decks and through enemy formations, all wreathed, all laughing. There was Leukas, who had been born almost in Hyperborea, and there was Seckla, in a magnificent robe of shining white and gold (loot, I suspect, from one of the Carthaginians), and he was from so far south of Thebes (Thebes of Egypt, that is) that he said it was as far from his home to Thebes as it was from Thebes to Athens. And there was Ka, who wore, instead of a himation or a chiton, the skin of a leopard, a fabulous spotted cat, or perhaps it was two, but it made him look even more exotic and even less Greek.

Of course, he was almost a foot taller than all the other men, as well. It made him easy to find, in a fight. Ka was a contrast to Moire. Ka never tried to be Greek; Moire was as Greek as he sought to be.

Anyway, I couldn't quite get my mind around the reality of it. The chariot rolled along well enough, and the horses, for horses, behaved themselves. Cimon was beside himself with what a fine team they were and how magnificent they'd be if he could only replace the off-side horse with a bigger one. They were all grey, unmatched and yet somehow matched, and it's true that the offside horse was smaller. But they filled the street, they obeyed me like slaves, and they didn't upset my magnificent himation. Listen, when I was a slave boy on Hipponax's farm, learning to drive a chariot, little did I imagine that the next chance I would have would be in the streets of a tiny town in the Peloponnese, on the road to wedding my master's daughter!

Cimon was striding along by the horses. He didn't seem to think I could be trusted with them. Did you know that when Themistocles proposed that the men of Athens put to sea and defend Attica in ships – that 'wooden walls' was the oracle of Delphi's way of telling them to fight at sea – Cimon went to the temple of Athena and sacrificed his bits and bridles and went from the altar straight to a ship? A magnificent act, and one that helped weld the richest men in Athens to the poorest.

Despite which, he didn't really think I was any good with horses. And he was right.

Then we were there.

At the last moment a little of my boyhood flowed into my hands, and despite my himation and my gilded sandals, I napped the reins. My four greys leapt forward – like most horses, they wanted to run. The street in front of me was empty; well, mostly empty, and I enjoyed making Cimon leap for a sausage stall, and we moved down the last hundred paces at a fast trot and I left my crowd behind.

The entrance to the yard of the house that Archilogos had rented was not very wide, and at right angles to the street. I had, naturally enough, never been in the yard, but I knew I was to take the chariot in. And I do like to make an entrance.

One of the tricks you learn when you learn to race a chariot, or to be a charioteer in combat – you paying attention, ladies? I trained for this as a slave – is to stop one wheel and pivot the whole chariot on the other. It takes great horses and good timing, and some terrible daimon of youth invaded me and made me try to do it entering the courtyard of the house of my bride.

I checked the horses with my voice, threw all my weight to the right, and reined in the lead horse, and he all but pivoted on his back feet.

By Poseidon, Lord of Horses, the gate seemed narrower than the wheels of my chariot. It was a foolish chance to have taken with a vehicle my friends and I had rebuilt from worm-eaten wood and rotted rawhide.

My right hub clipped the doorpost hard enough that white plaster fell like a little shower of snow, and then we were through, still moving very fast.

There's a thing you do, as a charioteer, to pick up your master: you pivot the chariot all the way around and rein in, all but scooping the man off his feet with the back deck of woven cords. The daimon was strong in me, and I now reined my offside leader and my back wheels skidded on the smooth marble.

It was almost perfect.

Unfortunately, the axle clipped a small, very elegant standing column.

And knocked it over. It took a long time to fall, and it broke into several sections and lay there, accusingly.

Archilogos – by the eternal irony of the gods, the master for whom I would have driven my chariot in combat, had the world ever gone that way – stood under the stoa of the courtyard and laughed very hard. He was beautifully dressed, and his ruddy curls bounced with his mirth. He tried to say something – and was off again in another paroxysm of laughter.

Behind me, my crowd of friends and about a thousand oarsmen approached the gate. They made a roar like the sea.

And then Briseis stepped out into the open.

It was not what she was wearing; it was not the magnificent gold earrings she had in her ears, the crown of a priestess on her head, the gold bracelet she wore or the gilded sandals that cradled her arched feet.

It was her eyes, which were only for me.

Somehow, in that moment, we were wed. Never before, not ever, anywhere, had those eyes been entirely intent on me and no one else – no 'next thing', no plot, no intrigue. Her brother was laughing, and as she passed him, her right hand reached out and viciously poked him in the side – a very sisterly act. Remember that they had not been together in many years.

He reached for her arm to respond in kind, and froze, aware that three hundred or more men were watching him.

They grinned at one another.

And then she reached out a hand, and the smell of musk and jasmine and mint embraced me. I took her hand and she rose into the chariot like Venus riding the dawn.

'Please do not hit another column,' she said very quietly. Her lips parted, and sound emerged, and it was all I could do not to stare at her for ever, or take her in front of all those people!

Instead, training and good breeding took hold, and I snapped the reins. My horses leapt forward and by luck – or the grace of Aphrodite – we sailed through the doorposts without blemish, although I was ashamed to note a long white gouge on the one as we passed. Men flattened themselves to be out of my way, and called out.

Oh, in those days, thugater, men and women said such things.

She swayed, and I put a hand around her waist. And the fingers of my left hand found that her chiton was open-pinned, not sewn down the side, and at the contact with the smooth skin of her hip, I almost lost my horses.

'Drive the chariot, my husband,' she said. 'Drive me later, if you will.'

And she laughed, and all the happiness that a man could feel, that the gods allow, flooded me. By Zeus Sator, by all the gods who sit in Olympus, what more can we ask? Victory in war, and the woman you love ...

The street cleared. I made the turn at the base of the hill and it was flat for two hundred paces until the promontory rose away with the temple of Poseidon sitting atop it, and I tightened my grip on her waist and snapped the reins and gave a shout – and my horses obeyed.

From a walk to a trot, trot straight to a gallop, and we tore along that stade of a street, scattering a few bystanders, and our clothes and hair billowed, dust rose in a cloud, and for the length of the time it takes a man to sing a hymn, we *were* gods. And then, as the horses began to take the rise in the road and I reined them in, perhaps not beautifully, but competently, and they slowed, so that they were shiny with sweat, composed and walking elegantly, as we entered the sacred precinct.

'That is my answer,' I said. And was rewarded with her smile, and her blush. Who knew she could blush like that?

And we walked up into the temple.

I had, of course, forgotten to bring a sword. But you need a sword for sacrifices, and I felt a fool until Eugenios stepped out of the crowd and put my own sword belt over my head as if the whole thing was planned.

I did not behead a bull. The chariot-driving had been as much adventure as I needed on my wedding day and I killed a ram fastidiously, raising the hem of my himation before the blood could flow.

But the auspices were brilliant, in birds of the air and in the livers of dead animals, and my sons made their kills and the smell of roasting fat rose to the gods. The sun on the pine trees all around the shrine – the last of the summer was ours for that day, and the scent of pines and the smell of cooking meat, the salt air, the spilled wine ...

We did not short the gods. Libations were poured to many gods and many absent friends: Paramanos, Onisandros, Idomeneus, and many others. We prayed and then we ate, we drank and then we danced.

I won't relate the whole. I could make it longer than the Battle of Salamis, for truly, it was better in every way. Weddings are about life, while battles are about death.

But I will say that the three brides, Iris and Heliodora and Briseis, danced together. And I confess that, for once, Briseis was not best. She was beautiful, and she was all I wanted, but the Brauron girls danced the dance of Artemis for the last time, and they were superb. And then we all danced together, men in the outside ring, women in the inside, and wine and the flash of limbs and the open sides of many a chiton began to work on me, so that passion became very like lust. I remember a woman, who looked very much like Gorgo but insisted that her name was Io, which made me laugh. She and Jocasta danced and talked and danced and talked. I saw the two of them with my bride at one point, and they all laughed together, and I worried.

I danced until my head was clear, and then I went and sat and I found myself with Cimon and Aristides, and Eugenios and Ka – a very eclectic group of couches indeed. I ate a barley roll, the white kind we call 'of Lesvos', and chased it with some wine.

'You should take your bride to your house,' Aristides said. He was watching his wife dance again. 'Because if you do not, there will be Lapiths and Centaurs on this very grass.'

'Indeed,' Cimon said, 'I just saw a lass with her back all pine needles, and I do not think she was napping.'

So I made my rounds, hugging Cleitus, embracing Agariste, who was, if not very drunk, certainly jolly, and Xanthippus, who suddenly, full of wine, began to propound to me a forward naval strategy – an attack on the Persians in Ionia.

His wife pulled him down on their couch.

And I kissed my new daughters-in-law, who watched me with downcast eyes, as my leaving would mean that they were to leave too.

We walked to the chariots and the noise increased so acutely that I knew we were in for a loud night.

There was a moment ... again, just as she mounted the chariot ... half a hush, and Briseis put her hand on my arm where it rested as if it had been there all my life. I thought she might admonish me like a wife – you know, that I was drunk and needed to drive slowly.

Instead, she smiled into my eyes. Her own were huge and deep. And in a voice suffused with emotion, she said, 'You are now related to two of the three most powerful families in Athens, my love.'

'So we are,' I said.

I didn't whip my horses to a gallop. I did move along briskly, however, purely to leave the more boisterous elements behind us, and I confess that I went down the hill a little too fast and almost missed the turn along the northern beach, but Poseidon stayed by me and I did not. And I let the horses run a few strides and then calmed them, my hand already searching in the folds of her Ionian chiton.

She leaned into me with her whole body. Until a women does this, no man knows what a kiss is. I was driving horses, but Briseis was always as mad as I, or madder. We kissed; the world went by in a blur, and only Eros, who protects lovers, kept us from a foolish death.

And then we rolled to a stop in front of 'my' house. I jumped down, and lifted her. Behind me there was shouting. Hundreds of men and many women were pouring down the hill, but the chariots had kept them back, and we had a stade or more head start.

I carried her across the threshold of my borrowed house. My hands were already on her pins.

I did not put her down until I crossed the garden. I carried her into the tiny house and past the table where Eugenios had set cakes and wine and, as I tore at her clothes, I said:

σφαίρῃ δηὖτέ με πορφυρέῃ
βάλλων χρυσοκόμης Ἔρως,
νήνι ποικιλοσαμβάλῳ
συμπαίζειν προκαλεῖται.
ἡ δ᾽ — ᾿ς ἐστὶν γὰρ ἀπ᾽ εὐκτίτου
Λέσβου — τὴν μὲν ἐμὴν κόμην —
λευκὴ γάρ — καταμέμφεται,
πρὸς δ᾽ ἄλλην τινὰ χάσκει.

Golden-haired Eros once again
hurls his crimson ball at me:
he calls me to come out and play
with a girl in fancy sandals.
But she's from civilised Lesvos:
she sneers at my hair because it's grey ...

I was quoting Anacreon. She rolled away from me on the bed and took off her magnificent sandals and threw them at me, laughing, and she reached between my legs and said, 'I am, however, unlikely to turn in wonder for another girl.' Then she was on me.

And it was she, not I, as the sound of copper pots and bronze ladles and wooden spoons beaten on iron kettle lids filled the garden outside our door, as voices suggested positions, and others asked how big I might be, and a few made ruder jokes at her expense – it was she, who, already astride me, gathered all our clothes, a fortune in dyed wool and linen, leaned back so that I could see every inch of her splendour in the moonlight, and cast the whole ball of Tyrian red and indigo blue, glinting with gold, straight out of our garden window to the crowd below.

They *roared*. They roared like oarsmen in the moment of victory and like hoplites in the last push at Marathon. And I looked up into her face, still crowned with Aphrodite's golden tiara, still wearing her earrings and nothing else ...

Ah ... Good night, friends. The rest you will have to guess for yourselves.

Epilogue

You'll make *me* blush if you demand more. Hah! Pour cool wine over
the hot coals of lust and tomorrow night, the last night, I'll tell you
one more tale, how the men of Greece, free Greece, stood against
the Medes and Persians and men of a hundred nations, spear against
arrow as my friend Aeschylus has said, and fought until the dust and
haze of Ares covered all. How the men of Plataea danced the dance
of Ares one last time. And how close we came to losing everything.
Indeed, many of us lost life, and others lost all they owned.

But leave me to remember the happiest night of my life. Because
although I never promised you a happy story, some days it was as
full of glory as sunrise over the ocean, and some nights, too. And if
there is sadness to come ... well, here's to your mother, my dear, the
love of my life.

Το τέλος

Historical Note

When I set out to write this novel, I thought that I knew a fair amount about warfare under oars and the Battle of Salamis. Today I completed the novel feeling considerably less sanguine. The Battles off of Artemisium and the Battle of Salamis were, almost inarguably, pivotal events for Greece, and quite possibly, despite hyperbole, for the whole history of the world. And I'm still not sure how many ships were engaged, how exactly the fighting went, or even, at Artemisium, who really won. I still can't tell you the names of most of the ships engaged, where they beached, or what, exactly, the intentions of the commanders were.

That's a little odd, as I find that the book I've written is more a fictional campaign history than a novel.

So I'd like to discuss the sources, some theories, and some of the evidence. And I'd like the reader – and I'm aware I have readers who read Ancient Greek and know these issues as well or better than I – I'd like all my readers to know that I did my due diligence, and if I didn't agree with your favorite theory, I'll bet I considered it.

First, a general caveat. When dealing with the dawn of the Classical era, we actually *know* very little. The lightest brush with the so-called 'Hoplites and Heresies' debate (and here a perusal of Josho Brouwers' excellent synopsis in the bibliographical section of *Henchmen of Ares* will help you better than I can) will show every reader how contentious every aspect of warfare in this era really is. A perusal of the literature on ancient sexuality will get you the same confusion; ship construction is beginning to edge towards consensus as underwater archaeology disproves some theories, but there's still lots of room for debate; dance and martial arts are both realms that appear open to the wildest speculation, and even as simple an (apparent) subject as the role of women in society is rent with quarrels whose real basis is in modern academia, not the ancient world. (But if you want to read my favourite book on the subject, which I regard as the best by far, try *Portrait of a Priestess* by Joan Breton Connelly.)

Second, a specific warning – I'm a novelist, and I really like to tell a good story. I'm pretty sure there really was an Arimnestos; I will bet he was at Artemisium, because the Plataeans were there. Quite frankly, it is unlikely he was at Salamis – more likely, he and the Plataeans, having evacuated their farms, were camped around Nemea or at the isthmus, or even at Troezen or Hermione. But I built him from the first to be one of those piratical captains that the Greeks had in plenty – Herodotus mentions several of them, and Miltiades as much as any – and those men had their own ships and crews. So in short – to make my story work, I have juggled some of my Plataean characters and sent them back to Salamis.

But that is all the juggling I have done a-purpose. Any other errors are errors, and I'll apologize in advance, because I do make them. For example, until I wrote this book, I was unaware of the difference between the relatively open rowing frames in the latest trieres re-constructions and the slab-sided ships that I had seen in pictures and imagined. So in this book, rowers row in frames – and I ask readers to 'edit' their memories to include frames and so on in my other naval actions. Likewise, close attention to the appendix on mooring and anchoring in the magisterial *Seagoing Ships and Seamanship in the Bronze Age Levant* by Shelley Wachsmann has indicated to me that I didn't know as much as I thought I did about anchors and their uses, and you'll find that gets a little more detail this time.

Anyway, I'm sure I've made new errors. Be merciful.

On to the Battle of Salamis.

There are really only two primary sources on the battle – Herodotus, in the main, and the opening of Aeschylus' play *Persians*. Of the two, Aeschylus was an eyewitness – he was *there*. He was, in fact, a hoplite, a veteran warrior who had fought at Marathon. As much as possible, I took his word as law. Of course, that wasn't always easy. And Herodotus – frankly, this whole series is based on Herodotus, and next to the Iliad, Herodotus' *Histories* is one of my favorite books. I love the humanity that shines through his work, and it is my belief that he never wittingly lied or shaded the truth. Rather, in a very Husserlian way, he gave us the truth as he experi-enced it, and it is we moderns who struggle with his endless tales of omens, the vengeance of gods and men, and the eternal turning of a wheel of fate. He sure knew how to help a novelist though. Look at Queen Gorgo of Sparta!

I also used two secondary sources that I enjoyed – for different reasons, but I liked both. One was Barry Strauss's *The Battle of Salamis* which I read back in 2004 when it came out – when, in fact, I was writing the first draft of what became *Tyrant*. The other is John R. Hale's wonderful *Lords of the Sea*, about the rise of Athenian sea power. Finally, I used the 'Ancient Map Book' as my bible on place names and distances, and I can promise you that I have been to most of the beaches on which Arimnestos lands – except Megalos. Never been there. It sounds wonderful, though.

The battle is a confusing welter from the first page – from the moment the Greek fleet leaves the beaches of Artemisium. Right away, the novelist is presented with a list of questions. Let me put one of them to you – because in it lies all the seeds of the confusion of the rest of the campaign.

When the Greeks knew that Leonidas was dead and the League Army at Thermopylae had failed – did they think they would fight again? Or did they only sail to Salamis together in a sort of route, preparatory to the fleet breaking up?

I realize this seems obvious, but if Herodotus is to be believed, the Corinthians and the Peloponnesians – and perhaps even the Spartans – were for going to the isthmus immediately, while the Athenians, at least, thought that a fight would be made in the plains of Boeotia and that the fleet should remain together. Why didn't the allied fleet break up immediately?

Asking this question gave me one hint about the campaign that I play throughout – that Eurybiades really was in command, and not just a shadow-puppet for Themistocles to keep the Aeginians and the Corinthians happy. If you accept that Leonidas and the Spartans had the foresight to want an alliance to save Greece, Eurybiades seems likely to have been a member of their party. And that means that the Greeks left Artemisium with their high command still willing to fight. I can't actually imagine that the Greek fleet that Aeschylus portrays on the morning of Salamis – a united fleet signing the paean and striking fear in the hearts of the Persians – was still wrangling the night before.

And yet – just to keep you in the picture of how this book developed – I was pretty deep in the book when I read Maurizio Arfaioli's book on *The Black Bands of Giovanni*, a book about the early 16th-century wars in Italy that included an appendix on a pivotal naval fight between galleys (Capo D'Orso in 1528). I enjoyed it, but I also noted that the winning side was nonetheless rent with dissension almost to the moment of action. And that the winning commander betrayed his 'side' later. After some soul-searching, I decided to accept that both Herodotus and Aeschylus were right, or at least, that they probably described a situation that was very complex, as real life all too often is. The upshot was that I changed the book, and chose to follow both. And that led to the rather careful examination of the personalities and arguments of the leaders as portrayed. And to the making of Themistocles as a more 'nuanced' character.

As to the day of battle, I am relatively confident that Strauss et al are correct, and that Xerxes' fleet intended to surround the Greek beaches to prevent flight – and to allow themselves to form a long line with a friendly coast at their backs, instead of being caught in a fight in the narrows by Psyttaleia. I am *still* unsure whether the Greek attack on Psyttaleia was pivotal to the battle, or merely made exciting by Herodotus to inflate hoplite vanities in the aftermath of a naval battle, and to make Aristides look good. But I chose the former, because, looking at the 'terrain' of the battle and the width of the channels, as I think they were in 480 BCE, possession of that island with archers would have been pivotal to the battle. And a brilliant commander might well have seen that if his left flank struck hard, he could turn the battle from a long-line fight to a choked fight in the narrows. That would, after all, have been sound strategy on land, and it is my perception that before the era of Phormio and true Athenian maritime greatness, fleet actions were viewed much as land battles where the losers drowned.

The aftermath of the battle is almost all my speculation, but again based firmly on Herodotus. Clearly the Greeks, who'd probably won at least one of the days at Artemisium, were not immediately aware that they'd finished Xerxes' fleet. And likewise, lest we exaggerate, it is also very possible that Xerxes finished the day at Salamis with more battle-ready ships than the whole league fleet had possessed *before* the fight. But they were at the very end of the sailing season, and I suspect there are several untold stories – the Egyptians, for example, didn't want to be there to start with and had the longest trip home; the Ionians might have been brave on the day of battle, but when they realized that they were the only fleet the Great King had left, it must have occurred to many of them, even the sailors of the Persian-backed tyrannies, that the day of judgment was at hand. To me, the steady defections recorded in Herodotus suggest deep fissures in the Persian fleet. Salamis was not a one-shot victory – it was the knock-out blow of a tough campaign, or so I see it.

And finally, as my brave Arimnestos runs across the sea to rescue his girl, let me remind you that contrary to Herodotus, many Athenians knew how to cross the sea to the coast of Asia. They'd been there in the Ionian revolt, and many of them had been to Egypt. While I love and trust Herodotus, in this I can only note that Greeks are great or terrible navigators as it seems to suit his story. I'm sure they had their share of both. Possibly Themistocles had a lot of trierarchs who had never been outside the harbours of Piraeus and Phaleron – but let's give Arimnestos and his friends the benefit of some practice. I hope you have enjoyed that Arimnestos was not born a good navigator, and in fact has taken nineteen years at sea to develop the confidence and skill to do something as daring as what I've written.

Ah, and in the end, we have a wedding. Hermione is a beautiful, magical place, and the temple of Poseidon (probably) sits on a magnificent promontory that instantly evokes the late Archaic, and smells of pines and the sea to this day. My wife and I stayed in a wonderful house their, and I confess it had a fig tree. And our daughter, and some cats. We stayed there in the days after we re-enacted the Battle of Marathon in 2011, and I will not soon forget the sights and sounds of that trip, many of which are in this book, and a few of which will be in the next. In the meantime, on to *Marathon* 2015!

If you'd like to see a few of these places for yourself, look at the Pen and Sword tour website at https://1phokion.wordpress.com/or just visit my author page on Facebook or my author site at www.hippeis.com and look in the 'agora'. I enjoy answering reader questions and I usually respond, and I almost never bite. And if you've always wanted to be a hoplite – or a Persian, or a Scythian, or a slave, or almost any ancient person – well, try re-enacting. Contact me, or visit our http://www.boarstooth.net/ website, and we'll find you a group. Maybe even ours!

Acknowledgements

Each year, since I was married in 2004, my wife and I have gone to Greece. It is from all these trips – and my oft-quoted brush with Greece and Troy and Smyrna and Ephesus from the back seat of an S-3 Viking in 1990 – that my love, even passion, for Greece, ancient and modern, was born. In this, the fifth book of my 'Long War' series, I tackle perhaps the best known battle in the whole of the Persian Wars – indeed, one of the best known battles of the ancient world. What I have written is heavily influenced by my trips to Greece, by days in Piraeus and by many views out the window of an airplane taking off from Athens or landing there. My wife Sarah is always kind enough to let me have the window seat if we're passing over the Bay of Salamis. My daughter Beatrice is not always so forgiving!

Salamis is a different book and I am perhaps a humbler man than when I wrote the first books of this series. First and foremost, I have to acknowledge the contribution of my friends and compatriots like Nicolas Cioran, who cheerfully discussed Plataea's odd status, made kit, and continues to debate issues of leadership and character. My good friend Aurora Simmons, an expert martial artist and a superb craftsperson with almost any media (but a jeweler by profession) has quite possibly had more input on my understanding of Ancient Greece than any other person besides Giannis Kadoglou, whose nearly encyclopedic knowledge of the Ancient Greek world of hoplites and oarsmen continued to support me to the last page, with vase paintings of wedding scenes produced on short notice! My trainer and constant sparring partner John Beck deserves my thanks – both for a vastly improved physique, and for helping give me a sense of what real training for a life of violence might have been like in the ancient world; as does my massage therapist Susan Bessonette, because at age fifty-two, it is not always easy to pretend to be twenty-six in a fight. And while we're talking about fighting – Chris Duffy, perhaps the best modern martial artist I know, deserves thanks for many sparring bouts whose more exciting bits find their way into these pages, while a number of instructors – Guy Windsor, Sean Hayes, Greg Mele, Jason Smith and Sensei Robert Zimmermann have helped shape my appreciation of the combat techniques, armed and unarmed, that were available in the ancient world.

Among professional historians, I was assisted by Paul McDonnell-Staff and Paul Bardunias, by the entire brother and sisterhood of 'Roman Army talk' and the web community there, and by the staff of the Royal Ontario Museum (who possess and cheerfully shared the only surviving helmet attributable to the Battle of Marathon) as well as the staff of the Antikenmuseum Basel und Sammlung Ludwig who possess the best preserved ancient aspis and provided me with superb photos to use in recreating it. I also received help from the library staff of the University of Toronto, where, when I'm rich enough, I'm a student, and from Toronto's superb Metro Reference Library. I must add to that the University of Rochester Library (my alma mater) and the Art Gallery of Ontario. Every novelist needs to live in a city where universal access to JSTOR is free and on his library card. Finally, the staff of the Walters Art Gallery in Baltimore, Maryland – just across the street from my mother's former apartment, conveniently – were cheerful and helpful, even when I came back to look at the same helmet for the sixth time. A helmet which I now own a faithful copy of, thanks to Manning Imperial!

Excellent as professional historians are – and my version of the Persian Wars owes a great deal to many of them, not least Hans Van Wees and Victor Davis Hanson and Josho Brouwers – my greatest praise and thanks have to go to the amateur historians we call re-enactors. Giannis Kadoglou of Alexandroupolis has now spent many, many hours with me, tramping about Greece, visiting ruins from the Archaic to as recent as the Great War, from Plataea to Thrace, charming my daughter and my wife while translating everything in sight and being as delighted with the ancient town of Plataea as I was myself. I met him on 'Roman Army talk', and this would be a very different book without his passion for the subject and relentless desire to correct my errors, and that of his wife Smaro, whose interest in all these things and whose willingness to wear ancient Greek clothes and debate them in the New Acropolis Museum kept me focused on the details that make for good writing. We are all now fast friends and I suspect my views on much of the Greek world reflect theirs more than any other. Alongside Giannis go my other Greek friends, especially Giorgos Kafetsis and his partner Xsenia, who have theorized over wine, beer and ouzo, paced battlefields and shot bows.

But Giorgos and Xsenia, Giannis and Smaro are hardly alone, and there is – literally – a phalanx of Greek re-enactors who continue to help me. (We are recreating the world around the Battle of Marathon with about 100 re-enactors this year in Marathon – that's late October 2015, if you want to book tickets.) Here in my part of North America, we have a group called the Plataeans – this is, trust me, not a co-incidence – and we work hard on recreating the very time period and city-state so prominent in these books, from weapons, armor, and combat to cooking, crafts, and dance. If the reader feels that these books put flesh and blood on the bare bones of history – in as much as I've succeeded in doing that – it is due to the efforts of the men and women who re-enact with me and show me every time we're together all the things I haven't thought of – who do their own research, their own kit-building, and their own training. Thanks to all of you, Plataeans. And to all the other Ancient Greek re-enactors who helped me find things, make things, or build things. I'd like to mention (especially) Craig and his partner Cherilyn at Manning Imperial in Australia, and Jeffrey Hildebrandt here in Ontario, who just made me a superb new thorax for Marathon 2015.

Thanks are also due to the people of Lesvos and Athens and Plataea and Marathonas – I can't name all of you, but I was entertained, informed, and supported constantly in three trips to Greece, and the person who I can name is Aliki Hamosfakidou of Dolphin Hellas Travel for her care, interest, and support through many hundreds of e-mails and some meetings. Alexandros Somoglou of Marathonas deserves special thanks, and if you ever find yourself in Molyvos (Ancient Mythemna) on Lesvos, please visit the Sea Horse Hotel, where Dmitri and Stela run my favorite hotel in the world. Also in Greece I've received support and help from professional archaeologists and academics, and I wish particularly to thank Pauline Marneri and her son John Zervas for his translation support.

Bill Massey, my editor at Orion, has done his usual excellent job and it is a better book for his work. Oh, and he found a lot of other errors, too, but let's not mention them. I have had a few editors.

Working with Bill is wonderful. Come on, authors – how many of you get to say that?

My agent, Shelley Power, contributed more directly to this book than to any other – first, as an agent, in all the usual ways, and then later, coming to Greece and taking part in all of the excitement of seeing Lesvos and Athens and taking us to Archaeon Gefsis, a restaurant that attempts to take the customer back to the ancient world. And then helping to plan and run the 2500th Battle of Marathon, and continuing as a re-enactor of Ancient Greece. Thanks for everything, Shelley, and the agenting not the least!

Christine Szego and the staff and management of my local bookstore, Bakka-Phoenix of Toronto also deserve my thanks, as I tend to walk in a spout fifteen minutes' worth of plot, character, dialogue, or just news – writing can be lonely work, and it is good to have people to talk to. And they throw a great book launch.

It is odd, isn't it, that authors always save their families for last? Really, it's the done thing. So I'll do it, too, even though my wife should get mentioned at every stage – after all, she's a re-enactor, too, she had useful observations on all kinds of things we both read (Athenian textiles is what really comes to mind, though) and in addition, more than even Ms. Szego, Sarah has to listen to the endless enthusiasms I develop about history while writing (the words 'Did you know' probably cause her more horror than anything else you can think of). My daughter, Beatrice, is also a re-enactor, and her ability to portray the life of a real child is amazing. My father, Kenneth Cameron, taught me most of what I know about writing, and continues to provide excellent advice – and to listen to my complaints about the process, which may be the greater service. Oh, and as we enter into a world where authors do their own marketing, my wife, who knows a thing or two, is my constant guide and sounding board there. And she is also a veteran re-enactor and a brilliant researcher and questioner, and the best partner a person could ask for.

Having said all that, it's hard to say what exactly I can lay claim to, if you like this book. I had a great deal of help, and I appreciate it. Thanks. And when you find misspelled words, sailing directions reversed, and historical errors – why, then you'll know that I, too, had something to add. Because all the errors are solely mine.

Toronto, March, 2015